A Grave Deception

Also available by Connie Berry

The Kate Hamilton Mysteries

A Dream of Death

A Legacy of Murder

The Art of Betrayal

The Shadow of Memory

A Collection of Lies

A Grave Deception

A Kate Hamilton Mystery

CONNIE BERRY

NEW YORK

Published in the United States by Crooked Lane Books, an imprint of The Quick Brown Fox & Company LLC.

Crooked Lane Books and its logo are trademarks of The Quick Brown Fox & Company LLC.

Library of Congress Catalog-in-Publication data available upon request.

ISBN (hardcover): 979-8-89242-209-3
ISBN (paperback): 979-8-89242-293-2
ISBN (ebook): 979-8-89242-210-9

Cover design by Alan Ayers

Printed in the United States.

www.crookedlanebooks.com

Crooked Lane Books
34 West 27th St., 10th Floor
New York, NY 10001

First Edition: December 2025

The authorized representative in the EU for product safety and compliance is eucomply OÜPärnu mnt 139b-14, 11317 Tallinn, Estonia, hello@eucompliancepartner.com, +33757690241

10 9 8 7 6 5 4 3 2 1

This book is dedicated to my parents, whose zest for life, endless curiosity, and unconditional love shaped my childhood and my life. They are on every page.

"Oh Pearl," quoth I, "with pearls bedight,
Art thou my Pearl that I have plained,
With yearnings through the long lone night
And bitter tears in secret rained!
Since earth received thee from my sight . . .
What weird hath brought hither the gem of my heart,
And set me in dole and great danger?
Since we two were sundered and set apart,
I have been a joyless jeweler."

From "Pearl," Anonymous Fourteenth Century Poem
Translated into modern English by
G. G. Coulton, M.A., 1906

Chapter One

Thursday, June 19
Long Barston, Suffolk

The body was discovered on an afternoon in early May when the bluebells were in bloom and the sky was the color of sapphires. I read about it the next day in the *East Anglian Daily Times*. "Archaeological Discovery of the Century!" was the headline. Now, a little more than a month later, I pulled up that original article on my computer:

> *Last Wednesday, excavations beneath the ruins of St. Margaret's Church, Egemere Close, revealed a previously unknown vault containing a lead coffin sealed with beeswax. Within the coffin, the team of archaeologists from the CMBA, the Centre for Medieval British Archaeology in Norwich, found the well-preserved body of a woman, entombed sometime in the early fourteenth century. Her remains had been wrapped in a fine linen shroud impregnated with a resinous substance, resulting in adipocere, or grave wax, a natural process that preserved the tissues and organs in such detail it was possible to determine the colour of her irises. They were blue.*

I took a drink of my coffee, contemplating death and grief and the strange turns life sometimes takes. A woman dies and seven hundred years later I'm involved. The Centre for Medieval British

Archaeology had asked us, meaning my colleague, Ivor, and me, to examine the grave goods, which consisted of two silver pennies; a collection of personal objects, including an unusual wrist cuff adorned with twelve small human heads of silver with blue glass eyes—the Twelve Apostles?—and a large, single pearl wrapped in a leather pouch, which had protected the *nacre*, the shiny, iridescent material known as mother-of-pearl, from deterioration.

The number and quality of grave goods indicated the woman had been wealthy, perhaps of noble birth, but the fact that items of such value had been interred with the young woman at all was unusual, as the practice had pretty much died out by the eleventh century. Were they mementos, like burying a child with a stuffed toy or a whisky lover with a bottle of his favorite single malt, or was there some deeper meaning?

The answer to that question wasn't our concern. Our job would be to date the objects, assess their values, outline a plan for preservation, and suggest methods of display. Naturally, we'd jumped at the chance. Ivor had done similar work in the past, but nothing with the notoriety of a miraculously preserved body.

It was a quiet morning at The Cabinet of Curiosities. Through the multi-paned shop window I watched Mr. Cox, the greengrocer across the street, setting out heads of glossy green lettuces and bunches of what looked like round red radishes. Ivor Tweedy, owner of the fine antiques and antiquities shop on Long Barston's High Street, hadn't yet emerged from his flat above the showroom, although I could hear him moving about. I'd gotten an early start, leaving my husband, Tom, at home to finish his breakfast and log on for a video conference with DCI Annabelle Scott, his counterpart in the Norfolk Constabulary.

I took another sip of coffee, which was cooling, and clicked on the second article, a follow-up interview published several weeks later with Dr. Simon Sinclair, head of the CMBA and a professor in the archaeology department at the University of East Anglia. In the weeks following the initial discovery of the body, a consulting bioarchaeologist from University College London had made several stunning discoveries.

> *"It was a once-in-a-lifetime experience," Sinclair said in answer to a question about his personal response to the discovery. "At first, we assumed the body must be relatively modern. The skin, where unstained by the resinous wrapping cloth, was still pink. Apart from the brain, the internal organs showed remarkably little deterioration. Liquid blood was found in her chest cavity." When asked about the cause of death, Sinclair said, "CT scans and 3D reconstructions of the skeleton revealed deep cuts on the woman's sternum, inflicted by a sharp object, most likely a knife or dagger. Her lungs and heart had been pierced, killing her quickly. And she'd been pregnant, the perfectly formed fetus having reached the point of viability."*

The article ended with the description of a small ceremony in which the bodies of the mother and child were reburied in the crypt beneath the south transept of the church, the place where they had originally lain.

I felt a pang of grief for this unknown woman, murdered with her unborn child. Someone had loved her. And someone had wanted her dead.

Sunlight streamed through the shop window, illuminating a collection of small Roman marbles, mostly busts of strikingly modern-looking individuals who'd lived during the Republican period when art was often startlingly realistic. Ivor had entered them in an upcoming auction of Roman antiquities. Who had they been, these long-ago luminaries, important enough to memorialize in stone? Their names had long been forgotten—like the woman in the grave. At least the village had a name—*Egemere Close*—although nothing was left of it now except the partial shell of the church and a few tumbledown stone walls. According to Ivor, the village had been abandoned in 1349 after the Black Death killed all but a handful of its citizens. The remains of Egemere Close lay in a field eighteen miles northwest of Long Barston, near the village of Hartwell, on the grounds of Ravenswyck Court, the estate of the commercial packaging entrepreneur Alex Belcourt.

"Good morning, Kate. Up and at 'em early, I see."

I turned to see Ivor trotting down the stairs. He was wearing a natty gray suit and a red velvet smoking cap with an elaborate gold tassel, the kind worn by Victorian men to keep their hair from smelling of tobacco smoke.

I tried not to laugh. "What's up with the hat?"

"Come the day, come the hat."

What that meant, I hadn't a clue.

Ivor Tweedy was a small man, not much more than five feet tall, with pink cheeks and sparse white hair frizzed out like a halo—straight out of a Victorian docudrama. He was also the most knowledgeable antiquities expert I'd ever encountered, with a lifetime's experience in the trade. Somewhere in his mid-seventies, he hadn't yet showed signs of slowing down. In fact, it seemed to me he was just reaching his stride. We'd become friends when I moved to Long Barston a year and a half ago. In that time, he'd become almost a second father to me. I loved him dearly, and I was sure he loved me, too, although given the English dis-ease with public expressions of emotion, this was never actually spoken. Ivor, who had no family of his own, had made me his business partner. One day, when he was gone, I would inherit the shop and everything he owned. I fervently hoped that day would be a very, very long way off.

"Tom had a video conference," I said, "so I thought I might as well come in early."

"Police business, I assume."

"Assault outside a pub in Thetford last night." I closed my laptop. "Witnesses say the attacker fled south in a white caravan. The Norfolk police have requested assistance in locating him—and a woman seen with him in the pub. She may be a hostage."

"So what's worrying you?" Ivor asked.

I swear that man could read my mind. Probably some telepathic technique he'd learned during his travels in the Merchant Navy—northern Mongolia, perhaps, or the rainforests of Ecuador.

"Tom won't be confronting the suspect himself," Ivor added, hitting the nail on the head, "now that he's a detective chief inspector."

"Probably not," I said, although my words lacked conviction. Tom was having a hard time leaving fieldwork to his subordinates. Not that he'd said so. He knew his new role as DCI was primarily strategy and coordination rather than hands-on investigation, but I'd sensed his frustration. Tom never liked being away from the action.

"What do you think about our latest commission?" Ivor asked.

"I've been rereading the original newspaper articles. One of them includes photographs of the grave goods. I'll print it out for you."

We had an appointment Monday morning to examine the grave goods, which were being stored at Ravenswyck Court, near where the body had been found.

"How were the archaeologists able to date the burial to the early fourteenth century?" I asked.

"The coins," Ivor said, shuffling through a pile of auction catalogs. "They found two silver pennies covering the woman's eyes, both struck near the end of Edward the First's reign in 1307. So the woman was buried sometime between that date and the summer of 1349, when the plague reached Suffolk."

"Where will the artifacts end up?" I asked.

"*That* is the question, my girl." Ivor looked up from a catalog he'd been perusing. "A bit of rivalry there. Dr. Sinclair wants to display them at the art history museum in Norwich. Alex Belcourt has been lobbying the Crown to allow *him* to display the grave goods in an exhibit he's set up at Ravenswyck. Something like the Egyptian exhibition at Highclere Castle but focused on the medieval plague village. Fancies himself an amateur archaeologist." Ivor strode over to the door, unlocked it, and flipped the sign to *Open*. "Monday we'll get our first peep at the artifacts. And tonight"—he waggled his eyebrows—"we'll get our first peep at the archaeologists."

Ivor and I had been invited to a dinner with the senior archaeologists at Finchley Hall, the historic stately home on the edge of Long Barston. Lady Barbara Finchley-fforde, the last of that once-influential family, knew one of them personally—Celia Whybrew, a university lecturer and the niece of one of Lady Barbara's childhood friends.

"I hope they'll tell us about finding the body," I said. "What an amazing experience that must have been."

"If they don't, Lady Barbara will. She's fascinated by the whole thing. The Finchleys were here in the fourteenth century, which, in her mind, makes the unfortunate young woman practically a neighbor." Ivor opened his laptop and turned it on. "Tom will be joining us, I assume?"

"He's meeting us there." I carried my mug of coffee to the small sink behind the sales counter and poured out the remains, then rinsed the mug and placed it upside down on the drainer. "Can you imagine the first glimpse of that preserved body? It must have been almost as exciting as Howard Carter peering for the first time into the tomb of Tutankhamun."

Ivor gave me the side-eye. "And like that esteemed Egyptologist, our Dr. Sinclair has earned quite a reputation."

"For what?"

"For brilliance, personal charm, and diplomacy as a cover for ambition, misogyny, and partisan academic politics. I hear he's trampled on more than one career to get to the top."

"Politics in academia?" I put a hand to my chest, feigning shock.

Ivor snorted. "You know what they say—the smaller the stakes, the more vicious the battle."

I laughed. "Who told you about Dr. Sinclair?"

"An old friend at the university. Expert in medieval languages. He also told me there's been some controversy at the dig."

"Like what?"

"Protesters accusing the archaeologists of disturbing the dead." Ivor tapped something into his computer. "Lots of people believe human bodies shouldn't be exhumed. But one of the protesters is calling down curses on everyone involved, saying they've unleashed malign forces. And there've been a few minor incidents, including a small explosive device placed under the field office caravan. Fortunately, all it did was create a loud bang and give off a foul-smelling smoke."

"That sounds serious."

"My friend says they're hoping the protestors will lose interest now the body's been reinterred." He pressed a key on his computer, and I heard the copy machine in the stockroom come to life. "Speaking of tonight's dinner, did you know Vivian's new lodger is one of the PhD students involved in the excavations?"

"She told me. She said the girl is brilliant but lacks confidence." Vivian Bunn, the bossy, exasperating, but quite lovable seventy-something who'd been my landlady before I married Tom, was . . . *opinionated* might be the word for it. Often wrong. Never in doubt.

Ivor pulled off the smoking hat, finger-combed the tassel, and placed it on the counter.

"Come on, Ivor. What's with the hat?"

"Won it in a card game in New Guinea. They gave me a choice—the hat or the village chief's daughter."

"His daughter?" Oh, this was going to be good.

"Marriage within the clan was considered incest, and they were running low on outsiders."

"You chose the hat."

"A bit sticky, that. I had to tell her father I already had three wives back in England. Three is apparently the limit."

I wanted to ask what a Victorian smoking hat was doing in a village in New Guinea, but I settled for, "And you're wearing the hat for . . . nostalgia?"

"Certainly not. Jeff Swift is stopping by this week." Jeff was one our reliable pickers—freelancers who purchase valuable items at estate sales, auctions, and street markets, and then sell them to dealers at a profit. "Jeff has a customer who collects vintage hats and antique rodent traps. Oh, and Victorian tooth extractors."

I laughed. "Well, England *has* been called 'the paradise of eccentrics.'"

"Eccentrics?" Ivor, looking slightly offended, plopped the hat on his head again, this time at a rakish angle. "I'm sure I don't know what you mean."

Chapter Two

It was almost six thirty when Ivor and I set out for Finchley Hall, a short fifteen minutes' walk from the village center. The sixteenth-century estate had been gifted to the National Trust the previous January when Lady Barbara had admitted she could no longer afford the massive maintenance costs.

That morning, knowing I wouldn't have time to drive home and change before dinner, I'd brought with me a mid-length, pearl-white satin skirt and a fitted black jacket. I changed clothes in the shop's single bathroom, brushed my dark shoulder-length hair into a ponytail, and slicked on a layer of the cherry-colored lip gloss I wore on special occasions. Tom had texted earlier in the day to say he'd meet us at seven unless the unexpected happened, which it did with disturbing regularity.

The path from the church car park led us through Finchley Park with its stands of old oaks. It was a beautiful summer evening. Drifts of purple iris bloomed along the banks of Blackwater Lake. In the farmer's field to the north, a small herd of black-and-white cows rested in the evening shade. Beyond that, on the far side of a fence, we could see rows of neatly hoed young turnip plants.

I cast a surreptitious eye at Ivor, who was puffing. He'd recovered well from his double hip replacement surgery a year ago, but I knew his stamina hadn't fully returned. "You all right?"

He said nothing, rather pointedly.

Ten minutes later, Finchley Hall rose before us, the old bricks glowing rose-red in the slanting rays of the sun. The property had closed to visitors at four o'clock, but a number of the National Trust staff workers were still there, emptying waste bins, scrubbing the picnic tables outside the café, and laying out bedding plants in the Elizabethan garden.

I carried my black slingback heels in a string bag, along with a bottle of wine for Lady Barbara. Ivor—who'd always been unconventional, so why stop now?—had wrapped up a mid-Victorian baby rattle in the shape of a cat playing a fiddle.

We entered the house, not through the main entrance, which was now locked, but through a side entrance leading directly to Lady Barbara's apartments in the east wing. A Portland stone staircase led us up to the first floor where we were met by Francie Jewell, Lady Barbara's cook and live-in companion. "Come in, you lot. They're waiting for you." She collected our jackets and scurried off with them.

Lady Barbara appeared, beaming. "Welcome, darlings." She looked me up and down approvingly. "Very chic. Perfect with those blue eyes." Lady Barbara looked pale but lovely in the rose-colored silk dress she reserved for special occasions. Like the former queen, Lady Barbara paid no attention to fashion trends, preferring instead what she called "timeless pieces," meticulously maintained but often slightly threadbare.

"How are you coping with all the visitors swarming the estate?" Ivor asked while I removed my flat shoes and slipped into my heels.

"Oh, I quite like them. This house was never meant to be lived in by one old lady. Now it's full of life again—and being cared for as it should." She added in a conspiratorial tone, "Sometimes, for a lark, Francie and I put on our old Barbours and headscarves and stroll around the grounds, listening to people talk. We feel like *spies*."

It was just like Lady Barbara, who'd had more than her share of sorrow in her six-plus decades on earth, to make the best of whatever pleasures life afforded her. I knew she was grateful the National Trust had agreed to take on Finchley Hall, saving her from the trauma of a public sale to a pop star or footballer or, worse yet, some multinational corporation with plans to turn the mansion into an executive leisure center. I knew she was grateful, too, for her lovely apartments in the east wing and for the help and companionship of Francie Jewell. If she grieved for the daughter she'd lost at birth, for the husband who'd died too young, for the son who'd thrown his life away for drugs . . . if she regretted being the last of the Finchleys or mourned the progressive loss of her vision, no one would ever know.

We handed her our small gifts, and she thanked us, unwrapping the silver baby rattle. "Well, my goodness," she said with a straight face. "I've always wanted one of these. However did you know?"

Ivor blushed.

Holding the gifts, Lady Barbara led us into the drawing room with its coral-pink walls and exquisite plasterwork frieze. Even in late June, a small fire had been lit in the Portland stone fireplace. A young woman in a black dress and white apron offered us each a glass of wine. I recognized her as the shop girl from the co-op in the village. Another young woman, one I didn't recognize, followed her with a tray of canapes. "Spiced pear in filo, madam."

I took one to be polite, but I was saving myself for Francie's dinner.

Vivian Bunn stood near the fireplace, chatting with three men and two women, the guests of honor. Two of the men had apparently been arguing because the oldest of the trio, a large man somewhere in his early fifties, put up a hand. "No offense, old chap, but you know as well as I do that plague pits are more folklore than history."

"It's *not* folklore." The youngest man's voice was tight with anger. "The discovery at Lincolnshire proves that, and we have good reason to believe—"

"No, Mark. It's no good." The older man shook his head. "We just don't have the—"

"Everyone, please." Lady Barbara shook the rattle, which turned out to be loud enough to traumatize an unsuspecting infant. "I'd like you to meet my dear friends." She transferred the wine bottle and rattle to Francie Jewell. "Please welcome Kate Hamilton and Ivor

Tweedy from The Cabinet of Curiosities. Kate, Ivor—you know Vivian, of course. I'll just go 'round the circle, shall I?"

Ignoring Lady Barbara, the older man stepped forward. "Your reputation precedes you, sir." He shook Ivor's hand. "Dr. Simon Sinclair, senior archaeologist and head of the CMBA." Sinclair was a solid, muscular man, well over six feet with dark hair going gray at the temples and the bronzed skin of someone who spends a lot of time outdoors, or in a tanning salon. A gold chain flashed below his open-collared linen shirt, and I caught a glimpse of what looked like a vintage Patek Philippe watch on his wrist.

Ivor had noticed the watch, too, because he whispered, "Worth a bob or two, eh?"

Sinclair turned his attention to me. "We consider ourselves fortunate to have the benefit of your expertise as well, Ms. Hamilton." He took my hand in both of his and gazed into my eyes. "Beautiful as well as brilliant. How perfectly charming."

I gave him what I hoped was a cool smile. I'd been warned.

Sinclair dropped my hand and turned his attention back to Ivor. "It's the pearl that interests us most, of course. I look forward to your thoughts."

"We'll do our best," Ivor said modestly.

There was an awkward silence in which it became clear Dr. Sinclair wasn't going to introduce the rest of his team. Lady Barbara stepped in. "Kate, Ivor—meet my adopted niece, Dr. Celia Whybrew." She took the woman's hand and pressed it to her papery cheek. "Celia's a lecturer at the university and deputy head of the CMBA." Celia Whybrew was a striking woman, somewhere in her thirties—slim, elegant, and tall, perhaps five-nine or -ten, with long blond hair pulled into a ponytail. She wore no makeup that I could see. She didn't need any.

"I've heard so much about you both from Auntie Barbara," she said. "I'm looking forward to working with you."

"This is Dr. Niall Nevin," Lady Barbara said. "He's also a university lecturer and part of the senior team. In charge of the *finds*, I believe—the artifacts you uncover. Do I have that right?"

"You do. The artifacts discovered during our excavations, no matter how small or seemingly insignificant, must be accounted for and listed, along with field descriptions, sketches, and photographs. It's mostly online work, I'm afraid. Less than glamorous." He blinked. "Delighted to meet you both." Nevin was a tall, thin man with a head that seemed too small for his wide, bony shoulders. He appeared to be somewhere in his mid to late forties, although he might have been younger. A fringe of brown hair flopped over his eyes, and he brushed it back with long, slim fingers. He stooped slightly, all knees and elbows. With his brown tweed jacket and moss-green turtleneck, he reminded me of a grasshopper.

"This young gentleman," Lady Barbara indicated the earnest younger man, "is Mark Lambe, tenth Baronet Kniveton. He's one of the student archaeologists in the PhD program at the university."

The young man's face reddened. "Just Mark," he mumbled. In spite of his grand title, Mark Lambe was dressed in ripped jeans and a hoodie. He had a pleasant, youthful face and thick, rather unkempt dark hair.

"We call him *Your Grace*." Sinclair tugged a forelock in mockery.

Lady Barbara's smile, the product of five hundred years of breeding, never wavered. "And this delightful young lady is Tamzin Oliver. Also a PhD student."

"Tamzin with a *Z*." Vivian traced the letter in the air. Vivian, another septuagenarian, was wearing her ubiquitous baggy tweed skirt and twinset, dressed up for the occasion with a strand of pearls. "She's lodging with me next term as well, aren't you, dear?"

"I hope so." Tamzin, a plump, pretty girl with pale, greenish eyes, looked to be somewhere in her mid-twenties. She was probably a natural redhead, but the neon orange of her hair was definitely not a shade observed in nature. Two thick plaits hung over her shoulders, fading in color from carrot to peach and ultimately pale pink. She wore a white lab coat belted over a short, gauzy pink skirt, purple flowered tights, and shiny white platform boots. Her clothes were what my daughter, Christine, would call *wacky-chic*, intended to shock the hopelessly conventional.

"You're in charge of the dig, then?" Ivor asked Sinclair. "How does it work—the division of responsibilities?"

"I'm the excavation director, yes. As he mentioned, Dr. Nevin is our finds manager. A real stickler for accuracy. Nothing gets past you, eh, Niall? He's a computer expert, lucky for us. Keeps us all in line—or is it online? *Ha!*"

Nevin wasn't smiling. Sinclair was baiting him, but why?

"Niall is our unofficial IT expert," Celia explained. "Everyone in the department ends up in his office at some point."

"And the first thing we see is the sign on his door." Mark laughed. "'Have you turned it off and back on?'"

"It often works," Nevin said a little defensively.

"Niall's also been doing research," Celia said, and I got the impression she was sticking up for him. "For a series of articles Simon is writing."

"Helping out where I can," Nevin said. "Simon's the writer."

"Publish or perish, as they say." Sinclair steepled his hands and made a little mock bow. "Now, Celia here works with the students—everything from recruitment to selection, training, supervision, dating advice." He barked a laugh. "She's a mother hen to them." He gave her an awkward side-hug. "And of course our two stellar graduate students, Mark and Tamzin. They supervise the student teams. They work well together—very well." He winked at us.

This time I got the subtext. Mark and Tamzin were a couple—or Sinclair thought they should be. He turned to Ivor. "We were talking earlier about the pearl. Amazing discovery, was it not?"

"Nearly unprecedented," Ivor agreed. "Pearls were rare in England before the sixteenth century and owned almost exclusively by the Crown. A single pearl the size and quality of the one found in the coffin would have come from the Persian Gulf or the shores of India, which begs the question, how did it get to England? You have a bit of a puzzle on your hands."

"That's what my team keeps telling me." Sinclair shrugged. "And I keep reminding them that solving puzzles is what I do best." He made a small self-deprecating gesture. "At least that's what people say."

I try to give people the benefit of the doubt. I really do.

By now, I was pretty sure I wasn't going to enjoy working with Sinclair, but if Ivor and I turned down a job every time we didn't like the client, we wouldn't be in business for long.

"Tamzin took her undergraduate degree in medieval history," said Vivian, who wasn't used to being ignored. "She's only recently switched to archaeology."

"How interesting," Lady Barbara said. "Is this your first dig, Tamzin?"

"Oh, no. I was part of the dig last year near Oakham in Rutland. A Roman villa."

"A *villa rustica* to be more precise," Sinclair said with a passable Italian accent. "A farm complex with both residential and agricultural buildings. Our students were uncovering a mosaic floor in what was once a dining salon. Tamzin was a real leader," Sinclair said. "This year I made her co-supervisor with Mark." He put his arm around the girl's shoulders and squeezed, pulling her slightly off balance. "She and His Grace here have been preparing for your visit Monday."

Mark Lambe's expression tightened.

"We're looking forward to meeting Alex Belcourt," Ivor said. "Will he be there as well?"

Sinclair snorted. "We could hardly avoid him if we wanted to. Seems to think he's a modern-day Lord Carnarvon. Naturally, we're grateful to him for allowing us to excavate, but he doesn't own the history."

The room fell silent.

"And to think," said Lady Barbara, saving the moment, "that such wonderful discoveries have been made practically on our doorstep. Celia, I know your Aunt Emily must be so proud of you." Lady Barbara dabbed her eyes with the handkerchief she'd tucked up her sleeve. "Emily Whybrew was my best girlhood chum. We've kept in touch, but she had a career in the diplomatic core. When she retired, she settled in the British Virgin Islands."

"I knew Emily Whybrew." Ivor raised a finger. "Splendid girl."

"I'll send her your greetings when next I write," Celia said.

"Virgin Islands, you say?" Sinclair perked up. "I was part of the dig at Cinnamon Bay." He began telling a story about his involvement in the prehistoric excavations on the island of St. Thomas.

I turned to Celia. "Will I see you at Ravenswyck Monday morning?"

"Yes, of course. We're between semesters now, so there's just a handful of us onsite—Simon, Niall, and myself, Mark, and Tamzin. The rest of the team, the students, have returned to college for their assessments and graduation. A few will rejoin us next term as post-grads, but most of the new team will be undergrads. We offer this kind of field experience twice a year. The excavations at Egemere Close could keep us busy for some time."

"So the work at the church is ongoing?"

"Oh, yes. Our first dig at Egemere Close was in 2016. This time we focused on the church—the south transept. That's where we found the lead coffin."

"That was almost ten years ago. Why the gap in time?" I asked.

"Simon chooses the sites." She shot a surreptitious glance at him. "But we're back now—and we may be next term as well. The CMBA wants us to excavate the north transept as well as the nave and chancel. It's possible we might uncover more burials, although the graveyard was relocated in the 1960s."

"If they moved the bodies, why leave behind the one you found?"

"That's part of the mystery. We suspect Egemere Woman—that's what we're calling her—was buried privately."

"Privately?"

"Perhaps secretly."

I tried to think of reasons why someone might bury a body secretly but couldn't come up with any. "Does Dr. Sinclair specialize in medieval archaeology?"

"Actually, he prefers prehistory and Roman England. In fact, he lobbied pretty hard to have this year's student experience at the Roman villa near Oakham again, but this time the CMBA put their foot down, and here we are."

"I thought Dr. Sinclair was head of the CMBA."

"He is in an operational sense, but the board has the final say. The power of the purse strings. And they were proved right. Even Simon has to admit that."

"I heard him mention a mound."

"There's a raised area, roughly circular, not far from the ruins of the village. Mark believes it's a plague pit."

"By *plague pit* you mean the mass burial sites during the Black Death."

She nodded. "Mark's been trying to talk Simon into requesting a full excavation."

"He isn't interested?"

"No, and I'm not sure why not." She lowered her voice. "In 2020, a plague pit with forty-eight skeletons was found at the site of a medieval hospital in rural Lincolnshire. To prove his theory, Mark needs ground-penetrating radar—which Simon refuses to authorize."

"I take it you don't agree with Dr. Sinclair's decision?"

"It's complicated." Her eyes flicked again to Sinclair. "So far, the mass burial at Lincolnshire is unique—the only confirmed plague pit outside London. But Immingham can't have been the only rural community overwhelmed by the Black Death, can it? Between 1348 and 1353, an estimated two to three million people died in England—nearly half the population. The Black Death was one of the worst pandemics in human history." She took a breath. "The mound could be Anglo-Saxon, of course—even Neolithic. But Mark found a reference to a mass burial site in a letter written in the sixteenth century from a woman in Hartwell to her son in London. There'd been another outbreak of bubonic plague, and the letter refers to the opening of an earlier pit to accommodate the bodies of the current victims." She raised her elegant shoulders. "Simon doesn't agree, and he's right about the cost. Funding is always an issue, but Mark's spent more than a year researching plague pits in rural England. He needs results. His dissertation topic hasn't been approved yet. Without Simon's support, it probably won't be, which means Mark will never get his doctorate in archaeology. At least not at the University of East Anglia."

"What does Dr. Nevin think?"

"Niall agrees with Dr. Sinclair. No surprise there."

"Could the pits be dangerous? I mean, could the plague be active after all these years?"

Celia shook her head. "The culprit is *Yersinia pestus.* After seven hundred years, there'd be no living bacteria, so no chance of spreading the infection. Good question, though, given what the world's been through recently. Mark's interest is not only the possible location of plague pits in East Anglia but also the methods of burial under such extreme conditions. In the past, scholars pictured carts loaded with plague victims—some still clinging to life—dumped into massive holes in the ground." She shook her head. "That's probably not true. The skeletons in Lincolnshire had been laid out with great care."

My phone pinged—a text from Tom.

Possible sighting of white caravan near Hart's Green. Give my regrets to Lady B. xoxo

Chapter Three

Voices from the hallway announced the arrival of our friends, the Reverend Edmund Foxe and his wife, Angela. Edmund and Angela had been married the previous September and were expecting their first child in a little over a month.

"I'm so glad you could make it, dears." Lady Barbara beamed. "Everyone, this is Edmund Foxe, rector of St. Æthelric's, and his wife, Angela, our local veterinarian."

"We apologize for being late," Edmund said, helping his wife out of her jacket. "Angela was called out at the last minute to supervise the birth of seven springer spaniel puppies whose mum was having rather a hard time of it."

"I didn't handle the pups myself, because of the baby—transmitted disease. The owner needed moral support, and she did great. They all made it." Angela accepted a glass of what looked like sparkling mineral water. "One little chap might need a bit of extra care, but he's a fighter. Crawled over several of the larger pups for a place at mum's table."

"Just like my Fergus." Vivian began telling a story about her pug's puppyhood.

"The baby will be here soon," I said to Angela and Edmund privately. "Are you ready?"

"As we'll ever be." Angela cradled her belly. "Edmund's parents came down last week with a carload of equipment. This wee one is going to be the best-turned-out infant in Suffolk."

"Do you know if it's a boy or a girl?"

"No," Edmund said, "and we don't want to." He put his arm around Angela's shoulder. "Either way is fine as long as it's healthy. That's why I'm trying to talk Angela into stopping work. Routine office cases are one thing, but she's occasionally called out for the large farm animals."

"Being pregnant means there are certain things I can't do," Angela said. "Lambing, for one. I missed lambing season entirely this year, and I love it. The locum's arriving next week. He'll take the large-animal work and the birthing and leave the small practice to me—routine checkups, injections, teeth-cleaning—all the boring stuff." She made a face. "I'll go back half-time after six weeks or so. Hattie can't wait to mind the baby. She's been knitting little caps and sewing flannel sleep sacks." Hattie Nuthall, the rectory housekeeper, had made the transition from overseeing a bachelor establishment to caring for a married couple—and now a family.

I couldn't help thinking about Egemere Woman. Had she been preparing a tiny wardrobe? Was her last thought for her unborn child?

Francie Jewell appeared, smiling broadly. "Dinner is served. Follow me, please."

We made our way into the dining room with its pale Edwardian paintwork and early nineteenth-century mahogany table of grand proportions. I was seated between Dr. Sinclair and Celia Whybrew. Ivor sat across from me, next to Dr. Nevin.

As always, the food was amazing. Francie had prepared roasted Finchley estate pheasants stuffed with truffles and crushed root vegetables, and her famous potatoes layered with Suffolk farmhouse cheese.

Dr. Nevin was quiet during dinner, and I got the impression his mind was elsewhere. Or perhaps he was simply content to let others do the talking.

Truthfully, none of us needed to say much. Conversation was dominated by Dr. Sinclair, who, perhaps fueled by Lady Barbara's excellent pinot noir, delivered a lecture on the evolution of burial practices in East Anglia. "That's why the discovery at Ravenswyck is so important." He gestured with his fork. "You can imagine our shock when the shroud was peeled back and we saw that face. She might have been buried a few years ago rather than centuries. I knew immediately we had only a short time before the remains would begin to deteriorate, so I phoned the coroner—old mate of mine. He located a refrigerated mortuary cabinet in Long Melford."

Vivian spoke up. "Tamzin explained why the body was so well preserved after all those centuries. Tell them, dear."

"*Erm*, well, no special mummification had been attempted, but the conditions—"

Dr. Sinclair cut across her. "Combination of factors. All a bit technical, I'm afraid. In layman's terms, the lead coffin, the beeswax seal, and the resinous coating—which turned out to be frankincense, by the way—excluded moisture and air, allowing the neutral fats in the bodily tissues to convert to fatty acids, which then dehydrated and acidified the tissues, killing off the bacteria and producing glycerol, a preservative."

Tamzin's face flushed, whether in anger or embarrassment, I couldn't tell.

"No one back then would have understood the chemistry of preservation, of course," Celia added. "You were going to say that, weren't you, Tamzin? Those who buried her did so with reverence and extraordinary care."

"Just as we do today." Dr. Sinclair made a dismissive gesture, and I noticed for the first time a curious ring on his left hand—an agate intaglio, the stone engraved with the image of the Roman god Mercury, recognizable by his winged helmet and staff. This was a man who liked jewelry. "Pointless. Bodies are meant to decay."

"Except this one didn't," Mark said quietly.

"And that rather *is* the point, isn't it?" Celia looked directly at Sinclair. "Whoever buried Egemere Woman went to great lengths to preserve her body. Anyway, I don't imagine preventing decay is what grieving families think about when they choose a coffin, do you, Simon?"

She'd openly challenged him, and I got the feeling she'd enjoyed it.

All eyes swung to Sinclair. His mouth opened to speak, but Lady Barbara got there first. "When did you say Egemere Woman lived, Dr. Sinclair?"

For a moment, he looked blank, processing the unexpected segue. "Ah . . . the evidence suggests she died sometime in the first half of the fourteenth century."

"Well, let's see, then." Lady Barbara furrowed her brow. "Sir Oswyn Finchley, who built the Hall as we see it today, died on the Eve of St. Æthelric in 1549. His father was Galfrid, who died in 1503, and his father was Thorold, who died in 1480-something, and *his* father was—" She frowned. "Oh, dear, I'm lost in the fifteenth century."

"Egemere Woman will rewrite the textbooks," Sinclair said, ignoring Lady Barbara. "A once-in-a-lifetime discovery."

"Your crowning achievement." Nevin's eyes were bright, making me wonder if wine was the only stimulant he'd consumed that evening. "Everyone is impressed."

"Apparently not everyone," I said, intending it as a joke. "We heard about the protesters."

The room fell silent. Mark coughed. Tamzin stared into her napkin.

"Who told you that?" Sinclair glared at me.

I gave Ivor a surreptitious glance. "I can't actually remember." I don't like lying, but no way was I going to throw Ivor's university contact under the bus.

"As it happens, you're right," Sinclair admitted. "Loonies. Happens all the time. Any archaeologist will tell you. Disturbing the dead. Awakening evil spirits. The curse of the pharaohs." He waggled his fingers to signal something spooky. "It's all nonsense. This is academic research. If people don't want historians digging them up, they should put 'Do Not Disturb' signs on their coffins." He roared at his own joke.

"That wouldn't work everywhere," Ivor said, steering the conversation away from the rocks. "I stayed once in a Torajan village in

Indonesia. The ritual of *Ma'nene* is a kind of annual meet-and-greet with deceased relatives. The mummified bodies are brought out, cleaned, dressed in new clothes, and then carried to the village for a good chin-wag."

"Fascinating." Dr. Sinclair leaned forward in his seat. "Reminds me of—" He began telling a story about funeral customs among the ancient Scythians.

I whispered to Celia on my left. "I'm sorry."

"You weren't to know," she whispered back. "We've been instructed not to talk about the protesters. Actually, that's one of the reasons Simon's so opposed to excavating the mound. He's afraid the protesters will increase their opposition. If there's controversy, and if the press gets hold if it, the university could pull their funding. The human remains debate is one of the most contentious issues in global archaeology today. People and institutions with the money to fund excavations don't want to end up on the wrong side of history."

"I've read about Ma'nene," Mark said. "You were actually there?"

"I rather saved the day." Ivor gave a modest smile. "One of the mummies lost an arm. Luckily, I had a tube of marine-grade epoxy and stuck the gentleman back together. Worked like a charm."

Ivor's tales of his days in the Merchant Navy were the stuff of legend, but were they all strictly true or did he embellish the truth now and again? Did it matter?

After dinner, Francie Jewell reappeared with a silver platter upon which rested a spectacular chocolate and praline ice cream bombe. I accepted a thin slice and felt like a stuffed pheasant myself.

When the plates were cleared, Lady Barbara stood. "Well, now. Who's ready for brandy in the drawing room?"

"Not us, I'm afraid," Vivian said, speaking for Tamzin as well. "Fergus will need his walkies. I brought a torch, Tamzin dear. We don't want you falling into the koi pond."

"Mind if we walk with you?" Ivor asked. "Kate left her car at the shop."

We gathered our belongings, thanked Lady Barbara, and told the others we'd see them on Monday morning at Ravenswyck Court.

Outside, the evening sky had clouded over, and the temperature had dropped. Rain was on the way, and I hoped Ivor and I would make it back to the shop before it began. At least I'd exchanged the heels for my flat shoes.

A mist was rising, sending tendrils curling around the old tree trunks and floating eerily over the walking path. Vivian strode ahead with the flashlight, the beam diffused by the mist. The rest of us trailed behind her like ducklings.

I walked with Celia. "Is something wrong with Dr. Nevin?"

"He's in pain a lot. He injured his back in a dig several years ago. That's why Simon put him in charge of the finds lists. He can't do the heavy fieldwork anymore."

"That's terrible," I said, wondering if an injury like that could damage his career.

"It really was kind of Simon to find him a place on the team. Uncharacteristically kind."

"Is Dr. Nevin married?"

"No, and I'm not sure he's interested."

"Dr. Sinclair is interested." I glanced over to see her reaction.

"He's interested all right—as long as there are no commitments. He was married, briefly. There's a daughter, but I don't think he sees her much. She attends one of those posh boarding schools."

"Tough on a professor's salary."

"Oh, he doesn't live on a professor's salary. Dr. Sinclair is in great demand as a speaker, and he's good at it—charming, erudite, and very funny. He has a wealth of experience and lots of entertaining stories. I've heard he makes more from his speaking engagements than he does from archaeology. Good thing, because he has expensive tastes."

That explained the vintage gold watch. "Maybe Dr. Nevin could do the same."

"Hardly. Niall isn't the most riveting lecturer in the world. He's a competent archaeologist—more than competent—but he lacks Simon's charisma."

Ivor caught up with Tamzin. "Anything we should know about the protesters?"

I hadn't had an opportunity to tell him what Celia had said about funding.

"Nothing to worry about." Tamzin shook her head. "It's just people marching around with signs asking if we'd dig up our grandmothers."

"How many are there?"

"Only six or seven, but they're determined to stop the digging. The leader is this creepy lady. Ancient—seventy, maybe. And weird. She keeps saying we're all cursed, and if we continue digging, someone will die."

"Has she threatened anyone?" Ivor asked.

"Not directly."

"Has Dr. Sinclair contacted the police?"

"No, but I think he should," Tamzin said. "It started out as a nuisance, but the incidents are escalating. No one's been hurt yet, so we've been warned not to say anything." She put a hand to her mouth. "I shouldn't have told you that."

"Why not?"

Tamzin just shook her head.

"Well, as you say, nothing serious." Ivor began whistling softly in the dark.

I felt a chill, hoping it was the cool night air, because I'd heard fear in Tamzin's voice, and that unsettled me. Who was she afraid of—the old woman leading the protest or Simon Sinclair?

Chapter Four

Manor Farm

By the time Tom got home, I was already in bed. Hearing the crunch of tires on the gravel drive, I got up, wrapped myself in my cashmere robe, a wedding gift from Lady Barbara, and hurried downstairs to meet him in the hall.

"Hullo, darling." He shrugged off his waxed jacket and hung it on a wall hook. "Sorry I'm late. Did I wake you? The fog is so thick tonight I wasn't sure I could make it home. Almost like those old pea-soupers back in the day."

"I was awake." I yawned, reaching out to kiss him. "How'd it go?"

"The victim in the Thetford incident didn't make it. We're looking for a killer now."

"You said there was a possible sighting of a white caravan."

"Turns out it wasn't the suspect, although we believe he's still in Suffolk. All the roads are being watched."

"He can't stay out of sight forever. He'll need food, supplies—especially if the woman's with him." *If she's still alive.* "Do you think he knows the victim died?"

"If he doesn't, he will soon enough. It'll be on the morning news and in all the papers."

"Cup of tea?"

"Exactly what I need." He smiled, and I could see he was exhausted. "How was the evening at the Hall? How were the archaeologists?"

"Come on. I'll tell you all about it." I took his hand and led him into our old-fashioned kitchen with the inglenook hearth. It was my favorite room in the house. Before moving in, we'd repainted the old wood cabinets a pale taupe color, installed a refurbished cream Aga cooker, and switched out the old vintage fridge for a modern American-style one. Everything else we'd left as it was, especially the original flagstones. They weren't perfectly level, but I'd memorized the trip hazards.

Our house, a lovely rose-brick, mid-Georgian on the edge of Long Barston, had been called "Waifs' House" in Victorian times because the owner, a wealthy widow, had taken in young girls in need of refuge and trained them for domestic employment. Doing a little research into the history of the property, I learned it had originally been called Manor Farm. I loved the name, and we'd rechristened the house.

I plugged in the electric kettle. Tom sat at the huge pine table that had rested on the flagstones longer than anyone could remember. Two or three centuries of history were etched into the top—burn marks where I imagined a candle had gone over; scratches made by generations of children practicing their letters; shallow cuts where loaves of bread had once been sliced, and deeper ones where a joint of meat may have been prepared for the turnspit.

A postcard lay on the table, showing a view of the French Riviera. Tom turned it over to read the few hastily scrawled lines. "From my mother. 'Fabulous! Wish you were here!'"

Tom's mother, Liz Mallory, was currently enjoying a cruise in the Mediterranean with one of her single girlfriends, to be followed by two weeks in Sardinia. From the looks of the clothes they had packed, I wondered if it was a singles cruise, although that didn't sound like Liz. Her brief marriage to Tom's father had put her off marriage altogether. I was just glad to have her out of our lives for a few weeks. Liz had never been a fan of mine and took every opportunity to make that clear.

"What do you hear from your mother and James?" Tom asked.

"They're still in Door County," I said, speaking of the peninsula between Wisconsin and Lake Michigan. "After that, they're spending a couple of weeks with James's daughter at her lake house in Vilas County." A year ago, after thirty years as a widow, my mother, Linnea, had married the dashing Dr. James Lund. In spite of their health issues, they were enjoying life to the full. We emailed, texted, and occasionally Zoomed, but the fact that we weren't communicating daily anymore was a sign to me that we were both very happy.

"So how was the dinner at Finchley Hall?" Tom asked.

"Brilliant," I said, opening a glass jar of tea bags. "Francie Jewell could have her own cooking show if she wanted—which I'm glad she doesn't because Lady Barbara needs her. I think she knows that. She's very loyal." I found a carton of milk in the fridge and poured some into a small creamware pitcher. "You asked about the archaeologists. The two PhD students are young, eager, and earnest. Tamzin Oliver is the one who boards with Vivian. The other student is Mark Lambe, tenth Baronet Kniveton." The kettle whistled, and I poured hot water into the teapot to warm it. "He took some teasing about the title, and I got the impression he's embarrassed by it."

"I knew his father casually—Julian, the ninth baronet. He died in a riding accident when he was just forty. His son, the one you met, became the tenth baronet at the age of twelve. Plenty of money there, all right."

"He's a serious scholar." I placed two cups, the pitcher of milk, and a bowl of sugar cubes on the table. "He wants to do his thesis on plague pits in East Anglia." I filled the teapot with steaming water and added three tea bags.

"Are there plague pits in East Anglia?"

"That's what he wants to find out—if his thesis topic is approved."

"And Lady Barbara's friend?" Tom poured milk into his cup. "What's she like?"

"Celia Whybrew. She's delightful—interesting, personable, smart. I can see why Lady Barbara has a soft spot for her." I swirled the teapot and poured out. "She's deputy head of the CMBA, in charge of training the student archaeologists. Dr. Niall Nevin is responsible for cataloging the finds—the artifacts uncovered during the dig. He's nice enough, but he didn't say much. I got the impression he's rather cowed by Dr. Sinclair." I added a splash of milk and two sugars to my tea. "Simon Sinclair is the senior archaeologist. I hate to be critical, Tom, but he's everything I can't stand—proud, opinionated, condescending, belligerent if he's challenged. The students are afraid of him. Nevin, too, I think. I can't imagine how a nice woman like Celia Whybrew can work with him so closely. Oh, and he drinks too much."

"I hope he wasn't driving." Tom stirred his tea and took a tentative sip.

I cradled my cup to warm my hands. Our house had been built in 1780, when there was no such thing as energy efficiency. Insulation and radiators had been installed in the 1960s, but the climate control was definitely not up to modern standards. Even so, I'd decided long ago that putting up with a few minor inconveniences was preferable to living in one of the soulless mini mansions that developers on both sides of the pond seemed to be throwing up everywhere.

"Did you learn anything that will help you and Ivor?" Tom asked.

"Not really, although Ivor heard they've had protestors at the site, accusing them of disturbing the dead. Sinclair warned his team not to talk about it. He's afraid the controversy will jeopardize their funding."

"Was Alex Belcourt at the dinner?"

"No. We'll meet him for the first time Monday morning. The grave goods found with the fourteenth-century body and the finds from this year's dig are being kept at Ravenswyck Court. There's a museum."

"The medieval exhibit. I've seen it. What do you know about Belcourt?"

"Nothing except he made a lot of money designing packaging systems."

"Tragic history there. In 2013, he married a woman named Carrie Holgate—a runway model from London. Three years later she vanished."

"She left him?"

"That's the question. Belcourt insisted she'd been kidnapped, even though the police found no evidence of it. She just disappeared. Their joint bank account was never touched. She never accessed her credit cards or used her mobile phone."

"What do you think?"

Tom shrugged. "Maybe she ran away, didn't want to be traced, but it isn't easy to disappear in this digital age. I think she's probably dead."

"Wouldn't a body have turned up?"

"That's what makes it so puzzling. It's not easy to disappear, and it's even harder to make a body disappear, and yet no trace of her has ever been found, dead or alive. At the time, the police suspected Belcourt of killing her. The SIO on the case was sure of it, but without a clear motive or a body, there was no case."

"Were there other suspects?"

"I'd have to look at the case notes again." Tom placed his empty cup in the saucer. "Cold cases are brutal. The police feel they've failed, the relatives have no closure, and the suspects can't clear their names."

"Did Belcourt marry again?"

"The High Court issued a declaration of presumed death a few years ago—but no, he's never remarried. Lives alone in that enormous house—with a large staff, presumably." Tom leaned back in his chair. "When Belcourt lost his wife, he poured himself into his work. He was rich before. Now he's one of the wealthiest men in England."

"He seems to have poured himself into his hobby as well—amateur archaeology. Ivor says he wants to display the grave goods in the museum at Ravenswyck Court. Bit of contention over that, according to Ivor. Dr. Sinclair wants the artifacts to go to a museum in Norwich."

"Who will win?"

"I don't know, but if there's a dispute, Ivor won't get involved. We're there to do the work we've agreed to—that's it."

Tom drew a hand down his face. "I'm knackered." Thunder rumbled in the distance. "It's going to rain tonight."

I stood and kissed the top of his head. "Go to bed. I'll clean up and join you in five minutes."

Chapter Five

Monday, June 23
Ravenswyck Court

At eight thirty Monday morning, I picked Ivor up at the shop and we headed in my Mini for Ravenswyck Court. My GPS led us through several tiny villages and along highways flanked by hedgerows thick with elder and the wild briar roses that thrive in England's summer. The overnight rainstorm had reduced to a fine, drizzly mist that petered out before we met the brick-and-iron fencing delineating the Ravenswyck estate.

At the entrance, electric wooden gates swung open. I drove along a pea-shingle lane, past a row of handsome stone stables with fenced-in paddocks. After a mile or so, we spotted the house with its early Georgian elevations, shallow tile roof, and small-paned sash windows.

A battered old Land Rover was parked near the entrance. A man with thick salt-and-pepper hair emerged from the house wearing jeans and a rough leather jacket. He shot us an unfriendly look before climbing into the old four-wheel-drive vehicle and pulling away.

I took the parking spot he'd vacated.

I expected a butler, but the man who met us at the door introduced himself. "You must be our art experts. I'm Alex Belcourt. Welcome to Ravenswyck." He wasn't much taller than me—maybe five-nine—with unremarkable features and mild, blue-gray eyes.

Ivor and I introduced ourselves, and Belcourt beckoned us inside a long, high-ceilinged hall lined with old portraits in oils. A massive and beautifully carved oak staircase rose to a landing before doubling back on itself. Ravenswyck was smaller than Finchley Hall but gave nothing away when it came to grandeur. "You just missed my farm manager, Peter Eley."

"He didn't look best pleased to see us," Ivor said.

Belcourt laughed. "That's just his way. He's been with me since the beginning. His father was farm manager before him, so he takes a proprietary interest in his job. Just what I need since I'm often away on business."

"This is a working farm, then," I said. "Do you grow crops?"

"Sugar beets and barley, but Eley's main work is the animals. My wife, Carrie, got me interested in some of the traditional breeds of sheep and cattle. And goats. We have a small herd of endangered species."

His wife, the one who disappeared.

Ivor was examining one of the portraits.

"Don't look for a resemblance," Belcourt said. "These are all members of the Wyck family, the original owners of Ravenswyck. They lived here for nearly seven centuries—until the 1870s when the line died out. I bought the estate in 2013—house, outbuildings, and a couple hundred acres. Decided the portraits should stay. These folk have been here a lot longer than I have."

Ivor handed him our card. "We're looking forward to seeing the grave goods."

"No time like the present." Belcourt grinned. "The others are waiting for us in the exhibition area on the lower level. We'll take the lift."

Belcourt led us along a wide corridor, past a formal reception room on the left and a library on the right. We stepped inside a small cage-style elevator. Belcourt pulled the metal doors shut and pushed a button. The elevator lurched and began a slow, shuddering descent.

"Do you get many visitors?" I asked.

"More every year. We're open only at the weekend, Friday to Sunday. Visitors enter through a separate, outside entrance and climb a set of stairs to the ground floor. The self-guided tour begins in the public rooms and ends on the lower level, with the medieval exhibit."

I glanced at Belcourt, trying and failing to picture him as a wife-murderer. Nor would anyone take him for one of the wealthiest men in Britain. He wore a pair of baggy moleskin trousers, an old tweed jacket with frayed cuffs, and boots sadly in need of polishing. His hair was light brown, going gray and thinning at the forehead. His face was pleasant but unremarkable, the sort of face no one remembers.

"I haven't seen the exhibit," Ivor said, "but I've heard it's impressive. You've invested considerable time and money here."

"We're partially funded by the British Heritage Fund and the local arts council, but yes—this exhibit means a lot to me. It was my wife's dream." Belcourt's expression softened. "Egemere was a tiny hamlet in the fourteenth century, of no importance to anyone except its inhabitants. What we document here are the lives of the vast majority of people living in England at that time. They were farmers, herdsmen, artisans. This is the real medieval Britain, the one many historians neglect." I saw passion in his face and understood why Alex Belcourt was fighting to display the objects buried with Egemere Woman here rather than the museum in Norwich. This was personal for him.

The elevator jerked to a halt, and we stepped into a sort of vestibule, the walls lined with drawings and photographs of the house and the Wyck family in the early to mid-nineteenth century. A sign read "Resurrecting the Medieval Village of Egemere Close."

"We've included some photographs from the dig in 2016," Belcourt said. "That one includes my wife, Carrie." He indicated a group photograph taken in front of the house.

It wasn't a great photo, shot partially into the sun. Standing in the middle of what appeared to be students, maybe twelve or fourteen of them, was a slim young woman with dark braided hair. She stood beside a younger and trimmer version of Simon Sinclair, looking up at him and laughing. He had his arms around her and another young woman who held what appeared to be a piece of stained glass, probably from the church.

We followed Belcourt into a large, open room, surprisingly high-ceilinged.

I could hardly believe my eyes. He'd actually created a medieval street, complete with the façade of a cottage, a forge, a bakery, a pigsty, and what looked like the corner of a tithe barn. It looked almost real, with life-size wax figures. An old woman hung out of an upper-story window, about to tip the contents of a bucket onto the street. A boy in a leather jerkin herded three woolly sheep along the cobbles. An old man with a single crutch begged for alms. Behind an enclosure of woven twigs, an enormous black sow nursed her litter of piglets. Medieval music played softly in the background.

Ivor was right. Belcourt had invested a small fortune here. It would take several lifetimes for the exhibit to begin generating a profit—which told me profit wasn't his motivation.

Celia, Nevin, Mark, and Tamzin were waiting for us.

"Isn't this wonderful?" Celia asked, and we agreed that it was.

"Carrie, my wife, planned the exhibit as an immersive experience for visitors," Belcourt said. "Peasant villages like this existed all over Britain from pre-Roman times to the Norman invasion and beyond."

"She got it right," Mark said. "This is no Disney fantasy. People associate the word *peasant* with poverty, ignorance, missing teeth, and poor personal hygiene. What it really means is simply a person who lives in the countryside and makes their living from resources available to them by their own labor."

"A few acres of arable land and a pasture were enough to keep a peasant family going," Belcourt added, "especially when supplemented by hunting and fishing or artisanal skills such as weaving or baking. Egemere Close was a small but vibrant community. This is what we're attempting to demonstrate here." He gave us a lopsided smile. "On my hobbyhorse again. Sorry."

"Don't apologize," Ivor said. "You'll never find a more interested audience."

"Egemere Woman was part of this community," Nevin said. "Exactly what part remains to be discovered."

"Well, I'm impressed," I said truthfully. "It's one thing to read about history in books. It's another to stand here in the middle of it."

The look on Belcourt's face told me I'd hit exactly the right note.

Tamzin and Mark had gone ahead of us, through a stone archway at the end of the reconstructed street.

"Where's Dr. Sinclair?" I asked Celia as we followed the students. "I thought he planned to meet us here."

"He always runs late. I'm sure he'll show up any minute now."

The next room was a proper museum filled with glass display cabinets, some freestanding, others lining the walls.

"Everything you see here was found on the property," Belcourt explained. "People discarded what was no longer useful to them. They lost things, as we all do. Lucky for us, when the village was abandoned in 1349, the few survivors seem to have left everything behind, perhaps considering the possessions of the dead to be unlucky or cursed."

The exhibit was just as Belcourt described it—the remains of a lost world. As I gazed at case after case of everyday objects—a clay pipe, a child's leather shoe, the bones of animals once cooked and served for dinner, coins, pendants, tools, jewelry—I felt as I had when I'd first read about Egemere Woman and her blue eyes, as if time was folding back upon itself. I could almost smell the effluvia and hear the rumble of wooden cart wheels on cobbles.

Ivor's voice brought me back to the present. "Were all these objects found in the archaeological excavations?"

"No, indeed," Belcourt said. "I began to collect soon after my wife and I bought the estate. Every time we ploughed the land, something would turn up. Then a group of local metal detectorists asked permission to search in my fallow fields. I agreed with the understanding that anything they found that could be dated before 1500, the beginning of the early modern period, would belong to me—for the collection. We knew it was the site of Egemere Close, but the number of items discovered exceeded our expectation. It was my wife's idea to create the exhibit. She was pursuing a degree in archaeology when she got her first modeling contract. She's the one who suggested contacting the university. She'd heard they were searching for locations for their semi-annual student work experience, and I thought, why not?"

"When was this?" Ivor asked.

"Summer of 2016, the year . . ." Belcourt left the sentence unfinished.

Was he about to say *the year Carrie died* or *the year Carrie disappeared*? I waited, hoping he would offer more details.

He didn't. Instead, gathering himself, he rubbed his hands together. "Well, let's have a look at the artifacts found with the body, shall we?"

"I expected to see Dr. Sinclair," Ivor said.

"He's probably on the way," Nevin said. "I'll phone him." Pulling out his mobile, he tapped in a few numbers and listened. His brow furrowed. "No answer. Not even a recorded message."

"That's not like him," Celia said. "He always picks up."

Mark tapped his forehead. "I'm sorry—I forgot to say. Last night at the pub, he told me he had something to check on this morning. It must have taken longer than expected."

"He didn't tell me," Celia said. "Niall?"

"No."

"Or me either," Tamzin agreed.

"He's probably at the site," Mark said. "Forgot about the time. You know how he can hyperfocus."

"Typical," Belcourt muttered. "In that case, we'll have a look at the artifacts without him."

"If he doesn't show up in thirty minutes or so," Nevin said, "we can meet him at the dig site. Kate, Ivor—I think you'll be interested to see what we've been doing there."

Chapter Six

The grave goods had been laid out on a table covered with a dark-blue felt cloth. Besides the two silver coins, there were personal items—a glass mirror protected by two hinged copper alloy discs; a gold cross set with garnets; a double-sided tortoiseshell comb, the teeth still intact; a shallow bronze dish that might once have held cosmetics; and the silver wrist cuff we'd seen photographed from every possible angle. These were personal items, things a woman might have valued, and the condition was remarkable—due, I supposed, to the fact that the lead coffin had been so effectively sealed.

Ivor handed me a pair of cotton gloves. Donning his own, he picked up the cuff and peered at it through the jewelers' loupe he always carried. "Hmm, yes." He held it up for me to see. "Look at the niello border design. I'd say mid to late thirteenth century."

The silver cuff had been divided into twelve segments, one for each head, bordered by a pointed Gothic-style arch incised into the silver and filled with a black sulfide alloy—niello, visible even under the dark tarnish.

"The twelve heads probably had religious significance," Ivor said, "and would have been almost antique in the early fourteenth century. It may have been a family piece, passed down from an earlier generation." He handed it to me.

The tarnished surface had darkened to an iridescent blue-black that set off the blue glass eyes in sharp contrast. Even without a loupe,

I could see that all the relief-molded faces were bearded. Each wore some sort of headgear or crown—or possibly a halo.

"What do you notice about the faces?" Ivor asked Celia.

"The eyes." She leaned in to look. "They really stand out, don't they?"

"Under magnification, I'm able to detect individual differences in the faces. I suspect they'll become more obvious when the tarnish is removed—if restoration is what you want." Ivor turned to Belcourt. "I suggest testing a tarnish remover in an inconspicuous area. That will tell us if restoration is recommended—or even possible."

"We'll have to check with the CMBA board," Celia said. "It's their call." She picked up a small leather pouch, roughly spade-shaped, with a drawstring that looked like silk cording. "And now for the prize." She looked at us, her eyes shining. "We found it lying near her heart." Turning the pouch upside down, she eased out a large, teardrop-shaped pearl, perfectly symmetrical and still so lustrous, it took my breath. I'd seen photos, of course, but seeing the pearl for myself was almost . . . mystical.

I gripped the edge of the table to steady myself as my mouth went dry and my fingertips began to tingle. A flush of heat rose in my cheeks. My heart thumped against my ribcage. An irrational impulse to weep made my throat ache with suppressed tears.

And then it came, that inner voice I'd come to recognize—with words as clear and sharp as flint glass. *Fear, terror.*

It was *my* voice and yet not mine, the words coming not from my throat or even my brain but from somewhere deep within my core. I heard, or seemed to hear, the clash of metal—*swords?*—and the sound of a horn, an insistent trumpeting above a cacophony of voices.

I blinked away tears, trembling as the voices and sounds slowly receded.

Ivor's arm brushed mine. "According to one legend," I heard him say, "the tears Eve cried when she was banished from Eden turned to pearls."

No one spoke. At that moment, anything seemed possible.

"It's worth a fortune," Ivor said in a hushed voice. "A pearl of great price."

I focused on his words, my breathing slowly returning to normal. Seven hundred years ago, someone had placed this precious, costly jewel—for it was worth a fortune then as now—in a coffin with a dead woman. For love, or . . . ? I couldn't make sense of it.

Ivor had moved on to the tortoiseshell comb, but I couldn't tear my eyes away from the pearl. It was perfectly formed, about the size of a wild rose hip. The silvery-white iridescence shimmered, its lustrous depths pulling me in. My breath caught.

"Ms. Hamilton . . . Kate." The voice belonged to Alex Belcourt. "Are you quite all right? You look ill."

"I'm fine." I tried a shaky laugh. "It's a little warm down here."

Ivor looked at me, and I saw curiosity in his eyes.

"Are you sure?" Belcourt looked concerned.

"Absolutely," I said, relieved my heart was returning to a normal rhythm.

I'd had these experiences from childhood. Some would call it a gift, the ability to experience the emotional atmosphere in which an object once existed, as if those emotions had lingered like the scent of strong perfume. Was it a gift? I thought of it as a curse. These episodes had no purpose that I could see. *Unless* . . . a thought floated into my brain. Unless they were meant to put me on my guard. Was that it? My subconscious mind, alerting me to some unknown danger?

Belcourt was still looking at me.

"Really, I'm fine." I was also a coward. In Devon, where it had been a bloodstained Victorian dress that had brought on another such episode, I'd promised myself I would tell Tom about my so-called *gift*. He was my husband. He deserved the truth. If only I could figure out a way to tell him without sounding like I was losing my marbles. Assuming I wasn't.

"If you're sure," Belcourt said, "would you mind a private chat? We can use the gift shop."

The others were still examining the grave goods.

"I'll be right back," I whispered to Ivor and followed Belcourt into an adjoining room. He flipped on the lights, revealing shelves stocked with gift items—books on medieval life, mugs shaped like castles, faux tapestries and goblets, coloring books for children along with small plastic knights and ladies. Curated. Tasteful. Just about every great house open to the public had similar things for sale.

"I'll make this brief." Belcourt perched on the edge of one of the tables. "I've done my research. I know your husband is a policeman, and I know about the incident in Devon. You helped the police solve a hideous crime." I started to explain that my role in Devon had been strictly peripheral, but he waved it off. "It doesn't matter. You know this exhibit means a great deal to me. Finding Egemere Woman in the ruins of the village seems a kind of miracle. My wife, Carrie"—his voice cracked—"disappeared in 2016. You may have heard."

"I did hear," I admitted, "but I don't know the details."

"The short version, then. I was flying to the Philippines and Vietnam, where we were building packaging plants. We had breakfast together. We kissed. She said goodbye, and that was the last time I saw her. The police were never able to explain what happened. For years I hoped she would turn up one day. Come back to me." He shook his head and blew out a breath. "I've given that up now. I'm no fool. I accept that she's dead. Must be. This exhibit is my tribute to her. You may think I'm obsessive, but the museum is what I live for. Not my business. Certainly not the money." His mouth twisted. "Here's the point: I'd like you to look into the history of this place, the village. See if you can find out who Egemere Woman was—why she was murdered. I want to bring her to life again, so to speak. It's what Carrie would have wanted."

I was touched, but I had to be honest. "You know what you're asking may be impossible."

"I know that, but if you can learn anything, however insignificant, it would be of immense value to me. No expectations." He met my eyes. "I'll pay you, of course. Whatever you require."

Reaching into my small crossbody bag, I handed him one of my business cards with the logo of Nash & Holmes, Private Investigators. "Any investigation would have to go through my employer. If they believe there's a chance of success, they'll email you a contract. If not, they'll tell you so."

Chapter Seven

Ivor and I followed Belcourt and the archaeologists along muddy footpaths and over metal stiles to the excavation site. We could have driven in two cars, Belcourt informed us, but walking was quicker.

The rain had stopped, but I was glad I'd worn my boots as the mud was inches deep in places. Ivor had worn his wingtip brogues, which were now caked with mud and possibly something more disreputable, as the fields were populated by the hornless, black-faced Suffolk sheep who grazed, unconcerned by our presence.

I was still thinking about the pearl. And my reaction to it—the trumpet, the clashing of swords, the *fear.* Where had that come from? More importantly, what did it mean?

"Watch your step," Ivor said, pulling me back to the present.

As the footpath narrowed, Belcourt led us single file with Dr. Nevin bringing up the rear. We'd gone about a half mile when we encountered a small, dispirited-looking group of protestors who moved aside to let us pass. They wore rain gear, which meant they'd prepared to stay for some time. I wondered why. The dig had been suspended, at least temporarily. No one was working, and yet there they were, carrying signs reading *Stop the Dig* and *Hands Off Our Heritage.* One sign threatened *Those Who Disturb the Dead Will Pay with Their Lives.* That sign was carried by a tall, elderly woman in a dark, rubberized mackintosh that looked like it might once have belonged to a man. A mass of thick white hair escaped from beneath a striped, knitted cap. She said nothing, pressing her lips together as we passed, but she made her sentiments clear by shaking her sign at us.

"They've been warned to stay on the footpath and not impede our work," Celia said. "The actual dig is strictly off-limits."

"One of them doesn't mind breaking the law," Mark said, shooting a guilty glance at Celia. "We should have reported the vandalism to the police."

I silently agreed. Things might escalate.

"Sinclair is probably in the field office and forgot about the time." Mark pointed out a caravan standing on a low rise overlooking a series of trenches marked with grid pegs and a perimeter surrounded by high-vis fencing.

I looked around the grassy site, seeing only a few stone foundations, the suggestion of several lanes, and the shell of a roofless church. Two of the walls remained standing, including the altar with the framework of what must have once been a stained-glass window.

"Not much left, is there?" I said to Celia.

"Most of the stones were carried away by locals in the eighteenth century," she explained, "until the Wyck family put a stop to it."

We approached a plot of land roughly twenty feet square where the soil had been graded and seeded. Clumps of grass were beginning to emerge.

"This is where we found the body," Celia said. "Beneath the south transept. The church was a small cruciform with a north and a south transept, both of which are now gone. Early on we used ground-penetrating radar, GPR, which indicated the presence of stairs. We excavated and found steps leading down to a lower passage and the crypt. That's where we found the coffin, and that's where we reburied Egemere Woman and her child."

"Where's the mound Mark hopes to excavate?" I asked.

"A half mile or so beyond those trees." She pointed out a clump of what looked like beeches.

Dr. Nevin unlocked the caravan door. "Simon, are you here?"

We stepped into a fusty office complex, crowded with three desks, some computer equipment, a bookshelf, and a filing cabinet. To the left was a small kitchenette, a sagging sofa, and several wire-mesh chairs—but no Dr. Sinclair.

"That's odd," Belcourt said, consulting his watch. "I can't believe he forgot the meeting this morning."

"Could he be working in the trenches?" Celia asked. "I mean, it doesn't seem likely, but . . ." She trailed off.

"One way to find out," Mark said.

I followed the others out of the caravan and down the rickety steps. Mark led us through an opening in the mesh fence. Trenches stretched over an area roughly equivalent to a square block.

"Simon?" Belcourt shouted.

No answer.

A scream pierced the air, and I felt the hair prickle on the back of my neck.

Tamzin stood at the edge of one of the trenches close to the barricade. "It's Dr. Sinclair," she shrieked. "He's *dead*."

We rushed to where she was standing and looked down. I saw blood, masses of it, and swallowed against a wave of nausea.

"Oh, my god." Celia put her hands over her mouth.

Dr. Sinclair lay at the bottom of the trench, his legs splayed, his right fist clenched, his left sort of clawing at the soil. The back of his head was matted with blood, which had soaked into his khaki anorak.

"His ring's gone," I said, not seeing the agate intaglio he'd worn on his left hand.

"Bloody hell," Belcourt muttered.

Tamzin was shaking. Mark put his arm around her. "It's all right," he said, although it plainly wasn't.

"He could be alive," Dr. Nevin said in a choked voice. "We have to check."

"He can't be alive," Belcourt said. "Look at his head, the blood. I don't think we should touch him."

"We have to know for sure." Nevin jumped into the trench, nearly collapsing as he landed. After righting himself, he crouched next to the body. He wrenched Sinclair onto his back and put two fingers on his neck. Nevin looked up. "He's dead. Has been for some time." His face had gone white, and his hands were shaking and covered in blood. He held them up as if waiting for someone to hand him a towel.

I reached for Ivor's arm. Our eyes met. *What have we gotten ourselves into now?*

"Call the police," Ivor said. "This is no accident."

Belcourt fumbled for his mobile, but I was already punching in Tom's direct number.

He picked up immediately. "What's happened?" He knew I wouldn't call him at work unless it was important.

"I'm at the Ravenswyck dig site." I took a breath and tried to speak clearly. "We found Dr. Sinclair. He's been murdered."

"Get everyone away from the crime scene now," he said. "We'll be there in fifteen minutes."

* * *

We waited in the caravan, silent and shivering—and not because it was cold. I sat on the sofa between Celia and Ivor. Nevin, Tamzin, and Mark sat at their desks. Belcourt had chosen a wire mesh chair, set off from the others. I'd seen dead bodies before, but nothing like that. *All that blood.*

Tamzin was sobbing quietly. Mark was holding her hand.

"Someone must have taken him by surprise," he said.

"But why was Simon here at all?" Celia demanded. "I don't understand."

The sound of sirens told us the police and EMS personnel had arrived. We filed outside to meet them.

Tom and Detective Inspector Amy Cartwright strode toward us from the small parking area, holding out their warrant cards. Near the trench, Detective Sergeant Matthew Ren and Detective Constable Holly Marsh were donning coveralls, masks, and booties.

Amy, who'd come from Suffolk Police HQ in Martlesham Heath, had been Tom's replacement when he accepted the role of DCI the previous January. She had a stocky frame and a plain, serious face. She wore a dark pants suit with a white shirt and low-heeled boots. Her light-brown hair was pulled into a neat bun. Efficient, professional.

DS Ren, a young man with close-cropped brown hair and a mischievous grin, had joined the team a month before Cartwright when Tom's old sergeant, DS Ryan Cliffe, passed his detective inspector's exam, married his girlfriend, and moved to the Eastern Division of the Suffolk Constabulary in quick succession.

DC Marsh was the newest member of the team, having come from traffic control in April. She was tall, athletic, and eager.

Tom greeted me with a kiss. "You okay? Need my jacket?"

"I'm fine," I said, trying not to shake.

"Tell me who's here."

Starting with Alex Belcourt, I pointed out the members of the archaeological team.

"I thought you were meeting Sinclair at Ravenswyck."

"He didn't show up. Mark Lambe—the young man speaking with DI Cartwright—told us he spoke to Sinclair in the pub last night. Sinclair said he had something to check on this morning. And before you ask, no one knows what that *something* was."

"When did you and Ivor arrive at Ravenswyck?"

"Just before nine."

"Who was there?"

"All of them except Sinclair. When we asked where he was, Mark remembered what Sinclair said in the pub. Everyone assumed he was here at the site and lost track of time, so we had a quick look at the grave goods and then walked over here to meet him. Tamzin spotted his body, and I called you."

"This way, please." DI Cartwright herded Ivor and the archaeologists back toward the caravan.

A few yards from where we were standing, DS Ren was spooling out the crime-scene tape. DC Marsh had joined several EMS officers in the trench. They were laying out yellow number markers and taking photos of the body in situ. It looked like Marsh was going through Sinclair's clothing.

"A forensic pathologist from the coroner's office is on the way," Tom said. "We'll speak with the others now, and I'd like you to be present, Kate. You and Ivor both. Once we get a time of death, we'll interview everyone again, individually."

I wondered if Tom would conduct the preliminary interview himself or let DI Cartwright take charge. Cartwright was competent, thorough, and ambitious. She wouldn't take kindly to any hint from Tom that she wasn't up to the job.

"What was your first impression when you saw the body—besides the blood?" Tom asked me.

I thought for a moment, trying to picture the scene. "His clothes were damp." The memory surprised me. "That means he must have been lying there for some time, because the rain stopped before nine. Did you find his watch? It's a Patek Philippe. Valuable. And the ring he wore on his left hand is missing."

"A robbery?" Tom said as we moved closer to the trench. "Have you found his mobile?" he asked DC Marsh.

"No sign of it, sir." She straightened. "We found this in his jacket."

Tom pulled on a pair of nitrile gloves. Marsh handed him a thin black notebook, which turned out to be a small calendar diary, not much larger than a postcard. Holding it so I could see, Tom turned to the current page, which was partially stained with blood. Scrawled across the previous day was a single word. *Safe.*

"What does that mean?" I asked.

"It could mean an actual safe," Tom said.

"There's a safe at Ravenswyck. Maybe here, too. Mark said something about Sinclair checking artifacts that hadn't yet been processed."

"It's a thought." Tom dropped the notebook into an evidence bag. "Any jewelry?" he asked DC Marsh. "Kate says he wore a watch and an unusual ring."

"No watch," Marsh said, "but we found this in his right hand." She held up the agate intaglio ring.

"Put it in an evidence bag."

"Wait a minute," I said, staring into the trench. "What are those little white things?"

DC Marsh reached down and sifted through the soil. Picking up several small spheres, she held them in her palm.

They were tiny pearls.

Chapter Eight

Twenty minutes later, after the arrival of the pathologist, I sat with Ivor and the archaeological team in the cramped sitting area of the field office caravan. DI Cartwright had dragged in two of the desk chairs, wedging them between the sofa and mesh chairs. She and Tom stood, leaning against the kitchen counter. DS Ren and DC Marsh had remained with the scene-of-crime team. They'd begun a search of the surrounding area for tire tracks, footprints, or anything else possibly connected with the murder. Unfortunately, the early rain was making that process difficult.

DI Cartwright began the interview. "My name is DI Amy Cartwright from the Suffolk Constabulary. This is DCI Tom Mallory. He'll be the SIO, the senior investigating officer in overall charge of the investigation." Was there a note of disapproval in her voice? "The rest of our team members are currently helping process the crime scene. We'll be asking each of you to make a formal statement later. For now, we'd like some general background information. We understand the body was moved."

"That was me," Nevin said in a slightly defensive tone. "I had to see if he was still alive."

"We understand, but we'll need to take a DNA sample, sir—to eliminate you from our inquiries." Cartwright glanced at Tom, who was taking notes. "Did Dr. Sinclair mention to anyone other than Mr. Lambe that he had some task to perform this morning?"

Everyone shook their heads.

"Thinking of others wasn't Simon's gift," Celia said.

"So you didn't think the change of plans was strange?"

"Of course it was strange," she said. "Simon was eager to hear the assessment of our art experts. He wanted to be there when they got their first look at the pearl. Whatever took him to the site must have been important."

"Or he expected to be back by nine," Mark added.

"I'm sure he wasn't expecting to be murdered," Celia said dryly.

Cartwright hadn't mentioned the notebook or the word *safe*, and no one besides me had noticed the pearls. Not surprising. Everyone had been riveted on Sinclair's body.

"Is there CCTV coverage here at the site?" Cartwright asked.

"No CCTV," Nevin said. "The caravan is alarmed."

"What about Ravenswyck Court?"

Belcourt answered. "We installed cameras a few years ago. They're on a three-day rolling repeat."

"We'll need the footage," Tom said. "DS Ren will be in touch."

Cartwright changed topics. "You say you were all at the pub last night?"

"Not me." Belcourt held up a hand. "Not my thing."

"Nor me," Nevin said. "I had work to finish up. End of term, you know. I remained at the cottage we share on the estate."

"Which cottage would that be?" Tom asked.

"It's called The Forge," Belcourt explained. "Large house. Four bedrooms, two baths. No CCTV."

Cartwright cut in. "So you were alone, Dr. Nevin, until the others returned from the pub. Do you remember when that was?"

"Well, I think it must have been around"—he shrugged—"maybe half eleven. Is that about right?" He looked at the others.

"Yes," Celia said. "We left the pub at eleven. It must have taken us twenty or twenty-five minutes to walk back."

"Which pub?"

"The Six Bells in Hartwell," Mark said, mentioning the village closest to Ravenswyck. "We meet there often in the evenings. Have a pint. Talk over the day's activities."

"And Dr. Sinclair was with you. How did he seem?"

"Same as usual," Celia said.

"But he *wasn't* the same," Tamzin said, causing the others to stare at her. It was the first whole sentence she'd spoken since finding the body. "I'm sure he had something on his mind."

"What made you think that?" Cartwright asked.

Tamzin glanced at the others as if for support—or permission. "Well, he seemed distracted—I mean, he was the same as always on the surface, but I noticed his eyes. Usually, he sort of pins you with a look, like he's waiting for you to say something stupid so he can correct you. Last night I remember thinking his mind was somewhere else. And then . . ." She hesitated. "Well, that's about it, really."

"And then what, Tamzin?" Tom asked. "It might be important."

The girl blushed. "He was . . . being especially nice to me, I suppose. Like he valued me as a colleague." She looked at her lap, clearly uncomfortable.

"I noticed that, too," Mark said. "Simon was always hard on the female team members, especially the newer ones. He's been really unfair to Tamzin."

"Was he ever inappropriate?" Cartwright asked.

Tamzin's face flushed in embarrassment. She shrugged. It wasn't a denial.

"Simon was a pig." Celia crossed her arms over her chest.

I could almost see the gears turning in DI Cartwright's brain. "I'd like each of you to walk me through your movements from last night until this morning when you arrived at Ravenswyck Court."

"Are we suspects?" Belcourt asked.

"We'd like to eliminate you from our inquiries if we can." Cartwright smiled.

"Fine. I'll go first," Belcourt said. "What do you want to know?"

"When was the last time you saw Dr. Sinclair?"

"Yesterday afternoon. He and Dr. Whybrew were in the museum, preparing for the art experts."

"That was . . . ?"

"I think they arrived around three and left a couple of hours later—five, maybe?"

"That's right," Celia said. "We left just before five. I remember looking at my watch."

"What did you do after they left, Mr. Belcourt?"

"I had an early supper, finished some work—I'm comparing proposals for an expansion to our plant in Mexico. After that, I read for a while in my study. I went to bed around nine thirty."

"Can anyone vouch for that?"

"Of course. My cook and my butler."

"How about this morning?"

"I was home."

"You didn't leave the house—even for a short while? You didn't take a walk, for example?"

"No."

"How about you, Dr. Whybrew? When did you last see Dr. Sinclair?"

Celia twisted the end of her blond ponytail. "I saw Simon at the pub last night, but I hardly spoke to him."

"When did you arrive?"

"Seven thirty, I think. We'd all walked over from the cottage."

"And when did you leave?"

"Eleven—as Mark said. Closing time."

"And you went where?"

"Back to The Forge. We each have a private bedroom, but we share the living spaces. Except for Tamzin, that is. She boards in Long Barston. There isn't room for everyone at The Forge, and she has a car."

"What kind of car?" Cartwright asked.

"It's a white Renault Clio," Tamzin said.

"Did Dr. Sinclair leave the pub with you at eleven?"

"Actually, no," Celia said. "He left before we did—maybe ten fifteen or ten thirty?" She looked at the others for confirmation.

"I wasn't paying attention," Mark said, "but that must be about right."

"Did he say anything when he left?"

"Not to me," Celia said. "He'd been drinking rather heavily. I assumed he wanted to sleep it off."

"Was that typical? Was Sinclair a heavy drinker?"

"He liked a pint," Mark said.

"Dr. Nevin, you say you were alone at The Forge all evening until the others returned at around half eleven."

"Right."

"Did you see Dr. Sinclair at any time last night? When did he get back to the cottage?"

"No idea. My room is on the second floor near the back of the house, so unless he shouted or knocked over a table or something, I wouldn't have heard him. And I was focused on my work. I'm preparing the final listing of our finds this term."

"You worked until what time—approximately?"

Nevin thought for a moment. "It was late. Well after midnight. Probably later."

"How about the rest of you? Did anyone see Dr. Sinclair at The Forge?"

"I didn't," Celia said. "I assumed he was there. His door was shut."

"Did anyone hear him leave the cottage during the night?"

"He might have done," Mark said. "I wouldn't know. I'm a sound sleeper."

"I didn't hear anything either," Celia agreed. "I went straight to bed. My room's on the first floor. The only room on the ground floor is Simon's."

"And what did you do this morning, Dr. Whybrew?"

"Got up, got dressed, and walked over to Ravenswyck."

"When was that?"

"Just after eight."

"Did you see Dr. Sinclair this morning?" Cartwright asked. "At breakfast, perhaps?"

"No. His door was still shut. I assumed he was still sleeping."

"Did you see anyone before you left?"

"Mark and Tamzin were having breakfast."

"Mark and Tamzin?" Cartwright looked puzzled. "I thought she boarded elsewhere."

Tamzin flushed. "I slept on the sofa at The Forge last night. I do that sometimes. I'd had something to drink, so I didn't think I should drive. And I don't like to disturb Miss Bunn if I'm going to be late. I'd texted to let her know."

"If Dr. Sinclair left the house during the night, would you have known?"

"Maybe. If he'd left by the front door."

"That's the only way out?"

"Well, there is a back door off the kitchen."

"So you might not have been aware of someone leaving?"

Tamzin flushed. "No, I suppose not."

"How about you, Dr. Nevin?" Cartwright turned toward him. "You say you worked late. What did you do after that?"

"Fell asleep."

"Did you hear anyone leave the house?"

"No, and I wouldn't have. As I said, my room is well away from either of the exits."

"When did you leave The Forge this morning?"

"Early—maybe seven fifteen. There were a few items I wanted to check for the listing. Make sure my numbering system was correct. Most of the finds are currently stored at Ravenswyck."

"Where exactly?" Tom asked.

"There's a large safe."

"Who has keys to the safe?" Tom asked.

"Simon, Celia, and I do," Nevin answered. "And Belcourt, of course."

"Did you see anyone at Ravenswyck when you arrived?"

"No. I went in through the visitors' entrance. There's a keypad."

"Did any of you leave the cottage last night?"

They all shook their heads.

"Let me get this straight." I could see Cartwright was frustrated but trying not to show it. "No one saw Dr. Sinclair after approximately ten thirty at the pub. You all assumed he was in his room at The Forge, sleeping off a hangover, but no one saw him or heard him. And no one saw him the next morning either. Weren't you concerned for his well-being?"

"Why would we be?" Celia asked. "We're not his keepers."

Mark looked at Tamzin. "I wasn't thinking of him at all, if you want the truth. Mr. Tweedy and Ms. Hamilton were due to arrive at Ravenswyck at nine. Tamzin and I went over around eight fifteen—just after Dr. Whybrew—to open the safe and make sure the grave goods were ready for inspection."

"Where did Dr. Sinclair keep his computer?" Tom asked.

"In his room, I suppose," Celia said, looking around the caravan. "It's not here."

"Has anyone entered Dr. Sinclair's room since last night?" Tom asked.

They all shook their heads.

"Make sure you don't until the forensics team has completed their work."

"One more question," Cartwright said. "Who might have wanted to harm Dr. Sinclair?"

"You mean besides everyone who's ever met him?" Celia said, crossing her arms.

DI Cartwright waited.

"The protesters?" Mark said at last. "I mean that old lady said if we didn't stop the dig, someone would die."

I pictured the woman's angry face and the sign she carried—*Those Who Disturb the Dead Will Pay.*

Coincidence or something more sinister?

* * *

It was almost noon when the preliminary interview ended. Before the others left, Tom explained again that they would be expected to show up at the police station in Hartwell to give their formal statements by Wednesday at the latest.

When the others had left, Tom asked me, "What did you think of the interviews? Did everything agree with what you and Ivor witnessed? Anything odd or off?"

"Nothing except Celia Whybrew's animosity toward Dr. Sinclair. I mean, she stood up to him at the Finchley Hall dinner, but she was defending Tamzin." I thought for a moment. "Actually, that's not true. At Ravenswyck, when we asked why Sinclair wasn't there, Celia made a point of saying how selfish he was, considering himself above others. I wondered why she would be so outspoken about a colleague. Someone might have reported her comments to Sinclair."

"Because she knew he was already dead?" Tom scribbled something in his notebook.

"I can't believe that."

"It's a possibility, Kate. Which brings me to Tamzin. What did you make of her story?"

"I think something happened between her and Dr. Sinclair—how serious, I couldn't guess."

Tom pulled an evidence bag out of his jacket pocket. Inside were the small pearls, perhaps four millimeters in diameter. "DC Marsh found more pearls in the trench. It looks as if someone scattered them on the ground and tried to dig them in." He handed me the bag. "How valuable are they?"

I didn't have to look twice. "They're worthless, Tom. Fakes—and not even good fakes." I showed him. "See that bead? Some of the pearlized paint has peeled off."

A question hung in the air: Why would someone scatter fake pearls at an archaeological dig?

Were they a message?

Chapter Nine

Tuesday, June 24
Manor Farm

After breakfast the following morning, Tom and I carried mugs of coffee into our small, ground-floor sitting room. We hadn't had a chance to talk since the murder—really talk, I mean—because Tom hadn't made it home from police headquarters until well after midnight. I'd spent the evening writing out the list of questions I knew he would expect. We'd started the practice in Scotland. Writing things out had always helped me organize my thinking, and Tom said it helped him, too, because I looked at things from a non-police perspective. So far, my questions were less than insightful, but in order to pose insightful questions, you need insight—which I didn't have. I'd begun with a couple of obvious assumptions. First, there'd been at least two people at the dig site—Sinclair and his killer. Second, whatever Sinclair's purpose in going there, he'd arrived at the dig site sometime after leaving the pub and before the rain stopped at nine AM the next morning. And then there were the pearls. What was that all about?

I handed Tom my list. "You're not going to be impressed."

"Let's see what we've got." He pushed up his reading glasses. "Question number one. *Who met Sinclair at the dig site? Was the murder planned or opportunistic?*" He cocked his head to one side. "Well, that is the question, isn't it? The second person will have left something behind, even if it's only DNA."

"DNA from all the archaeologists will be there," I said.

"And Belcourt's as well. We'll be looking for unknown DNA."

"Second question," I said. "*Why was Sinclair at the site and when did he arrive?*"

"We know he got there between ten thirty PM when everyone saw him at the Six Bells and nine AM the next morning. The coroner should be able to pin that down some. As far as Sinclair's reason for going to the site, he told Mark Lambe he had something to check on. Which brings us to your question three: *What was the task he told Mark he had to do that morning?*"

"I've been thinking about the word written on the note in his pocket," I said, turning to look at Tom. "*Safe.* Sinclair must have meant a physical safe. There's one at Ravenswyck, and another at the field office—a smaller one."

"Was he checking the security of the finds or . . . ?" Tom shrugged. "Or was he reminding himself of something as simple as changing the combination between terms?"

"In that case, it might not be related to his death at all. But I'm wondering if he caught someone burgling the field office safe or scattering the pearls. That would mean the attack was unplanned."

"Which leads directly to question number four. *Motive? People don't kill someone just because they're arrogant and unpleasant.*"

"I suppose that depends on *how* arrogant and unpleasant they are," I said. "Ivor's friend at the university said—his words—that Sinclair 'trampled on a few careers' on his way to the top."

"Means, motive, and opportunity. Motive is the most important question. If Sinclair trampled on someone's career, we'll hear about it, and from more than one source."

"Question number five," I said. "*What happened to Sinclair's watch and mobile phone?*"

"We found the watch in his room last night, along with a gold neck chain and his computer. We have high hopes for the computer."

"No robbery, then." I took my pen and scratched out the part about the watch. "Did you find his mobile? Celia said he always picked up."

"No, which means it was probably taken by the killer. We've requested the logs." He dropped a kiss on my head. "We make a good team, you and me."

"We do."

"Last question," Tom said. "*Who scattered the fake pearls? Were they a message for Sinclair or for us?* It's a start, Kate. We'll know more when we get the results of the autopsy."

"I just thought of another question," I said, jotting it down in the notebook as I spoke. "*Why was Sinclair's ring in his hand and not on his finger?* Not much to go on yet, is there?"

"No." Tom raked his fingers through his salt-and-pepper hair. He sighed deeply. "These late nights are brutal. I must be getting old."

"We're all getting old. What you need is coffee." I poured us each a second cup from the sleek, black, insulated French press we'd received as a wedding gift. "There's something I want to tell you," I said, settling beside him again and tucking my feet under me. "About Alex Belcourt."

"Oh, yes?"

"Yesterday at Ravenswyck, before we left for the site, Belcourt pulled me aside and asked me to look into the identity of Egemere Woman. He knew about the case we solved in Devon last January."

"What exactly does he want you to do?"

"Find out who she was and why she was killed."

"He wants you to solve a seven-hundred-year-old murder? I'm mean, you're good, Kate, but even so."

"Tell me about it." I took a sip of coffee. The previous January, the Canadian-based private investigations firm, Nash & Holmes, had offered me occasional work, researching cases involving antiques and antiquities. I'd agreed, but this case wasn't about antiques, and I had no clue where to begin. Yet, I had to admit, it appealed to me.

"Did you agree to take it on?"

"Not yet, but I'm tempted." I hesitated, wondering how to explain the effect Belcourt's grief for his missing wife had on me. I knew all about grief, the pain of losing someone you can't live without. "The thing is," I started again, "the medieval exhibit—you've seen it—is a tribute to his wife, Carrie. Did you know she was studying archaeology before she got her first modeling contract? She was the one who got Belcourt interested in local history. He thinks he failed her—failed to keep her safe. If he can't find justice for his wife, he hopes he can find it for the young woman found in the crypt."

"Justice?" Tom gave me a skeptical look. "Even if you do find out who she was and who killed her, we can't bring that person to justice, not after seven hundred years."

"No, but I suppose he thinks that making her fate and the fate of her child known would be a kind of justice."

"Belcourt was never cleared in his wife's murder, you know."

"I know. All I can say is he sounded sincere. I gave him my card and told him to contact Nash & Holmes. There's a chance they won't want to get involved."

"True." Tom nodded. "They're not in the business of profiting from people's grief, and I don't believe they'd take a case if they thought there was no chance of completing it." He looked at me, raising his eyebrows. "What *are* the chances of finding the information he wants?"

"Slim. I'm sure records from that period in history exist, but I'd have to find out where they're located and how to access them. There is a chance I could identify the woman, Tom. Egemere Close was a tiny hamlet. The population in East Anglia in the fourteenth century was far smaller than it is today, and the fact that she was buried with valuable items tells me she was an important person. But identifying her killer? That may be asking too much."

"What's the next step?"

"I left the ball in his court. If Nash & Holmes are interested, they'll issue a contract."

"And will you sign it?"

"I don't know."

Tom's mobile rang.

He stood. "Cartwright—what have you got?" He paced, rubbing the back of his neck. He stopped and looked at me as if I'd heard the message. "You've got to be kidding. Well, that's a turn-up for the books. They're sure about it? It couldn't have happened after death? No, I can't think how. It's just . . . well, odd." He shook his head. "Okay. I'll be there as soon as I can."

Clicking off, he grabbed his jacket. "I have to go."

"Tom—what is it? What's wrong?"

He looked at me with his shrewd hazel eyes. "The coroner says Sinclair died early Monday morning, between midnight and three AM." He pulled on his jacket. "And remember the pearls you spotted in the trench? There were more of them—a lot more. Some in his fist, some in his mouth, and some in his stomach."

"*What?*" Had I heard him right? "You mean he *ate* the fake pearls? On purpose?"

"Or someone forced him."

* * *

Tom got home late again that night—eleven PM. This time I waited up for him with a bottle of his favorite cabernet, hoping the melatonin and resveratrol would help him sleep.

We curled up on the sofa. He put his arm around me, and I leaned back against his chest, watching the flames dance in the log burner. I knew from experience that the first days of a serious investigation were always long and unsatisfying

"Did you learn anything new from the formal interviews with the archaeologists?" I asked.

"You mean apart from the fact that if any of them is grieving Sinclair's death, they're hiding it rather well?" Tom took a sip of his wine. "I wonder how Sinclair got to be head of department. He certainly wasn't popular with his underlings."

"People like Sinclair are good at what they do, Tom. They flatter those above them on the ladder and step on those below."

"Three of them showed up for their interviews today—Niall Nevin, Mark Lambe, and Tamzin Oliver. Actually, we did learn one thing. Dr. Nevin was telling the truth when he said he was working the night of the murder. We asked him to bring his computer, and the tech team checked it out. The log-in history shows he was active until about two thirty AM."

"Which means he couldn't have made it to the dig site by three. But can't that be faked?"

"It can, but there were detailed user actions and time stamps. Plus, Mark Lambe remembers hearing Nevin's printer working around quarter past two. His room is directly below Nevin's. The sound woke him up."

"That lets Nevin out." I felt a bit disappointed. It wasn't that I actually suspected Dr. Nevin, but he was the only one I hadn't taken to immediately. "Where do you go now?" I asked. "Who are the main suspects?"

Tom crossed one long leg over the other. "At the moment? Everyone who knew him. DS Ren will interview the protesters, and we're getting contact information for the archaeology students who recently left to go back to college. One of them might have returned."

"How about his university colleagues?"

"They'll all have to be interviewed as well. We're putting together a list. Ivor's friend, the linguist, will be a priority. The main thing right now is piecing together Sinclair's life, both academically and personally, and constructing a timeline of the hours leading up to his death."

"Celia mentioned a daughter."

"She attends a boarding school in Switzerland. The mother lives there as well. We've confirmed that neither of them left the country."

"What about girlfriends or partners?"

"Sinclair lived alone in Norwich. There might be girlfriends. We'll find out, but my gut tells me his death was connected to the dig. I could be wrong."

"I don't think you are. I can't prove it, but I think the killer is someone staying on the estate. Who else would have met Sinclair at the dig site after midnight? Who else would have scattered those pearls? I think they point directly to the pearl found with the fourteenth-century body."

The argument between Sinclair and Mark Lambe at Finchley Hall sprang to my mind, but I decided not to say anything. First of all, if Tom and his team hadn't already heard about it, they would; and second, I wasn't going to be the one to throw Mark under the bus. He reminded me too much of my son, Eric.

Tom kissed the top of my head. "You are a treasure, Kate. Did you know that? 'The prettiest Kate in Christendom.' I read that somewhere."

"Shakespeare." I laughed. "And I believe that Kate was a shrew."

"No offense intended." He ruffled my hair. "Did you hear anything from Nash & Holmes today?"

"Not a word."

"If the contract is approved—and if you sign it—you'll be busy."

"I like busy."

"That's a good thing, because I have something to ask you."

"Oh?" I turned my head to look at him.

"Once again, like it or not, you're involved in a murder investigation."

"Not by choice."

"I know, but you are involved, and I need your help—unofficially."

"Help with what?"

"You and Ivor are in a position to learn things people never tell the police. Investigations like the Thetford killing are different—there's no way you'd be involved in that. But in the case of Sinclair, you have an insider's advantage. I trust your judgment, Kate, and circumstances have placed you in the middle of this. I'm not going to waste an asset. What I'm asking is that you keep doing what you're doing with the . . . what are they called—grave goods? If Nash & Holmes issues a contract, I hope you sign it."

"That's what the police in Devon said. 'Keep doing what you're doing.'"

"Yes, and in Devon, you were the one who found the missing piece of the puzzle because you looked at things from a different perspective."

"That was a one-off, Tom. It's not going to happen again."

"Police are trained to collect evidence and build a case based on that evidence. It's possible Sinclair's killer had a motive we know nothing about yet, which is why we'll follow every line of inquiry, both personal and professional. But Sinclair was killed at the dig site. I agree with you. The pearls were scattered there for a reason. Now, could it be that's what the killer wants us to believe? Of course. They could be a red herring."

"What if Sinclair scattered the pearls himself? And consumed them." I shuddered. "It really does boggle the mind."

"What I mean is the killer might be pointing us in the wrong direction on purpose."

"Yes, but the pearls have to mean something, even if the message was meant only for Sinclair."

"Which brings me back to my request," Tom said. "You're good at seeing patterns and connections, so do what you would do anyway. Work with Ivor on the grave goods. Get to know the team members. Look into the identity of the woman in the crypt. Keep your eyes and ears open."

"They all know I'm your wife. Why would they tell me anything?"

"They might not. I'm just saying, if you see or hear anything that might help us identify the killer, tell me. I'll take it from there." He reached out to caress my cheek. "I told you we make a good team."

I couldn't argue with that. And the truth was, I didn't want to.

Chapter Ten

Wednesday, June 25
Long Barston

The day promised to be dry and seasonably warm, a welcome change from the cool, drizzly weather of the previous days.

I threw a load of wash in the machine and phoned Angela Foxe, the veterinarian. She'd called and left a message. Was I free for lunch today? We'd become good friends in the past year, and I'd been one of the first to know about her pregnancy. As a first-time mother, Angela had lots of questions, some of which I could even answer. I'd raised two children of my own, which certainly didn't make me an expert, but at least I'd walked in her shoes twice. My goal was to encourage Angela in her new role as parent. *Don't expect yourself to be perfect. This is on-the-job training.*

This time, however, I suspected Angela's questions would be less about her pregnancy and more about the murder of Simon Sinclair. The story had appeared on the front page of the local newspaper. Everyone in town would be eager for information, and Angela had actually met Sinclair at Lady Barbara's dinner.

I returned Angela's call, and we agreed to meet at the vet clinic just north of Long Barston. From there, we would walk to a lovely café along the River Stour.

When I finally left the house, I stopped first at The Cabinet of Curiosities and found Ivor disassembling a Louis XV gilt-bronze clock we'd recently taken on consignment.

"Do you need me this afternoon?"

"Not until four thirty." Clock parts were spread all over the sales counter, and I hoped he remembered how to put them back. "I have an appointment to view a collection of Russian silver. Pre-revolution."

I saw the anticipation on his face, and I couldn't blame him. Nineteenth-century Russian silver was becoming increasingly rare, and he was lucky to get a chance to view the collection.

"I promise to be back before four thirty. I'm having lunch with Angela Foxe."

"Say hello from me."

I left him happily cleaning the inner mechanism of the fine old clock, a task he loved. I had some time before meeting Angela to devote to a little preliminary research on Egemere Woman. Did records from the fourteenth century exist? If so, what were they, where could I find them, and—most importantly—were there translations in modern English? My knowledge of Middle English was spotty, and my ability to read Latin even worse.

Even if I did find records, would they shed light on the identity of the woman in the crypt? Was I wasting my time? Maybe. But then Alex Belcourt might have changed his mind about hiring me. Or Nash & Holmes might refuse to issue a contract. Even so, it wouldn't hurt to be prepared.

I started at our local branch of the Suffolk Libraries system. In Devon, it had been a librarian who'd ferreted out information that had put us on the right track.

Behind a desk marked Resources sat a middle-aged woman, thumbing through what looked like a large gazetteer, a geographical index. Seeing me, she smiled. "May I help you find something?"

"I'm looking for local history sources from the fourteenth century."

"The fourteenth century? Well, that's a request we don't get every day."

"Where would I start? I mean, are there parish records of births, marriages, and deaths, for example? Family genealogies?"

"What a lovely accent you have. American?"

I smiled. "Yes, but I live here now." I was still getting used to the idea that in England, I was the one with the accent.

"Fourteenth century?" she said again, frowning. "I'm not an expert, dear, but I believe it wasn't until later that clergy were required to keep parish registers. Are you interested in a particular parish?"

"The ruined church at Egemere Close."

"Oh, dear." Her brow creased with concern. "That's where that archaeologist was killed. I read about it in the paper this morning."

"I'm interested in the excavations. The body of a young woman was found in the crypt of the church last spring."

She brightened. "I read that in the newspaper as well. The Year Five students at the local primary did a project on it. The church was called St. Margaret's—originally attached to the small Abbey of St. Margaret near Hartwell. Nothing remains of the abbey now. It closed in the eleventh century when the Anglo-Saxon abbot refused to pledge allegiance to William the Conqueror."

"Do records from the church or the abbey still exist?"

"I'm sure they do. Only we don't have any of them here in our collection. Now, we did have a man speak about the abbey and the village a few years ago. Lovely older gentlemen he was. Very knowledgeable."

"Is there a way for me to contact him?"

"I may still have his card somewhere. I'd have to look for it." She smiled. "It was a wonderful lecture. I remember a tragic story about a woman of great beauty and pious character."

"Really?" This sounded promising. "Do you remember the woman's name?"

"Sorry, no." She put a hand to her chest. "I'm afraid I don't remember any of the specifics."

"If you find the lecturer's contact information, will you please let me know?" I gave her my card and left her staring at the logo of Nash & Holmes, Private Investigators.

* * *

Angela and I chose a table on the café's outside patio. Below us, the River Stour burbled along on its circuitous journey to the North Sea.

"I was shocked to read about the murder," Angela said. "We just had dinner with Dr. Sinclair, and only days later, he's found dead. I can hardly believe it. Do the police have a suspect?"

"A bit early for suspects," I said. "No motive yet."

"Well, I hope they catch the person responsible." She looked at the menu, sighing. "Oh, dear. I've gained two and a half stone already, and I've got a month to go."

"You're healthy and active. It will come off."

I ordered a smoked chicken salad with avocado and Suffolk farmhouse cheese. Angela ordered something called a *tartiflette*, which turned out to be a baked casserole of Brie cheese with bacon and roasted potatoes.

Angela tucked in, the sunlight gleaming off her red-blonde hair. "When did you say the locum will arrive?" I asked, referring to the freelance vet who was supposed to be filling in for Angela during the last month of her pregnancy.

"Would you believe the guy who was supposed to come has a broken leg? He was kicked while trying to examine a cow with an inflamed udder." She swirled a chunk of roasted potato in the cheesy sauce and popped it in her mouth. She chewed for a moment. "The agency's finding someone else, but they said it might take another week or so."

"Oh, no—I'm sorry."

"It's fine. The belly does get in the way sometimes, but I can deal with it." She wiped a smear of cheese from her lip. "Sinclair was a brute, wasn't he? I mean the way he treated those students that night at Finchley Hall—Tamzin and Mark." She pulled off a chunk of the whole-grain loaf they'd brought on a wooden bread board. "I hope *they're* not suspects. I really liked them—and Celia Whybrew. She's a class act."

"I thought so, too. What did you think of Dr. Nevin?"

"I couldn't tell if he was antisocial or just painfully shy." She buttered the bread thoughtfully. "What about the protesters they mentioned? Maybe Sinclair caught one of them vandalizing the site."

"It's a possibility." It really was. The pearls might very well have been an act of vandalism. But then how had they ended up in Sinclair's throat and stomach?

"I ran into them a couple of weeks ago." Angela took a bite of the bread.

"Who?"

"The protesters. The farm manager at Ravenswyck invited me to see their latest acquisition. She's a Golden Guernsey, one of the goats on the rare breeds watchlist. Her name's Hazel." Angela poured herself a second cup of tea. "She's a lovely girl—beautiful long, golden coat. Alex Belcourt has a soft spot for goats—or his late wife did. Anyway, I stopped afterward for lunch at the Six Bells, a lovely old pub in Hartwell. The protesters were there, having some sort of meeting."

"How did you know they were protesters?"

"Had their signs with them, didn't they?" She laughed. "Most looked like retired schoolteachers, but there's one young guy, scruffy, and this weird old woman who seems to be the leader. I asked the server who they were—I hadn't heard about the protests then. She said they usually stop at the pub after marching at the dig site."

Tom would be interested in that bit of information. "Did you speak to the protesters?"

"Heavens, no." She broke off another piece of bread. "Anyway, they left soon afterward. The server said the old woman is a local eccentric—into divination and fortune-telling. Always trying to warn people about their futures."

That was even more interesting. The protesters had warned the archaeologists about a death at the dig site. Then Sinclair was murdered. Some coincidence.

"Do you know the old woman's name?"

"No." Angela took a sip of her tea and flinched, grimacing in pain.

"Are you okay?"

"Fine." She wiped her mouth. "Braxton Hicks contractions. False labor. I've been having them for a while. Perfectly normal." She checked her watch. "Gotta go, Kate. Full schedule of appointments at the clinic this afternoon."

Twenty minutes later, we said goodbye outside the vet clinic. Although I knew Braxton Hicks contractions were common in the last trimester of pregnancy, I felt a twinge of anxiety. Was Angela's husband, Edmund, right? Was she doing too much so late in her pregnancy?

I didn't have to be back at the shop for another two hours, which gave me plenty of time to check out the pub in Hartwell, a short ten miles away. The protesters probably wouldn't be there. In fact, they might have given up altogether. After all, the archaeological site was now a crime scene, and with the death of Sinclair, who knew if the dig would even continue?

Even so, I might learn something useful. It wouldn't hurt to try.

* * *

The Six Bells in Hartwell turned out to be a treasure. Located just outside the village center, the pub combined two adjoining buildings, a gray stone two-story and a long, low pebbledash in a pale yellow limewash. Outside, three wooden tables shaded by red umbrellas were currently vacant. A plaque beside the entrance door told me the original part of the building dated from the late fifteenth century, possibly earlier, and the name, Six Bells, was taken from the village church, which had six bells in its belfry.

At two thirty in the afternoon, there were only three patrons inside, two of them rather dejected-looking older men who sat at the bar nursing pints of beer. The third man, younger, in his late twenties maybe, was throwing darts. All three stared at me with undisguised curiosity.

"What'll you have, duck?" A middle-aged woman stood behind the bar, polishing pint glasses. She wore a smock with the logo of Greene King, a popular local beer. Dark curls framed her round, cheerful face.

"Mineral water with lime, please." I chose a stool as far away from the older men as possible.

The barmaid filled a glass from a handpump—probably seltzer water, but oh well—plopped in a lime slice, and placed it on a coaster in front of me. "Haven't seen you before. Passing through?"

"No," I said. "I'm local, working on a project at Ravenswyck Court."

"Ravenswyck?" Her eyebrows flew up. "That's where that archaeologist chap was murdered."

"Unfortunately." Every eye in the place was now on me.

When I didn't offer any additional information, the barmaid said, "He came in here just about every night—him as got murdered, Sinclair. One for the ladies, he was. Bothering one o' my servers. My husband had to set him straight. We own the place." She put her hands on her hips. "Police caught the killer yet?"

"I don't think so."

"Knew 'im yourself, did ya?"

"Not personally. I met him only once."

The answer was clearly a disappointment. "Something to eat?" She shoved a menu at me.

I wasn't in the least hungry but decided I should probably order something. "How about the avocado toast?" I said, choosing one of the starters.

"Sourdough or whole grain?"

"Whole grain, thanks."

She disappeared into what must have been the kitchen and returned some minutes later with two thick slices of toasted bread spread with guacamole, slices of mozzarella, and ripe red tomatoes.

The woman picked up her towel and resumed polishing glasses. "Heard those archaeologists found a great huge pearl. Big as the one Burton gave Elizabeth Taylor for Valentine's Day. Seen it, have you?"

"It's impressive, all right." I took a bite of the toast, feeling a slight uptick in my heart rate as I remembered the intense reaction I'd had, seeing the pearl for the first time. "This is really good."

"Thank you kindly." She was pleased at the compliment. "I'm Brenda, by the way."

"I'm Kate. Lovely to meet you."

One of the men at the other end of the bar signaled for another pint. Brenda pulled it, letting foam spill over the sides before handing it to him.

"Here's to you, luv." He winked at me and raised his glass.

"Don't mind 'im," Brenda whispered. "Harmless."

"I hear the protesters stop in here sometimes."

"If they want to eat, they do. Only pub in the village."

"Ever have trouble—I mean between the archaeologists and the protesters?"

"Nah. Wouldn't stand for it. They eye each other but keep their distance."

"The protesters are local, then?"

"Mostly. A few come over from Sudbury." She adjusted her headband. "Can't feature one o' them as the killer, if that's what'cher getting at."

"No, of course not." I shook my head to emphasize the point. "But I know there's been some vandalism at the dig site."

"I don't take any o' them for criminals. Determined is all. They believe human remains should be left in peace. Can't say as I disagree with that."

"What about the leader—the old woman?"

"Oh, her. Name's Edlyn Dark. Mad as a box of frogs."

"Why do you say that?"

"Got herself a reputation, don't she? Claims to be some sort of psychic. Well educated, though. Her father taught history at one of the secondary schools 'round here and, I believe, at one of the local colleges. He died—well, must be three years ago now."

"Does Edlyn Dark live in the village?"

"Just down the road." Brenda picked up her towel again. "She used to come in here passing out cards, offering to do her readings. We put a stop to that." She tapped her cheek. "Might'a kept one of 'em, though." She went to the cash register and opened the money drawer. "Here it is. Keep it."

She handed me a grubby white card with the logo of an eye surrounded by rays. GET ANSWERS NOW! was printed at the top in all caps. At the bottom I read *Edlyn Dark, Psychic Medium*, with a website and a telephone number.

I slipped it in my handbag. "Were you working the night Dr. Sinclair was murdered?"

"I'm here every night, luv. Can't afford good help these days."

"The archaeologists say they stopped in the night of the murder. Did you see them?"

"A'course I did. As I said, can't get good help."

"Did you happen to see Dr. Sinclair leave?"

"I saw him checking his mobile around half ten. Coming out of the loo. Pulled the thing out of his pocket and stared at it—like he'd got a text or something."

From his killer?

"One o' the women he was with cornered him. Angry, she was. He pushed her away and hightailed it out o' here."

"The younger woman with the orange-and-pink hair?"

"No. The attractive one. The blonde."

Chapter Eleven

Long Barston

I made it back to The Cabinet of Curiosities with thirty minutes to spare. Ivor was shoving his commissions book into his old leather briefcase.

"Good luck with the appraisal," I said. "I'll close up at five thirty unless we get any last-minute customers."

The shop did get walk-ins from time to time, mostly tourists, but most of our sales—the ones that paid our salaries and kept the lights on—came from the online auction trade. At the moment, we were working on the Roman marbles, setting reserve prices, taking photographs, and writing up detailed descriptions for the catalog. The collection would be included in a forthcoming sale of Roman antiquities by a well-known auction house in Glasgow.

Ivor consulted a Venetian gilt-frame mirror and straightened his tie. "Any news on Sinclair?"

"I might learn more tonight." I really wanted to tell him about the pearls, but I'd have to get Tom's approval.

Ivor gave me a skeptical *hmm*. He knew I was withholding information.

"Ivor," I said as he closed the latch on his briefcase. "What do you think of people who claim to foretell the future?"

He gave me a sharp look. "People in general, or someone in particular?"

"I stopped at the Six Bells in Hartwell today. The owner told me the old lady who leads the protesters—Edlyn Dark—gives psychic readings."

"Dark, you say? Old West Country name. How does the pub owner know?"

"She stops in just about every night." I handed Ivor the card, wondering what he would make of it. He'd encountered plenty of strange practices in his years with the Merchant Navy. Once he'd hypnotized Vivian Bunn using a retrogression technique he'd learned in northern Mongolia.

"Attempting to foresee the future is as old as civilization," Ivor said. "Plenty of medieval manuscripts include charms—words and rituals meant to predict the future or influence the future in your favor. If someone stole something from you, for example, you'd write a series of letters and symbols on a piece of parchment and place it under your pillow at night to see the face of the thief in your dreams."

"You believe it?"

"Certainly not. There are laws about advertising psychic powers in the UK. You can't claim to know the future."

"She doesn't actually say that, though, does she? It's just 'get answers now.' But she did predict someone on the dig team would die." I pulled up the stool behind the sales counter.

"A prediction or a threat?" Ivor laid the card on the counter.

"Good question." I opened the shop computer. "I wonder if the dig will be shut down permanently now Sinclair's dead."

"Not so." Ivor headed for the door. "I spoke to my friend at the university today. He says the dig will continue next term with Niall Nevin as head archaeologist. Celia Whybrew's been appointed temporary head of the CMBA. Silver lining and all that, eh?" He grabbed his briefcase and started for the door. Stopping, he turned back, a strange look in his eyes. "The Six Bells in Hartwell, you say?"

"Only pub in town."

"That's where our local psychic drinks?" He smiled angelically. "What do you say we check out their menu one night this week?"

* * *

Manor Farm

That evening, with Tom gone again, I polished off the leftovers from my two lunches and did a computer search for medieval records in Suffolk. Some were held privately in the libraries of the county's stately homes, but most were kept at The Hold in Ipswich, the central repository for Suffolk's nationally significant archives. The Hold had a searchable online database, as well, which meant the name of Egemere Woman might be discoverable—if records from Egemere Close existed. I'd ask Alex Belcourt about it the next time I saw him. They could be at Ravenswyck Manor for all I knew.

Tom got home at the semi-reasonable hour of nine PM. "There's been progress on the Thetford murder." He peeled off his jacket and hung it on one of the hooks in the entrance hall.

"Hungry?"

"Knackered."

"Let's go up, then. You can tell me all about it."

He followed me up the stairs to our bedroom on the first floor. It was a large room, almost square, with lovely, glossy white woodwork and walls the color of the velvety moss that grew in the woods beyond our property. Windows on two sides looked out over the countryside. On one of the interior walls, a fireplace with a veined marble chimney piece featured carved scrolling and garlands of fruit.

Tom and I sat facing the fireplace, side by side in two cushy armchairs. "Tell me about the Thetford case," I said, propping my feet on the upholstered fireplace fender.

"The good news is we know where he is—approximately. He's heading south, probably hitchhiking from time to time, probably trying to get to London. Plenty of places there to disappear."

"I thought he was driving a caravan."

"Abandoned in a field near Whepstead. Forensics are going over it now. It's registered to someone called Derek Quinn. We're checking to see if he's our suspect or if the caravan was stolen."

"How's he living, eating?"

"Sleeping in barns and outbuildings, stealing food. We've been getting phone calls. That's how we're tracking him."

"What's the bad news?"

"He could be dangerous. The chief constable went on TV today, warning citizens not to approach him but to notify the police with any sightings."

"Description?"

"Middle age, medium height, dark clothing." Tom gave me an ironic grin.

"That's helpful." I laughed. "Is the woman still with him?"

"No one's reported seeing a woman."

"If she's smart, she's ditched him. By the way, did you get the coroner's report on Sinclair?"

"Struck from behind with significant blunt force trauma. No defensive injuries. Wood fibers in the wound. One odd thing—there was mud on the back of his clothes as well as the front, which means he moved about after falling. He died from the blow to his head but not immediately. Bleeding continued for a while. He may have been conscious for some time."

"The pearls?" I shivered involuntarily, picturing Sinclair lying in the cold, muddy water, stuffing pearls into his mouth.

"That's a complete mystery." Tom folded his arms behind his head and let out a slow breath. He was relaxing.

"Did you conduct more interviews today?"

"Everyone's given their statements now, including Alex Belcourt and his farm manager, Peter Eley. The archaeologists confirmed what they said initially. They were together at the pub that night, except for Dr. Nevin. Belcourt was home, seen by his butler and cook, but they didn't stay with him all night. Eley lives on the estate. He was home alone. The time of death has been established as between midnight and three, but with the body lying outdoors, the timing could be off. Which means that with the possible exception of Nevin, we can't eliminate any of them as suspects."

"How about the CCTV footage at Ravenswyck?"

"We're waiting on that now. In the meantime, the forensics team took DNA samples from everyone." Tom stretched out his long legs, propping them beside mine on the fender. "Tell me about the archaeologists. Any of them capable of murder?"

I laughed. "You mean did I catch one of them rubbing his hands together and mumbling about evil schemes?"

"No, Kate." He shot me a look.

"I'm sorry. It's just I can't imagine any of them as murderers."

"We need a break—one piece of evidence that will open up the case. There always is one, you know. Ren and Marsh have been interviewing Belcourt's neighbors, people whose land lies adjacent to the dig site. We're hoping someone saw something the night of the murder, even if it was only the lights of a car. So far, no one has."

"What about the protesters?"

"We're putting together a list of names."

"I can help you there." I pulled the grubby white card out of my pocket and handed it to him.

Tom frowned. "What's this?"

"I stopped at the Six Bells in Hartwell today. Brenda, the owner, gave it to me. This woman, Edlyn Dark," I tapped the card, "is the leader of the protest group. She claims to do psychic readings—telling people what their future holds."

"Does she now? Lives in Hartwell?"

I shifted so I could put my feet in Tom's lap. "Same cottage where she was born. Ivor and I thought we might give the pub a try one evening. If she's there, we'll strike up a conversation."

"You could ask her to tell your future."

"*Pfft.* Right. Even if she could see into the future, which I don't believe, I wouldn't want to know mine."

"Really?" Tom closed his eyes and put two fingers on his temple. "Kate Hamilton, I believe I can predict your future tonight."

"Are you chatting me up, Tom Mallory?"

"Guilty as charged." He ran the back of his hand over the arch of my right foot. "Come on. Let's go to bed."

I thought again, as I did so often, that I was the luckiest woman on earth. When I lost my first husband, Bill, I was sure all joy in life was forever beyond my reach. Never, ever could I have imagined my life in England with Tom. He was my greatest blessing, but I had so many others—my children, even though I didn't see them that often, and my mother and her new husband, James. We'd spent a wonderful two weeks together in the spring, after which I'd seen them off on the Aegean cruise they'd missed in January. And then there was Lady Barbara and Vivian and Angela and so many other dear friends in Long Barston. I had my work at The Cabinet of Curiosities, and I had Ivor, my mentor, my dear friend. Which reminded me.

"Tom, is it all right if I tell Ivor about the pearls at the murder scene?"

He was unbuttoning his shirt. "Just make sure he knows we're not releasing that information to the public."

"He's good at keeping secrets." I pulled the curtains shut. "I had lunch with Angela Foxe today. She's the one who told me about the Six Bells in Hartwell. She was there recently and saw the protesters. They weren't there today, but the pub owner, Brenda, told me she saw Sinclair at the pub on the night he was killed. She said it looked like he got a text from someone around ten thirty. Do you think it was from the killer?"

"Who knows? His mobile's probably in a landfill by now. Or at the bottom of the Stour. We've requested his phone logs, but that will take time, and we'll probably get only the metadata."

"She also said that Celia Whybrew tried to speak to Sinclair. She was upset. He rebuffed her and left the pub. Did she happen to mention that in her statement?"

"No, she didn't."

"It probably isn't important." I kicked off my shoes. "It's weird, isn't it? Edlyn Dark predicted someone on the dig would die. It's almost as if she knew."

Tom looked at me. "Does that make her a prophet or a murderer?"

Chapter Twelve

Thursday, June 26
Ravenswyck Court

Ivor and I planned to spend a good part of the morning at Ravenswyck, examining the grave goods in greater detail, making notes that would help us when writing up our final report, and taking photographs with a portable light box. Ivor was also eager to test a chemical solution on the silver cuff. The goal was to remove the tarnish while preserving the silver. Fortunately, tarnish itself isn't corrosive. In fact, it can actually protect the silver. What we didn't know was whether the silver had been alloyed with some other metal, a common practice in medieval times. If so, it might require a slightly different form of treatment. Or the CMBA might opt to leave the silver cuff as it was. I hoped not because that might eliminate the possibility of identifying the heads as the apostles, and I, for one, wanted to know.

Ivor and I started out for Ravenswyck at nine. Another overnight rainstorm had weighed down tree branches and beaded the hedgerows along the way. Everything glistened with the leafy green perfection of an English summer.

I lowered my driver's-side window a couple of inches and took a deep breath of the crisp morning air. "I love the smell after a rain."

"What does England smell like?"

I looked at him. Had he been dozing off? "Are you asking me what England smells like?"

"Sorry. I was thinking about air freshener."

"What are you talking about?"

"Air freshener. You know—those tree-shaped things that hang from your rearview mirror. A few years ago, a company claimed their new fragrance evoked quintessential Britishness. Naturally, that set off a national debate—what does England actually smell like?"

"What was the answer? Sheep? Tea bags? Fish and chips?"

"I believe the winning answer was 'Brexit,'" he said without cracking a smile. "A blend of confusion, regret, and the faintest whiff of burning bridges."

British humor, I'd learned from my first husband, a Scot, is a combination of irony, understatement, a healthy dose of the absurd, and the uniquely British aversion to taking yourself too seriously.

Ivor did doze for the rest of the twenty-minute journey. I woke him when we got there.

Once again, we were met at the door by Belcourt himself. Where was that butler he talked about? "Come in, come in," he said. "Let me take your jackets."

I studied the impressive entrance hall. The first time we'd been there, I'd been taken by the proportions and the lovely staircase. This time it was the portraits that caught my eye. "I believe you said these are all members of the Wyck family."

"A gallery of Wycks, yes. The Wyck family lived in this house, or one of its iterations, for more than seven hundred years. The house—not the one we see today, of course—is mentioned in the Little Domesday Book."

"Where did the name come from?" I asked. "I know *wyck* means *settlement*, but why Ravenswyck?"

"Because of the ravens who nested for centuries in the great trees. There's one on the Wyck coat of arms. Odd, really, because ravens were considered omens of death and misfortune. Ornithologists will tell you ravens were driven out of Suffolk in the nineteenth century, but we still see them occasionally at night." He gave an ironic smile. "Or we think we do."

"How far back do the portraits go?" Ivor asked.

"Come. I'll show you." Belcourt led us through the long gallery to the library with bookshelves lining the walls. Above them, following the line of the ceiling, were what looked stylistically like the oldest portraits. Early medieval portrait painters, I knew from a previous case, were less concerned with reproducing the precise facial features of their subjects and more concerned with depicting their wealth and status through clothing, heraldry, and significant objects.

"This is the oldest portrait we have." Belcourt indicated a painting that hung over the door we'd come through. "Meet Sir Henry Wyck. His father was born in Hertfordshire and married the daughter of a Suffolk man who'd become wealthy in the Ninth Crusade. When he died, his widow took their son, little Henry here, and returned to her own father at Ravenswyck. As he had four daughters and no sons, little Henry took the name Wyck and became the heir."

The half-length portrait showed a handsome young man in full plate armor. His short blondish hair was worn in ringlets, and his direct gaze created an impression of confidence and strength. In his left hand, he held a sword; in his right, a dagger. On a table beside him were a candle, an open book, a scroll, and a black quill pen. A coat of arms appeared in the left upper corner and, near the top of the wood panel, the words *Sir Henry Wyck, 1304–1348.*

"Look at the dates," Ivor said. "Henry died in 1348, just before the Black Death reached Suffolk."

I felt a frisson of excitement. "That means Henry Wyck may have been alive when Egemere Woman was buried in the crypt. He might have known her."

Belcourt's face lit up. "I hadn't considered that, but it's true."

"Do you know Sir Henry's wife's name?" I looked again at the handsome man with ringlets and armor. "Do you have portraits?"

"Henry had two wives. The first was Matilda, and the second was Julia. We were given a general history of the house when we bought it. Sadly, there are no portraits or descriptions of them."

"Kate," Ivor said. "Look at the triangular space between Henry's chest and his cocked left arm, holding the sword."

Peering closely, I saw a tiny figure—a man on horseback, wearing a black hooded cloak and carrying a scythe. "It's the Grim Reaper." I thought of the mechanical clock I'd seen in Devon, the hooded figure reminding everyone of the brevity of life.

"We had an art expert weigh in," Belcourt said. "He said portraiture of this time was highly symbolic. The painter was telling a story. Everything here speaks of wealth and power. Henry's armor and weapons indicate success in battle—the Hundred Years War with France, it would have been. The open book and the quill pen tell us he was a scholar and a poet. The hooded figure probably means an untimely death—or misfortune of some kind."

"Do you know where the Wyck manorial records are kept?" I asked.

"I don't even know if they exist. I've never seen them."

"Could they be held at the Suffolk County Archives?"

"It's quite possible. Carrie took care of all that."

Don't get your hopes up, I warned myself. Even if Ravenswyck's archives had been transferred to the Suffolk County Archives, they might contain nothing more than lists of household servants and the rents paid by tenants.

"I do remember people asking about the history of the estate," Belcourt said. "I believe one of them was writing a chronicle of the plague village."

"Do you remember a name?"

"No, I'm sorry."

Leaving the portrait gallery, we rode the creaky antique elevator down to the recreated village.

We found Tamzin and Mark in the museum. Mark was dressed in jeans and a blue shirt with the sleeves rolled up. Tamzin was her quirky self in plaid pajama bottoms, an orange Superman T-shirt, and red high-tops. They'd laid out the grave goods again, the objects lined up on the table with the dark-blue felt cloth.

"Dr. Nevin and Dr. Whybrew send their apologies," Mark said. "Niall's completing his databases"—he was always doing that, it seemed to me—"and Celia's in Norwich, meeting with the CMBA board."

"Where's the pearl?" I asked, not seeing the leather pouch. I'd been steeling myself for a second look.

"Celia took it with her, to show the board," Tamzin said. "I think it's a funding meeting."

"Since the discovery of Egemere Woman," Mark said, "interest in the CMBA has increased. Donations are up. They intend to make the most of it."

I gazed at the grave goods—the coins, the objects of precious metal and jewels, the tortoiseshell comb. I bent down to examine the comb, almost expecting to see a fine hair of jet black or spun gold caught in its perfect teeth. My mouth went dry. Heat rose in my cheeks. These were literal time-travelers, created seven or in some cases eight centuries in the past—survivors of a lost world populated by vibrant human beings who'd lived extraordinary lives in a time of danger and fear. They'd faced their challenges and left their mark, even if that mark was only a footnote in the history books. But these objects remained, objects they'd handled and valued.

I put a tentative finger on the spot where I'd first seen that glorious, ancient pearl. The oddest feeling came over me, a kind of thrumming, as if I'd touched a mild electrical current. Whatever it was, I didn't like it. I tried to calm myself, analyze my feelings. Was I experiencing the aftershock of my previous experience, a kind of PTSD? The faint sound of metal striking metal echoed in my brain . . . cries of pain and terror . . . the rushing of many feet. And a small, tremulous voice—*Please, no.*

And then, as suddenly as it had come, it was gone, leaving me slightly breathless and very confused.

"I'll leave you to get on," Belcourt was saying. "I promised my farm manager we'd finish a proposal for the autumn season. I'll be back in an hour or so."

I took a few deep breaths and focused on Ivor.

"Let's get to work, then," he said, pulling out two pairs of white cotton gloves. "Photograph the silver cuff first. When you've finished, I'll try removing a small section of tarnish from the inside band."

Still reeling, I began, almost mechanically, to set up the light box and camera. I needed time to think, to make sense of things, but that would have to wait. I had a job to do.

Tamzin and Mark watched with interest as Ivor took precise measurements of the goods and recorded them in our notebook, along with the detailed descriptions and thumbnail sketches we'd already made.

Once I'd photographed the cuff, Ivor set to work with his mini chemical lab. A series of bottles held various tarnish removers with different chemical compositions. The idea was to use the gentlest solution necessary to do the job.

"Put these masks on, please—just while I'm using the solution." Ivor handed out the industrial N95 masks we'd brought with us from the shop. "There's no real danger, but the vapors are slightly toxic. Best to play it safe. If we decide to treat the whole cuff, we'll do it in a laboratory setting with proper ventilation. Today will take only a minute or two."

Masks in place, we watched as Ivor applied a cotton swab soaked in a solution to the inside of the cuff.

"Normally a silver object would be submersed," Ivor said. "I don't want to do that. The glass eyes might be damaged or dislodged."

A small area of black tarnish was staining the swab. If successful, the solution could be applied carefully to the outside of the cuff, allowing the details of the heads to become visible. The decoration was unusual. The heads had been cast separately and soldered to the cuff—an ancient and usually reliable technique. Cleaning would also reveal if repairs were needed.

"Now we clean the treated area with ionized water and a mild detergent." Ivor closed the bottle of chemical solution, dropped the swabs in a plastic bag, and sealed it. We removed our masks, and I collected them. Ivor opened another of the bottles and applied the rinse water with a cotton cloth.

The tiny patch of silver gleamed. A good omen.

Tamzin was interested in the photography. She watched as I placed each object in the light box and positioned the camera through the aperture at the top. By turning the box on its various sides, I could photograph each object from several angles.

She started to say something, then went silent.

"What is it?" I asked. "Do you have a question about the photography?"

"It's not that." Her cheeks turned pink. "I've been wondering about the investigation into Dr. Sinclair's death. We know you're married to that detective. Is there any news? I mean has anything significant turned up?"

It had—the pearls—but that was confidential information. "Significant as in . . . ?" I left the sentence hanging, hoping she'd finish it.

"I don't know. Forget it. I'm not myself." She hugged herself, tucking her hands under her arms.

"Of course you're not. We're all in shock." Well, that was true. But I looked at her, seeing something else in her expression. Fear? Was she worried about her own safety? "The police will get to the bottom of it, Tamzin. I promise. If they think there's any possibility of danger, they'll tell you."

She smiled, but I wasn't sure I'd comforted her.

When we finished our work, Ivor and I began packing up. Tamzin and Mark were putting the grave goods back in their storage containers in the safe.

I thought about the word Sinclair had written in his daily diary—*Safe*. "Did Dr. Sinclair say anything to either of you about a safe?"

"You mean this one?" Tamzin asked.

"Or the one at the field office. Was he worried about theft?"

They both shook their heads.

We heard the elevator descending.

"Ms. Hamilton," Belcourt said, "may we have another chat before you leave? It won't take long."

"I'll finish up here, Kate," Ivor said, giving me a curious look. Was my face still flushed? "Take your time."

* * *

In the gift shop, Belcourt said, "Yesterday I received a contract from Nash & Holmes. I signed it. All that's left now is for you to sign as well—if you haven't changed your mind." He reached into his jacket, pulled out a folded sheet of paper, and handed it to me.

I scanned the contract, noticing a renewal clause. Anything I learned, it said, would be presented to Belcourt after a period of two weeks. At that point, he could either renew for another two weeks or let it go.

"Are the terms acceptable?" I asked. "The cost?"

"I'm not concerned about that." He shifted his weight, and I got the impression there was something he wanted to say. "I need you to understand why this means so much to me." He pulled out his wallet and opened it to a photograph of possibly the most beautiful woman I'd ever seen in my life. It was obviously a high-fashion shot, perhaps an advertisement for the silver chandelier earrings that grazed her shoulders.

Carrie Holgate had an oval face with perfectly symmetrical features—huge eyes, a straight nose, sculpted bone structure, and full scarlet lips. Her dark hair was parted in the middle and pulled back, offering neither enhancement nor competition for her gorgeous face. Her expression was that bored, almost contemptuous look high-fashion photographers seem to love.

"It doesn't really look like her," Belcourt said. "She was always smiling, always friendly, interested in other people, you know?"

"She's stunning," I said, feeling it was an understatement. "Absolutely beautiful."

He smiled. "She *was* beautiful, inside and out. And brilliant. And kind." He held out his arms. "Look at me. Why would a woman like that love me?" He met my eyes. "She could have had anyone she pleased . . . *anyone*. But she chose me—God knows why. It wasn't the money. She was on her way to becoming an icon in the fashion world. *No.* She loved me. We were happy—more than happy. We were in love. She wouldn't have left me."

Belcourt showed me a second photo, a selfie of the two of them on a beach. With no makeup and her hair tousled by the wind, Carrie was even more lovely than she'd been in the ad. She wore a white shirt, unbuttoned at the neck to reveal an unusual gold necklace.

"Is the necklace Roman?" I asked. I could just make out the loop-in-loop chain and what looked like an irregular, unworked emerald pendant.

"Second century. Carrie fell in love with it on our honeymoon. We bought it at a shop in Malta." His arms fell to his side. "I know it sounds overly romantic, but we were soulmates. We really were. We talked about everything and nothing. No secrets. I know she's gone. If not, she would have come back to me—" His voice broke, and he turned away. After a moment, he turned to face me. "That's why this project means so much to me. It was her dream. She was so excited about the excavations and the prospect of building a museum. If only she'd lived long enough to see what they found."

"Are you sure you want me to sign the contract?"

"Very much."

I had one more point to make. "What if the truth can't be found?"

"Then so be it. I'll have done my best." He handed me a pen.

I signed the contract.

Chapter Thirteen

Manor Farm

I got home early that night as Ivor decided it wouldn't be worth it to reopen the shop for an hour or so at the end of the day. His decision was more than welcome as Tom had texted to say he'd be home by six thirty, which left me only about an hour alone to sort through the disturbing reaction I'd had in the Ravenswyck museum.

I'd had these experiences since childhood. They were familiar to me, and growing up, I'd even wondered if my father experienced something similar. For some unknown reason, I seemed to be sensitive to the emotional atmosphere in which an object once existed—whether that atmosphere had been pleasant and joyful or just the opposite. Like radio waves from the deep universe or glimmers of light from distant stars, my brain had been created as a sort of receiver. That was the way I'd explained it to myself anyway. The emotions felt real at the moment, but until now, the gap in time provided a sort of insulation.

This time had been different, and I didn't like it one bit. I'd seen the pearl with my own eyes only once. Why had the mere memory of its lustrous beauty and mysterious past touched off a full-blown . . . *experience? Encounter? Attack?* I couldn't think of an appropriate word. Maybe there wasn't one.

Since living in England, I had realized one important truth. I used to believe it was objects of great age and beauty that brought on these internal reactions—and they did. Working just about every day with valuable antiques and antiquities was a pleasurable experience, a little like the feeling one gets after that first glass of fine wine. But lately I'd begun to realize it wasn't the value of an object that touched me so much as the intensity of the emotions in which that object once existed. And that led me to another thought. Now, without a doubt, I knew the pearl had witnessed the clash of swords, the heat of battle, and the agony of certain death. And the woman upon whose breast it had lain for seven hundred years had known terror, for herself and for her unborn child.

I shivered at the thought and might have begun to weep, but I was saved from another wave of pointless sorrow by the sound of Tom's car in the driveway.

All I wanted was to feel his solid warmth. This was my reality, not hers.

That evening Tom and I made dinner together, something we hadn't done since before the Thetford murder. Most nights now, Tom stayed late at police headquarters. His team was working flat out to locate the fugitive, who might or might not be Derek Quinn. Whoever he was, he'd fled the scene of the crime, desperate and possibly armed. The police were under growing pressure to bring him into custody before some innocent person got hurt.

Tom was tossing a green salad. I was heating up a lamb curry with basmati rice I'd made earlier in the week. I poured us each a small glass of Australian Shiraz.

A small bubble of joy burst in my heart. Whatever evil had befallen those long-ago people had been buried with them centuries ago. This was now. Tom and I were safe.

"So, you signed the contract," Tom said. "Good. That gives you another reason to hang out with the archaeologists."

"I knew you'd feel that way," I said. "I can read your mind."

"I'm not sure I like that." Tom gave me a mock frown. "I deserve a few secrets."

I laughed, but a trickle of guilt ran down my spine. I was the one with a secret, and it was getting harder to keep. Ivor had witnessed my initial reaction to the pearl at Ravenswyck, and if I knew him at all, he'd bring it up sooner or later. I couldn't lie to him, and yet Tom deserved to be the first person to know about my so-called gift. I really did have to come up with a more accurate word for it.

As soon as this whole thing is over, I'll tell him, I promised myself.

"Almost done." Tom smiled at me.

I watched him measure olive oil and lemon juice into a glass jar. "Do you really consider the archaeological team suspects in Sinclair's death? They all seemed so shocked to find his body."

"We haven't ruled anyone out yet—not completely."

"They have alibis."

"Except for Nevin, unproven." Tom added a clove of garlic and a tablespoon each of honey and Dijon mustard to the dressing. Capping the jar, he shook it. "They all claim they didn't hear anyone leave The Forge that night, but there's a back exit, off the kitchen. Any of them could have left the cottage without the others knowing."

"And Belcourt?"

"Same thing. Belcourt could have left Ravenswyck that night. He's not a prisoner. His employees say they didn't see or hear anything, but a lack of evidence isn't evidence."

I told him about the conversation I'd had with Belcourt, and about his beautiful, missing wife. "He's still devastated by her loss."

"Yes—he gives that impression."

It was a curious way to put it. "Have you viewed the CCTV footage yet?"

"The download came through today. The IT team will check to see it hasn't been edited."

Tom's mobile buzzed. We looked at each other, hoping it wasn't an emergency.

"Tom Mallory." He listened, looking surprised. "Say that again?" He nodded slowly. "I see. Well, I suppose we can be there in, say, forty minutes." He looked at me and I nodded, wondering about the *we*.

"Who was it?" I asked when he'd clicked off.

"Alex Belcourt. He wants us to drive over to Ravenswyck tonight. As soon as possible, as a matter of fact. He's learned something he thinks we should know."

"Did he say what?"

"No, but when someone volunteers to talk to the police, we listen."

I quickly plated our dinners, and we left for Ravenswyck twenty minutes later.

Belcourt met us at the door again, but this time a man in a black suit took our jackets. He did have a butler after all.

"Thank you for coming at short notice," Belcourt said. "There's someone in the drawing room waiting to speak to you."

We followed him along the long gallery, but instead of turning right into the library as Ivor and I had, we turned left into a large drawing room with a vaulted Tudor ceiling. Belcourt's farm manager, Peter Eley, stood with his back to the fireplace, his arms crossed over his chest. He didn't look happy, but then maybe he never did.

Belcourt didn't look happy either. "Tell Detective Inspector Mallory what you saw, Peter."

Eley stood there, a scowl on his face.

"This isn't an interview," Tom said mildly, "but if what you have to say concerns Sinclair's murder, you are legally obligated to tell the police. I assume it's something you failed to mention earlier?"

"T'were the lights, sir," Eley said grudgingly. "What sort of lights?"

"Torches, probably," Eley said, meaning flashlights. "I can see the excavations from my house. Struck me as odd. No one's meant to be at the excavations at night. Why would they be? And the lights sort of bounced about, as if people were walking."

"When was this?" Tom asked.

"The week before Dr. Sinclair was murdered."

"You told Mr. Belcourt."

Eley cleared his throat. "No, sir. I didn't. Not at first. I told Dr. Sinclair."

"Why didn't you tell me?" Belcourt demanded. "That's what I want to know. Everything that happens on this estate concerns me."

"Well, sir, I thought t'were more likely the concern of Dr. Sinclair. Very grateful, he was, too. 'Nighthawkers,' he called 'em."

"Nighthawkers?" Tom looked at me.

"It's a term for people who use metal detectors at night," I said. "Treasure hunters. They steal artifacts from archaeological sites and sell them online or through the black market. It's illegal."

"I'm sorry, Mr. Belcourt." Eley looked embarrassed. "I know how busy you are, and I didn't want to distress you. Sinclair said he'd take care of it." He wavered. "Oh, hell. The truth is he made me promise to keep it to myself. He said bad publicity might close down the dig, and I know how much it means to you, sir."

"What about the night Sinclair was murdered?"

Eley shifted his weight, looking uncomfortable. "I did see lights that night, yes."

"Do you think that's why Sinclair was killed?" Belcourt asked Tom. "He caught these nighthawkers in the act?"

"It's a possibility," Tom said and turned to Eley. "You should have told the police."

"I realize that now, sir," Eley muttered. "Don't like to get mixed up in things that aren't my business." He looked at Belcourt. "Am I free to go, sir?"

"Yes, go," Belcourt said, "but if anything else happens on my land, I'd better be the first to know about it, not the last."

"We'll need a formal statement," Tom told Eley. "Stop in at the police station in Hartwell tomorrow. You can revise your statement."

Eley shot us a black look and turned on his heels.

When he was out of earshot, Belcourt said, "It's not like Peter to keep something like that from me. I can't imagine what got into him."

"He's a trusted employee?" Tom asked.

"With me since the beginning. I told your wife. He's lived on the estate all his life, and his father before him. He was devoted to Carrie and her animals. Absolutely devoted. Her disappearance hit him almost as hard as it hit me."

* * *

Tom and I sat in the Tudor drawing room on one of the two sofas flanking the fireplace. "This room is stunning," I said, taking in the arched beams interspersed with floral medallions.

"It's the oldest part of the house." Belcourt stood at a drinks tray. "Carrie fell in love with this room. The history, you know."

"I was in the Suffolk CID when your wife disappeared," Tom said. "Not working on the case, but I remember it well. A tragedy."

"Yes, it was. What would you like to drink, Kate?"

"Mineral water with lime, if you have it," I said.

"Tom?"

"Same for me."

A table between the sofas held books on archaeology—the excavation of Roman Britain, Anglo-Saxon culture in East Anglia, Viking York. I opened the one on top and saw the nameplate. *This book belongs to Carrie Holgate.*

"I've ruined your evening. I'm sorry." Belcourt handed me a tumbler. "I thought you should know about the lights."

"You were right to call me," Tom said. "It could be important."

"It was this very week, nine years ago, that Carrie disappeared." Belcourt opened a second bottle of mineral water. "I'd been away on a business trip—almost two months, eager to get home. I was able to catch an earlier flight. Carrie wasn't expecting me until the next day. It was late, and I didn't want to wake her—she'd been tired the previous few weeks—so I slept in the guest bedroom." His hands twisted in his lap. "If I could go back and do it again—" He left the sentence unfinished. "By the time I awoke in the morning, she was gone. I assumed she'd be at the dig site, but no one had seen her. I tried phoning. No answer. And then . . . nothing. I called the police late that afternoon. They asked if her car was gone. It wasn't."

"Were any of her possessions taken?" I asked. "Toiletries? Clothing?"

"Nothing was missing." He handed me my drink. "There was something on her mind, though. She'd mentioned it on the phone, said it would keep until I got home. We never had that talk. It haunts me."

"Do you have any idea what it was about?"

"At the time, I assumed it had something to do with the dig, although I'm not sure why." Belcourt handed Tom his drink. "Sinclair's death brings it all back—the waiting, the mind-numbing terror, being a suspect in my own wife's disappearance." He poured himself a generous shot of whiskey. "It's almost as if this place was cursed."

"As far as we know, the two cases are completely separate." Tom crossed his legs. "For what it's worth, I don't believe the house is cursed. Think of what you've accomplished here, how you've brought the past to life."

"That's what bothers me." Belcourt drained his glass. "The past may not want to be resurrected. Carrie said something once about a legend connected with the house, something sad. She must have read it somewhere." He looked at me. "I was reminded of it when your colleague, Mr. Tweedy, noticed the figure of Death in the portrait of Henry Wyck."

"Did Carrie say where she read about the legend?" I asked.

"I wish I'd paid more attention. I was busy with work. But with her disappearance and now this murder, I can't help thinking of it."

"Understandable," Tom said. "If we find anything relating to your wife's disappearance, you'll be the first to know."

The door opened. "You have a visitor, sir." It was the man in the black suit. "She says it's important."

* * *

Vivian Bunn strode into the room, a large carryall on her arm. "Sorry to barge in."

"Vivian?" I was astonished. "What are you doing here? Did you drive?"

"No, I walked. Only took me three hours." She cocked her head. "Of course I drove."

Vivian had a car—an old Vauxhall sedan—but she rarely used it except for shopping at Tesco or driving to church in a hard rain.

"Aren't you going to introduce me?" Vivian asked.

"Yes, of course. Alex, this is my friend, Vivian Bunn. Tamzin Oliver boards with her. Vivian, this is Alex Belcourt, the owner of Ravenswyck Court."

"A pleasure, madam," Belcourt said, looking lost. "Is there some way I can help you?"

"It's nothing like that." Vivian plopped the carryall on a side table and opened the zip. "This is for Tamzin. Her laundry. She's been stopping at The Forge since the *unfortunate incident.*" She put the words in virtual italics. "I thought she might need her clothes."

"I'll see she gets them." Belcourt reached for the carryall, but Vivian kept her hand firmly on the handles. "I didn't know how to get to The Forge, you see, so I thought you were my best bet."

I watched all this with fascination. Vivian never did anything without a specific purpose. She'd eventually tell us what that was, but she wouldn't be rushed.

"As I said, I'll make sure she gets it," Belcourt repeated. "Very kind of you, I'm sure."

"You see, I've been worried about the girl. I feel responsible—to her parents, you know. I feel that way about all my lodgers."

I could vouch for that. *In loco parentis* was Vivian's house motto. Even when the guest was in her mid-forties like me.

"I can see that," Belcourt said. "Would you like me to—"

She ignored him. "When I saw her laundry basket was full—she does her own, you know, but like I said, the basket was full, and I thought I'd just throw her things in the washer-dryer. So they'd be ready if she wanted them."

"I see." Belcourt tilted his head in confusion. "And you did that, yes?"

"I did." Vivian nodded once. "The thing is, I need to apologize."

"For doing her laundry?"

"No." She reached into the carry-all and pulled out a plastic baggie. "They must have been in the pocket of her anorak. Quite ruined, as you can see. Most were caught in the filter. Obviously, they weren't meant to get wet."

My mouth dropped open. They were pearls—fake pearls, identical to the pearls found with Sinclair's body in the trench.

Tom pulled out his mobile phone.

"Ren," he said. "I need to speak to Tamzin Oliver tonight. She'll be at The Forge. Caution her. I'll meet you at the station in Hartwell."

Chapter Fourteen

Hartwell

Tom and I drove directly from Ravenswyck to the police station. Somehow, we'd persuaded Vivian to go home. She was tearful, blaming herself for getting Tamzin into trouble with the police. She'd had no idea the ruined pearls had anything to do with Sinclair's murder. Feeling responsible, she'd called Tamzin's parents from Ravenswyck. They were living in Spain, but promised to contact a solicitor in Ipswich.

Tamzin arrived with DS Ren thirty minutes later. She hadn't been charged with a crime, but I knew they could hold her for twenty-four hours without a charge. Tom waited to begin the interview until her solicitor arrived. When she did, the woman looked less than happy. She was wearing a cocktail dress. Her evening out had been ruined.

"Kate, I'd like you to observe," Tom said. "There's a monitor in that office at the end of that hall."

DI Cartwright shot me a look of stern disapproval. It was far from normal procedure. I was a civilian after all, but I knew Tamzin and was familiar with the team and their work at Egemere Close. And I knew Tom. His priority wasn't administrative procedures. It was finding the killer.

After giving Tamzin and her attorney time alone, DI Cartwright and DS Ren began the interview. Tom sat in, and I think that irritated Cartwright, too.

Tamzin looked scared to death.

After reading Tamzin her rights, Cartwright began. "I'm Detective Inspector Amy Cartwright. This is Detective Sergeant Matthew Ren. Do you need anything? A glass of water?"

Tamzin shook her head.

Cartwright produced the bag of ruined pearls. "Do you know what these are, Miss Oliver?"

"Beads," Tamzin said.

"What kind of beads?"

"They look like pearls."

"They were found by your landlady, Miss Vivian Bunn, in your laundry. Do you know how they got there?"

"No."

"Are they yours?"

Tamzin glanced at her attorney. "No comment."

"Did someone give them to you?"

"No comment."

"Did you scatter pearls like these in the trench where Dr. Sinclair's body was found?"

"No comment."

"We found pearls exactly like these near Dr. Sinclair's body. Someone put them there. Why would they do that, do you think?"

"How should I know?" Tamzin looked terrified and, in the orange Superman T-shirt, so young. She reminded me of my daughter, Christine, in her teen years. *Deny, deny, deny.*

"Where were you the night of Dr. Sinclair's death?"

"I've already told you. I was at The Forge."

"Did you leave at any time during that night?"

"No."

"Did you visit the excavation site that day?"

"No." Her eyes flickered.

"But I thought you were the one who found Dr. Sinclair's body."

"I thought you meant earlier."

"Let's get back to the pearls. Why were they found with your things?"

"I don't know."

"Why did you buy them?"

"I didn't." She was clasping and unclasping her hands.

"Who did?"

"No comment."

Cartwright used the edge of her fingernail to lift the corner of a sales sticker. "They were purchased at a craft shop in Hadleigh. Will we see you on their CCTV footage?"

"No." Tamzin was faltering. If Cartwright kept up the pressure, she'd probably fold.

Her attorney must have realized the same thing, because she spoke up. "My client has answered your questions, Detective. She doesn't know anything."

"The fake pearls were found at Rose Cottage in her laundry basket. How does she account for that?"

"She doesn't. It's not her job to prove otherwise."

She was right about that.

"I'd like Miss Oliver to speak for herself, please," Cartwright said. "Tamzin, how do you account for the fact that fake pearls were found amongst your things in the laundry basket?"

Tamzin looked on the verge of tears.

"Do you need to take a break, Miss Oliver?" Cartwright asked.

I heard loud voices coming from the outer office and moved into the hall for a better look. Mark Lambe had arrived and was trying to shove past one of the local constables. "This is all a mistake. Let me talk to her. I can straighten this out."

"That's not possible, young man. She's being interviewed."

"But this isn't her fault. I can explain. Let me talk to someone." He saw me. "Ms. Hamilton, please." He clutched my arm.

"Let her go, son," the constable said. "This isn't helping."

"It's all right," I said. "I know him."

"Tell your husband I can explain everything." Mark was almost wild. "It's all a mistake. It was my fault."

"The pearls?"

"They were *my* idea. It was nothing—a prank. That's all. We had nothing to do with Sinclair's death, I swear it."

Did he know Sinclair had ingested the pearls?

"Get DCI Mallory," I told the constable.

"If you're sure you're all right, miss." He trotted out of the waiting room and returned in minutes with Tom and DI Cartwright.

"Let me talk to her," Mark said. "This is a mistake."

"Calm down, Mr. Lambe," Tom said. "We'd like very much to hear what you have to say."

We sat in the local sergeant's office around a metal desk nearly overwhelmed with papers and a framed photograph of a young boy in his school uniform.

"Where's Tamzin?" Mark demanded. "She must be terrified."

"Her lawyer's with her," DI Cartwright said. "Just explain your part in this. Tell us about the pearls."

"We knew you'd find them eventually." Mark's face was pale and serious. "We hoped you wouldn't know it was us."

"You put the pearls in the trench? Why?"

"I told the sergeant. It was a prank."

"A *prank*? You're a scientist, not a schoolboy."

"We didn't do it as a lark," he said. "We wanted to get back at Sinclair."

"Why? What had he done?"

"He was blocking my thesis topic, for one thing. It wasn't fair. I've spent more than a year researching. There's more than enough evidence to justify excavating the mound." He explained about Sinclair's refusal to investigate.

"That's the reason you put fake pearls in the trench?" Cartwright held up her hands. "You thought the pearls would persuade him to approve your thesis topic? That doesn't make sense."

"My thesis is just the beginning. Sinclair tried to . . . he assaulted her."

"Who assaulted whom?"

"Sinclair assaulted Tamzin. In the field office. She stopped it, but it was traumatic."

"How would putting fake pearls in the trench help?"

Mark sneered. "Sinclair was drunk with the accolades he'd received over the medieval body. He acted like no one else had any part in it, and he wanted more recognition—another body, more treasure, anything that would end up on the front page of the newspapers. But he's an archaeologist. He doesn't know pearls. That's why he hired Ms. Hamilton and Mr. Tweedy. We hoped he'd see the fake pearls and immediately issue some sort of press release which he would then have to retract. We wanted to embarrass him, hurt him."

"What if he recognized them as fake?" Tom asked. "It was pretty obvious."

"In that case, we figured he'd blame the protesters. Assume it was more vandalism. They'd deny it, of course, and the whole thing would be bad publicity. Exactly what he hoped to avoid." Mark spread his hands. "Look, I'm not proud of this, but we had no idea he would be murdered, did we? We've been living in fear, wondering why no one mentioned the pearls. It seemed unlikely you hadn't found them, but when nothing was said, we began to hope it would all blow over."

"We've kept it out of the press," Tom said. I could see he was watching Mark's reaction. "There's something you need to know, and I'm going to ask you to keep this to yourself for now. Some of the pearls were found in Dr. Sinclair's mouth and in his stomach."

"*What?*" Mark leapt to his feet, the blood draining out of his face. "Why?"

"We're hoping you can tell us," Cartwright said.

"But I have no idea—none at all." Mark held the sides of his head with both hands. "We didn't do that. Why would we?" He stared at Tom. "Are you saying that's what killed him? He choked on the pearls?"

"He died from a blow to his head."

Mark let out his breath. "Thank God for that."

"Were you and Tamzin at the dig site the night Sinclair was murdered?"

"No—of course not. We seeded the pearls earlier that day. Dug them in, hoping Sinclair would find them and leap to the wrong conclusion. He was always the last to leave the site in the evening and the first to arrive in the morning."

"Where did the pearls come from?"

"I bought two bags at a shop in Hadleigh. We didn't need the second bag as it turned out. Overkill." He winced. "Sorry—bad choice of words. Tamzin must have forgotten she'd left them in her anorak."

"Where were you the night Sinclair was murdered?"

"We told you. At The Forge. It's the truth—well, almost."

"What do you mean?" Cartwright asked.

"We waited up to see if Dr. Sinclair had found the pearls. He wouldn't keep it to himself. But it got late, and we fell asleep. The next morning, it seemed a stupid thing to do. And then when Sinclair's body was found—" He shook his head. "We should have come clean right away."

"Yes, you should have," Tom said.

"Have you and Miss Oliver ever gone to the dig site at night?" Cartwright asked.

Mark looked confused. "No—why would we?"

"Never mind." Tom turned to Cartwright "Give Tamzin a chance to corroborate what Mr. Lambe has told us. If she does, let her go."

Twenty minutes later Tamzin appeared at the door of the office. Seeing Mark, she burst into tears. "I'm sorry. I didn't mean to get you involved."

"No worries, kid," Mark said. "I told them everything."

"Miss Oliver," Tom said, "Mark told us you were assaulted by Dr. Sinclair. Is that right?"

Tamzin pressed her fingers to her lips, as if trying to prevent the words from escaping. "He asked me to stay behind one afternoon—to go over the finds list, make sure it was in order. He came up behind me and put his hands on my shoulders, sort of massaging me." She shivered. "I jumped up and asked him what he was doing. He said I knew very well what he was doing, that I'd been giving him signals. I denied it, of course, but he pretended not to believe me. He came at me again. There was a teacup on the desk. I threw it at him. He screamed at me and called me a tease and said if I breathed a word of it to anyone, he'd see that my career was ruined."

"He would have done it, too, the scum," Mark said. "But we didn't kill him."

"One more question, Miss Oliver," Tom said. "You haven't been entirely forthcoming, have you, and I want to give you a chance to correct the statement you made earlier. You said that on the night Sinclair was murdered, you and Mark fell asleep on the sofa at The Forge. You said you were together the whole night and didn't see or hear anyone coming or going. Is that the truth?"

Tamzin blinked. "I . . . well, I said—" She broke off and looked at Mark.

"Not quite," Mark said. "I woke up around midnight. Loo. When I got back, Tamzin was stretched out on the sofa. She looked so comfortable, I covered her with the afghan and went up to my room." He put his arm around Tamzin's shoulders. "It's okay."

"Around midnight?" Tom asked. "Did you see or hear anything then—anyone moving about, for example?"

"No. I heard Niall's printer, but that was it."

"We'll prepare a revised statement, Miss Oliver. Mark, take her to Rose Cottage. Vivian will be beside herself with worry."

Chapter Fifteen

Friday, June 27
Long Barston

I took Friday off at The Cabinet of Curiosities as Ivor had several appointments lined up, which meant he'd be in the shop all day. Angela Foxe had invited me to the rectory for lunch. She wanted to show me the baby's nursery. Sharing her joy was the very thing I needed to distract me from the murder investigation.

I spent the morning at home, doing a final read-through of the descriptions of the Roman marble busts that would be included in the auction catalog. Then I drove into the village.

The rectory, a Victorian house near St. Æthelric's Church, dozed elegantly in the sunshine, the cool gray stone set off by masses of white roses and frothy purple clumps of catmint.

I found Angela on the porch, watering flower baskets. "Lunch is almost ready," she said, "but do you mind if I show you the nursery first?"

"I can't wait to see it."

Angela and Edmund had chosen a small bedroom next to their own for the nursery. "What do you think?" she asked. "We've gone rather neutral, not knowing the sex."

"Oh, Angela—it's gorgeous." The woodwork glistened white, and the walls had been painted a soft, neutral blue-green. The wall behind the walnut crib was papered with a forest mural populated by adorable woodland creatures. A vintage dresser had been converted into a changing table, and in the corner, under the eaves, sat a beige striped chair and ottoman. The little room was like a stage set, ready for the appearance of the star. I didn't know why, but every time I thought of the baby, I pictured a girl.

"Thank Edmund's mother. She has the best taste and can do anything. She and Edmund's father put up the mural—it's the sticky sort that can be taken down without damaging the wall. And the cot bed can be converted into a toddler bed when the time is right."

"It's perfect." I was sure the dresser drawers were already stocked with tiny soft sleepers and stacks of diapers. "You and Edmund must be so excited."

"Oh, we are. I'm trying to hang in there until the new locum arrives."

"They found one?"

"Yes, recently qualified."

"When does he arrive?"

"That's the bad news. He can't start until mid-July. By that time, it'll hardly be worth it. Except if he works out, I might hire him. I could use a second vet in the practice."

"Which means you're on your own for another two weeks?"

"I'll be fine." She patted her belly. "Moving a little slower these days, but I'm strong as an ox."

We made our way downstairs. Angela stopped halfway, grimacing. "Oh, these contractions are a nuisance." She laughed. "Although maybe I can get the labor over with now, and when the time comes, she'll just pop out." I noticed Angela was using the feminine pronoun, too.

"It'll be a breeze," I lied, but in jest. Angela had medical training, after all. She knew what birthing babies entailed.

Hattie Nuthall, the housekeeper, served us lunch on the wide covered porch, a delicious pea soup with egg and cress sandwiches cut into triangles. She carried in a pitcher of lemonade with sprigs of mint and a plate of her famous macarons.

A gentle breeze brought the scent of roses. "Thanks for the tip about the Six Bells in Hartwell," I said. "Ivor and I plan to stop in one night soon. We're hoping to run into the protestors."

She stared at me. "You're investigating the murder, aren't you?"

"Not investigating," I said. "Keeping my eyes and ears open."

"Does Tom think the protesters killed Dr. Sinclair?"

"They don't have a suspect yet—or a motive."

"Well, be careful." She reached for her third macaron.

Hattie Nuthall peered out of the door. "Phone call for you, dear. An emergency, I'm afraid."

"I'm sorry, Kate." She hurried into the house.

She returned a few minutes later. "It's Leda at the alpaca farm. One of her animals is in severe pain. I'll have to attend." She put her hands on her cheeks. "I hate to ask, but could you possibly come with me? Edmund has parish meetings this afternoon. It's just I have a hard time carrying all the equipment. I could use another pair of hands."

* * *

Brockley

Ten Acres Alpaca Farm near Brockley combined the sale of raw fibers with a yarn shop and classes in knitting, crocheting, and felting. The owner, Leda Thomas, was a sturdy, no-nonsense sort of woman in her fifties.

"How many alpacas do you have?" I asked, puffing slightly. I was carrying Angela's medical bag, which was heavier than I'd expected.

"Twenty-two now. We started six years ago with five," she said as we walked to her barn. "All of them are still with us and producing fiber. Ebony, the one who's ill, is our newest purchase. She's been with us only two weeks, and it's been a difficult transition. She has the most beautiful dense coat, a true black, but her previous owners didn't know anything about alpacas. She was kept alone in their barn, which is emotionally traumatic for alpacas. They're herd animals. Buying her was a rescue, but now she's having a hard time bonding with ours. Several of the females spit at her, poor thing. There's a pecking order in the herd, and she hasn't found her place yet."

"Symptoms?" Angela asked.

"She's rolling some, kicking at her stomach, and doing quite a bit of vocalizing, which isn't like her. She's normally pretty quiet." Leda bit the side of her lip. "I hope it isn't colic."

"Is she eating and drinking normally?"

"Not for the last couple of days."

"I'll take a look and see what we're dealing with."

The barn was small. "Alpacas prefer sleeping outdoors year-round," Leda said. "We bring them in here only if they're sick or giving birth or if there's a really wicked storm."

Ebony was a gorgeous animal, but she was clearly in distress, pacing around the large stall and humming, a sort of *wooo* sound.

"*There now, there now,* Ebony. Good girl. Lovely girl." Leda spoke in a soft, low voice. "Doctor's here. She'll put you right."

"Why don't you two take a look at the herd while I examine her?" Angela said, donning gloves and a mask. I think she wanted us out of there.

The herd was in the field. Leda and I stood leaning on a wooden fence.

"These are the females and the *crias*, the babies," Leda said.

We watched the animals graze. They were lovely, all colors. One of them, a large white animal, wandered over to greet Leda, carefully avoiding me.

"This is Helen." Leda extended her face, allowing Helen to nuzzle her. "They're very smart," Leda said, "and they each have their own personalities. Helen is the matriarch of the herd. She's calm, kind, and tolerant, but she won't put up with any nonsense—like spitting. If something's going on in the herd, she'll tell me. Just hums and hums like a real conversation. This whole thing with Ebony has been upsetting for her. She considers it her job to make peace and keep everyone in order." Leda glanced at the barn. "I do hope Angela can do something."

We ended up in the shop, which carried a gorgeous range of yarn and all sorts of specialty gift items. "I could use a cuppa. How about you?" Leda asked, putting the kettle on. "Angela tells me your husband is a policeman. Have they located that fugitive yet?"

"Not yet."

"He was here, you know. Dossing in our barn."

"Did you report it?"

She shook her head. "I assumed it was a tramp. By the time I heard about the fugitive, he was long gone."

"Did he threaten anyone? Cause harm?"

"Nah—I think he needed somewhere safe to sleep. A few loaves of newly baked bread went missing from the porch."

"You should report it. The police are tracking his movements. Knowing he was here will help."

"I'll do that."

After about thirty minutes, Angela joined us, looking exhausted. "It's a fecal impaction," she said, "probably brought on by stress. I've given her a muscle relaxant and a pain reliever, which I'll leave with instructions." She handed Leda two small boxes. "And I've given her an oral dose of mineral oil. Walking her with a halter and lead will help that work. If there's no result tonight, you can give her another."

"Is she going to be all right?" Leda asked.

"I think so. Impaction can be serious, but you called me in early. I think she'll be fine. Make sure she drinks water. Use a funnel if you have to—and call me if things don't improve by tomorrow morning."

"And going forward? How do we treat the stress?"

"You know the animals better than I do, but you might try isolating the troublemakers in a separate field. Let Helen help Ebony assimilate. The other females will follow her lead. Then let the snippy ones back in one by one. I suspect Helen will discipline them, although it might take a couple of weeks."

As we stood to leave, Angela's smile froze. She clutched her stomach. Leda, who was putting a few trinkets in a gift bag for us, didn't notice.

"Contractions?" I whispered.

"Don't worry—they never last long." Angela took in a breath and blew it out slowly.

"Why don't you settle in the car?" We'd taken Angela's four-by-four from the veterinary surgery. "I'll get your things from the barn."

On the way back to the surgery I said, "You have a great job, you know. And you're so good at it."

"I've never wanted to be anything else." She sighed. "Poor little Ebony. She's been mistreated all her life. She's lucky to be in Leda's care now."

"And Helen's," I said, thinking of the sweet-tempered matriarch of the herd.

"You met her, did you? She's an incredible animal. Oldest female. Very wise. Honestly, if one or two of the alpacas can't accept Ebony, it would be better to get rid of them, sell them I mean, rather than put the whole herd under stress."

I considered that statement. Dr. Sinclair had been a troublemaker. From what I'd observed and heard, everywhere he had influence, he had used it to hurt people, to embarrass them, to belittle them—most importantly, to enhance himself. Someone had decided life would be better without him, and they'd made it permanent.

Back in my own car, I checked my phone. I'd missed two texts. The first was from someone named Hilary Kemble, a name I didn't recognize.

> *Hilary here, from the library. I found the name of the historian who gave the talk on the church and abbey at Egemere. It's Grenville Dark. Unfortunately he's no longer with us. He died three years ago.*

Grenville Dark. That had to be Edlyn's father, the one Brenda at the Six Bells said was a history professor. Had he been one of the people who'd requested access to the Ravenswyck archives? If so, what had happened to his research?

The second missed text was from Tom.

Can you stop at the police station in Hartwell this afternoon? We found something in Sinclair's room at The Forge. I'd like you to take a look. Bring Ivor if you can.

* * *

Hartwell

I phoned Ivor, and as I feared, he was stuck at the shop. "Sorry, Kate. I have appointments at two and three thirty. At four, Jeff Swift's customer, the one who collects Victorian smoking hats, is stopping by to pick up his purchase."

Oh, would I love to witness that. "I'll let you know what the police found."

At the police station, Tom ushered me into the tiny interview room. "Where were you today?"

"An alpaca farm near Brockley—and no, I didn't buy one, although I was tempted. They're adorable. I was helping Angela. The owner, Leda, told me someone slept in her barn for a few nights. I told her to report it."

"Thanks. That will help. He seems to be moving from farm to farm on foot."

"What's this?" On the table was an ordinary carton, about the size of a shoebox.

"We went back for a second search of Sinclair's room last night. We found it hidden behind a wood panel in his closet."

Tom handed me a pair of nitrile gloves and opened the box.

Inside was a pile of gold, not coins but jewelry and jewelry parts, lots of them—gold rings, brooches, and pendant frames that had once held coins or stones. "I'm sure it's gold," I said, "and high quality. We can test it."

"Is it from the Egemere Close dig?" he asked.

"Maybe. Ivor would know. I'll check for marks." I took out my magnifier and studied the objects. "No marks, which tells me—" I stopped because I'd noticed something. "Wait, there is a mark on this one." I showed him the impression of a leopard's head stamped into the back of a ring. "This means it was made in England. The design should tell us the approximate date." I examined another piece, an earring. An oval frame of hammered gold, fringed with gold beading in a distinctive pattern, was now empty. Whatever it had once held was gone—lost, perhaps, or removed at some point. A gold ring hung from the bottom, ending in a small natural pearl.

"What is it?" Tom asked.

"It's an earring—see the hook?" I held it up to my ear. "The frame held something once. May I text a couple of photos to Ivor? He can tell you more than I can."

I took several photos and attached them to a short text.

What can you tell us about this earring? Roman? I know the ring is English, but how early? If you're busy, we can talk later.

His reply appeared almost immediately.

Between appointments. The leopard's head tells us the ring was made in England sometime after 1300 but before 1363 when Edward III required a maker's mark as well. Obviously, the earring once held something. A precious or semiprecious stone?

Why take the stone out? I typed back.

Not unusual. If a family's fortunes went south, they might sell the jewel and keep the gold. Or maybe it was lost. There's only one earring?

Perhaps the reason it was broken up.

I thanked him and ended the exchange.

"What would Sinclair have been doing with a box of gold jewelry parts?" Tom asked. "And why hide it?"

"You hear of archaeologists who can't resist snatching a piece or two for themselves. Howard Carter did. So did Schliemann. Even a former curator at the British Museum couldn't resist, but I can't imagine someone like Dr. Sinclair doing it. Too risky these days. He thought too much of his reputation."

"So what was he doing with a box of Roman and medieval gold in his room? Could he have bought the gold legitimately as an investment?"

"I don't know. People do that. It is interesting, though. If the pieces were found during excavations funded by the university and the CMBA, they should have been listed as finds. I mean they list iron nails, for heaven's sake. I could ask Celia if they found gold at Ravenswyck."

"Don't tell her about the box. I don't intend to make this public until we know more."

My opportunity to ask Celia about the gold came sooner than I anticipated. When I got back to the shop, I found a phone message from Lady Barbara, inviting me to tea the following day at Finchley Hall—a party of sorts. Celia had been named the new head of the Centre for Medieval British Archaeology, a surprise because the appointment hadn't been expected so quickly. According to Lady Barbara, the position almost certainly meant a professorship at the university. "Considering recent events," Lady Barbara stressed in her message, "it won't be a celebration. Simply a quiet observance of Celia's new position."

Was there a difference?

Chapter Sixteen

Saturday, June 28
Finchley Hall

Before heading to Finchley Hall the next morning, I spent a couple of hours at the shop. Ivor and I had turned in our listing for the Scottish auction. The catalog proofs would be sent out soon, giving us an opportunity to view the other items to be included in an auction billed as "The Art & Antiquities of Roman Britain."

I arrived at Finchley Hall exactly at eleven. Vivian was already there, and I found the two older ladies waiting for me in Lady Barbara's sitting room. The midmorning sun streamed through the deep-set windows that looked out over the Elizabethan garden below. A glass vase of flowers in pinks and reds stood on a side table.

Last winter, when the cost of maintaining the Elizabethan country house had been assumed by the National Trust, Lady Barbara had reupholstered the fraying armchair and sofa and replaced the threadbare carpet with a gorgeous Persian rug in shades of ice blue, cream, and scarlet.

Today, she looked almost youthful in a pale blue cotton shirtwaist and cardigan, the sleeves pushed up to her elbows. Vivian, whose costume never varied, wore her signature tweed skirt with a lavender cashmere twinset. She'd acknowledged the warmth of the day by removing her long-sleeved cardigan and draping it over the back of her chair. I'd never seen her do that before. Standards must be maintained at all times.

"This is very exciting," Lady Barbara said. "Dear Celia deserves this after all she's been through."

"Do you mean Dr. Sinclair's murder?" I asked.

"Yes, of course, that too, but I was thinking of earlier. Celia went through a rather trying period when she was at university. The stress, you know. But that's all in the past now."

I would have liked to hear more, but at that moment, Francie Jewell introduced the guest of honor. "Miss Celia Whybrew."

Celia looked cool and classy in an ecru linen skirt and a crisp white blouse, open at the neck. "What a lovely treat, Auntie Barbara," she said. "I can't think of anyone I'd rather celebrate with."

"Congratulations," I said. "You'll do an outstanding job."

"You deserve the honor." Lady Barbara gave her a kiss on both cheeks.

Vivian shook her hand. "Well done, my dear."

Francie Jewell carried in a tea tray laden with china cups and saucers in a rose-garland pattern, along with a selection of miniature scones and a small cake decorated with pink roses.

"Celia told me about the plans going forward at Ravenswyck," Lady Barbara said. "Changes are on the way."

Celia placed her teacup in the saucer. "One thing will change anyway. It's good news, Kate. Mark's proposal to excavate the mound has been approved—within limits. The board has authorized the use of ground-penetrating radar, capable of indicating the possible presence of skeletal remains. If we get results, the team will dig a test pit. If human remains are found, the CMBA will probably choose the mound as the next student experience." She crossed one elegant leg over the other. "Niall's not pleased. He's pushing to excavate the north transept instead."

"I'm sure Mark is over the moon," I said, thinking privately that Celia must have been Mark's advocate with the board.

"They're sending a group of experienced volunteers next week, so we should know something soon," Celia said. "The chances of the mound being a plague pit aren't great, but Mark did find that letter about the reopening of an earlier burial pit. At least we'll know, one way or the other."

"Well, I hope they get to the bottom of the biggest mystery," Lady Barbara said. "Who killed Dr. Sinclair? I admit he wasn't my favorite person in the world, but he didn't deserve to die like that."

"Imagine the police suspecting Tamzin." Vivian shot me an accusatory look, but I noticed the slight wobble of her chin. She was still feeling guilty about the bag of ruined pearls.

"It turned out for the best," I said. "Tamzin and Mark told the truth." Vivian looked doubtful, so I added. "In a police investigation, it's important to know what isn't important." I wasn't the whole truth. Exactly how the pearls had ended up in Sinclair's mouth and stomach was important—and it was still a mystery, one I couldn't talk about.

"How is the poor girl?" Lady Barbara asked.

"She'll be fine." Vivian sniffed and straightened her back. "Needs to stand up for herself is all."

"She is a timid thing," Lady Barbara agreed. "Maybe we can bolster her confidence."

"What a good thought, Barb." Vivian was the only person I knew who called Lady Barbara *Barb*. "Let's do that. I'll come up with a plan."

Their conversation was beginning to worry me, and I wanted to get back to the excavation of the mound. "If the volunteers arrive next week," I asked Celia, "when do you think they'll begin?"

"Right away. The Centre provides room and board and a daily stipend for the volunteers, so the radar will probably happen Tuesday. If there's reason to excavate, it will happen that day or the next."

"Is the dig off limits," I asked, "or could I watch?"

"I don't see why not." Celia smiled. "You and Ivor are practically part of the team."

Lady Barbara and Vivian had moved on to the subject of Tamzin and Mark. Young love was one of their favorite topics.

"A perfect couple, if you ask me," Lady Barbara said.

"But will his family accept her, do you think? I imagine Mark's mother has someone a little higher on the social ladder in mind."

"If only we could have input in the *wardrobe* department."

Vivian slapped the arm of her chair. "My thoughts exactly."

I took the opportunity to ask Celia about the gold. "I have a question—pure curiosity. Besides the grave goods, which are spectacular, have you found anything of real value in the excavation of Egemere Close? Coins, perhaps, or precious metals?"

"Interesting question, Kate." She paused a moment before continuing, and I got the impression she was carefully formulating her answer. "I should say that everything we find from the past has real value, and that's true, but I know what you mean. We have found coins. Not a hoard, mind you. Just random coins, lost by somebody with a hole in their pocket. And some jewelry, although ordinary people usually wore lesser metals like copper or pewter—but the designs are often wonderful. You saw some of them in the Ravenswyck exhibit. Apart from the lord of the manor and his family, any gems would have been glass or semiprecious stones. That's what makes the discovery of Egemere Woman so extraordinary. The objects buried with her were priceless—especially the pearl. I wonder if we'll ever solve that mystery." Almost as an afterthought, she added, "I believe Mark did say one of the students found a gold ring, but most of the items we find are everyday things—utensils, tools, pottery, glass, knives, textiles. Their importance to history isn't the monetary value but the picture they paint of medieval life in rural Suffolk."

I was picturing the gold ring found in the box in Sinclair's room. According to Ivor, it was medieval. "How do you keep track of the finds? I know Dr. Nevin records the lists on a spreadsheet, but there must be written lists made on site."

"Yes, of course. All finds are brought by our students to either Mark or Tamzin, depending on the team. They're recorded on a handwritten finds sheet—Mark keeps that—which is then checked against the items themselves. Once it tallies, the lists are entered into the spreadsheet by Niall. His lists are then rechecked against the inventories of stored goods at Ravenswyck. He's a stickler for accuracy."

"I'd love to see the written records. Would that be possible?"

"Why, Kate?" Her brow furrowed. "The lists have nothing to do with the grave goods."

I arranged my face in a bright smile. "As you know, Ivor and I deal in antiquities. We try to be careful, checking the items we purchase or take in on commission with lists of stolen goods provided by the police. We find stolen goods more often than you might think. It would be helpful to see the procedures you follow in the field so I can compare them with ours." I held up a hand. "I can be a real nerd about details like this."

"I understand," Celia said, although I was pretty sure she didn't. "Stop by the field office one afternoon. Text me first to make sure I'm there. We keep everything in the files."

"Thank you. I'm impressed with the way you run things."

"But I haven't been running things, Kate," Celia said. "Dr. Sinclair kept those files. I've never actually seen Niall's spreadsheets, just the summaries printed up with the final dig documents."

"Then we'll both learn something," I said, wondering if Celia had been uninterested in the technical aspects of the job. If so, that was something else that was going to change.

It was nearly twelve when Vivian rose to her feet. "I should go. Fergus doesn't like being home alone."

Celia looked at me, puzzled.

"Her pug," I whispered.

"I should be getting back myself," Celia said. "There's so much to learn in my new role at the CMBA."

"We're proud of you, dear," Lady Barbara said, taking her hand. "I know your Aunt Emily will be simply bursting. She always told me you could do anything you put your mind to."

"I appreciate the confidence."

"I must be on my way as well," I said, hoping to catch Celia alone.

* * *

Outside in the sunshine, I walked Celia to her car, a lapis-blue Kia. "You and Dr. Nevin were here in 2016 when Carrie Holgate disappeared, weren't you?"

"Oh, that was an awful time."

"What was she like—Carrie Holgate?"

"Lovely in every way. And smart. Intensely interested in everything we did. She actually took part in the dig herself that year. She would have made a fine archaeologist. It was her first love."

"Was her disappearance a complete surprise?"

Celia studied me for a moment. "I don't mind the question, Kate, but why now? It's history. The facts will be in the police records. It can't have anything to do with the present inquiry."

"True, but Sinclair's death has brought the tragedy of Carrie's disappearance up again—in Alex Belcourt's mind, I mean. He was and still is completely devastated by it. He's accepted the fact that she must be dead, but that's cost him something."

"Yes, but maybe not what he wants you to believe, Kate."

My mouth fell open. "What do you mean?"

"Alex is a collector. He collects factories and money and valuable objects." Her eyes met mine. "Carrie was the most astonishingly beautiful creature I've ever seen. She was a prize. Like the pearl. Personally, I got the impression she was unhappy. I know for a fact there was something badly wrong that last week. She confided in me. We were friends."

"What did she say?"

"She said, 'Things aren't always what they seem, are they, Celia?' She looked like she was carrying the weight of the world on her shoulders. That's why I was so sure at first that she'd left willingly. A bid for freedom—something like that, anyway."

"Do you still feel that way?"

"Not after all these years. I think someone killed her."

"Who?"

Celia didn't answer, but I could see on her face what she was thinking. "You think Alex Belcourt killed her?"

"I didn't say that. But I think she knew something."

"Did you tell the police?"

Celia slid into her car. "I had nothing to go on except a feeling, an impression—and who would credit that?"

A question I'd asked myself more than once.

"Celia," I said, hoping I wasn't overstepping my bounds. "Do you mind if I ask you a personal question?"

"You can ask."

"You haven't exactly hidden the fact that you disliked Dr. Sinclair. Why?"

"You were with him for an evening." She tilted her head to one side. "Surely you were able to see what sort of man he was."

"I won't deny that, but given his character and the difficulty of working with him, why did you stick it out? Why not cut ties and go your own way?"

"That *is* a personal question, Kate." Celia shielded her eyes against the sun with one hand. "But I'll answer it. Why not? He's dead. Simon was well connected in the field. Very well connected. He had a gift for ingratiating himself with those above him. He always had, from the first time I knew him. And he had another gift." Her mouth twisted. "Binding his inferiors to himself. Somehow, he would worm his way into your life—your professional life, I mean, praising you to others and making sure you knew whatever good things came your way were down to him. He was my tutor and thesis advisor. Niall's as well. He made both of us supervisors on that first dig at Ravenswyck, and then he helped me publish a journal article, my first professional credit. He got me the position at the CMBA by telling the board he couldn't do it without me at his side. He was doing the same thing with Mark and Tamzin." She shook her head. "I tried to warn them without actually coming right out and saying, 'Don't trust him. Get out while you can.'"

"You mean his help was an illusion?"

"Oh, it was real, all right, but at the same time, he made a point of undermining your confidence. If you made a mistake, he never let you forget it. Implied that he was a saint for giving you another chance. But some of those mistakes were—" She broke off. "I'm getting off track here. The point is, he made sure my professional career and the careers of everyone who worked for him were under his control. Every act of kindness or favor was like glue, trapping you, and if you started pulling away, he would lay down another strip of glue. Like those horrible mouse traps where there's nothing the poor creatures can do but give up and lay there until they die. Horrible." Tears welled in her eyes. "I didn't just dislike him, Kate. I hated him. I didn't kill him, but I could have done. And not just me."

"Are you talking about Dr. Nevin?"

"You'll have to ask him. Niall and I have never really got on. He was Simon's perfect victim—brilliant but insecure, craving praise and recognition. How he felt about Simon personally, I couldn't say."

"What was Sinclair implying that night at Finchley Hall—going on about Dr. Nevin's computer skills and the meticulous records he kept?"

"I don't know. Something between the two of them, but it wasn't meant to be kind. I can tell you that for sure."

"What about you? How did Sinclair try to control you?"

"Me?" She gave a small laugh that was intended to be casual. "I'm not so easy to control. Ask my ex-boyfriends."

I had one more question, and it was even more personal. "Was Sinclair ever inappropriate with you, Celia? Aggressive sexually?"

"Never."

Had her answer come too quickly?

She slid into the driver's seat and closed the door.

Watching her drive off, I had a strong feeling she wasn't telling me the whole truth.

Chapter Seventeen

Long Barston

I spent the rest of the day at the shop. As there were no walk-ins, I decided to dust, a tedious task, but one that gave me time to consider what I'd learned from Celia.

The picture she'd painted of Carrie Holgate, beautiful but troubled, didn't agree at all with the idyllic picture of true love I'd gotten from Alex Belcourt. Which version, if either, was the truth? Was it possible Belcourt really had killed his own wife? Was his grief real or manufactured? Or was it guilt? The whole thing made me feel sick.

And what about the murder of Dr. Sinclair? Celia had described the devious way Sinclair used his subordinates to advance his own reputation and then bind them to himself with a kind of emotional blackmail. Sinclair had demanded absolute loyalty like a medieval lord demanded fealty from his vassals. The idea was disturbing to say the least—especially the image Celia used of the mouse caught in the sticky trap. Had someone reached a tipping point and lashed out? Was it someone on the leadership team? One of the students? And then I couldn't get Celia's quick *no* to my question about sexual assault out of my mind, although she didn't strike me as the kind of person who would cover up something like that.

I pictured the faces of Lady Barbara and Vivian. If Celia became a suspect in Sinclair's murder, if she were actually guilty—

No. I couldn't go there.

At four I began packing up the Roman marble busts for delivery to the auction house in Glasgow. At four thirty, Tom called. "Let's have a quiet, early dinner at the Three Magpies. Maybe take a walk afterward."

"I'd love that. Progress in the Sinclair case?"

"We've narrowed the suspects. He had no family in England and no serious love interest. And we've contacted all the students on the dig. Alibis, good ones, every one of them. We still have to interview his colleagues at the university, but it seems a long shot."

"So either the killer is someone we know nothing about or he's a person we do know—one of the protesters or one of the archaeologists or someone at Ravenswyck."

"Or she," Tom said. It was usually my line. "Oh, and we've located the woman—the one with Derek Quinn outside the pub in Thetford. Quinn is our man, all right, which means we have a good description, but she wasn't a hostage. The woman's called Willow Gale—ex-dancer, his girlfriend. She says Quinn dropped her off at her mother's house in Thetford. That's where she is now, lying low. Insists it was an accident. She's terrified something will happen to him."

"Has he been in touch with her?"

"She says not. I'll give you the whole story tonight. What's your news?"

"Not much." I would have to tell him about Celia, about her hatred for Sinclair, but I'd yet to work out how to do it without making her sound like a suspect. She'd been honest about her feelings, but maybe telling me was a case of admitting something you know is bound to come out anyway.

"Shall I pick you up at the shop in about an hour?" Tom asked.

"Meet me at the pub. First one there gets a table."

With an hour to fill, I turned my mind back to Sinclair's murder. Putting the members of the archaeological team aside for the moment, I had to admit that no enlightening patterns had emerged. Except for the curious pearl theme. Pearls everywhere. Was the universe trying to tell me something?

One intriguing fact was that Grenville Dark, who was almost certainly Edlyn Dark's deceased father, had done extensive research into the history of Egemere Close. He'd died before Egemere Woman was found, but he might have learned something that would lead me to her identity. If Ivor and I ever met up with Edlyn, I'd ask about her father's files.

That could wait. Pulling out the notebook I carry in my handbag, I reread my original questions:

1. Who met Sinclair at the dig site? Was the murder planned or opportunistic?
2. Why was Sinclair at the site and when did he arrive?
3. What was the task he told Mark he had to do that morning?
4. Motive? People don't kill someone just because they're arrogant and unpleasant.
5. What happened to Sinclair's mobile phone?
6. Who scattered the fake pearls? Were they a message for Sinclair or for us?

Two questions had been answered in part. The first concerned the pearls. We now knew Tamzin and Mark had scattered them, and if they were telling the truth, their reason for doing it. They wanted to get back at Sinclair, tempt him to do something that would damage his reputation. It hadn't worked because he'd been murdered. Maybe it never would have worked. Sinclair wasn't a fool. But why had he consumed the pearls? No answer there.

The second partially answered question concerned motive. The actual motive for Sinclair's murder could have been anything from professional animus to personal revenge—or something the police knew nothing about yet. But I'd been wrong in my first assumption that Sinclair's character alone hadn't been enough to cause his death. As Celia described it, Sinclair's cruelty was more than enough to goad someone into murdering him. I still couldn't get the image of that hopelessly struggling mouse out of my head.

I needed to go deeper.

Ripping the page out of the notebook, I crumpled it up, tossed it in the bin, and began again.

1. Did Sinclair go to the dig site to meet the person who texted him at the pub? Was that why his mobile was taken? Ask Tom about phone logs.
2. Who was at the dig site when Peter Eley saw lights? Nighthawkers? Sinclair himself?
3. Sinclair was a miserable human being, a bully, but this wasn't new. Why did he have to die at this particular time? Had something changed?
4. Was Celia telling the truth when she said Sinclair never attacked her?

I sat for a moment, tapping my pen. A vague idea floated at the back of my mind, but I couldn't make it land. Frustrated, I wrote:

5. Why would Sinclair swallow the fake pearls—and why was he holding his agate ring? Was he trying to tell us something?
6. Is there a connection between Sinclair's murder and the disappearance of Carrie Holgate? Revenge? Payback?
7. Was it the discovery of Egemere Woman and the fabulous pearl that precipitated Sinclair's death?

That last question was a real longshot, but it made me think of something I'd read once—that if all sounds could be stilled, we might actually hear the echoes of the past.

Echoes of the past were the last things I wanted to hear at that moment, so I began to sing, rather loudly, an old song I'd learned as a child—in a Norwegian accent.

Da north vind doth blow, and ve shall have snow,
And vat vill da birdie do den (da poor t'ing)?

I laughed, remembering those golden days when all I'd had to worry about was . . . actually, I couldn't remember what I'd worried about as a child.

Shutting down the computer, I grabbed my jacket and handbag and left the shop, locking the door behind me and still humming the tune all the way to the pub.

* * *

I found Tom at the Three Magpies, waiting for me at our usual table near the fireplace. He stood and gave me a kiss. "Hullo, darling. You look wonderful."

"Eye of the beholder," I said. After an afternoon of dusting and packing, I was feeling less than wonderful. "I'm glad you suggested this. We haven't had a date in almost two weeks."

"Not since the incident in Thetford." Tom took my jacket and hung it over the back of my chair. "Things have been brutal at work. I won't deny it. But we're finally getting somewhere. At least we know who we're dealing with now—and why."

"What do you mean?"

"Willow, Derek Quinn's girlfriend, told us the victim—his name was Conor Pike—attacked her two months ago. She was walking home from work, a late shift at a food-packaging plant near Lakenheath. She and Derek knew Pike casually from the pub. Pike offered her a ride home, and she foolishly accepted. Only he didn't take her home. He took her to an abandoned lot. She was able to fight him off. Got out of the car and ran, but not before he'd roughed her up. Black eye. Cracked ribs. Lots of bruising."

"Did she report it? Get medical help?"

"Neither. She didn't want Derek to retaliate, so she made light of it. But when Conor showed up at the pub that night, Derek decided to teach him a lesson."

"Quite a lesson."

"Pike had a record as long as your arm. Everything from shoplifting to grievous bodily harm. His ex-wife took out a restraining order. Willow swears Derek had no intention of killing Conor. It was an accident, and he panicked. She's afraid he's going to get himself into more trouble."

"I hope you locate him before that happens."

"The trouble is he keeps moving. The last sighting was north of Glemsford. By the way, thanks for telling the lady from the alpaca farm to call us. It fits a pattern. We know approximately where he's going—unless he changes tack."

"Glemsford isn't that far from Long Barston."

"At least he's keeping away from villages or towns. Willow told us Derek grew up on a farm. That's where he'd feel most comfortable. He's been seen at a few petrol stations, buying food, but he's probably out of cash by now—or will be soon."

The pub was busy for a Sunday night. One of the owners, our good friend Jayne Collier, came in person to take our order.

"How are my two favorite customers? Don't tell Lady Barbara." She winked. "Specials tonight are the lemon whitefish and the treacle-glazed pork loin."

We both ordered the fish, and Jayne brought us a basket of sourdough bread and the herbed olives that had become the pub's signature starters.

We took a few minutes to enjoy the pre-dinner treats.

"Did you learn anything more about the gold jewelry?" Tom dipped a piece of sourdough into the herbed oil.

"I asked Celia if they'd found any gold at Egemere Close. She said gold jewelry would have been uncommon in a village like that, but she remembered Mark Lambe saying something about finding a gold ring in the south-transept excavation. It could be the ring in the box. I've asked to see the finds lists. There might be a sketch."

"Did she say anything else?"

"Yes, and I think it's important." I told him what Celia had said about Sinclair's bullying and the control he maintained on his underlings. "Sinclair was a horrible person, Tom, and he's still controlling people, even after his death, because no one wants to admit how trapped they were. Celia denied it herself, but I wonder."

"She didn't mention that in her statement, but then people rarely tell us the whole truth the first time we interview them. They keep things back—things they're ashamed of or embarrassed about. Sometimes they just don't want to get others in trouble."

"Tom," I said, feeling guilty. "I'm not saying I suspect Celia of Sinclair's murder, but I do have the feeling she's hiding something."

One eyebrow went up. "Like what?"

As soon as he said it, I remembered what my brain had been trying to tell me. "I don't really know. I could be wrong, but Lady Barbara mentioned a trying period in Celia's life—when she was in graduate school. I wondered if it had anything to do with Sinclair. He was her thesis advisor. But whenever I bring up the subject of Sinclair acting toward her in a predatory way, she's always quick to dismiss it." I felt like a snitch. "It's probably nothing, but it's been bothering me."

"I'll look into it. See what I can find. Did you ask her about Niall Nevin?"

"She says he was loyal to Sinclair. Or maybe hadn't realized how trapped he was." *In for a penny.* "There's something else. Celia and Carrie Holgate were friends. Celia told me Carrie's marriage wasn't as ideal as Belcourt would have us believe."

"On what evidence?"

"She says Carrie was unhappy in the weeks leading up to her disappearance. When Celia asked her about it, Carrie said something about things not being as they seemed."

"Why would Carrie Holgate have confided in Celia?"

"Why not? They would have been around the same age then and Carrie probably needed someone to confide in."

"Does Celia think Carrie left her husband?"

"She did at first. Now she believes Carrie was murdered, and she hasn't ruled out Belcourt." I should have felt better after coming clean, but I'd just thrown suspicion on both Celia and Alex Belcourt. At least I knew Tom wasn't one to jump to conclusions.

"We'll check it out." Tom dipped another piece of sourdough into the olive oil. "And we won't mention you."

"Thanks," I said, still feeling miserable. "Have you found anything significant on Sinclair's computer?"

"Yes. All the emails in the week leading up to his murder were deleted."

"Did he do it himself?"

"Or someone with access to his devices. His door at The Forge was locked, but the lock was one of the old sort that can be released with a credit card."

"Wouldn't the emails be on his mobile as well? Have you had any luck getting the phone logs?"

"Not yet. Soon, I hope."

A light rain began to fall outside, quickly turning to a real soaker.

"There goes our walk," I said. "Maybe tomorrow?"

"I'm sorry, Kate," Tom said. "I'll be gone for a couple of nights—Sunday through Tuesday. Meetings in Ipswich."

"I'll miss you."

He reached over and touched my cheek. "I'll miss you, too."

I thought of Ivor. On one of those two nights, we could visit the Six Bells in Hartwell.

Chapter Eighteen

Monday, June 30
Ipswich

The Hold, which contained the bulk of Suffolk's nationally significant archives, was housed in a modern brick, glass, and steel building facing Neptune Quay, Ipswich's scenic waterfront. I found a spot for my car in the public car park, and since I'd already registered online for a reader's ticket, all I had to do was present myself to the archives staff.

An overnight rain had ushered in a tropical air mass from North Africa, and the day was even warmer than it had been over the weekend. Entering through a garden courtyard facing New Street, I felt a welcome rush of cool air. Signs directed me along an arcade to the reception counter.

I handed my ticket to a woman behind the counter. "I'm interested in a plague village near Hartwell called Egemere Close. The church was called St. Margaret's. How would I find out if there are records from the village or the church from the fourteenth century?"

"Egemere Close?" The woman removed her glasses and looked at me with interest. "That's where archaeologists found that miraculously preserved body, isn't it? I followed the story closely. My husband says I'm ghoulish, but it isn't true. It's like time travel." She stood and held out her hand. "I'm Lois Upton, one of the archivists."

"Kate Hamilton. I'm researching Egemere Close and the Wyck family who lived at Ravenswyck." I expected her to say, *Well, that will take some time.*

She surprised me. "I know exactly what you're looking for. There was a gentlemen interested in the same thing some years ago—when the records were held in Bury St. Edmunds. I was an archivist there before we moved everything to this new building last year."

"Was the gentleman's name Grenville Dark?"

"Well, yes. How did you know?"

"I've been told he gave talks on the subject."

"Ah, I see. I'm not surprised. Quite an enthusiast, he was. Gathering information for a book he was writing on the subject. Sadly, he died before he could finish it."

"That is sad. Do you know what happened to the manuscript?"

"I couldn't tell you, but I can tell you which of our records he accessed. You can look at them yourself if you'd like."

Had I heard her correctly? This was amazing.

She tapped some words into her computer. "Here we go. I'll print out a list. Just fill out a request form for the documents you wish to view." She handed me one of their forms. "The original records are very old, as you know. None can be checked out. Some can be examined here—with gloves. A few can be viewed only as PDFs." She tapped on the computer again, and I heard the sound of a printer coming from a back room somewhere.

Was it really going to be this easy? Was I about to find the information I needed today?

"I'll be right back with the list," she said and disappeared.

In a few minutes she returned. "Here you are." Lois Upton handed me several sheets of paper, which contained a list of documents. "Professor Dark was thorough—I can tell you that. " She smiled at me. "Perhaps you'd like to begin with the Wyck genealogy."

"There's a genealogy?"

"Allow me to show you."

This was getting better and better. Alex Belcourt would want a copy for the museum.

Lois Upton turned to another woman behind the counter. "Dotty, can you handle things for a few minutes? I'll be in the search room."

I followed her up a few steps to a lofty, library-like space with glazing in the pitched ceiling, letting in the natural light. Heads were bent over tables. Hushed coughs and the soft clearing of throats combined with the sound of pages turning. I'd always adored libraries, the fragrance of books and old documents, smelling of dust and mildew and, surprisingly, the suggestion of almonds and vanilla. I took it all in—the quest for knowledge and the tantalizing promise of discovering information that could answer questions, settle arguments, even change history—or our perceptions of it.

We moved to one of the computer stations. In moments a family tree filled the screen. An actual tree with trailing branches and leaves adorned the margins, but the people were indicated by small, embellished circles.

"I remember viewing this when Professor Dark was doing his research," Lois said. "The tree begins with Richard of Hertfordshire and his wife, Elizabeth d' Flory. Some of the dates are approximate—Richard's birth, for example. But we know he died in 1310 when Henry, their only child, was six."

"I heard the story of Richard's death and Henry's adoption by his grandfather in Suffolk."

"And here he is," she said, indicating a circle near the top. "Sir Henry Wyck, 1304 to 1348."

"I know he was married twice," I said, looking at the chart, "Matilda in 1345 and Julia in 1348."

"No children by Matilda," Lois said. "Henry's second wife, Julia, produced the only heir."

I looked at the dates. "Henry remarried, had a son, and died, all in the same year—1348?"

"He didn't die of bubonic plague. We know that because the plague didn't reach East Anglia until the summer of 1349, and Henry was already dead by then. His son, also named Henry, was probably born after his father's death. The baby and his mother survived the plague. She died in 1379, and he lived until 1394."

I squinted at the screen. "What does that mean—the *A* beside Matilda's name and then *R. Ufford, 1347*?"

"I thought you might notice that," Lois said, grinning. "It means Matilda was abducted by someone named Ufford while Henry was in France."

"Abducted? You mean stolen?"

"It wasn't uncommon at the time. I know that's surprising, but it's true. Often it was an excuse for adultery. The woman's honor was at stake, after all, so it would have had to look like the elopement was against her will. I'm not saying that's what happened in this case, but Henry fought in France, and he *was* gone a very long time." She smiled again. "I remember Professor Dark commenting on it. I don't have the dates to hand, but we could probably piece them together."

"What happened to Matilda?"

"I wish we knew. If records exist, they're probably moldering in the Ravenswyck archives—or perhaps in the archives of the Ufford family. So much has been lost. That's why Suffolk created this central repository."

"So Henry was free to remarry, even when his wife was still alive?"

"People weren't as fussy about those sorts of things in the fourteenth century. Henry's goal was to produce an heir—and he managed that."

It was tempting to think of Matilda as Egemere Woman, but she'd been abducted in 1347 and probably lived to a ripe old age with Ufford somewhere. Grenville Dark may have traced her, and I might find the information in his files. If I could ever find them.

Of course, Egemere Woman could have been anyone of high status—the daughter of one of Henry Wyck's aunts, for example. All I knew for sure was she'd been about to deliver a child when she was murdered.

"I'd like to look over these records," I said.

"Take your time. If you need me, I'll be at the front desk."

I carried the papers to a nearby table and, with a growing sense of anticipation, pulled out a pencil. The list filled two and a half pages and included the confirmation of charters, all sorts of legal documents, and something quaintly titled *Feet of Fines*, which turned out to be court records regarding property disputes. At first glance, the records appeared to have nothing to do with my area of interest—Egemere Close and St. Margaret's Church—but Grenville Dark had consulted these documents, and he'd been the expert. The sheer volume was overwhelming. I'd have to prioritize and pare them down.

One way, I saw, would be to trim the list by date, where dates were listed. I was looking for records covering the period roughly between 1307, when the silver pennies found in the coffin had been minted, and 1349, when the bubonic plague arrived in Suffolk—a period of forty-two years. Then I scanned the list for any mention of Egemere Close or the Wyck family. Seven documents looked the most promising. I marked them, telling myself I could always expand the search later.

I took my list to Lois Upton. "These are the records I'd like to view."

She looked up from her computer. "There's no charge for access to the search rooms, but you'd have to book a microfilm or -fiche viewer in advance."

I had to get back to the shop by lunchtime. Ivor and I were expecting a busload of seniors, and they always had tons of questions. "I don't have time today. May I purchase copies?"

"Of course." She looked at my list. "If you mean photocopies, it won't be cheap, and it will take time."

"I'd rather have downloads if that's possible."

"Of course—if they're available. Just fill out this form. If any of the records aren't available to download, they'll let you know. You can always return when you have more time." She handed me a form.

I filled it out, requesting the seven records I'd marked, plus a copy of the Wyck genealogy. I handed the form to her and tapped my credit card.

"We should have the downloads for you later today. Tomorrow at the latest."

Chapter Nineteen

Long Barston

Returning to the shop, I saw that Ivor had plugged in the box fan we use on especially warm days. Air conditioning was rare in the historic buildings lining Long Barston's High Street. Until recently, it hadn't been needed for more than a few days a year.

Ivor was eating shrimp rolls, his favorite treat from the Chinese takeaway a few doors down. Mine too.

"Hullo, Kate." He pushed the container toward me. "Hungry?"

I selected one of the rolls, still wrapped in paper. "Thanks."

"How did it go at The Hold?" Ivor asked. "Any luck?"

"I hope so." I took my first bite of the shrimp roll, savoring Mrs. Liu's secret sauce, the recipe a closely guarded secret. "The archivist told me an elderly gentleman named Grenville Dark—he has to be Edlyn's father, right?—was working on a history of Egemere Close when he died. And that's not all. Listen to this." I told Ivor about the Wyck genealogy and the abduction of Sir Henry's first wife. "The archivist showed me the documents Grenville Dark accessed as part of his research. I purchased a few downloads. The problem will be deciphering the language. It's been years since I studied Middle English, and my Latin is pitiful."

Our conversation ended when a busload of seniors from a retirement village in Cambridge entered the shop. They were frequent customers, stopping in every three months during one of their planned social outings.

Thirty minutes later, the pensioners streamed out of the shop, chattering about the latest retirement village gossip—who was making a play for the new male resident and who was in the early stages of dementia. They were headed for their tea break at the Suffolk Rose.

My phone pinged. The documents had arrived in my inbox. Opening my computer, I downloaded the files onto my desktop. There were five of them. The other two, I was informed, could be viewed in person only.

"Look at this, Ivor." I pulled up the first document and turned the screen toward him. "Can you read it?"

Ivor adjusted his glasses. "Seems to be a list of men recruited for the king's army by—" He peered at the screen. "—Sir Henry Wyck in . . . *hmm*, 'the year of our Lord 1345.'"

I remembered the Wyck genealogy. "If Wyck left for France in 1345 or early 1346, he was away from home several years. He was still in France in 1347 when his first wife, Matilda, was abducted."

"That's one way to get a wife." Ivor wiggled his eyebrows.

"You mean besides winning her in a card game in New Guinea?"

Ivor ignored this.

I scrolled through two more documents, feeling increasingly hopeless. "Even if I could read the handwriting, I'd have to dig out my old Middle English dictionary and go over everything word for word."

"You're forgetting about my friend, Kate. The expert on medieval languages. He might help you."

"I had forgotten. Do you think he'd be willing to translate? It would save me a lot of time."

"I'll find out."

The bell on the door jangled, and we were surprised to see Niall Nevin stoop to enter the shop. He was dressed in tan trousers and a brown turtleneck and carried a leather satchel over his shoulder.

"Hullo." He tucked a strand of his light-brown hair behind his ear.

Surprise left me momentarily speechless, but Ivor walked across the room, his hand outstretched. "Welcome to The Cabinet of Curiosities. Looking for a gift?"

"I was in the area and thought I'd stop by to see your shop. I'm always interested in antiquities."

"You're welcome to browse," Ivor said. "We're here to answer questions."

Nevin hesitated, and I got the impression there was something he wanted to ask.

"You mentioned an auction. Roman antiquities, I believe." He slipped his hands into his jacket pockets. "*Erm*, may I ask when the auction is to be held? I'd like to view the catalog when it comes out."

"Of course," Ivor said. "Glasgow. Last week in July. The catalog should be available online in the next couple of weeks." He wrote the name of the auction house on one of our cards and handed it to Nevin. "Are you a collector as well as an archaeologist?"

"No, no." He waved the suggestion away. "Matter of interest only. I like to keep up with everything in my field. Personally, I think most of these objects should be in museums rather than private collections."

"We agree," Ivor said. "No way to control that, of course, but we've been notifying our museum contacts about the auction."

Nevin moved away from the sales counter, then turned back as if he'd just thought of something. "Any news on the police investigation?"

I'd been waiting for that. "They're following every lead. These things take time." I'd mastered police talk.

"Yes, of course."

I decided to take advantage of the situation. "Dr. Sinclair was a complicated man, wasn't he?"

"Most definitely," Nevin agreed. "Complicated."

"You said you admired him." I gave Nevin my innocent look.

"Oh my, yes. He was a first-rate archaeologist and a much-loved professor. He had quite a following among the students. Well-respected in the profession. His death is a great loss. Did I say he was my mentor in graduate school? I owed him a lot. My entire career, in fact."

So far, we'd heard exactly the opposite. Why did Nevin have such a different view? "I'm sure you're responsible for your own success, Dr. Nevin. You've worked very hard."

"I'm dedicated and meticulous, but I'm not what you'd call an outgoing person. Rather backward, I'm afraid, when it comes to social interaction. Dr. Sinclair paved the way for me. When I was injured, he was the one who encouraged me to get involved in research. Archaeology is one thing, but most ordinary people are interested in the human stories behind the technical stuff."

"I think you're right," I said. It was true, and I wanted to keep him talking. "That's what makes the museum at Ravenswyck so fascinating. Can you tell me what you've been working on?"

"I was helping Dr. Sinclair with a series of articles about Egemere Close. A whole village destroyed by the plague. That intrigues people, and of course the discovery of the body adds to the mystery. I don't know what will happen with the articles now."

"Where did you do your research?" I asked, wondering if Nevin had seen Grenville Dark's files. "Did you consult the Suffolk County Archives?"

"The Hold? No, I used published sources," he said. "Dr. Sinclair always said the secret to success isn't coming up with new theories or uncovering previously unknown facts as much as it is putting things in context—and presenting them in a way people can relate to. He was good at that—taking historical facts and making them both relevant and entertaining."

"You could write the articles yourself," I said.

"I might do. I don't know."

Ivor was looking at me. *Are you going to tell him about Grenville Dark?*

The answer was no—not yet, although I couldn't have told you why. "Was Sinclair an easy man to work with?" It was the same basic question I'd asked before, but he didn't seem to notice.

"Easy? I'm not sure what you mean. He was a great man and a mentor."

"Now, that's interesting," Ivor said, "because we've heard the opposite—that he could be quite unpleasant. Vindictive and controlling."

Nevin stared at us. "That wasn't my experience. Simon was a friend to me when I needed one. I owe my career to him." His prominent Adam's apple bounced up and down.

"Celia told me that Dr. Sinclair helped you find a niche after your injury," I said.

"That's right. He kept me on when others wouldn't have. I owed him a lot."

"We've heard very different accounts of him," Ivor said.

"I really couldn't comment on the opinions of others." Nevin consulted his wristwatch. "Oh, dear. I must be on my way."

From the window, I watched him hurry down the street. Well, darn. I'd wanted to ask him about the gold.

"Why do you think he came here?" I asked Ivor.

"Not to check our stock."

"No." I closed my computer. "By the way, do you have plans tonight? Tom's out of town. What do you say we visit the Six Bells in Hartwell?"

Chapter Twenty

Hartwell

Ivor and I left directly from the shop. The small parking area at the Six Bells was full, but I found a spot in the overflow lot just across the road. Outside, the three tables with red umbrellas were fully occupied by families with small children. Inside, every seat at the bar was taken as were most of the tables in the dining area.

Brenda greeted us. "Welcome back, luv. Brought your father, have you?"

"This is my colleague, Ivor Tweedy."

Ivor gave her a little bow. "Kate tells me the food here is top-notch."

Brenda smiled broadly, obviously pleased. She grabbed a couple of menus and ushered us to a table not far from the dart board, where the scruffy young man I'd seen on my previous visit was throwing darts again. "We're out of the lamb tonight," Brenda said. "Specials on the board."

She must have seen me eyeing the young man because she tilted her head in his direction, "One o' the protestors. Zach Valentine. Regular here. Throws darts like he were gettin' paid for it."

We sat, and Brenda handed us each a menu.

"Is Edlyn Dark here—or the other protesters?" I asked, looking around the room.

"The protestors haven't met since the murder at Ravenswyck, at least not here. Edlyn usually toddles in around seven."

"Is Zach Valentine local as well?"

"Local as they come. He's a bit, well, *simple* might be the word for it." She pulled on her lower eyelid. "A few cards short of a deck."

Ivor and I settled ourselves at the table. Brenda brought a carafe of water and left us to contemplate the menu.

I felt eyes on my back and looked around.

Zach Valentine was watching us. "You're archaeologists," he said.

"No, we're not," I said. "We're—"

"But I saw you at the dig."

"We were *with* the archaeologists, yes," Ivor said. "We're appraisers, hired to assess the artifacts found with the fourteenth-century body."

"Shouldn't have dug her up. Desecration. Eddy tried to warn them."

"You mean Edlyn Dark. She warned them about what?" I was interested to hear his version of things.

"Told them someone would die, didn't she? And then someone did."

"Dr. Sinclair didn't die," Ivor corrected him. "He was murdered."

"Police think we did it." Zach was holding one of the darts, which was making me nervous. "Can't pin it on me. No evidence."

"I don't think the police want to pin it on anyone," I said.

"Eddy tried to tell them. Wouldn't listen."

"Who wouldn't listen—the police or the archaeologists?" I was losing the thread of the conversation.

"They think Eddy's making it up, but she isn't."

"Making what up—Zach, isn't it?"

"How do you know my name?" He shot me a suspicious look.

"I saw you here last week."

"Are you watching me?"

"Of course not. Why would I do that?" *Was he paranoid?*

"Who's he?" Zach asked, meaning Ivor.

"Ivor Tweedy. A pleasure to make your acquaintance."

"You think I killed that man, too, don't you? You've been watching me." Zach was becoming agitated, and that dart was really starting to worry me.

I glanced toward the bar where Brenda was pulling pints and laughing with customers.

"No, Zach, I don't think that." I tried a smile. "Could you please put that dart down?"

Out of the corner of my eye, I saw Ivor get to his feet.

"Eddy said you're married to that policeman."

"I am married to a policeman," I admitted, wondering how Edlyn Dark would know, "but that's not why—" I closed my mouth. He'd raised the dart to his shoulder. The point was aimed directly at my neck. It probably wouldn't kill me, but it would hurt like heck.

"Pretty good at darts, aren't you, son?" Ivor said in a friendly voice. "You know, that's something I've never mastered. What's the trick? Could you show me?"

The young man stepped back, but he didn't lower the dart.

"*Zachary.* Put that down at once." Edlyn Dark stood with her hands on her hips. She was wearing the same striped wool cap I'd seen before. A plaid cotton skirt hung below what looked like a man's trench coat. Why she wasn't sweating to death I couldn't imagine.

Zach dropped the dart. It hit the floor and rolled under the table.

"Why are you talking to those people?"

"They're talking to me," Zach said.

"I told you—she's with the police."

"I'm not with the police," I said. "My husband is a detective, but I have nothing to do with that." It was close to the truth.

Ivor retrieved the dart and slipped it in his pocket.

"Then why are you here, bothering the boy?" Edlyn stood with her large feet planted.

"Actually," Ivor said smoothly, "We're here to see *you*. Brenda told us about your gift."

Edlyn's brow furrowed. "My gift?"

"Seeing the future. We have one of your cards."

"You want a reading, is that it?" She looked at us sideways, clearly not buying it.

"We're hoping you might advise us. We're working with the archaeologists, appraising the grave goods, and my colleague here, Ms. Hamilton—Kate—has been asked to identify, if possible, the fourteenth-century woman whose body was found."

"That's right," I said, realizing where he was going. "I heard your father was a respected historian. One of the archivists at The Hold told me he was working on a history of this area—a book. I was hoping you might point us in the right direction—with research, I mean."

"My father was a great historian," Edlyn said "A genius. He'd been working on a history of Egemere Close for ten years when he died. Sadly, his death came before he could publish the manuscript."

"Now that is remarkable isn't it, Ivor? Her father may have discovered the very information I've been looking for." I tried a casual chuckle. "Sometimes the answers we need are right under our feet."

Zach Valentine peered at us over Edlyn's shoulder.

"I can't help you." Edlyn crossed her arms over her chest.

Zach crossed his arms as well.

"Why not?" I asked. "Are you thinking of publishing his work yourself? I'm not here to steal his research, you know. I would give him proper credit."

"I can't help you because his manuscript and his research notes are lost."

"You can't find them?"

"Lost. Irretrievable. I did consider publishing his work myself, but I couldn't access the files. Old computer. Different operating system. Called in a computer repair chap. He told me the hard drive was permanently damaged. Files corrupted. No way to reconstruct them."

"That's terrible," I said, meaning it passionately. "All those years of research."

Edlyn took a resigned breath. "He told me not to take it to heart. Protesting the dig was my life's work, not publishing."

"The computer expert said this?"

"My father."

It took me a moment. "You mean before he died."

"After I learned his files had been destroyed. I was upset. I suppose Father wanted to encourage me. He was like that."

"When was this?"

"Last spring."

I stared at her, speechless. Edlyn's father had died three years ago.

Ivor took over. "Now, this is interesting, Edlyn. May I call you that? By the way, please join us at the table. You and Zachary both. Round's on me."

"Don't mind if I do." Edlyn shrugged off her coat.

"Ta muchly." Zach slouched into the chair next to Ivor, still wary but not about to turn down a free pint.

Ivor signaled for Brenda. I needed food, but that would have to wait.

Edlyn, Zach, and Ivor ordered pints of the local brew. I ordered a glass of pinot noir and hoped Brenda might bring some munchies.

"Now, then," Ivor said. "Unless I'm mistaken, you're telling us your father communicates with you from beyond the grave. I've heard of such things. How exactly does it work, if it's not too personal a question?"

"We chat on the computer. The hard drive's blinkered, but he gets through."

"You log on and . . . ?" Ivor raised his eyebrows in a question.

"I log on, and he speaks to me."

"What does he say—besides not to worry about the documents?"

Brenda delivered our drinks.

Edlyn took a long swig of ale, wiping the foam on her sleeve. "It started after the dig at Ravenswyck was announced. Father told me to get up a protest, make a fuss. He said the spirits of the dead at Egemere Close wish to remain undisturbed."

"He would know, wouldn't he—being dead himself?" Ivor nodded encouragingly. "What exactly did Father tell you to do?"

"Protest." Edlyn gave Zach a meaningful look. "Nothing violent."

"Never hurt nobody." Zach slouched in his chair, and I imagined he'd been the one to plant the smoke bomb under the field office caravan. Probably without Edlyn's knowledge.

"What else did Father tell you?" Ivor asked.

"He said if the archaeologists refused to stop digging, someone would die."

"He was right about that, wasn't he?"

"Father's always right. We chat almost every night. He's very concerned about the dig, all those souls."

"But I heard all the bodies had been removed," I said.

Edlyn looked at me like I was daft. "I said *souls*, not bodies. Different thing."

"Have you mentioned this to anyone else?" I asked, wondering if she'd told the police, and if they'd contacted the National Health Service to arrange a competency assessment.

She frowned. "Everyone says I'm mad or a fantasist."

"That must be frustrating." Ivor smiled benignly.

"It's just so extraordinary," I said. "Things like that don't happen every day."

"I suppose they don't," she conceded. "Father was always extraordinary. I don't know how it works. It just does."

"Would it be possible to see it?" Ivor asked. "It would be a great honor to speak with your father."

Edlyn's brows drew together. "He might not want to. You're strangers."

Ah yes—there's her way out. "On the other hand," I said, "he might be delighted to know someone else is working on the history of Egemere Close. Does he know about the discovery of Egemere Woman?"

"Of course. I tell him everything."

"Did he mention a name?" I asked. "Does he know her identity?"

"I don't know about that. I do know Father was upset about the death of that archaeologist. He'd warned them after all."

"Let me get this straight," Ivor said. "Your father told you Dr. Sinclair would die."

"He didn't tell me who. Only said if the archaeologists disturbed the dead, the spirits would claim one of theirs. They should have listened to me."

"Obviously," Ivor agreed. "Would it be possible to contact your father tonight?"

Edlyn shook her head. "He'd have to agree first."

"Of course. You must ask him," Ivor said. "Please tell him we're friends."

"No promises."

Ivor handed her his card. "Contact me when you have Father's answer."

She tucked it inside her top.

"Now," Ivor said, rubbing his hands together. "How about another round?"

* * *

I dropped Ivor off at his flat above the shop. "Is she making it up or is she crazy?" I asked him.

"Neither one."

"Then it's true? You don't believe that."

"No, but it's possible she believes it's true. That's not the same thing as making it up. And if she has evidence, she's not crazy."

"What are you saying, Ivor?"

"I'm saying let's keep an open mind. If she agrees to let us witness the phenomenon, we'll know what we're dealing with."

"How about the young man, Zach. He was afraid."

"Yes, but was he afraid of us, the police, or Edlyn Dark?" Ivor released his seatbelt. "Oh, and my friend at the university, the medieval linguist, says he'd be happy to take a look at your documents. Here's his card. I said you'd contact him."

"Thanks, Ivor."

"You are most welcome. Good night, Kate."

I watched him enter the shop through the rear entrance. Before driving off, I looked at the card. It read *Dr. Duncan Price-Davies,*

Professor of Medieval Languages, then his email and the address of his office at the University of East Anglia.

As soon as I got home, I emailed Dr. Price-Davies, thanking him for his time and attaching the files I'd downloaded from The Hold.

I'd just pushed *send* when my mobile rang. It was Tom.

"Hello, darling."

"I'm glad you called. Ivor and I were at the Six Bells in Hartwell tonight. We had quite a conversation with Edlyn Dark and another protester, a young man named Zach Valentine."

"I know the one. DS Ren interviewed the lad. Impressionable. Under the spell of Ms. Dark by all accounts."

"She's quite something, Tom. Have you seen her?"

"Not personally. DI Cartwright described her as a bulldozer."

"I wouldn't disagree, but that's not all she is." I told him about her claim of speaking to her dead father. "She says he speaks to her through his old computer, even though the hard drive is damaged. Ivor asked if we could witness it. We'll see if she agrees."

"She won't agree if she's making it up."

"One thing was clear. The young man, Zach Valentine, is afraid of something. He kept repeating that he hadn't done anything and there was no evidence he did. I think he's feeling guilty."

"Ren said the same thing. He may have mental health issues."

"How are things at headquarters?"

"The Thetford killer's still on the move. We're contacting all the farmers in the area to be on the lookout, lock their outbuildings if possible, and stay clear of him. He can't remain hidden forever, and London is still seventy-five miles away. If that's where he's headed, he'll probably try to hitchhike or jump a train."

"I hope you catch him before he hurts someone. Fear can make people do things they wouldn't do otherwise." Naturally I thought of Sinclair's murder. Had fear been a motive there?

"We're trying to convince Quinn's girlfriend to go on TV, ask him to give himself up."

"He won't have access to a TV, and if he has a mobile, it'll be out of charge by now."

"Yes, but it will be front page news in all the local papers. Chances are, he'll see it sooner or later."

"Will she agree to speak on camera, do you think?"

"I hope so. By the way, Celia Whybrew got in touch. We'd asked her to inform us of any proposed activity at the site. She says the radar scan on the mound is scheduled for tomorrow afternoon."

"I'm surprised she hasn't contacted me. She knows Ivor and I would love to witness the procedure."

"Have you checked your texts?"

"Good point. Give me a minute." I checked my inbox. "You're right. Celia says Ivor and I are welcome to observe.'"

"Make-or-break time for Mark Lambe, eh?" Tom said.

"Speaking of Celia, have you looked into her college days?"

"Not yet, but I will. As you say, it's probably nothing." I heard him sigh. "I miss you, Kate."

"I miss you, too. Sleep well. When will I see you?"

"Wednesday night unless something comes up."

After we'd rung off, I realized I'd forgotten to tell him about Niall Nevin's rather odd visit to the shop.

Chapter Twenty-One

Tuesday, July 1
Ravenswyck Estate

The day began with a cloudless blue sky and temperatures in the mid-twenties—around eighty-two degrees Fahrenheit. The GPR team from Norwich, a technician to operate the equipment and a geophysicist to interpret the results, had arrived around ten in the morning. We'd been told it would take them several hours to survey the site and set up the equipment.

Ivor and I met Celia Whybrew at the field caravan just before one o'clock. She looked chic even in her working clothes—khaki jeans, a white long-sleeved T-shirt, and a straw hat trailing down her back. "This technology changes everything. In the past, we had to rely on manual excavation and luck. Now we have a way of looking beneath the soil surface before we dig."

"How does it actually work?" Ivor asked.

"A tiny pulse of energy is directed into the soil. A computer then records the strength of the signal and the time it takes to reflect back. It works best in dry sandy soil, but we should get useful information even in Suffolk's lime-rich loam and clay."

"Can the radar detect a buried body?" I asked.

"It doesn't distinguish bones from other objects, but it can detect places where the soil has been disturbed in an unnatural way, which may indicate a burial. We'll see." She put on her hat. "Come on. We don't want to miss a thing."

As we walked to the mound on Belcourt's grazing land, the sun beat down, releasing the scent of chalky soil and sheep. I kept my eye on Ivor but refrained from taking his arm. He was wearing his polished wingtip brogues again, and his only concession to the warm weather was rolling up his shirt sleeves.

The rest of the archaeologists were already at the mound, where an awning had been erected for observers.

Dr. Nevin was there, chatting with a man in jeans, a blue cotton shirt, and a ballcap—the geophysicist, I guessed. Mark Lambe was pacing the perimeter. Tamzin, dressed in shorts with neon pink leggings and a Daffy Duck T-shirt, was watching the technician prepare the radar equipment, which looked something like a large, clunky push mower.

Ivor joined her. I saw him chatting to the operator and examining the mechanisms. Ivor loved machinery.

"That's the computer," Celia said, indicating what looked like a tablet attached to the handle.

"I expected to see Alex Belcourt," I said.

"Away on business. I promised to text him with the results."

Dr. Nevin greeted us. He, too, wore a straw hat with a thin green hoodie and baggy shorts that exposed his long, bony—and I couldn't help thinking *insect-like*—legs.

"This is exciting," I said. "Do you think we'll know something today?"

"Hard to tell in this soil." Nevin pursed his lips. "Probably a waste of time."

"How long will it take?"

"With a site this size, it could take up to four hours," Celia said, "but we may not have to wait that long. The goal isn't to map the entire mound but to find signs of unnaturally disturbed soil. That could happen at any time. If we get results, the board will probably authorize a test pit. If the test pit yields a body, and if it's medieval, the whole mound will be mapped and excavated—but not until next season. This is the first step." Her eyes went to Ivor. "We did bring chairs, by the way."

The technician began, guiding the heavy machine slowly over the mound. He walked in long, straight lines, as if he were mowing grass. The only sound was made by the wheels moving over the uneven field.

"It's so quiet," I said, surprised.

"The machine uses high-frequency magnetic waves, which are essentially silent to the human ear."

We watched and waited.

Mark Lambe was still pacing, raking his fingers through his hair. I couldn't blame him for being nervous. His thesis and more than a year of research were on the line. I could imagine how my son, Eric, who was currently working on his PhD thesis, would react if his theory about a promising new method of radioactive waste disposal was suddenly proved false. He'd be back to square one, years of research and development wasted.

Tamzin looked miserable, her eyes constantly darting to Mark. Was she afraid of his response if nothing was detected?

Nevin was also pacing, loping back and forth in line with the technician.

"It really would be sensational if plague victims are found here," Celia said. "The second plague pit discovered outside greater London—and the glory would definitely go to Mark."

"What are you hoping for?" I asked her.

"The truth, of course, but it would be awfully nice for Mark. He's worked so hard to convince his colleagues to believe him."

An hour went by and then a second with no results. Mark was looking increasingly distraught. Ivor and I sat under the awning with Celia while Mark, Tamzin, and Nevin continued to follow the progress of the equipment.

Ivor dozed. I played Sudoku on my mobile.

It was nearly three thirty when Nevin wandered over. "It's probably an Iron Age burial, and the bodies will be too deep to detect."

"We're going to give them more time," Celia said. "The CMBA is paying for this."

"Your call, Celia."

We all looked toward the mound where the technician had stopped moving forward. He signaled to the geophysicist, who joined him. They peered at the computer screen. "We've got something," the man in the ballcap called out. "Shallower than we were expecting."

Celia, Mark, and Tamzin raced up the mound.

We heard a hoot of joy as Mark Lambe picked Tamzin up and swung her around. He set her back on her feet, then pressed his thumb and forefinger into the corners of his eyes.

She hugged him and ruffled his hair.

Celia squeezed his shoulder.

Nevin joined them around the computer tablet.

Celia held up her mobile, apparently searching for a signal.

"Good news?" Ivor called to her.

She made her way down. "I'll have to wait for a better signal. It may not be a body, but it's enough to authorize a test pit. The volunteers can be here as early as Thursday morning. Then we'll know for sure."

Ivor and I were almost back to the shop when he got a message from Edlyn Dark.

Two words. "Come tonight."

Chapter Twenty-Two

Hartwell

By eight o'clock, our agreed-upon arrival time, the sun was already low in the sky, casting long shadows across our path. I'd parked my Mini near the pub. Ivor and I followed Edlyn Dark's directions, walking past the old buildings lining Hartwell's main street. From somewhere, we heard the whoop of a child, perhaps relishing a few final minutes of freedom before bedtime.

I wondered if Mark and Tamzin were celebrating. The discovery of a possible burial on the mound was an exciting development, and I couldn't wait to see what the test pit revealed.

Edlyn's cottage, three blocks south of the Six Bells, turned out to be one of Suffolk's famous pink cottages, this one a salmon color with a beamed upper story and a fairly modern roof. In front, a viburnum hedge was so overgrown it nearly covered the ground-floor windows.

The nameplate at the door said *The Old Schoolhouse.* We knocked and waited.

Edlyn opened the door. "You'd better come in."

Inside, the cottage was old-fashioned but clean and exceptionally tidy. The furniture sat at right angles. Piles of books on the coffee table were arranged in order of size and shape. A dozen or so glass paperweights were lined up precisely on the living room mantel.

"This is an experiment, mind," Edlyn said. "Don't get your hopes up. Father may not cooperate."

"Oh?" I said. "I thought your father had no objection to meeting us."

"He didn't object or approve, either one, so like I said—it's an experiment. Although he was never averse to guests if he wasn't working."

"We wouldn't like to disturb him if he's working," Ivor said.

"*Working?*" Edlyn looked at Ivor as if he'd gone mad. "He's dead."

Ivor and I exchanged we've-fallen-down-the-rabbit-hole glances, but he continued to smile blandly as if the conversation was perfectly normal.

"Tea?" Edlyn asked.

"Don't go to any trouble," Ivor said.

"Already made."

"In that case, thank you," I said, wondering if the tea would be good old Yorkshire Gold or some hallucinogenic herbal variety.

"Make yourselves at home. Back in a tick."

Ivor and I sat in matching armchairs upholstered in a seventies-style brown geometric pattern.

Edlyn was right about the tea being ready because she returned in minutes with a tray. Happily, the tea turned out to be Earl Grey, which she served with honey. She placed the tray on the coffee table and poured Ivor a cup.

"How did you get started telling fortunes?" Ivor asked in the way you might ask someone how they got started selling encyclopedias.

I stirred my tea. Where he was taking this, I hadn't a clue.

"I don't tell fortunes," Edlyn said. "I pass along information."

"And you get this information from . . . ?" He raised his eyebrows.

"From Father, naturally. He lives in the spirit realm now, so he knows things, doesn't he? That's the advantage of being dead. I ask him questions, and he gives me answers—usually."

"Sometimes he refuses?"

"Sometimes he doesn't answer. In that case, I have to tell my clients the future is uncertain, and I don't accept a fee. Wouldn't be fair."

"Always best to be fair," Ivor agreed.

She believes this. She's telling the truth as she knows it. "What happened to your mother?" I asked.

"She died giving birth to my brother. They both died. I don't really remember either of them. I was only three at the time." She shook a finger at us. "Don't feel sorry for me. I couldn't have had a better life—or a better education." She suddenly looked confused. "I've never been alone, you see. He knows I need him." She got to her feet, took a framed photograph from a cabinet, and handed it to me.

The photo showed a thin, elderly man in a blue-collared shirt under a darker blue cardigan. Loose skin around his neck and jowls gave the impression he'd once carried more weight. He had a large nose, a receding chin, and dark, bushy eyebrows even though his hair was pure white. The resemblance to Edlyn was remarkable.

"Taken several months before he died," Edlyn said.

"How did he die, if you don't mind me asking?" Ivor placed his empty cup on the tea tray. "How old was he?"

"Eighty-two. No age at all these days. Cancer, the doctor said. He died at home. Right there as a matter of fact. The chair you're sitting in. Found him the next morning. Stiff as a board."

Ivor slid his hands from the arms of the chair and folded them in his lap.

"We'll go into Father's study now," Edlyn said, confiscating my cup even though I hadn't quite finished. "The computer room."

The study was a small, wood-paneled room toward the rear of the cottage. A large desk took up most of one windowless wall. On its light wood surface sat two laptop computers, side by side, one bulkier than the other.

"Take Father's chair," Edlyn told Ivor, indicating a desk chair upholstered in brown faux leather. She moved the only other chair in the room, a wooden straight-back, beside him.

I stood behind them.

"You were speaking earlier about your father's research," Ivor said. "You decided to publish his unfinished manuscript."

"That was last spring." She switched on the larger computer. A light flickered on the screen, and I heard an internal fan working. "The manuscript was essentially complete, so I purchased a new computer." She indicated the slimmer, newer unit. "I thought it would be easy to transfer Father's files to the new hard drive, but I couldn't get it to work—security updates, compatibility issues, operating system upgrades. Confusing. I must have done something wrong."

I could sympathize with her. My understanding of computers was pretty basic. Ivor's was worse. "Are you sure his files are lost? Could he have printed them out?"

"No."

"How about his research notes? Didn't he have notebooks, papers?"

"Probably. I looked. They're not here."

Well, I tried. At least I knew which documents he'd accessed in the county archives, and I had Dr. Price-Davies to translate them.

"Shall we begin?" Ivor asked. "How does it work?"

"Father uses his own computer, naturally." Edlyn's hands went to the old keyboard. She clicked on the Windows start button. A blue screen appeared. And a warning.

A fatal exception has occurred at— The series of letters and numbers meant nothing to me. *The current application will be terminated. Press any key to terminate the current application. You will lose any unsaved information in all applications. Press any key to continue.*

Edlyn pressed a key. The blue screen disappeared, and I took a sharp intake of breath as a shadowy face appeared, the black-and-white image shifting and morphing against a blurred background.

I held on to the back of Ivor's chair. The image was clearly a man—an elderly man with white hair, glasses, and a receding chin. *Edlyn's father.*

The image spoke. "Hullo, child. I've missed you." The lips moved in a sort of jerky motion, but the voice was clear, cultured, and local.

This couldn't be real, but I was seeing it with my own eyes.

"I've missed you, too, Father." Turning to us, Edlyn whispered, "He always says that."

I put my hand on Ivor's shoulder and squeezed.

"We have guests, Father. Mr. Tweedy and Ms. Hamilton. They're antiquities dealers, working with the archaeologists at Ravenswyck. Is it all right if they visit?"

"You must tell the archaeologists to stop digging."

"I know, Father. I've done that. Just as you said. I don't think they believe me."

"Someone will die."

"Someone *has* died."

"I was right."

"I do beg your pardon for interrupting," Ivor said in a genial tone. "Ivor Tweedy here. I'm delighted to meet you, by the way. Grenville, isn't it? Are you saying someone *else* will die?"

"The spirits are unhappy. A body will be found."

The hair lifted on the back of my neck. *Another body?*

"Where will the body be found?" Ivor asked the image.

"At the dig site."

I saw Ivor take a breath. "Is there a way to prevent it?"

"None. The spirits will not tolerate this desecration."

"Should we warn someone?"

"Of course. They must give up their plans at once."

"I think that's pretty clear. We have our orders."

"Is Mother with you?" Edlyn asked.

"She is always with me, child."

"And little Charles?"

"Of course. We are together, and one day you will join us."

"Not just yet," Edlyn clarified.

"No, not yet."

I wanted to object. *This can't be happening.*

Ivor spoke. "Ms. Hamilton is researching the history of Egemere Close. We know you were doing the same when you, *er*, passed on. Is there a way to access your manuscript? She would be very grateful and intends to give you credit."

"Everything's gone now. I'm with the spirits of all those who died at Egemere Close. They are grateful to be remembered, but they wish to be left in peace. The things we cared about in life mean little to us now."

"I suppose that's true," Ivor said reasonably. "But don't you want to be remembered as the great historian you were?"

"And your work, your book," I said over Ivor's shoulder. "Your daughter could publish your research."

"History was my life's work. I made a living teaching children who cared more about pop stars and video games than academics. That's all forgotten now. Unimportant. I live in the present, and I watch over my daughter."

Edlyn sniffed. "I love you, Father."

"I love you, too, child. I must leave now." The image seemed to smile, the lips pulling back in a rictus, grotesque and more than a little troubling.

The screen went black.

"More tea?" Edlyn asked. Without waiting for an answer, she left the room.

"Ivor, what did we just witness?"

"It has to be a *bot*, doesn't it?"

"What's a bot?" I asked, wondering how Ivor, who was definitely old-school, would know.

"Short for 'robot.' It's a software program that performs tasks online, mimicking human behavior without human intervention."

"How would you know that?"

"I wouldn't, except I happened to read an article recently about something called 'grief bots,' a new AI technology, artificial intelligence, that mimics your dead relatives. It's meant to help the bereaved deal with grief by letting them chat to the bot as if they were talking to the person."

"But it was so real. The image was actually having a conversation with us."

"Yes," Ivor said slowly, "and I don't believe the grief bots include a visual image and an actual voice."

Edlyn appeared in the door frame. "Kettle's on."

"Edlyn," Ivor said. "Have you signed up for any computer apps recently—a grief care group, perhaps?"

"Why would I need an app to deal with grief?" she asked. "I have Father."

"Yes, of course you do. But perhaps you've unknowingly or inadvertently subscribed to some kind of program."

"I think I'd know if I had."

"Tell me again. When did your conversations begin?"

"I told you. Last spring. Shortly after the dig at Ravenswyck was announced. Father told me I should stop them. I tried. I warned them."

"I'm sorry," I said. My head was spinning. "I don't think I want more tea."

"It's late," Ivor said. "Perhaps we should leave."

"Yes, it's probably best. Now you know it's real, and I'll thank you to keep it to yourselves."

It wasn't a question, which was a good thing because the chance of us keeping this to ourselves was zero.

On the way out, I noticed an old metal detector propped against the wall. "Look at that, Ivor."

"Are you a metal detectorist?" Ivor asked Edlyn.

"Father was. Hobby of his. The thing isn't working, though. I thought Zach might like to repair it."

"Zach Valentine?" I asked. "Is he interested in metal detecting?"

"He's keen, all right. I gave him Father's new unit. No use for it myself."

As soon as we were outside, I said, "Ivor, Peter Eley saw lights at the dig site in the week leading up to Sinclair's death—and on that very night. I think Zach had been doing a little nighthawking. No wonder he thought we were spying on him. He's afraid the police will find out and arrest him."

"He's a big lad," Ivor said. "What if Sinclair caught him out there, nighthawking, and things got out of hand?"

"I see what you mean, but I don't think Sinclair's murder was a random act. Something else was going on." We were standing in front of the Six Bells. "If Zach knows something, he could be in danger. He needs to tell the police."

"He's probably inside, throwing darts. Let's find out."

Chapter Twenty-Three

Even on a Tuesday night, the Six Bells was crowded with patrons eating and drinking. In its own way, the pub in Hartwell was as popular as the Three Magpies.

Zach Valentine was there as we'd hoped, throwing darts as Ivor had suggested. Seeing us, he gave us a tentative wave.

"What can I get you, son?" Ivor clapped him on the back. *The way to a man's heart . . .*

We found a table. Ivor and Zach ordered pints. Since I was driving, I ordered a mineral water.

"We heard something interesting tonight, Zach—from your friend, Edlyn. She told us you're an avid metal detectorist."

His eyes narrowed. "Why d'you want to know?"

"Because we think you might be able to help us solve a mystery. Kate here will explain."

Thanks, Ivor. I gave him a meaningful look as I scrambled to come up with a logical story. Or any story. Nighthawking was against the law. "Well, it's like this," I said, having no idea where the sentence was going. "We, *ah*, heard that lights were seen at the excavations a few weeks ago and wondered if you'd heard anything from your detectorist friends about it."

"Are you saying I was nighthawking?"

"No, I didn't say that, but it would be really helpful if someone *had* been at the dig site the night Dr. Sinclair was murdered—for some perfectly innocent reason, of course."

"Why?" he asked suspiciously.

"Well," I swallowed, "because that person might have seen or heard something important."

"And that person would be arrested."

"I don't think so. The police aren't interested in nighthawkers at the moment. I know that for a fact, Zach. They're trying to find a killer, and if someone just *happened* to be there that night, that person could be a real hero." I watched his reaction, surprised to see he was on the verge of tears.

"If you were there that night," Ivor said, "if you were afraid and tried to protect yourself, the police would understand."

"I wasn't there."

"If you were there, the police will find out, son. Much better to come clean before they take you in for questioning."

"It wasn't me." He looked from Ivor to me, his eyes huge.

Someone started the jukebox, and we heard Cliff Richard singing "Devil Woman."

"Do you mean you weren't there that night, or do you mean you weren't the one who attacked Dr. Sinclair?"

"I was there, but I didn't do anything wrong. I'm no killer." Several nearby patrons looked over.

"You were there." Ivor shrugged. "That's not against the law. Did you happen to have your metal detector with you?"

Zach's mouth twisted. "I knew they were finished with the dig, and I thought they might've left something behind. Something I could sell for a bob or two. It weren't really nighthawking."

"Have you done that other nights as well?" Ivor asked.

Zach gave us a wary look. "May have."

That accounted for the lights Peter Eley saw at the dig site around the time of Sinclair's murder. "That's not important now, Zach," I said. "No one cares about that. The important thing is for you to tell us if you saw anything—or anyone."

"It were a foul night. Raining, thick fog. Hard to see. I had my torch, but it was bouncing off the mist. I decided to go home and try again another night. That's when I saw them."

"Who?" Ivor asked.

"Don't know, do I? Two people—men, I think. Not sure. Come from the direction of the caravan. They were arguing."

"How did you see them in the dark?" I asked.

"They had torches, too. Turned mine off."

"What time was this?"

"Midnight? Maybe later."

"What were they arguing about?"

He eyed us. "Is it important?"

"It could be," I said.

"Will the police come and take me away?"

"Not if you tell the truth."

Zach blinked.

"What did you hear, son?" Ivor said. For someone who'd never been a father, he had the dear-old-dad thing down pat.

Zach squared his shoulders. He'd made a decision. "They were shouting. Couldn't help hearing, could I? One of them said, 'You stupid fool. You've started again, haven't you?' Angry, like. The other one must have been crying 'cause his voice was high and scratchy. He said, 'You don't know what I'm up against. You'll ruin me.'"

"You said *he* twice, Zach," I said. "Did you think it was a male voice at the time?"

"Nah—you just say that, don't you?"

"So it could have been a woman?"

"Could have, easy. A tall one."

Celia was tall. So was Tamzin—well, tall-ish.

"Did you hear anything else?" Ivor asked.

"I was scared. I ran."

* * *

Back in the car, I sat in the driver's seat for a good five minutes before I felt competent enough to drive. Finally, I fastened my seat belt and drove away from the village of Hartwell. "Is it possible to get PTSD in one night?" I asked Ivor. "First that *thing* in the computer, then Zach."

"There will be an answer for that *thing*. We just don't know yet what it is." He looked at me. "Are you all right?"

"I think so." Along the horizon, a line of soft, dusky blue faded into the deep blue of the twilight sky. A man on a bike passed me. "You'd best speed up a bit, or we'll get rear-ended by a horse cart."

"At least we know Edlyn isn't making it up."

"Will you tell Tom about all this?"

"Of course. He'll think I've lost my mind."

"I doubt that."

After dropping Ivor off at the shop, I drove home and phoned Tom immediately. When there was no answer, I kept trying.

He picked up on my third attempt. "What is it, Kate?" he asked in a hushed voice. "I'm in a meeting." The background noise faded. "What's wrong?"

I told him everything, every tiny detail of what Ivor and I had witnessed that night.

The line went silent for a moment. "Let me get this straight," he said, skipping over the computer thing and going straight to Zach Valentine. "The boy saw two people arguing at the dig site the night Sinclair was murdered."

"He couldn't see who they were. One was probably Sinclair, but he couldn't tell if the other one was a man or a woman."

"And this was midnight?"

"Or possibly later."

"Within the window of death. It has to be Sinclair and his killer. We'll have to interview Zach again."

"Could you do it unofficially? He's terrified you'll arrest him. And don't mention nighthawking."

"No problem." I pictured Tom's half-smile. "Now, about Edlyn Dark's father. You saw a face and heard a voice. Did it sound mechanical?"

"It sounded exactly like a well-educated older man from a village in Suffolk. Edlyn said it was her father, and she's known his voice her whole life."

"She wants it to be true."

"Yes, but she asks him questions, and that thing answers her. Ivor spoke to it." My voice sounded shaky. "I saw it with my own eyes, Tom, and it freaked me out."

"There is an answer, Kate," he said, echoing Ivor. "Someone is pretending to be her father. And he says someone else will die. We need access to that computer."

"Good luck with that. Edlyn won't want to give it up, that's for sure."

"She may not have a choice."

"She told us a computer repairman came out. I think it started happening soon after that."

"Try to find out who that was."

"Okay. Will you be home Thursday?"

"I will. I love you."

"I'm going to dream about that awful face, that creepy voice."

"Listen to me, Kate. There will be a logical explanation. We'll find it."

We ended the call, and I felt a sudden chill.

I wasn't sure which was worse, a killer from the beyond the grave or a flesh-and-blood murderer who was about to strike again.

Chapter Twenty-Four

Thursday, July 3
Ravenswyck Estate

Thursday was the day set for the test pit excavation. The excitement was palpable. Soon we'd know if Mark Lambe's theory about a plague pit near Egemere Close was real or simply wishful thinking on his part.

Unfortunately, I hadn't slept well for two nights in a row. Every time I closed my eyes, I saw that strange, flickering computer image of Grenville Dark, and when I did manage to drift off, I dreamt about it—not the benign fatherly figure Edlyn saw but something unnatural and evil, pretending to be him.

I picked Ivor up at nine.

I'd intended to park at the field office caravan, but the narrow access road had been blocked off, probably by the police, so I circled back and parked the car at Ravenswyck, next to Tamzin Oliver's little white Renault Clio.

Ivor and I walked to the dig site, making our way along the hedgerows on the footpath. The morning sun beat down, bringing the fragrance of the sweet peas that scrambled over the wild privet and blackthorn.

Approaching the mound, I looked back toward the trenches at Egemere Close. If Zach was right, and I had no reason to doubt it,

Sinclair had argued with someone at the dig site the night he was murdered. That person had to be his killer, but what had they been arguing about? What had started up again, and how would the second person be ruined?

A male voice whisked me back to the present.

The voice belonged to Niall Nevin. "I say we excavate at the upper site where the radar showed a cluster of images. It makes no sense to—"

"You forget, Niall," Celia Whybrew cut in, "the test pit is funded by the CMBA, of which I am now head. I say we begin there, where the image was closer to the surface." She indicated a spot about halfway up the side of the mound where a large tarpaulin had been laid. "We can always expand the operation later."

"Fine." Dr. Nevin turned back toward the mound. I watched him take something out of his pocket, toss it in his mouth, and take a swig from his water bottle. Pain pills?

In the distance, we saw Alex Belcourt and his farm manager, Peter Eley, standing under the portable awning. Belcourt raised a hand in greeting.

The mound was humming with activity. In addition to the archaeologists, the team included the promised volunteers from Norwich, three men and two women ranging in age from their twenties to their fifties. One of the volunteers held what looked like several long-handled spades. Another volunteer, with Mark Lambe's help, was setting up a perimeter with wooden stakes and string. Two others were securing the tarpaulin. A man wearing a plaid shirt and some sort of canvas hat held what looked like a camera.

Seeing us, Tamzin jogged down the side of the mound. She grinned. "You missed the excitement."

"Have they found something already?" I asked.

"I meant the argument."

"We heard the tail end of it."

"A question of authority?" Ivor asked.

"I suppose. The problem is, with Dr. Sinclair gone, the balance of power has shifted."

"Does Dr. Nevin take pain pills?" I asked.

"Sometimes. I know he's in constant pain. I think that's why he can be impatient at times. It's not a criticism," she added quickly. "Niall's been great to Mark and me. So has Celia. I'm sure they'll work well together eventually."

We watched two of the volunteers carefully strip a layer of turf. It came off in several pieces, which they laid on the tarp.

"The test pit will be approximately a meter square," Tamzin said. "As they remove soil, they'll put it through that screen sieve to capture any finds." She pointed out what looked like a rough wooden table on legs that had been positioned over the tarp. "Once they locate whatever created the image, everything will be put back exactly as it was. Archaeologists are as meticulous with the closing of an excavation as plastic surgeons are closing a wound. When we're finished, you'll never know any digging ever took place here."

"Who's the man in the plaid shirt?" Ivor asked.

"Dr. Nelson. He's a forensic anthropologist. We were lucky to get him on short notice. If they find a body, he'll examine it before they remove it to the lab."

Mark Lambe shouted something.

"I'm needed—sorry." Tamzin jogged up the mound.

Ivor and I joined Alex Belcourt and Peter Eley under the awning.

Eley acknowledged our presence with a brief nod.

"This is quite something, isn't it?" Belcourt said. "I've been told we should know something, one way or the other, in an hour or so."

"How deep will they have to dig?"

"No more than a meter and a half, apparently."

We stood watching for a few minutes.

Peter Eley unfolded the chairs they'd brought from the field caravan, and we sat, watching the excavation on the mound proceed at a snail's pace, the volunteers removing small clumps of dirt and depositing them on the screen sieve.

As the sun rose higher in the sky, Tamzin brought us paper cups and poured out tea from a large thermos. "Oops, sorry," she said, nearly spilling mine. "It's the nerves."

"Mark is excited, isn't he?" I said.

"He's sure he's right and afraid he's wrong." She placed the thermos on a large, insulated cooler. "He's grateful to Celia for the opportunity—at last." Tamzin blushed, which made me wonder if she was thinking the same thing I was: For Mark Lambe, Sinclair's death had an obvious plus side.

We continued to watch and wait.

Belcourt and Eley chatted about farm business and the needs of the livestock.

Ivor and I sat in companionable silence, watching the mound of soil on the tarp grow as the volunteers and the archaeologists took turns with the spades. After an hour or so, they exchanged the long-handled spades for trowels. The pit had deepened, and they worked on their knees and bellies.

The sun beat down. I was glad we were under the awning.

Tamzin returned. "More tea? It should still be hot."

We all shook our heads.

I leaned back in my canvas chair and crossed my legs. Conversation on the mound had ceased, leaving only the sound of metal trowels slicing through soil. It was surprisingly soporific—or maybe it was the warm breeze and the fact that I hadn't slept well.

My phone pinged. A text from Dr. Price-Davies. I opened it and showed Ivor my screen. "It's your friend from the university." I read him the text:

> *Well, this has been an interesting exercise. Two of the five files you sent appear to have no bearing on the mystery of Egemere Woman. One is a copy of the will naming Henry Wyck as the heir of his late maternal grandfather. The other is an inventory of lands belonging to the estate. The third file, the Patent Roll for 1345, authorizes Wyck to raise an army of fifty-five men to fight in France. The fourth is a record of the pensions*

he pledged to the widows or parents of men killed in battle. Since only forty-seven are listed, I assume he fell short of his mandate. The last file, the fifth, is the most intriguing—a letter Henry wrote to his wife, Matilda, on the ninth of September 1346, shortly after he arrived in France. He comforts her on what sounds like a miscarriage she suffered shortly before his departure.

If you were hoping Egemere Woman might be Matilda, I can almost guarantee she wasn't pregnant when Wyck left England, and according to the genealogy you supplied, he returned two years later to find she'd been abducted. I intend to do a little more digging. If I learn anything of interest, I'll let you know. Perhaps we could meet somewhere for coffee.

I responded. *I'd like that. Thank you for your help.*

I shut down my phone. "No progress on identifying Egemere Woman."

"Too bad," Ivor said. "But at least you know—"

"—what isn't the answer," we said in unison.

I yawned and closed my eyes, feeling disappointed. I needed that one discovery that would open things up—the one small detail Tom talked about that would point me in the right direction.

A warm breeze ruffled my hair. I leaned back in the chair.

I must have drifted off because Mark Lambe's voice startled me.

"We've got something," he shouted. "*Bones.*"

A flurry of activity broke out on the mound. The volunteers quickly erected an awning over the test pit as the archaeologists scrambled into white protective coveralls. It reminded me of a crime scene.

"What's going on?" I asked Tamzin.

"Protecting the bones from contamination." She was excited. "Once the bones are partially exposed, they'll use brushes to remove the remaining dirt. What happens next will depend upon the forensic anthropologist."

"Tamzin," Mark called to her. "Come see this."

She joined the others on the mound.

Mark, Celia, and the forensic anthropologist lay on their stomachs along the edges of the test pit. The others stood, arms crossed, looking down into the pit, watching the slow, meticulous brushing.

I stood, craning to see, my heart in my throat.

"It's a human skeleton." The forensic anthropologist clambered to his feet, his expression grim. "Definitely not medieval. Step away from the pit, everyone. Dr. Whybrew, I suggest you call the police."

* * *

While we waited for the police, I thought about the warning issued by that thing on Edlyn Dark's computer: *A body will be found at the dig site.*

How could he—or *it*—possibly have known?

Everyone had to be thinking about the one person who wasn't there—Carrie Holgate. Ivor and I exchanged glances. This could be the tragic end of a nine-year-old mystery.

A few meters away, Alex Belcourt paced back and forth. He didn't seem to know what to do with his hands, shoving them in his pockets, then pulling them out and crossing them over his chest.

Peter Eley sat in his chair, his tanned face as expressionless as marble.

The archaeologists and the volunteers milled about, unsure what to do.

Mark Lambe sat on the ground near the tarpaulin, his head in his hands. Tamzin crouched beside him, her hand on his back.

Celia Whybrew and Niall Nevin perched side by side on the cooler, unspeaking.

Ivor and I sat in the folding chairs, watching the forensic archaeologist snapping photographs and making notes on a clipboard.

DI Amy Cartwright and DS Matthew Ren arrived in less than thirty minutes, accompanied by a white forensics van. The team scrambled out of the van and began preparations to secure what was now a crime scene.

DI Cartwright met us under the awning. Niall Nevin and Celia Whybrew stood to greet her. "Dr. Sam Nelson is our bones expert," Celia told them. "Sam," she called, "the police are here. Can you come down?"

Dr. Nelson picked his way down the side of the mound. He shook hands with DI Cartwright. They moved away from us, but I could hear their conversation.

"I'm pretty sure it's female," Nelson said.

"How do you know the skeleton is modern?" Cartwright asked.

"Teeth," Dr. Nelson answered. "She had a fixed retainer."

At the other end of the awning, Belcourt stood half in the sunlight and half in shadow.

"There's something you should see," Nelson told DI Cartwright.

They climbed up to the test pit and stood talking for several minutes. Nelson gestured toward the pit. Cartwright nodded and slipped on a pair of nitrile gloves.

Nelson lay on his belly at the edge of the pit. He reached for something with his gloved hand and gave it to Cartwright, who stared at her palm. She looked in our direction, as if deciding on a course of action.

Returning to the observation awning, Cartwright addressed Alex Belcourt. "I am sorry, sir, but I must ask. Do you recognize this object?" In her hand, she held a broken gold chain and an irregular green stone.

Belcourt turned white. "It's part of a necklace. It belonged to my wife."

"Did she wear any sort of orthodontic appliance?"

His pale face froze. "She . . . she had a permanent retainer on her front teeth."

"There's something else, sir," Cartwright said. "The skeleton is female. Among the remains, Dr. Nelson has identified the partially ossified skull of a fetus. This woman was in the first trimester of pregnancy."

Belcourt's collapse was so sudden, none of us saw it coming. He fell to his knees, convulsed by grief. "Oh, God, no. Please, no."

"Sir," Cartwright said, trying to help him. "Allow me to—"

I looked for Peter Eley. He was nowhere to be seen.

Chapter Twenty-Five

By the time Tom arrived at the dig site, Ivor and Mark Lambe had managed to get Alex Belcourt into one of the folding chairs. He sat with his head down, sobbing.

Tom, who'd been required to break tragic news many times in his police career, pulled up a chair beside him and sat there in silence for a few minutes. Then he said, "I'm sorry for your loss, Alex. I can assign a family liaison officer, but I suspect what will help most right now is information. We'll have to make a formal identification, but I won't beat around the bush. We believe the body is your wife—Carrie Holgate. The remains will be removed to the coroner's office where an autopsy will be performed. We hope this will confirm her identity. It's possible we'll learn how far along she was in her pregnancy, and perhaps the child's gender."

Belcourt looked up. "I'd like to go home."

"Of course," Tom said. "I'll drive you there now."

"There's something you should know," Belcourt said. "I want Kate to hear."

Tom looked at me, and I nodded. "Cartwright," Tom said, "please drive Mr Tweedy back to Long Barston."

"Of course, sir," DI Cartwright said, but the tone in her voice told me she wasn't happy about being excluded from an interview with Belcourt.

Twenty minutes later, Alex Belcourt, Tom, and I were seated in the formal drawing room at Ravenswyck Court.

"You didn't know about the pregnancy?" I asked Belcourt. "That must have been what she wanted to tell you."

"Probably."

"I assume you were in touch with her during the two months you were away," Tom said. "She didn't drop any hints during that time?"

"Never." Belcourt shook his head and huffed out a breath.

The look on his face broke my heart. "I'm sure Carrie wanted to give you the wonderful news in person. Celebrate once you were home."

"*Celebrate?*" Belcourt got to his feet, his hands in fists at his side. "You don't understand." His face twisted in anger. "She didn't tell me because I wasn't the father."

Tom and I stared at him in disbelief.

"What are you talking about?" I asked.

"I was married once before Carrie—briefly. My wife had a career. She didn't want children, so I agreed to have a vasectomy. Carrie knew that when she married me." He took a shaky breath. "It wasn't easy for her. She loved children. We talked about having the procedure reversed, but the chances of success were slim. We were going to talk about adopting a child when I got home from the trip." He dropped onto the sofa opposite us.

I saw both grief and anger in his face. He'd been so in love with his beautiful wife. He'd trusted her, convinced that her love for him was beyond question. An unwelcome thought came to me. What if he was lying? What if he *had* known about the pregnancy? I looked at Tom, pretty sure he was thinking the same thing.

"I'm sure you realize, sir," Tom said, "the investigation into your wife's death will be reopened. We'll need to take new statements from everyone involved at the time. Stop in at the station in Hartwell as soon as it's convenient. In the meantime, perhaps you'd make a list of all your employees who were here in 2016. We'll need to speak with them as well."

"Yes, of course. There weren't many."

"We'll leave you, then," Tom said. "Is there anything I can do before we go?"

Belcourt shook his head.

I followed Tom to the door. "Do you mind if I stay for a few minutes?" I whispered. "I don't think he should be alone."

Our eyes met. *And Belcourt might say more once you've gone.*

Tom leaned down to kiss me. "CCTV footage of the night Sinclair was killed shows someone leaving Ravenswyck just before eleven PM."

"Who?"

"Hard to tell. It could have been Belcourt." He squeezed my arm. "Be careful."

* * *

The man in the black suit appeared. "Shall I bring tea, sir? Or something stronger?" He knew something had gone terribly wrong, but he'd perfected the incurious and unjudgmental expression of a well-trained butler.

Belcourt frowned at the question as if he didn't quite comprehend.

"That's a good idea," I said. "Tea with lemon and honey, please—and whiskey." Tea toddies were Vivian Bunn's all-purpose cure for everything from a hangnail to multiple gunshot wounds.

"Very good, madam."

I sat next to Alex Belcourt on the sofa. "I thought I'd make sure you're okay. Do you mind? You've had a bad shock."

He started weeping again, this time allowing the tears to run unchecked down his cheeks. "You can't imagine. Well, maybe you can after all I've told you." He pulled a handkerchief out of his jacket pocket and wiped his eyes. "I can't get my mind around it. How could it possibly be true—the pregnancy, I mean?"

"We all make mistakes. You know that. You also know Carrie wanted to tell you. She was going to explain."

"*Do* I know that?" His eyes flashed. He got to his feet and began pacing, running his fingers through his hair. "She wanted a child. I knew that. I wanted one, too. We were making plans. We were—" He stopped abruptly and stared at me. "Will they do DNA testing on the child? Will I know who the father was?"

"I don't know. I can ask."

"He must have killed her—the father. He must have wanted her to terminate, and when she refused, he—"

The butler carried in a tray and placed it on the table between the sofas.

"Thank you, er . . ." I said, realizing I'd never known his name.

"It's Hodgkins, miss." He glanced at Belcourt, then me, bowed slightly, and left.

"Did Hodgkins know Carrie?"

"No. He's a relatively new hire. I never wanted a butler—pretentious—but with my travel schedule, it made sense." He wiped his eyes again and then blew his nose.

I poured him a cup of tea, adding lemon, honey, and a generous shot of whiskey. "Sit down and drink this. It will do you good."

He made a dismissive sound but did as I suggested.

I poured myself a cup of tea—without the whiskey.

Between sips, Belcourt continued to speak. "What I can't understand is *why.* I know I was gone a long time, but we spoke every day. Every single day. Carrie was always the same, I swear it. She was busy with the dig, a little tired, maybe, but excited about each day's finds, participating in the dig herself whenever she could."

I thought about what Celia had said—that Carrie had been troubled; she'd had something on her mind. Well, an unplanned pregnancy with a man who isn't your husband would do that. "You said you were gone almost two months. Was the separation difficult for Carrie? Was she unhappy?"

He didn't answer right away. "Possibly, looking back at it now. But if she was unhappy, it was only in the last couple of weeks. I thought it had something to do with the dig."

"Did she say that?"

"I wish I could remember. It was an impression. I haven't thought of it in nine years."

The forensic anthropologist estimated that Carrie had been in her late first trimester—eleven or twelve weeks. If proven true, it meant she'd become pregnant *before* Belcourt left on his long business trip. That put a different light on things. She could have known she was pregnant for at least six weeks before her death, maybe more.

I poured him a second cup of tea, adding more whiskey. He was starting to relax. Was that a good thing or not? "Is there someone I can call, Mr. Belcourt?" I asked. "What about Peter Eley? Would you like him to stay with you?"

"No."

"Hodgkins?"

"I need to be alone. I need to think." He was up again, pacing.

"I'll check on you tomorrow." I rose and moved toward the door.

I was almost out of the room when he said, his voice breaking, "I would . . . I would have forgiven her, you know."

* * *

I was unlocking my car when I caught a glimpse of Peter Eley's battered old Land Rover, parked near one of the outbuildings. The low stone structure had probably been a stable block in years past. The presence of the vehicle didn't mean Eley was there, of course, but I had nothing to lose by finding out.

My instincts were right.

The building turned out to be a repository for animal feed and equipment. Eley was sitting on a bale of hay, his shoulders slumped, his forearms resting on his thighs.

"Peter," I said as gently as I could. "I know this is a terrible time for everyone. Is there anything I can do?"

He looked up. He'd been crying. "You can leave me alone."

"Okay." I put a hand up. "I'm sorry. I just wanted to make sure you're all right."

"All right?" he said, his eyes flashing. "How can I be all right? She's dead. Never coming back."

"Did you think she would?"

"Not really." His face crumpled, and he began weeping again. "She was so beautiful, so lovely, and now—" He broke off.

I tried to remember when he'd left the dig site, but I'd been focused on Belcourt.

"Were you and Carrie close?"

"She was a friend." Now that he'd begun, the words tumbled out. "We talked—you know, about the animals mostly. But sometimes she confided in me about other things. She needed someone to listen. I could do that."

"Did she seem troubled or unhappy in those last weeks?"

His forehead wrinkled, as if it was a question he'd never considered. "I think she was, actually. She'd always been so sunny, so ready to laugh. Then she wasn't."

"Did you tell that to the police at the time?"

"They didn't ask."

"Do you know why she was unhappy?"

"No. I know there was something she had to tell her husband. Something difficult. He wasn't going to like it."

No, he wouldn't, I thought, and I wondered again when Eley had left the dig site.

"Peter," I said, hoping my use of his given name wouldn't offend him. "Did you know Carrie was pregnant?"

He nodded. "They found the baby with her remains."

"Yes, but did you know while she was still alive?"

He nodded again.

"She told you?"

Another nod. His face twisted.

"Was she unhappy about the pregnancy?"

"No." He met my eyes. "She was happy about the baby."

She probably was, except for the little matter of telling her husband. "Was that the difficult thing Carrie had to tell her husband? Do you know?"

He just shook his head, his face a mask of pain.

"You loved her, didn't you?"

He nodded again.

I looked at him, and for the first time, I realized that under the rough manner and rough clothing, Peter Eley was a very attractive man. He was also shutting down. I'd watched Tom interview people often enough to know that when you have a reluctant witness, it's time to stop asking questions and just listen.

We sat there in silence for a few uncomfortable minutes. Then I made a decision, one I was probably going to regret. "Peter, were you the father of Carrie's baby?"

He stood, his nostrils flaring. "*Get out.*"

Back in the car, I realized he hadn't denied it.

Chapter Twenty-Six

Manor Farm

Tom and I sat on the patio, sipping glasses of white wine. The night was balmy, the air fresh and dry. On the heels of Monday night's rainstorm, a high-pressure system had stalled over the British Isles. Lucky us.

A fox barked in the woods behind the house. We'd seen him from time to time—a handsome fellow with a gorgeous tail and a very pretty wife. I hoped they had some kits hidden away in a nearby den. From above us came the *hoo hoo twoo* of a tawny owl, and then in the distance, the female's answering call.

I told Tom what I'd learned from Alex Belcourt and Peter Eley. Tom had reread the file from 2016. Belcourt's statement when his wife disappeared agreed essentially with what he'd told us today. Eley's hadn't. In 2016, he'd left out the part about knowing Carrie was pregnant.

"We'll have to bring Eley in," Tom said.

"Is he in trouble?"

"He withheld important information. It's called *obstruction*, and there are penalties. If he tells the truth now, I can probably get the penalties waived. Always assuming he wasn't the father of Carrie's baby and had nothing to do with her death. That remains to be seen."

"I think he was protecting her reputation."

"Any reasonable person would know something like that would be important in a murder investigation. Why did Eley neglect to tell the police? Because he was the father? We can't ignore the possibility."

"Alex Belcourt asked if the coroner will be able to establish paternity."

"We'll have to wait and see. They've called in a specialist."

"At least Belcourt's statement hasn't changed."

"The problem with his statement, then and now," Tom said, "is we only have his word for it. We checked his flight from Manila. He was on it, all right, but who's to say Carrie was asleep when he got home that night? What if she told him about the pregnancy and he lost his temper?"

"I don't think so, Tom. He was shocked when her body was discovered."

He gave me a skeptical look. Police are trained never to believe anyone.

"Besides, he would have had to get her body out of the house and bury it on the mound. A difficult job for one person."

"But not impossible."

"Was there CCTV then?"

"No. Not installed until later. And if Belcourt didn't kill her, how was Carrie able to leave the house without his knowing?"

"He said he took a sleeping pill."

"Yes, but did he? We don't know what either of them did that night. I hate to say it, but he's a suspect in her death—again."

"Oh, Tom. That's awful."

"Especially if he's not guilty." He consulted his watch. "Willow Gale will be on TV at nine PM. She's going to make a plea for Derek Quinn to give himself up."

We moved inside to the small library where we'd installed our one, not-so-large-screen television set. Tom turned it on to the local BBC channel. Willow Gale stood beside a tall, impressive-looking man in a police uniform. She had huge dark eyes and a mass of auburn hair. In her arms, she held a little girl who looked to be around two.

"I didn't know she had a child," I said. "Is it Derek's?"

"She says so."

Willow Gale looked terrified. She bounced the child up and down as if to comfort her, but I got the impression she was trying to comfort herself.

The chief constable introduced her, and the camera panned to Willow's pale, pretty face. "Derek, I don't know where you are," she said in a high, almost childlike voice, "but I'm asking you to turn yourself in. I told the police what happened that night in Thetford, that you didn't mean to harm Conor. It was an accident. You were trying to protect me. The police say they'll listen to you, but you must give yourself up now before anyone gets hurt. Please, Derek." Her voice rose to a squeak as she fought tears. "Rosie needs her daddy. Please, come home."

The camera panned back to the chief constable. "We're asking you to turn yourself in at the nearest police station, Derek. If you have a mobile, call us. Get word to us any way you can. We'll send someone to pick you up. You can only make things worse for yourself by staying away. We will be fair, I promise."

The screen went dark before returning to the regularly scheduled program, a documentary on forced labor in China and the impact on UK tomato imports.

Tom clicked off the TV. "Now we can only hope Quinn hears this and makes a wise decision."

"Tom," I said. "I want to go back to Simon Sinclair. I assume you haven't found his mobile, but you were going to request his phone logs. That was almost ten days ago. Have you learned anything?"

"Nothing, except the metadata shows that a week's worth of emails, phone messages, and texts were deleted. Like Sinclair's computer. Someone, and I'm betting it was his killer, made sure no digital footprints remained. That takes special knowledge."

I downed the final ounce of wine in my glass. "Have you learned anything about Celia—the *trying time* at university Lady Barbara mentioned?"

"Her records show she missed most of her second postgraduate year."

"Really? Why?"

"The records say *personal reasons*, but the absence was highly unusual. Postgraduate research students are expected to be in attendance for the entire year, except when research requires remote learning *and* has been specifically approved. Celia left abruptly at the end of March that year and didn't return until the following September. In essence she lost a whole year."

"It wasn't approved?"

"Oh, it was—I saw the signature."

"Don't tell me. Simon Sinclair."

"Got it in one. And the place on the form where an explanation should have been given—outlining her remote course—was left blank." Tom stretched out his long legs. He leaned back and turned his head to look at me. "Why would a young woman leave university so abruptly?"

"Illness?" I suggested. "Either physical illness or some form of mental stress. Sinclair was her supervisor. Maybe he realized she was in trouble."

"Isn't that the euphemism given by an older generation to an unplanned pregnancy?"

"Oh." I sat up, remembering Celia's curious response to my questions about Simon Sinclair. "And you suspect Sinclair was the father?"

"It's happened before."

"And would probably have meant the end of his career."

"No way to prove it after all this time. You might be able to get her to open up."

"Why would Celia tell me anything?"

"Because people tell you things, Kate. They do. Think about it. And if an opportunity presents itself—" He didn't finish the sentence.

He didn't need to.

Chapter Twenty-Seven

Friday, July 4
Manor Farm

It was the Fourth of July. Memories of sparklers, hot dogs, and root beer floats filled my mind.

My mother and her husband, James, would be at his daughter's lake house in Wisconsin. I imagined them sitting on the dock after dark, watching the pyrotechnics reflected in the dark water below. As much as I loved my new life in Suffolk, my history would always have its roots elsewhere.

Tom and I sat at the kitchen table over breakfast. He was reading the local paper. *Police Admit No Leads in Murder of Archaeologist* was the headline. Another article on the front page had the heading *Thetford Fugitive Still At Large*. I was reading the preliminary report of the forensic examination of the skeleton found on the mound. It confirmed the victim had been a female in her mid-twenties, that she'd been approximately thirteen weeks pregnant and had most likely been strangled. Dental records identified her as Carrie Holgate. An attempt to extract DNA from the fetus had been made, but because microbial activity had significantly degraded the infant's remains, identifying the father might be impossible.

I handed the report back to Tom. "We may never know the identity of the baby's father."

"Probably not." Tom was moving his eggs around with his fork.

"You think the pregnancy was the likely motive for Carrie's murder?"

"In the absence of another motive, yes. Why would someone kill a woman everyone agreed was not only beautiful but also kind and generous? What possible offense could she have caused? What possible threat could she have posed other than the fact she was pregnant?"

I handed him a cup of coffee. "You're making a case against Alex Belcourt."

"Circumstantial. After nine years, the chances of uncovering new direct evidence are practically nonexistent. Unless someone confesses or we stumble upon another motive, the case might never be solved."

"And Belcourt will live for the rest of his life under the shadow of suspicion."

"We'll do our best, Kate. Now, our chances of solving Simon Sinclair's murder are better, and there we do have direct evidence—the pearls, the CCTV footage of someone leaving Ravenswyck Court that night, the missing phone and computer data, the box of gold, the lights seen at the dig site, the argument Zach Valentine heard the night of Sinclair's murder, the protesters' threats—"

"Warnings, not threats, according to Edlyn Dark."

"The already-dead warning the about-to-be dead." Tom took a tentative sip of the hot coffee.

"Are you still planning to interview Zach Valentine this afternoon?"

"If I can find him. I'd like to stop at Edlyn Dark's cottage as well."

"Without an invitation? Good luck."

"You and Ivor got in."

"We were invited, but I think that was down to Ivor's charm. I can ask him to broach the subject with her, but I don't think she'll talk to you unless Ivor is able to convince her it's in her best interest."

"At some point, Kate, she won't have a choice."

"Still, I think she'd tell you more if it's voluntary." I took a bite of my toast and chewed thoughtfully. "What Ivor and I saw at Edlyn's cottage was impossible. I know that. But it was also convincing. I can see how a lonely person like Edlyn might be taken in. The question is, how was it done? The computer image spoke to us. It answered questions, said the appropriate things, responded naturally. Could a real person have been at the other end of the conversation, manipulating it over some sort of online chat room?"

"In that case, he or she would have had to sit at their computer day and night, in case Edlyn wanted to talk."

"I see what you mean." It made sense. Nothing else about the experience did.

"We're interviewing Belcourt's farm manager, Peter Eley, today as well. I'd like you to listen in—if you're free. So far, you've got more out of him than we have."

"How will your new DI react to that?"

"Let me worry about Cartwright. My concern is finding the truth, and I'll use every asset I have. You are an asset. You are involved—just not officially."

"When and where is the interview?"

"Ten AM. Police station in Hartwell."

"I'll check to see if I'm needed at the shop."

I was interested to hear what Eley would, or wouldn't, tell the police. Tom was good, but Eley didn't strike me as a man easily manipulated.

"By the way," Tom said, grinning at me. "Happy Fourth of July. Are you planning to celebrate?"

"In my heart only." I laughed. "Ivor texted me this morning. He said, 'We always knew you'd be back.'"

* * *

I arrived at the police station in Hartwell a few minutes before ten. Amy Cartwright was moving around behind the glass wall in the public waiting room.

She slid open the divider. "If you're here to see your husband, I'm afraid you'll have to wait. He's conducting an interview—or he will be in a few minutes."

"He asked me to come," I said, watching her eyebrows go up. Tom hadn't told her.

"I'll let him know you've arrived." She gave me a disapproving look.

In minutes, Tom appeared, and I followed him to the same office I'd used before, when Tamzin Oliver had been interviewed about the pearls.

Peter Eley showed up thirty minutes late. "This is a massive waste of time" were the first words out of his mouth—heard by everyone in the building, including an elderly man who'd come to report his missing dog.

I watched the monitor as Tom, DS Ren, and Peter Eley took their seats in the interview room. After fiddling with the recording machine, Tom introduced himself and DS Ren. "This is an informal interview, Mr. Eley, but it will be recorded. You're not under caution. If at any point you feel the need of a lawyer, you just have to say so."

"Is there anything we can get you?" DS Ren asked. "Coffee? Tea?"

When Eley declined, Tom began. "We met briefly at Ravenswyck, which means you know Kate Hamilton is my wife. She told me about your recent conversation, which is why I've asked you to come in today. What you told my wife differs significantly from the statement you gave to the police in 2016." He opened a file folder and removed a paper. "This is a copy of the statement you made at that time." He placed it on the table and turned it so Eley could read. "You said you spoke with Carrie Holgate in the days leading up to her disappearance about the rare-breed goats she'd recently purchased. She wanted them tested for certain diseases and asked you to call the vet. Is that correct, Mr. Eley?"

"That's what I said." Even through the monitor, I could see the tightness in his jaw.

"When was this conversation?"

"We talked about the goats several times."

"When was the last time?"

"The day before she disappeared."

"She was concerned about the health of her goats, and yet you assumed her unexplained disappearance was voluntary?"

"I didn't know what to think."

"Yesterday you told my wife that Carrie confided in you. She told you she was expecting a child. Is that correct?"

"Yes."

"Why did you withhold that information in 2016, Mr. Eley, when it could have been important in our investigation?"

"Because it was no one's business, that's why," Eley growled. "Carrie told me in confidence. At that point, we all thought she'd run away. She'd been tired. Needed a break. It was hers to tell, not mine."

"You've withheld that information for nine years. At some point, you didn't think you should come forward?"

Eley shifted in his chair. "I did consider telling the police."

"Why didn't you?"

"Because of Mr. Belcourt."

"You're going to have to explain that."

"Because I knew he wasn't the father."

"How did you know that?"

"Because I knew he'd had a vasectomy." Eley thrust out his chin. "If Carrie wasn't coming back, how could I add to Mr. Belcourt's grief by telling him his wife had been unfaithful? I couldn't do it."

"It's time to tell the truth now, Mr. Eley. The whole truth. What exactly did Carrie Holgate tell you about the baby?"

"Just that she was expecting."

"Was she happy about it or upset?"

He pressed his lips together and shook his head. "Both, I think."

"Did she tell you the identity of the baby's father?"

"I was meant to believe Belcourt was the father, wasn't I? Carrie didn't know I'd driven him to hospital for his procedure, and I wasn't going to bring it up."

Tom sat back, folding his arms across his chest. He looked at Peter Eley appraisingly, as if debating with himself. Finally, he said, "We've taken DNA samples from the fetal remains." He didn't add they were probably useless. "Mr. Eley, were you the father of Carrie Holgate's unborn child?"

Peter Eley shot him a black look. "No. I swear it."

"But you were in love with her."

"Yes, God help me. I would have given my life for her. I wish I had."

"You never told Alex Belcourt about the pregnancy?"

"Never."

"You'll be given a chance to sign a revised statement. Consider yourself lucky."

Eley acknowledged this with a grunt, and Tom ended the interview.

Several minutes later, he appeared in the office doorway. "Let's go. Have some lunch."

We were on our way out when DS Ren stopped him. "Boss, I've got Alex Belcourt in the second interview room. He says he's here to give a statement."

"Shall I see your wife out?" Amy Cartwright looked triumphant.

I touched Tom's arm. "See you at home. Good luck in Hartwell."

On the way to the car, I thought about Peter Eley's admission. He said he'd withheld the information about Carrie's pregnancy from the police in 2016 in order to protect Alex Belcourt from further grief.

I believed him.

Chapter Twenty-Eight

Long Barston

When I arrived at The Cabinet of Curiosities, I found Ivor studying the proofs of the auction catalog—an important task because if we were inaccurate, we could be sued later by a buyer claiming he'd been misled. This was a major sale of Roman antiquities. The full-color catalog would be mailed to more than three thousand subscribers and emailed to thousands more, not only in England but around the world. Museums would send representatives to bid. So would wealthy collectors from the Continent, the Americas, and Asia.

"Do you need my help?" I asked, feeling guilty. My contract with Alex Belcourt was taking time away from my responsibilities at work. Not that Ivor had ever complained.

"Thank you, Kate, but I'm almost finished. Everything looks in order." He stretched. "This auction is going to be a sensation. The number of objects and their importance is quite impressive. I may bid on some of them myself." His cherubic face shone with excitement.

Ivor was a buyer at heart. Sometimes an emotional buyer, and I knew he had a soft spot for Roman antiquities. I could have pointed out that our bank account wasn't in great shape, but the business was Ivor's, after all, and he did have a gift for sniffing out items that were selling well under their retail value.

"Do you plan to attend?" I asked, meaning online. Glasgow was a thirteen-hour train ride from Long Barston. Fortunately, we could log on and bid by computer.

"I think we both should attend. Once we get the final catalog, I'll mark some of my favorites. You can do the same."

"Yes, let's do that." Seeing Ivor so happy was a balm for my soul. In the years I'd known him, he'd weathered serious cash-flow problems, major surgery, the theft of a priceless Chinese jar, insurance claims, and, I suspected, loneliness. All that was behind him now, and I intended to do everything I could to keep it that way.

"Tom plans to interview Zach Valentine this afternoon," I said. "He'd like to see Edlyn Dark's computer. I told him his chances of getting inside her cottage were slim to none."

"I agree. We were lucky to be admitted. I think it was because of your interest in the history of Egcmere Close."

"Do you? I think it was your irresistible charm. I told Tom I'd ask you to intervene. I hope that's all right. If Edlyn contacts you again, could you ask her if she's willing to talk to Tom about the computer tech guy she hired? She already knows Tom's a policeman."

"I can try," he said. "Wouldn't like to get his hopes up."

Almost exactly what I'd said to Tom.

Defying expectations, two groups of women entered the shop within ten minutes of each other, but the rest of the day was quiet.

Ivor and I were thinking about closing up early when Tom appeared. "May we be of service, sir?" Ivor asked as if Tom were a customer.

"Actually, you can—or I hope you can." Tom pulled a small box out of his jacket pocket and opened it. Inside was Simon Sinclair's agate intaglio ring, the one he'd been clutching when he died. "I'd appreciate any information you can give me about the ring."

"I know the ring," Ivor said. "Sinclair wore it on his left hand." He looked at me. "Kate?"

"Go ahead, Ivor. You're the expert."

I was dying to ask if Tom had interviewed Zach Valentine, but since he hadn't brought it up, I thought I'd better wait until we were alone.

Ivor donned a pair of cotton gloves and held the ring up to the light. "The stone is older than the setting. Actually, the setting is fairly modern. Give me a moment. I'd like to examine the carving under magnification." He clipped one of his jeweler's loupes to the frame of his glasses and positioned the instrument. "I'm not a certified gemologist, you understand, but I do have some experience." That was an understatement.

He examined the ring closely, making occasional small murmurs of approval.

Finally, he flipped the loupe out of the way and replaced the ring in its box. "The classical design is certainly Roman or Greco-Roman, but that in itself isn't proof of age. Classical themes have been popular many times in history." His eyes sparkled. "Except in my opinion, it isn't a repro."

"You mean a reproduction?" Tom asked.

"Close. A reproduction is an item created to look like an original. Perfectly legitimate—like purchasing a newly made chair in the Chippendale style. In the trade, a 'repro' is a new item created purposely with the intention to deceive. I don't believe this stone is a repro. First, the engraving shows clear signs of hand-tooling. And the stone has a patina, a weathering of the surface—tiny scratches and abrasions such as would occur with great age. A professional gemologist would study the intaglio under a microscope, analyzing it for signs of modern polishing techniques and artificial enhancements, but even with this loupe, I can see the kinds of inclusions and natural variations not typically seen in modern materials. I'd say this might have been an ancient seal ring, used to authenticate documents, probably Roman."

"Would the ring be valuable enough to kill for?"

"I hope not," Ivor said. "I'd say it might sell for four or five thousand pounds."

"But the killer didn't take it," I said. "Sinclair had the ring in his hand when he died."

"The more we learn, the deeper the mystery," Ivor said. Then, "Why don't you two get out of here? Have a nice evening together."

"Are you sure?" I asked. "Do you want me to close out the computer?"

"I'll do that." Ivor walked to the door and flipped the sign to *Closed*. "I'm meeting an old friend at the Magpies tonight. Gentleman in his upper eighties. He had an antiques shop in the village for years. We were friendly rivals. He's retired now, but he likes to keep his hand in, hear all the gossip."

"Thanks, Ivor," Tom said. "Did Kate ask you about intervening on my behalf with Edlyn Dark?"

"She did, and I will. No guarantees."

* * *

Since the evening was lovely and neither of us was hungry, we decided to take the walk we'd had to postpone the previous weekend. It was one of our favorite walks—the footpath along the River Stour that meandered gently through Long Barston.

"Tell me about Zach," I said as we strolled down the High Street, past the shops and the Suffolk Rose Tea Room to the Stour bridge. "Did you find him?"

"At the pub, as you suggested. He was alarmed at first, but when I told him I was your husband and you'd said he had important information, he relaxed a bit. He confirmed what he told you but added nothing new except to say he thought the first man to speak, the one who mentioned starting up again, was probably Dr. Sinclair. Zach was pretty sure he recognized the voice."

"Did he say anything more about the second person?"

"No. He doesn't know if the voice was male or female."

"Did you believe him?"

"I did, actually. His testimony places Sinclair at the dig site just after midnight with a second person. Given the coroner's evidence, Sinclair must have been murdered soon afterward."

The footpath along the river, ten feet or so below the road, was accessed by a series of zigzag steps built into the bridge abutment. The river was shallow there, tumbling lazily over rocks and fallen limbs. The trees created a cool green canopy.

"What did you think of Peter Eley's statement today?" Tom asked. "Did I miss anything?"

"Amy Cartwright's outrage?" I watched him for a reaction. "She practically shoved me out the door."

"I wish I had missed it. She had a *word* with me after Belcourt left. She thinks I have it in for her. I told her the others on the team were getting tired of her attitude."

"What did she say?"

"She said they were welcome to their attitudes as long as they didn't stand in her way. I think she has a real problem. No wonder headquarters was so keen to approve her transfer."

The path was wide enough for two there, and I took his hand. "What did *you* think about Peter Eley's statement?"

Tom raised his shoulders and let them fall. "It made sense, didn't it, but Eley has the face of a marble statue. He could be lying."

"He could be, but I don't think he is." I picked my way over a tangle of exposed tree roots. "How about Alex Belcourt's interview? Did you learn anything new from him?"

"Not about Carrie Holgate. Belcourt's statements then and now are virtually identical. Carrie was asleep when he got home from the airport—or he assumed she was sleeping. It was late, and her door was shut. They didn't speak, anyway. He took a sleeping pill, which he says he rarely does, but his body clock was eight hours ahead, and he wanted to get some rest as he had a meeting with his board of directors the following day. A meeting he never made, of course. When he got up, around ten, Carrie was gone. He called her mobile. No answer. He looked for her at the dig site. No one had seen her. He organized a search of the property without results. Finally, he called the police."

"Oh, Tom." I felt a chill. "By that time, she was already dead and buried."

"At that point, everyone assumed she'd left voluntarily—an extraordinary assumption, given the fact that nothing had been taken—no clothes, toiletries. We've heard from three people now that Carrie was troubled in the last weeks of her life. Celia Whybrew thought it had to do with her marriage. Peter Eley assumed it was because of her pregnancy and the prospect of telling her husband. Belcourt thought she was tired, doing too much."

"Belcourt told me he got the impression something was bothering her and that it had to do with the dig."

"He mentioned that, but he couldn't say why." Tom stopped walking as a shrill *whee-eep* came from the field beyond the opposite bank "Listen," he said. "It's a flycatcher." We stopped to watch a small black-and-white bird dipping and soaring, hoping to catch an insect in mid-flight. On our side of the bank, in the shade of an old oak, a few wild violets were still pushing out their small, fragrant blooms.

I was struck with the beauty of nature in stark contrast to the ugliness of murder. Not that nature couldn't be cruel at times. I knew that. But human cruelty was usually planned.

"You said you learned nothing new about Carrie," I said as we started walking again. "Does that mean you learned something else?"

"You do listen, don't you?" Tom grinned. "I told you the CCTV footage the night of Sinclair's murder showed a shadowy figure arriving at Ravenswyck just after eleven PM and leaving approximately twenty-five minutes later. The camera had infrared capabilities, but the resolution is poor. We showed it to Belcourt. The figure was male, on the tall side, wearing a light hooded jacket, but that could describe just about anyone—Belcourt, Peter Eley, Niall Nevin, Mark Lambe, even the butler, Hodgkins, or another member of staff. Belcourt swears it wasn't him."

"What did you learn?"

"We learned the camera that captured the image was the one covering the public entrance to the museum, not the house itself."

"A break-in?"

"Probably not. There was no damage, nothing was taken. It appears the person knew the key code. That includes Belcourt, of course, and the butler, and all the senior archaeologists."

"Not Peter Eley?"

"Not unless he found the code or guessed it. Which is possible."

"What was the code?"

"Carrie, on the alpha-numeric keypad—227743."

"You're right. He might have guessed it. May I see the footage?"

"I thought you'd ask. I have a copy on my computer. Come on. Let's go a bit farther before we turn back."

We'd walked as far as the next bridge, about a half mile, when I heard my mobile ping with a text. "Wait, Tom. This could be important." We stopped, taking a seat on one of the benches provided at intervals for people who need to catch their breath—or perhaps just enjoy the scenery.

The text was from the medieval languages expert, Duncan Price-Davies.

I've found something rather remarkable. Can you meet me at The Hold? I'll be there tomorrow afternoon doing research. If that doesn't suit, I can make time later.

I typed back:

Perfect. I'll be there around two.

"Who was it?" Tom asked.

"The professor Ivor knows, the expert on medieval languages. He says he's found something interesting. I'm meeting him tomorrow afternoon in Ipswich."

"You might learn Egemere Woman's identity after all."

"It was a very long time ago."

"True," Tom said. "And the murder of Carrie Holgate was nine years ago—that's a long time in a police investigation. Right now the murder of Simon Sinclair is my major concern, and I think it's time to consider the suspects. I'd like to hear your thoughts. Who's the most likely suspect at this point?"

"Someone who was actually here, for starters."

"Meaning someone we know and have already interviewed."

"That's what I think. Niall Nevin, for example. Everyone says he idolized Sinclair, but I saw how Sinclair baited him at the Finchley

Hall dinner. Nevin doesn't strike me as a violent person, but even a mild-mannered person can be pushed too far."

"True, but Zach Valentine's evidence strongly suggests Sinclair was murdered shortly after midnight or twelve thirty. Nevin's computer logs show he was at The Forge, working, at that time."

"And Mark Lambe heard his printer," I said. "But what if Nevin had an accomplice—someone who used his computer to make it appear he was actually there?"

"Who would that be?"

"Celia or Mark, I suppose. They were present. Even Tamzin."

"Tamzin helping Nevin commit murder? That sounds pretty far-fetched."

"Yeah." I had to agree. "How about Celia, then? She says she didn't leave The Forge, but we know now that any one of them could have left by that back entrance. And the pub owner at the Six Bells told me there was a minor altercation between Sinclair and Celia that night. She said something to him as he came out of the loo, and he pushed her away."

Tom pursed his lips in thought. "And then there's that unexplained absence from university, permission granted by Sinclair. What if Celia was pregnant and she blames Sinclair?"

"Even if that's true, why would she wait all this time to get revenge? The argument may have been about something completely different."

"That's why you need to talk to her. Find out what was really going on between them."

"Easy for you to say." I gave him a playful shove. "I will try though."

"All right—let's get back to Mark and Tamzin, either separately or together."

"They certainly had motive—Sinclair's sexual advances toward Tamzin and his refusal to approve Mark's thesis. Celia said it would probably mean the end of his PhD track at the university. He'd have to start from scratch somewhere else."

"They had strong motives, but they would have had to work together."

"Not necessarily, Tom. Tamzin admitted she fell asleep that night. Mark says he went to his room, but maybe he didn't. Maybe he knew Sinclair would be at the dig site and went there to confront him instead."

"What about Alex Belcourt? What if he killed his wife, and Sinclair knew it and was threatening to tell the police?"

"And never said a thing for nine years? That really is far-fetched."

"I agree," Tom admitted. "You said Belcourt and Sinclair were fighting over the display of the grave goods."

"I can't believe that would be a motive for murder. Besides, the matter hasn't been decided yet."

"What if Belcourt killed Sinclair in revenge for Carrie's pregnancy?"

"That assumes Sinclair was the father," I said, "and Belcourt knew it."

"Peter Eley was in love with Carrie. He would have had the same motive for killing Sinclair."

"That doesn't explain why either would have waited all that time. And we both saw their reactions to the discovery of Carrie's body. I'm sure their shock was real."

"So who does that leave?" Tom asked.

"The protesters, I suppose. Edlyn Dark and/or Zach Valentine."

"Zach wasn't the killer. I'd bet my warrant card on it."

"There's something we don't know, Tom. And this won't be solved until we find out what that is." I stood and stretched. "Shall we walk as far as the church?" All Saints' Church in the next village was a picturesque site. We could hear the peal of bells in the distance. The bell ringers were practicing, one of my favorite sounds.

"I say we turn back," Tom said. "That way, you can view the CCTV footage before dinner."

* * *

We drove home in separate cars, arriving a little after six PM. I'd put a whole chicken in the slow cooker that morning with carrots, onions, and potatoes. It could wait. While Tom set up his computer, I pulled out some aged cheddar I'd bought at the artisan cheese shop in the village, along with a package of crispbread crackers and our favorite ale chutney.

"Don't be surprised if you can't see much." Tom pushed *enter* and the screen filled with dark, grainy images. The resolution was terrible, which made me wonder why someone with Alex Belcourt's money wouldn't go for top-of-the-line security cameras.

"Here goes," Tom said. "It's motion activated. The time stamp says eleven ten PM."

A dark shape crossed directly in front of the camera, which had been mounted on the adjoining wall. The shape was human, a man wearing a light hooded jacket. He approached the door, blocking our view, and seemed to hesitate for a moment, as if he was having a hard time seeing the keypad or remembering the combination. Finally, the museum door opened inward, and the man disappeared. The screen went blank.

"You're right," I said. "That could have been anyone."

"Whoever it was, it looks like he knew about the security camera and took care not to reveal his face." Tom clicked a few more keys. "Here's the next reel, captured just short of thirty minutes later. The time stamp says eleven thirty-eight PM."

This time there was more to see. The man emerged from the museum entrance door. He was facing the camera this time, but he kept his head well down so all we could see was the bridge of his nose. Then, unexpectedly, he raised a hand to his hood, pulling it farther down on his forehead.

"Wait," I said. "Back up and stop the image."

"You saw something?" Tom set down his cracker and backed up the reel, image by image.

"That's it—right there." I squinted at the image of the man's left hand. "What's that?" It wasn't much and certainly wasn't clear, but it looked like a tiny patch on the man's hand.

"We noticed that. It could be a shadow."

"Can you pull in closer?"

"Not without degrading the resolution even further."

"Try it."

He did. This time the patch took a definite shape. It was oval.

"Tom, I think that's the ring. Sinclair's intaglio ring. I think the man is Sinclair."

Tom frowned. "What would he have been doing at the museum at that time of night?"

An answer, whether true or false, came instantly. "The *safe*. Tom—he was checking the safe. Putting something in or taking something out. Remember the note on his calendar?" It was pure conjecture, and yet I had a strong feeling I was right.

I had another thought. "If Sinclair opened the safe at the museum—"

"We don't know that."

"*If* he did, maybe he also decided to open the safe at the field office that night."

"And you're saying someone followed him or met him there."

My mind was spinning, but things were beginning to add up. "Listen, Tom. On the night he was killed, Simon Sinclair got a text and left the pub between ten fifteen and ten thirty. By eleven ten he was caught on camera, entering the museum at Ravenswyck and taking care not to be recognized. He'd written the word *safe* on his calendar."

"Why would he need to make a note about it in his calendar?"

"I don't know. To remind himself? Or maybe because that particular date was significant in some way. Whatever the reason, he left the museum just before eleven forty, so he was there for almost thirty minutes. By midnight or slightly after that, he was spotted by Zach Valentine at the dig site where presumably he met his killer, perhaps by appointment."

Tom nodded slowly. "You're saying someone lured him to the dig site in order to kill him. He was hit from behind, taken by surprise, which means a strong woman might have done it. The coroner says Sinclair was killed where his body was found, but we have no idea why he was in one of the trenches. Had he noticed the fake pearls? He was clutching his ring when he died. Why? To prevent his killer from stealing it? And then the biggest mystery of all: In the short time Sinclair had left to live, he ingested some of the pearls scattered earlier by Mark and Tamzin."

"The ring and the pearls," I said. "It doesn't make sense. Unless . . ." An idea had begun to form in my mind, a landscape emerging from the mist. "Dr. Sinclair wasn't a nice person. He used people to enhance his reputation and his career. He couldn't stand being upstaged or bested, but he was highly intelligent and good at connecting small details to form a larger picture. That's what archaeologists do. In the last moments of his life, he did two strange and inexplicable things. He removed his ring and held it in his fist, and he swallowed some of the fake pearls he'd found scattered in the trench. Those actions weren't random. There must be an explanation—if we can find it. Actually," I said as the landscape became clearer, "I think that was the point—that the police would notice and look for an explanation. Tom, I think Sinclair was trying to tell us who killed him."

Chapter Twenty-Nine

Saturday, July 5
Ipswich

I spent the morning at the shop as Ivor had a dentist appointment. When he returned, around eleven thirty, I filled up with fuel at the BP station at the roundabout, grabbed a sandwich in the little shop, and pointed the car in the direction of Ipswich, where the linguist, Duncan Price-Davies, had asked me to meet him. I couldn't wait to find out what he'd discovered.

Lois Upton was at the reception desk again. She greeted me warmly. "Dr. Price-Davies said you'd be arriving. You can find him in the café. Just inside the Fore Street entrance. Look for a man in a blue jumper and gray tweed jacket."

I'd pictured an older gentleman, around Ivor's age, with neatly combed white hair, wire-rimmed spectacles, and a thoughtful expression. Instead, Price-Davies was in his early to mid-forties, around my own age. He was a trim, attractive man with a warm smile, very blond hair, and very blue eyes. He was sitting at one of the tables, finishing a salad. He stood and held out his hand. "You must be Ms. Hamilton. Ivor's told me so much about you—and your very interesting commission. I was shocked to hear about the murder of Dr. Sinclair—and then finding the body of that young woman. I can't imagine."

"Yes, Carrie Holgate. Everyone was horrified."

"Can I get you anything—a coffee?"

When I thanked him and said no, he gathered up his lunch things. "I'm finished here, anyway." He placed his dish and silverware on a tray and tossed the paper into a bin. "Let's do this in the search room. I can plug in my computer. May I call you Kate?"

"Yes, of course."

"Please call me Duncan."

"I'm grateful to you, Duncan. I know your time is valuable. As you know, Grenville Dark was researching a book about Egemere Close—never published. His manuscript and all his research notes have disappeared, so knowing which files he accessed is important."

We claimed one of the larger spaces and pulled up two chairs. Price-Davies set up his computer and removed a stack of papers from his briefcase. "After reading what you sent, I thought I'd take a look at the list of files you *didn't* request. One of them was listed as a medieval poem, which naturally caught my attention."

"Yes, I remember seeing that. I didn't think a poem would help me identify Egemere Woman."

"You may change your mind." His eyes sparkled. "First, though, let's go over the translations of the files you sent me." He pulled up a document, in Latin, on his computer. "As I said in my text, this is part of the patent roll for 1345. Technically, it's a *letter patent*, meaning an official document carrying the authority of the king. This one authorizes Henry Wyck of Ravenswyck to raise an army. These are digital images. Do you see the texture and variations in the background? The original texts were copied onto sheets of parchment, which were then stitched together, head-to-tail, to form long scrolls, one for each year in the mid-fourteenth century." He scrolled down a list of names with ages and occupations. "You can see most occupations say *servus*, meaning serfs, or *agricola*, meaning farmers or plowmen. The king had asked Wyck to recruit fifty-five men of fighting age to join him for the siege of Calais. Fifty-five would have been quite optimistic for this area. The population wasn't great, and the youngest and oldest would have had to stay behind to grow crops and perform other tasks considered in the male purview at that time."

He pulled up a second document, another list, also in Latin. "In this manuscript, Wyck pledges to give the parents or widows of men killed in France the average sum of one or two pounds a year, depending on the son's or husband's social status and land holdings. It was fairly generous. He wasn't required to give them anything."

"How many of his men were killed in France?"

"Out of the original forty-seven—he didn't make the requested number—twenty-nine never made it home. I learned that Wyck himself was severely wounded, but he obviously recovered as his name is listed as alive in court records later."

I thought of the symbolic figure of Death lurking in the background of Henry Wyck's portrait. Misfortune had certainly been his lot—severely wounded in France and then returning home to find his wife abducted.

"Now here's what I want you to see." Price-Davies pulled up a third document.

"That's Middle English," I said, recognizing the patterns. "I studied it in college, but I haven't kept up."

"It's a poem, Kate, written by Henry Wyck—or so it claims. The title is 'The Pearl of Wyck.' " He was watching me for a reaction.

" 'The Pearl of Wyck,' " I repeated, marveling. "You know about the pearl found with the body of Egemere Woman."

"Oh, yes. I remember reading about it at the time, and Ivor has filled in some of the details. I knew you'd be interested." He moved the slider at the bottom to 150 percent.

"I see now," I said, recognizing the special, stylized characters, the lack of uniform spacing, and the idiosyncratic punctuation typical of medieval handwriting. "I hope you translated."

"I did. Fortunately, the poem is short." He handed me a sheet of paper. In the left-hand column was the original and on the right his translation. "The meter is iambic tetrameter. I could have done a better job had I more time, but I thought you'd want to see it right away."

I glanced at the original language—

O Pearl, in theæ mīn fatæ waſ sealede
th' adai thī beautī piercede mīn hearÞ
a'd bounede mīn wretchede līke bihofþe woæ.

—and quickly switched to Price-Davies's modern English translation:

O Pearl, in thee my fate was sealed
The day thy beauty pierced my heart
And bound my wretched will to woe.
For pity, pride would not admit
The mercy due a truer heart.
Thou Pearl of Wyck, one day mine own,
For whom I'd giv'n my prince's soul
Had fate not claimed his doleful share.
The clay I sought to cheat of death
Now holds thee in its miry grip.
For thee I gave what I hold dear;
Those joys now mock my lofty pride.
O dare I ask with trembling lip
Where I shall lie when earth has fled
In realms of joy or prisons dread?

"Wow," I said, momentarily speechless.

"Wow, indeed," Price-Davies said. "What do you make of it? Who or what is the Pearl?"

I scanned the poem again. "The Pearl of Wyck is either a pearl or . . . a woman."

"Or both?" he added with an enigmatic smile.

"It sounds like the author claimed what wasn't his own and feared an eternal penalty. I wonder if he abducted Matilda first, only to have her stolen back by her rightful husband."

"That's an interesting take. How would you interpret clay's 'miry grip'?"

"It sounds like the grave." I felt like one of his students and decided his courses must be popular.

"I think so, too, so who or what is in the grave's 'miry grip'?"

"Well, either the pearl or the woman."

"Or both?" he said again with the slight quirk of his eyebrow.

It was a stunning thought. "The Pearl of Wyck could be Egemere Woman *and* the pearl buried with her."

He shrugged. "He also mentions pride, pity, fate, mercy—or the lack of it. When I have a chance, I'm going to check the court records, the *eyres* they're called, for the years in question. I already know Wyck's name is listed." He closed his computer and wound up the cord. "I should get back. I have tutorials this evening. Where are you parked?"

"Public car park—why?"

"I am as well. Do you mind if we walk together? There's something I want to ask you. It's personal."

* * *

We exited into what they'd called a "physic garden," with raised planters displaying historic medicinal plants.

"There won't be a place to chat at the carpark," Price-Davies said. "Shall we stop here for a few minutes?"

"Yes, of course."

It was a pleasant choice. We sat on a low wooden bench near a profusion of thyme and rosemary, which gave off delicious herby scents. Price-Davies lowered his backpack to the paved terrace. He sat there, silent for a moment.

"I'm grateful for your help, Duncan. This is an amazing bit of history."

"We're collaborators now, aren't we?" His blue eyes twinkled.

Duncan Price-Davies was really very attractive, and it wasn't only his looks. I could imagine more than one of his students forming a crush on him.

"You said this was a personal matter?"

"Yes." He hesitated. "It's about Dr. Whybrew—Celia. How is she? After Dr. Sinclair's murder, I mean."

"It was awful for everyone, of course, finding his body. But I get the impression Celia isn't in mourning."

"She wouldn't be."

It was an interesting comment—one I wanted to pursue. "You're worried about her?"

"I know how she comes across—confident, analytical, cerebral, and she is all that. But underneath that cool exterior, she can be sensitive, even vulnerable. I've been concerned about her."

"It sounds like you know Celia well."

"Quite well—at least I did." He looked down at his hands.

I could see I'd touched on a sensitive topic and didn't want to hurry him. "She's a very beautiful woman."

He nodded, acknowledging the point. "We were seeing each other for a while. She ended it. I don't know why."

I smiled, trying Tom's silence technique again. This time it worked.

"We met when I helped the CMBA team translate runic inscriptions on the Isle of Man. We were compatible—on the same wavelength, you know? We never argued—except about Sinclair. I suggested she'd be better off, academically, on her own. She disagreed."

"Ivor told me what you said about Sinclair—about his reputation in the department and the way he treated his subordinates. I've heard similar things from most of the team members since his death—including Celia. Why would she put up with it?"

Price-Davies was focusing on something miles away from the physic garden. "I wondered the same thing, but then Simon was a force of nature. He liked to get his own way and generally did, using the proverbial carrot-and-stick technique—dangling the carrot to make sure you stayed in line, and if you didn't, he produced the stick, which you quickly noticed was a flick-knife."

"I witnessed it myself."

"Celia wouldn't like me telling you this, but she was writing an article for one of the archaeological journals. It was a major piece, one her colleagues would have noticed. I'm sure it would have meant promotion. The university loves that kind of recognition. Celia had done extensive research at the site—it was Roman. I won't bore you with the details, but Sinclair had been the leader on the dig, and he—I admit I'm showing my bias here—couldn't stand the fact that Celia would receive the credit. He undercut her, publishing an article on a similar subject in another journal, using her data . . . well, the data she'd gathered for the team. His article came out first, which pretty well made hers irrelevant."

"Why didn't Celia call him out?"

"She couldn't. To accuse a colleague, a supervisor, of that kind of thing would label her a troublemaker. Plus, Sinclair had credited her in the article. He'd praised her work and her meticulous research methods. It made him look generous. If she'd said anything, she would have appeared ungrateful. It's the way he works . . . *worked*, I mean." He gave me a quick glance. "I don't blame Celia for hating him—and she did. She really did. Sinclair used her like he used everyone else in his life."

"So why wouldn't she have simply left the team?"

"I'd like to know that myself. He must have had some hold over her, but she always denied it." I could see the muscles in his jaw working. "I don't know a single person who's sorry Sinclair is dead."

"What about Dr. Nevin? Had Sinclair done similar things to him?"

Price-Davies made a dismissive sound. "Probably, but Niall's attitude toward Sinclair was something like hero-worship. He was content to live in 'the great man's shadow'"—he put air quotes around the words—"and to take whatever favors Sinclair tossed in his direction. And Sinclair did toss favors. *Bribes.*" He swore softly under his breath.

"I appreciate your honesty," I said, feeling uncomfortable. "And now I must be honest as well. My husband is the SIO, the senior investigating officer, on the Sinclair murder case."

Price-Davies stiffened. "Ivor neglected to mention that."

"The police need this information."

"And you're going to tell them."

"No, I'm not," I said, making a quick decision—one I might regret. "I happen to know the police are in the process of interviewing everyone who knew Sinclair at the university. Your name will be on the list. When they contact you, and when they ask if Sinclair got on with his colleagues, you're going to have to tell the truth."

"And betray Celia."

"You won't, Duncan. Not unless she's guilty."

Chapter Thirty

Long Barston

It was late afternoon by the time I got back to the shop. Ivor took one look at me. "What's wrong?"

"Nothing," I said unconvincingly. "I think your professor friend may have discovered the identity of Egemere Woman. No name, though."

"That's good news. Tell me."

I explained about Henry Wyck's military career and the fact that if his first wife, Matilda, had become pregnant, he couldn't have been the father. "Price-Davies translated a poem and just listen to the title—'The Pearl of Wyck,' written by none other than Henry himself. It was on the list of documents Grenville Dark consulted—not the title, just that it was a poem. I didn't think it would be important. Boy, was I wrong." I pulled out the copy of the poem and the translation.

Ivor read the translation, raising his eyebrows and giving a soft whistle. "I see what you mean."

"Your friend says the Pearl could be both Egemere Woman and the pearl buried with her. Medieval poets liked that kind of ambiguity."

"Which brings us back to the question of why someone would bury a great fortune."

"I don't have an answer for that, but if Henry murdered his wife, maybe giving up the pearl was a kind of penance. People in that time thought they could make atonement for sin by inflicting pain on themselves."

"The poem mentions fate and trying to cheat death, and there's an undercurrent of irony. It reminds me of *Oedipus*. I don't mean the story. I mean the idea of pride as the fatal flaw—that believing he could outrun Fate, Wyck inevitably caused the very thing he was trying to avoid." He handed me the poem. "So, what's troubling you?"

I couldn't tell him about Celia Whybrew and the rival journal articles. "The murder inquiry, I suppose."

He gave me a look. *I don't believe you, but we'll let it go for now.* Aloud he said, "I think I'll walk down to the Chinese takeaway. Pick up something for dinner. Anything for you?"

"Thanks, but I don't know when Tom will be home. You go ahead. I'll finish reading through the catalog proofs and then lock up."

As soon as Ivor left, I began second-guessing myself. Should I really have promised Price-Davies not to tell Tom about Simon Sinclair's betrayal of Celia Whybrew? It gave her a motive—and people have killed for less. Price-Davies admitted that Celia kept her emotions concealed behind a cool exterior. Had she concealed her anger toward Sinclair, allowing the initial spark of resentment to blow up into a full-fledged conflagration? Maybe. The problem was I really liked Celia Whybrew. So did Lady Barbara. That brought another wave of self-doubt. Maybe I should have stayed out of it, not forced Price-Davies to inform the police. It was their job to uncover the truth, not mine.

Coward, said my inner critic.

Mind your own business, I shot back.

Which struck me as funny.

I was still chuckling when Tom texted to say he'd booked a table for six PM at the Three Magpies. Perfect, I texted back. *See you soon. xxx*

I started on the catalog proofs but couldn't focus. My mind was on Tom and what, if anything, I *could* tell him without violating my promise to Price-Davies. Finally, I gave up and wasted forty-five minutes searching for *Henry Wyck* on the internet. There were seven of them living happily in Suffolk.

* * *

Once again, Tom beat me to the pub. He was waiting for me in the bar. "We were lucky to get a table," he said. "Saturday night. They squeezed us in."

"I'm glad. I didn't feel like cooking tonight."

The pub owners, Jayne Collier and her husband, Gavin, had a rare weekend off, we were told. One of the newer waitresses showed us to a corner table. "Sourdough and olives on the way," she said, filling our glasses with water from a chilled carafe. "I can recommend tonight's special—breast of chicken, pan-seared with wild mushrooms, garlic, and shallots, flamed with vermouth and finished with brown sugar and fresh lemon. Served with new potatoes and green beans."

Who in their right mind could resist that? We both ordered the chicken and paired it with glasses of sauvignon blanc.

"How did it go today with Duncan Price-Davies?" Tom asked.

"Pretty well, actually." I decided I could tell Tom one thing. "Duncan told me he and Celia Whybrew were seeing each other. She broke it off."

"That's interesting, but what did he say about the fourteenth century?"

I told him what I'd learned about Henry Wyck and his poem. "Egemere Woman could be 'The Pearl of Wyck,' and she could be Henry Wyck's first wife, Matilda, the one who was abducted. Or she could be someone else entirely—a mystery woman like Shakespeare's Dark Lady. I still don't know who killed whom or why, but at least I'll have something to tell Alex Belcourt. There's less than a week left in our contract."

"If he wants to extend the contract, will you agree?"

"If there's a chance I might learn more. Price-Davies is going to search the court records. If he finds anything, he'll text me."

"You're interested, though, aren't you?"

"Of course. I love information, and I love solving mysteries. Speaking of which, how are you coming with the murder investigation?"

"Which one?"

"Either—both."

"The Thetford case is going nowhere. There've been no further sightings of Derek Quinn. He's holed up somewhere."

"The Sinclair murder?"

"There I do have news—such as it is. The tests on Sinclair's body and clothing came back. No surprises. Pretty much what we expected to find." He took a drink of his wine. "More importantly, the crime-scene team found the murder weapon a half mile away. A wooden mallet with Sinclair's blood and hair on it. Part of the archaeological equipment."

"No fingerprints, I assume. Have you interviewed Sinclair's colleagues in Norwich yet?

"Next week."

I looked at him. "There's something I can't tell you."

"Oh?" Tom looked amused. "So you thought you'd announce it?"

"You'll find out what it is when you interview Sinclair's colleagues at the university. It could be important."

"You promised someone not to pass along information."

"I thought it was best at the time. Now I'm not so sure."

"I assume it has to do with Dr. Price-Davies."

"I didn't say that."

Tom opened his mouth to reply, but at that very moment, the door to the pub opened, and the rector, Edmund Foxe, and his very pregnant wife, Angela, entered. Seeing us, they waved.

Edmund consulted the bartender, who shook his head. No available tables.

"Let's ask them to join us," I said to Tom. "We can just about fit in two more chairs."

Tom approached the bar and shook hands with Edmund, reaching around to clap him on the back. "Why not join us?" He looked at the bartender. "If you can feed two more diners."

They could, and one of the young waiters brought two chairs from the dining room.

Angela looked lovely but tired. "I had a full schedule today," she said as she lowered herself into her seat. "I couldn't face cooking, so we thought we'd take a chance."

"Where's Hattie?" The rectory housekeeper, Hattie Nuthall, was a wonderful cook, rivaling even Lady Barbara's Francie Jewell.

"Gone for two weeks. Her older sister in Cambridge just got home from hospital. She lives by herself and can't yet manage without help."

"You really are on your own then."

"I'm managing. I just wish we'd thought to book a table ahead."

"It turned out for the best, didn't it?" Tom said. "Now we can spend an evening with you. By the way, we just ordered the special—lemon chicken. It sounds amazing."

Edmund signaled the waitress. "Two more orders of chicken," he said. "Mineral water with lemon for my wife. Half pint of Suffolk's Finest for me."

"How are you—besides tired?" I asked Angela.

"I'm fine."

"Blooming," Edmund said, putting his arm around his wife's shoulders. "The doctor says she's healthy as a horse and on schedule to deliver in mid-August, which is why I've agreed to attend the Church of England's General Synod meeting in York next week. It's a big deal, opened by the king. I'm on one of the standing committees. They tell me I'm needed, but I am worried about Angela—with Hattie away."

"You mean if she's called out?"

"Exactly. It's getting harder for her to manage on her own."

"Better now than next month," Angela said, poking a finger into Edmund's chest. "I'm not having this baby alone."

"Wouldn't miss it for all the standing committees in England." Edmund kissed her hand.

"You can always call me," I said. "We made a pretty good team last time."

"Last time?" Edmund asked.

"The alpaca farm." Angela broke off a piece of the sourdough and dipped it in the olive oil. "Didn't I tell you? Kate went with me. Drove the car. Carried all the equipment."

"Would you, Kate?" Edmund looked relieved. "I mean, could you be 'on call,' so to speak? You do realize veterinary emergencies don't often happen during working hours."

"Kate's terrific in an emergency," Tom said, smiling. "I could I tell you stories." He gave my hand a squeeze.

"Of course I'll be on call," I said. "Any time—day or night. In fact, I'll make a point of keeping my phone near me until Edmund gets back from York."

"What about your work?" Angela asked.

"No problem there. Ivor would insist."

With that settled, we spent the rest of the evening telling baby stories and coming up with silly names for Baby Foxe. Swift-Brown was the winner.

I had no doubt that Edmund and Angela had already decided on names. And I had no doubt they were going to be amazing parents.

Chapter Thirty-One

Sunday, July 6
Ravenswyck Court

With the police investigation ongoing, the archaeological team was preparing to take a break before the next student dig. In light of this, Ivor and I requested a final look at the grave goods. We'd been finalizing our comprehensive report, which included not only our appraisals but also our (mostly Ivor's) recommendations for cleaning, restoration, preservation, and display. That was his area of expertise, not mine, but man, was I learning a lot. One piece of good news was that the CMBA board had authorized the cleaning of the silver cuff. The lab in Cambridge had made arrangements to pick it up.

In the meantime, the archaeologists, Celia Whybrew, Niall Nevin, Mark Lambe, and Tamzin Oliver, had been filing their various reports with the CMBA board and reorganizing the field office caravan in preparation for the incoming students. Next term, in September, Dr. Nevin would take Dr. Sinclair's place as both head archaeologist and finds manager. Celia, who might have taken the job herself, decided instead to continue working with the students. She loved it and was good at it. Mark and Tamzin had agreed to return as supervisors. Given Mark Lambe's as-yet-unproven plague-pit theory, the best news was that the CMBA, on Celia's recommendation, had decided to make excavations on the mound their new focus. Dr. Nevin, in a complete about-face, agreed.

Ivor and I met the team, all but Dr. Nevin, at the Ravenswyck museum, which, because of the murder, had been temporarily closed to the public. Mark and Tamzin had laid out the grave goods again, including the pearl. I wouldn't tell them about "The Pearl of Wyck" until I'd had a chance to report to Alex Belcourt.

I was bracing for another of my episodes when Celia said, "You asked about the finds lists, Kate. Are you still interested in seeing them?"

When I said I was, she added, "I thought you'd say that. I've laid out copies of Niall's spreadsheets in the gift shop."

"Go ahead, Kate," Ivor said. "I'll do one final check and meet you there."

Celia had cleared one of the display tables for the database printouts.

"Can you explain your procedure?" I asked.

"Of course. Each dig lasts six weeks. Daily, the students bring their finds to either Mark or Tamzin. Mark compiles a handwritten finds list, and the objects are temporarily stored in the field office safe. At the end of each week, the objects are transferred to the museum safe, and the lists are given to Niall, who enters everything on the official spreadsheet. After verifying and cross-checking, we email the spreadsheets to the CMBA. Finally, at the end of the dig, the senior archaeologists and the students produce an interpretive document, and Niall develops a summary. Over these past six weeks, our students have excavated more than two thousand objects ranging from pottery shards, glass, iron, and non-ferrous metal objects to jewelry, leather and textiles, and portions of the church's stone structure."

"I know the south transept of the church was your focus this time. Do you mind telling me what you were looking for in the 2016 dig?"

"The village itself—mapping the streets and footpaths, the cottages and other structures—reconstructing village life."

"Did you find human remains?"

"No, and we weren't looking for them. Sixty years ago, in the 1960s, a team of archaeologists excavated the church graveyard. They unearthed almost four hundred skeletons, dating from the eleventh through the mid-fourteenth century. They've since been reburied at St. Mary's Church in Hartwell."

"Yes, I heard that. A small hamlet, then."

"Very small, but the excavation made headlines because of what they called 'efforts to resist the living dead.'"

"What does that mean?" I made a face.

"They found evidence of the burning of body parts and the deliberate breaking and mutilating of bones after death."

"Why?"

"Medieval folklore claimed the corpses of people who'd committed evil deeds in life or who were generally disruptive people died with what they thought of as 'a malevolent life force,' which enabled them to rise from the grave at night, spreading disease and attacking any unfortunate person who happened upon them. The way to deal with this, apparently, was to dig up the offending corpse, decapitate or dismember it, and sometimes burn the pieces in a fire. This isn't the only medieval village where such a practice has been documented."

"Good grief. Could that have happened to Egemere Woman?"

"No. Because of the extraordinary preservation of her flesh, we know her fatal wounds were delivered while she was still alive."

"I don't know which is creepier." I was thinking about malevolent life forces. If Dr. Sinclair had died in the fourteenth century, his body would definitely have been dug up and mutilated.

"Anyway, I think the finds lists should be self-explanatory." Celia gave me a warm smile, and once again I felt guilty. If Duncan Price-Davies told the police about the rival journal articles—and I felt sure he would—Celia would be interviewed again by the police. And she would blame me. I tried telling myself I'd had no choice in the matter. Celia had already been questioned about her relationship with Dr. Sinclair. Withholding the information about his betrayal was a choice she'd made, and that could only create suspicion. I also thought about Tom's request. He wanted me to talk to Celia about her time at university—and her unexplained absence. How I might broach the subject was unclear to say the least.

"If you have questions," Celia said, "Niall's finishing up at the field office. He should be here soon."

I thanked her and settled in to study the lists. There were six of them, one for each week of the dig, each several pages long and printed in a tiny font. I began to scan the pages, looking for any mention of gold or—as Celia had put it—"non-ferrous metals."

An hour later, apart from the grave goods, I'd found no mention of gold. And yet according to Celia, someone had found a gold ring and Mark had recorded it. So why hadn't the ring been included in the database?

I was trying to think of an explanation when Celia appeared at the door. "Getting along all right? Any questions?"

"Yes, as a matter of fact. You told me someone found a gold ring, but I don't see it listed anywhere."

She frowned. "Let me take a look." It took her a few minutes to scan the computer printouts. "Maybe I was mistaken. We can ask Mark."

In the museum, Ivor was packing up his gear. Mark and Tamzin were returning the grave goods to the safe.

"Kate's been looking at Niall's finds lists." Celia held them up. "Mark, didn't you tell me someone found a gold ring in one of the trenches?"

He looked up. "One of the students. A little smashed and no stone but definitely gold."

"Why isn't it included on the spreadsheets?"

"It should be. Tam—what week was that? Do you remember?"

"I think it was week four—or maybe three." Tamzin appeared as confused as the others.

Celia handed her both lists. "I think you should check."

Mark and Tamzin examined the lists. "You're right. It's not here," Mark said. "I can't imagine why not. We found a few other gold objects as well—a bit of chain near the old vestry, for one. I know they were on my original list."

"Do you have the original lists?" I asked. "Could we check them?"

"Sure," Mark said. "They're in the safe at the field office. Niall's bringing everything over here." He looked at me. "We always empty the field office safe between terms. Start fresh."

A few minutes later, Nevin appeared, carrying a banker's box. "This is the lot." He dropped the box on the table, wincing. "By the way, did one of you begin clearing out the field office safe?"

"No, why?" The others looked at each other, shaking their heads.

"Never mind. I'm probably mistaken."

"About what, Niall?" Celia asked.

He shrugged. "It looked like someone had been moving things around. Forget it. I'm probably mistaken."

"May we see Mark's original finds lists?" Celia asked.

Nevin frowned. "They weren't in the safe. I thought Mark took them."

"Not me," Mark said.

"Tamzin?" Celia asked.

"Of course not." She looked offended.

"When was the last time you saw them?" I asked Dr. Nevin, earning a curious look from Celia.

"When I last entered the raw data, so . . . a couple of days after the students left."

"There's a discrepancy in the lists," Celia said. "Mark says gold was found."

"Gold?" Nevin looked confused. "There was no gold on Mark's lists."

"Well, I wrote it down," Mark said.

"If you did, someone altered the list," Nevin said, "although I don't know how anyone could tell. They're not easy to read, you know—cross-outs, erasures, revisions. Takes patience to sort through them. You really need to be neater, Mark."

"Neater? I'm not working on a computer, you know. Students are handing me objects, everyone talking at the same time, but I know I documented the gold. Someone changed the lists." He looked at

Tamzin. "But when did that happen? I keep the lists with me at all times—except when they're in the safe."

"We're the only ones with access to the safe," Tamzin pointed out.

"No, we're not," Celia said. "There was someone else."

"Dr. Sinclair," said Mark and Tamzin in unison.

I thought of the box of gold the police had found in Sinclair's room. Had he been stealing gold from the safe and then altering the finds lists to cover the thefts? Was that why he went to the museum the night he was murdered—for gold? But why kill him? Why not just report him to the police?

Whatever the truth, the original finds lists were missing, and that meant the discrepancies couldn't be verified.

I studied the four faces in the room, searching for telltale signs that one or all of them were lying. I didn't see any.

What I did see on Celia's face was satisfaction.

* * *

Manor Farm

Driving home that evening, it occurred to me that Celia must have known or suspected the gold was missing—and she wanted *me* to find it rather than herself. The question was why. Perhaps as the new head of the CMBA, she didn't want to invite questions. Either way, there would now have to be some sort of investigation, and the best outcome for everyone would be to keep it in-house. The publicity thing again. The CMBA was a nonprofit, dependent partly on donations from the public. Who would donate money to an organization whose ex-head had been pilfering?

Tom had been right. I *was* involved in the investigation into Sinclair's murder. I knew the prime suspects personally, had conversations with them, heard things they would never tell the police. My dual role as an antiquities expert and private investigator gave me an advantage. Tom considered me an asset. I hoped I was, but my concern was that Tom's team—actually, DI Amy Cartwright—didn't appreciate my involvement. My conversation with Duncan Price-Davies, for example, had uncovered important evidence, evidence that had been withheld from the police. How had Cartwright reacted to that? I decided I should say something to Tom. Warn him. My husband was the very best of men, and he knew policing, but he could be a bit naïve when it came to women.

I was surprised to see his car in the drive.

"Home early?" I called out as I entered the house. I laid my briefcase on the kitchen table and went in search of him.

I found him in the sitting room, his computer open on his lap. "Hullo, darling." He patted the sofa. "Come, sit. I want to show you something." He turned the computer screen toward me. "What would you think about a weekend away—just the two of us? Look at this place."

He'd pulled up the website of an exquisite and pricey self-catering property near one of Suffolk's nature reserves. "It looks amazing," I said, "but don't you have two murders to solve?"

"I know." He sighed. "Just thinking about it makes me feel better."

"What's wrong?" I reached over and stroked his hair.

"You mean besides budget cuts, a lack of resources, tensions on the team, intrusive journalism, public pressure, and the unrealistic expectations of headquarters?" He gave a bitter laugh. "Actually, it's Cartwright. She asked to see me today. She said I don't trust her, that I've been undermining her, taking interviews myself and giving Ren and Marsh more responsibility than they deserve." His eyes shifted. "She also mentioned you."

"I'm not surprised. Is she right?"

"Probably, but she's not a team player, Kate. She's ambitious—not a bad thing in a cop, but her ambition is for herself, not the team. If I'm honest, I really don't trust her—not the way I trust the others. I hadn't realized it showed. Now I'll have to decide what to do about it. She's on the team, and that isn't likely to change anytime soon."

"What did you say to her?"

"I said her concerns were valid and that I'd consider them seriously. I also said she would do better to treat her colleagues as team members, not rivals. She isn't well liked, Kate. She's prickly, easily offended, slow to let things go. She's not lacking in intelligence or skills. It's her attitude. Unless she's willing to change, I'm afraid she's not going to make it in CID."

"I'm sorry," I said, thankful that Tom had introduced the subject himself. He would be fair, but he would think first of his team. "What happened today—besides Amy Cartwright?"

"Based on what you *didn't* tell me"—he smiled—"I sent DS Ren to interview Duncan Price-Davies. Luckily, he was willing to talk. Eager to get it over with, I suspect. We know about Celia Whybrew and the journal articles. She was foolish not to tell us. We're going to interview her again, first thing in the morning."

"Oh." I felt a wave of guilt. "I'm sure I've ruined our relationship."

"You haven't, as a matter of fact. Price-Davies kept your name out of it. The three of us are the only ones who know you pressured—well, let's say *encouraged* him to tell Ren."

"I knew I liked him," I said, "and for the record, I didn't pressure him."

"I'd already asked DS Ren to conduct the interview with Dr. Whybrew. I think that's what set Cartwright off. She wants to be the one to solve the case."

"She reminds me of Simon Sinclair."

"Bottom line—I had to backtrack, tell Ren that Cartwright will now be in charge of the interview."

"How did he take it?"

"Like the team player he is."

I stood. "What do you want for dinner?"

"What have we've got?"

"Smoked salmon and a green salad?"

"Perfect."

We made supper together and continued to talk.

"Remember the box of gold you found in Sinclair's room at The Forge?" I drizzled some of Tom's special lemon dressing on my salad. "I searched through the official finds lists from the dig today—printouts that Niall Nevin produces from a database he keeps. No gold was listed, even though Mark Lambe insisted that several pieces had certainly been found. And that's not all. Sometime in the last two weeks, Mark's handwritten finds lists disappeared from the field office safe."

"How did Nevin explain that? Doesn't he work from Mark's lists?"

"He said the gold wasn't on the lists, although he admitted there were cross-outs and erasures. Someone altered the lists, and they all assume it was Sinclair. I didn't mention the CCTV images of Sinclair at the museum."

"Good, but if Sinclair removed gold from the safe, he didn't do it that night. First, the image doesn't show him carrying anything. And second, the timing doesn't work. No gold was found on his body, and he wouldn't have had time to return to The Forge to stash it before heading over to the dig site."

"Maybe he found gold in the field office safe."

"If he did, the killer must have taken it."

"There's something else. I got the impression Celia already knew about the missing gold and was glad it had come out. They all suspect Dr. Sinclair. What I can't figure out is why that would have gotten him killed."

My mobile pinged with a text.

"It's Ivor," I said, reading the text. "He says Edlyn Dark contacted him. Her father has stopped communicating. She blames us."

"What does she expect you to do?"

"Apologize. Explain we weren't trying to steal his research."

"Apologize to a computerized image?"

"I know."

"I don't suppose Ivor asked her about an interview with me."

"Not exactly the ideal time. Tom," I put down the pepper grinder. "Do you think Ivor and I should go back to Edlyn's cottage?"

"Absolutely.

I texted Ivor.

"What about Derek Quinn?" I asked.

"Still no new sightings."

"He must not have heard Willow's TV appeal."

"I think he did, Kate. I think he's laying low, considering his options. He has to know the police all over Suffolk are looking for him. I think he's found somewhere he feels safe."

"Or he was so desperate he—" I pictured the face of Willow's little daughter and couldn't finish the sentence.

"Let's hope not," Tom said, understanding my unspoken fear. "If what Willow told us is true, there's a chance the charges against Quinn will be downgraded to involuntary manslaughter."

"I just hope he doesn't do something stupid."

Chapter Thirty-Two

Monday, July 7
Long Barston

Our preview copy of the auction catalog arrived in the morning mail. This time, instead of just text, full-color photographs were included. On Friday the catalog would be mailed out to interested collectors and dealers all over the planet. A week after that, it would be available online.

I perched on a stool behind the sales counter and sipped a cup of dark roast while thumbing through the photos. This was going to be some auction. Most of the sellers were galleries and shops like ours in the British Isles, but a number of objects were being offered for sale by individual collectors or pickers. Still others represented the estates of wealthy individuals. These were often the most intriguing, the collections having been out of the public eye for decades, even lifetimes. All the items dated from the Roman occupation of Britain. The conquering armies had settled in, brought their families over, and made themselves thoroughly at home, recreating the culture of their homeland.

One object caught my eye—a bronze oil lamp from the second century AD in the form of a seated satyr with a laughing face, pointed ears, and a long beard. I was about to put a sticky note on the photo when I noticed the estimated sale price was ten to fifteen thousand British pounds.

"See anything you want to buy?" Ivor strolled in, chewing a piece of buttered toast.

"Want or can afford?"

"Want, of course." Ivor waggled his eyebrows. "We can always find the cash for something really important." He looked over my shoulder at the catalog. "Jeff Swift has some items in the auction." Jeff was the picker Ivor had met with the Friday before last, the one we trusted and had dealt with for some time. His main business was selling to dealers and a few private customers, but sometimes, if he'd acquired something really special, he would offer it at auction himself. "Jeff's pieces are mostly miniature bronzes, small marbles, and jewelry," Ivor said. "He has a source, a collector who wishes to remain anonymous. Posh bloke. Family stuff."

"Show me."

The objects offered by Jeff Swift were on pages thirty-four through thirty-six. I was looking through them when my mouth dropped open. "Ivor—look at that earring. Is that what I think it is?"

Item number 268 was a single earring, a fishhook holding an oval frame of hammered gold, fringed with gold beading. Suspended from the bottom was a gold ring that ended in a small natural pearl. The bezel held an agate intaglio, the stone engraved with the image of the Roman god Mercury. The winning bid was expected to be in the neighborhood of three thousand pounds.

"Well, well," Ivor said. "We've seen that image before, haven't we?"

"The intaglio in Simon Sinclair's ring."

"I'd have to examine both stones to be certain, compare the carving quality and patina, but they look to me like a matched pair. Do you see that lighter banding on the left side? There was an identical banding on the right side of Sinclair's ring. I think they came from the same rock."

"I've seen the setting before, too, Ivor. The police found it in a box of gold jewelry parts in Sinclair's room at The Forge." He raised his eyebrows, and I said, "That's confidential, by the way."

"At some point, the earrings must have become separated. I wonder who owned this second one?"

"Could you ask Jeff?" This felt like too much of a coincidence.

"Jeff's an old friend. If he can give me a name, he will." Ivor went to his computer and tapped out an email.

I closed the catalog. "When does Edlyn Dark expect us to apologize to her father?"

"As soon as possible. I felt sorry for her. Those computer conversations were a lifeline. She feels as if she's lost her father a second time."

"Whoever did that to her, making her believe her father was really speaking, has no conscience," I said. "I can't imagine what they'd get out of it, except to confuse a vulnerable old lady."

"I agree, although how we're going to deliver an apology is a mystery. I thought we might close early today and drive to Hartwell. We should be back by five thirty. Does that suit?"

"Sure. Let's get it over with. And Ivor—"

"Yes?"

"If we get a chance to bring up Tom, you take charge. You might be able to persuade her to talk to him. I think Edlyn has taken a shine to you."

"I do seem to have that effect on women."

At three, we were preparing to leave for Hartwell when the shop door burst open. Vivian Bunn marched in followed by Lady Barbara.

"They've arrested her." Vivian stood, her face flushed, her hands on her hips.

"Who?" I asked.

"Celia, of course," said Lady Barbara, who'd been trained never to raise her voice except in the case of imminent death. "She's being held at the police station in Hartwell."

"You have to do something," Vivian said.

"Why did they arrest her?" Ivor asked.

"I can't imagine," Vivian said. "She hasn't done anything."

How Vivian would know this was beside the point. "How did you find out?"

"She phoned Dr. Nevin. He phoned Mark and Tamzin, Tamzin phoned me."

"And Vivian phoned me." Lady Barbara's voice quavered. "We really must do something. Get her a lawyer. Protest. *Something.*"

I remembered that DI Cartwright had been scheduled to interview Celia that morning about the journal articles. I felt sick. *Had Celia confessed to murder?*

Lady Barbara pulled out a white handkerchief. Vivian, who denied even possessing a soft spot, coughed to cover a sob.

"All right," I said. "Let's calm down. I'm sure Tom wouldn't have let this happen if there had been any alternative. Maybe Celia hasn't been arrested, just questioned. I know they're interviewing several people for a third time."

"Nope," Vivian said. "They've arrested her. She was cautioned. They're keeping her on remand."

"Did they charge her with something?" Ivor asked.

"I don't know." Vivian waved away the question. "What's the difference? She's being held prisoner. They'll do a mug shot, take fingerprints, treat her like a common criminal."

"We're on our way to Hartwell," Lady Barbara said. "We thought you might want to come along, dear. You might be able to talk to your husband." Her eyes filled.

"Ivor, you'll have to tell Edlyn Dark we can't meet her today." I looked at the two elderly women. "Come on, you two. I'll drive."

* * *

By the time we got to the police station in Hartwell, Celia Whybrew was already being released. DI Cartwright and DS Ren were there. So was Tom, and he appeared to be apologizing. "We really are very sorry, Dr. Whybrew. I'm afraid this whole thing has been an unfortunate misunderstanding."

DI Cartwright was fuming.

DS Ren handed Celia her handbag.

"My solicitor is on the way," Celia said. "He's going to charge me for his time, you know."

"Ren," Tom said, "provide Dr. Whybrew with a claims form and her reference number." To Celia, he said, "Again, I apologize. You can claim compensation. I hope you do. May we offer you a ride back to The Forge?"

"I'll wait for my solicitor, thank you," Celia said in a clipped tone. She noticed Lady Barbara and Vivian. "You two shouldn't have come." She must have seen their faces because she added, "Oh, I do appreciate it." She reached out and touched Lady Barbara's shoulder. "Thank you."

"I knew Tom would straighten things out," Lady Barbara said kindly.

"I should hope so," Vivian huffed. "Kate, perhaps you'll drive us all back to Finchley Hall. Poor Celia needs some liquid reinforcement." I had no doubt she meant one of her tea toddies.

Tom caught my eye. *I'd like you to stay if you can.*

"We'd be a bit squashed in my Mini," I said.

"I'll wait for my solicitor," Celia said. "He'll want to speak with me in private."

"I left my car at the antiquities shop," Vivian said. "You can drop us off there, Kate."

"DI Cartwright will drive you," Tom said before I had a chance to respond. "I've asked Kate to stay, and I'm sure you two have better things to do than hang around a police station."

"We all have better things to do," Celia said tartly.

"I'm sure DI Cartwright would like to apologize," Tom said. "Wouldn't you, Amy?"

Cartwright shot him a furious look before turning to Celia. "I apologize for any inconvenience I may have caused." The words came out through clenched teeth.

"Ren," Tom said, "would you show Dr. Whybrew into the room with the sofa and chairs? Make her comfortable. Get her something to drink. Let her know when her solicitor arrives."

When they'd all gone, Tom and I moved into one of the empty offices. "What happened here?"

"Cartwright overstepped her authority. She made a mistake—a bad one."

"Why?"

"I assume her eagerness to solve Sinclair's murder overpowered her better judgment. You know I decided to let her run the interview, but when Celia admitted withholding the information about Sinclair's journal article, Cartwright cautioned her and advised her to call an attorney. Then, without consulting me, Cartwright booked her on suspicion of Sinclair's murder. It was uncalled for, Kate. There was never any real evidence of wrongdoing, nothing that would stand up in court. Cartwright was grandstanding, and it was a serious breach of procedure. If this becomes public, the police will look overzealous and incompetent." He shook his head. "It's a disaster."

"I'm sorry, Tom. Does this mean Celia isn't a suspect?"

"It does not. We haven't ruled anyone out yet, especially not Celia Whybrew—which doesn't mean we're ready to charge her."

"What will happen to DI Cartwright?"

"I'll have to report this. She'll probably be suspended, pending a hearing." There was regret in his voice. "The best she can hope for is a transfer."

"Sounds good to me." Through the office window I caught a glimpse of DI Cartwright wedging herself into the driver's seat of a small panda car. I was glad I wasn't with them. I could only imagine the conversation on the way to Long Barston. I had no doubt Vivian was planning to deliver a few home truths.

Tom had perched himself on the edge of the metal desk. "Thanks for staying behind."

"Of course. But why?"

"Celia Whybrew. She might talk to you." He dashed to the door as DS Ren walked past carrying a steaming cup. He took the mug and handed it to me. "It's worth a shot."

* * *

I knocked softly on the door of the small interview room—the one they used for witnesses, not suspects.

"Come in."

"Tea—milk and two sugars." I smiled as warmly as I could.

"Thanks." Celia took the mug and cradled it in her hands. "I didn't have time for this, you know. We're beginning to pack up to leave, and I've lost an entire afternoon."

"Tom is very sorry."

"I don't blame him, but that DI of his is a piece of work. I omitted to mention something that happened years ago, and she decided I was guilty of Simon's murder." Celia blew on the steaming cup.

"Things that happened in the past can be relevant," I said, trying to figure out a way to broach the subject of her unexplained absence from the doctoral program. "Carrie Holgate's death, for example." I wasn't sure where I was going with this, but the words kept coming. "That's the problem with life. Something happens, and it stays with us forever."

"*Damn.*" Celia had spilled some of the hot tea on her lap.

I grabbed tissues from a box on the side table to help her mop up the liquid, but when I did, I saw she was weeping. "Celia, what's wrong?"

She shook her head. "I've had a few things in my life." She wiped away tears. "And you're right. They never leave you."

I moved beside her on the sofa and spoke as gently as I could. "As part of the investigation, the police have looked into the backgrounds of everyone involved, including you. Standard procedure. They know you had a hard time at university, that you left your course abruptly and didn't return for many months." I watched to see her reaction.

"And Tom allowed you to ask me about it," she said with a small, sad smile. "Kind of him, really."

"If it has no bearing on Dr. Sinclair's death, they'll let it go—I promise. They're not out to hurt you or humiliate you, but they have to know. Police are like that, and this is a murder investigation. It might be best to get it over with." I handed her several clean tissues.

"You're right." She wiped her eyes and blew her nose. After taking a couple of deep breaths, she met my gaze. "Fourteen years ago I was beginning my doctoral program. Simon was my advisor. I fell for him—it's as prosaic as that. We had an affair, all very hush-hush, of course. I became pregnant. He wanted me to terminate. I couldn't do it, and he agreed as long as I consented to give the baby up for adoption. Which I did, and I don't regret that. There was no way I could have cared for a child at that time. She was a girl." She lifted her mug and took a long drink. Then she cleared her throat and began again. "I'm thirty-six now, almost thirty-seven. My chances of ever having a child are poor, and I find . . . I *find* that I want more than anything in the world to know the daughter I gave away." She waved a hand in front of her face. "I don't want to ruin her life or come between her and her adoptive parents. I'm grateful to them. She'd be fourteen now, a teenager. I just want to see her, and when the time is right, when she's eighteen, if she wants to know me—" She shrugged and broke off, tears springing to her eyes again.

"I'm sorry," I said, "but what does this have to do with Simon?"

"Both biological parents have to agree to end their anonymity. Simon refused to give his consent."

"Is that the reason for your interaction at the Six Bells?"

"You heard about that, did you? It's true—and I was so angry. I wanted to follow him out of the pub, shake him, force him to agree."

"Did you follow him, Celia?"

"I considered it, but he'd had so much to drink. I decided to wait and try later."

"Where did you go?"

"Back to The Forge as I've already testified." She gave me a sad smile. "I lied about going right to sleep. I couldn't. I stayed up for hours, writing a letter to my daughter. One she'll probably never see."

DS Ren poked his head around the door. "Your solicitor's here, Dr. Whybrew. He'd like a word."

Celia stood and brushed off her damp skirt. "I'm glad I told you, Kate. And I'm glad Simon's dead. Now I'm free to do whatever I choose."

I wasn't glad—not one little bit. Because Celia Whybrew had just given herself the perfect motive for murder.

Chapter Thirty-Three

Tuesday, July 8
Hartwell

"First you say you're coming, then you say you're not coming, and now here you are." Edlyn Dark stood scowling in the doorway of her cottage.

"We're sorry to disturb you," Ivor said. "May we come in?"

Edlyn stood there for a few seconds as if debating the question. Then she stood aside and allowed us to enter. "You'll have to wait while I take the pot off the hob."

"Of course," I said. "Take your time."

She disappeared for a few minutes, then returned. "This isn't like Father." Her lips quavered. "We were such good friends always, the two of us. I can't lose him."

"When exactly did he stop communicating?" Ivor asked. It was a good question.

"A week ago, right after you were here. That was our last conversation."

"Have you checked the computer?" Ivor asked. "Is it plugged in?"

"I'm not an idiot."

"Of course not. Faulty connections can happen."

"Well, let's find out." She led us into the small, wood-paneled study.

Ivor located the power cord. "You're right. It's plugged in. Perhaps the internal battery has failed. Try turning it on."

"It isn't the computer. It's Father." She clicked on the Windows start button. The same blue screen appeared and the same warning about a fatal exception. Then she pressed a key as she had before, but this time nothing happened.

"Did you press the right key?" I asked.

"Same one as always. He isn't there."

I couldn't argue with that. "Did anything else happen after our last visit?"

"Like what?"

"I don't know. Did you . . ." I tried to think. "Did you call the computer guy again?"

"Why would I?"

"Let me take a look," Ivor said. He sat at the desk and tried pushing a few more keys. Nothing happened. The blue screen remained. "Let's turn the computer off and back on. That works sometimes."

"I've done that ten or twelve times."

"Let's try once more."

She did with the same result.

Ivor tried typing something onto the blue screen, but no words appeared. "Maybe your father can hear us," he said. "Mr. Dark, Ivor Tweedy here. I'm visiting your daughter, Edlyn, again, with Ms. Kate Hamilton—the one who's researching Egemere Close, remember? We spoke last week about the archaeological dig. You said a body would be found. You were right. We'd like to thank you for the advance warning and apologize if we've done anything to offend you. Edlyn would very much like to continue your little chats. Would that be possible?"

We waited and watched the screen. Apart from a slight blip, which was probably due to Edlyn's internet access, nothing happened.

"Father, please." Edlyn spoke into the screen. "Please talk to me."

Again, there was no response, which was for once, I reminded myself, entirely normal. Nevertheless, I felt sorry for Edlyn Dark.

"I'd like you to leave," she said. "This is your fault. I should sue you."

"I can understand how you feel," Ivor said, "and we apologize if we've done anything to cause this. You told us before, but would you explain again exactly how this all came about?"

Edlyn sniffed, pulled a tissue from the sleeve of her cardigan, and blew her nose. "I don't know what good it will do. I was attempting to download father's files so I could transfer them to my new computer, but I kept getting warnings about operating systems and security issues. Some kind of update was required, but I couldn't make sense of it, so I called the computer lab at the university."

"Which university?" Ivor asked.

"East Anglia, naturally. Father's alma mater. They sent out an expert, but he couldn't help. He said the hard drive had failed, and the files were irretrievable. I suppose he felt sorry for me, so he helped me set up my new computer. He asked if I wanted him to take the old computer away, but I said no. It was all I had left of Father. He understood."

"Do you remember his name?"

Edlyn wrinkled her nose. "No. He left his mobile number. Said if I had any problems with my new computer, I should call him directly."

"Have you called him?"

"No. I will now, after what you've done." She gave us a stern look. "If I can find that piece of paper."

"We should leave you now so you can have your supper," Ivor said. "Do you still have my card?"

"Yes."

"Will you get in touch if your find the number for your computer technician?"

"So you can warn him off?"

"We wouldn't think of such a thing. I might need him myself one day." Ivor held up one finger. "By the way, Kate's husband, Tom, would very much like to see your computer and talk to you about all this. May I have him phone you—or text?"

"No."

We followed her to the door.

She gave us the kind of look one might give a teenager who'd just egged your house. "I am going to sue you."

* * *

Back in the car, Ivor said, "Something fishy going on there."

I laughed. "You think?"

"Father stopped communicating right after our visit. Whoever's doing this must have got the wind up." He clicked his seatbelt. "I still think it's some kind of grief bot."

"How could a computer repair guy install a grief bot on her father's old computer?"

"I don't know."

"And if he did, why shut it down now?"

"Yes, that part is puzzling. Unless he knows we're on to him—or them. There might be more than one person behind this."

"We are on to him," I said. "If Edlyn can find that phone number, we'll know who it is."

"What I want to know is why. What was this person's motivation? To drive her over the edge?"

"No." A thought occurred to me, one that finally made sense. "What was Father's main message?"

"Stop the dig. The spirits of the dead are not amused. Someone will die."

"Exactly. I think the person who did this wanted to stop the dig."

"Why?"

"I don't know. To stop the desecration of human remains? To discredit the archaeologists? To hurt Dr. Sinclair?"

"And when it didn't work, they killed him?"

"It's the only thing I can think of at the moment."

"There is one thing we can do. It's only five o'clock." Ivor typed something into his mobile phone. "Someone will be at the computer lab at UEA." A few moments later he looked up. "There seems to be more than one lab. Most are attached to one of the colleges. Private."

"Isn't there one the public could access?"

"There's one called 'Student, Faculty, and Staff IT Support.' Maybe they reach out to the public as well."

"Try it."

Ivor tapped in the numbers and put his phone on speaker. Someone answered almost immediately. "Computer lab," said a youngish male voice. Probably a student.

"Hello. I have a question about computers. I'd like to speak with someone in your repair department."

The voice was directed away from the phone. "Some guy wants to speak to our repair department." Raucous laughter.

Another voice, male but older, came on the line. "Sorry, mate. We don't make house calls." More laughter.

We heard a click, and the line went dead.

* * *

Manor Farm

"Do you see those bright stars?" Tom asked me. We'd taken our decaf coffee out to the stone patio. "It's called the Summer Triangle. Do you see it in the States?"

"I don't know," I said. "I've never heard of it."

"Vega is on the right." He pointed out a star with a bluish tint. "Look up from there to Deneb at the apex, then down to Altair on the left. Each is an alpha star, the brightest star in their individual constellations."

"I didn't know you were an amateur astronomer."

"I'm not. I've just always been fascinated. Uncle Nigel had a powerful telescope. He taught me about the stars and the constellations." As a boy, Tom had spent his summers at his uncle Nigel Hartley's country house deep in rural Devon. "Those three stars make up the Lyra constellation. Do you know the story?"

"No, tell me." I leaned back against him.

"It's Roman mythology. Orpheus, the son of Apollo, played the lyre so beautifully he could charm the wild creatures, make the trees and rocks dance, and divert the course of rivers. He fell in love with a beautiful wood nymph, Eurydice. When she died of a snake bite, Orpheus descended into the underworld to rescue her, playing his lyre. The melodies charmed the king and queen of the underworld, who agreed to let him take Eurydice back with him. But he broke his promise not to look back until they'd reached the surface. Eurydice was lost forever, and Orpheus, overwhelmed with grief, died, although his lyre continued to play mournful music. To honor Orpheus, Zeus set the lyre in the sky, creating the constellation Lyra."

We were silent for a moment.

"Orpheus couldn't live knowing he'd caused Eurydice's death," I said. "Reminds me of that poem, 'The Pearl of Wyck.'"

"And Egemere Woman—so beautiful someone went to great lengths to preserve her body."

"We don't know she was beautiful, Tom. She wasn't that well preserved. But she must have been loved. I'm still curious about why she was buried with a priceless pearl."

"An attempt to atone for killing her?"

"That's what I thought."

"What will you tell Alex Belcourt? Your contract ends in two days."

"I'm still waiting to hear from Duncan Price-Davies. If the court records from that time tell us nothing, I'm at a dead end. I can tell him what I suspect, but I'm not entirely convinced myself." I placed my empty cup and saucer on the wicker arm of the sofa. "Will you interview Celia Whybrew again?"

"After what she told you, of course." He reached over and ruffled my hair. "I told you she'd talk to you."

"And she knew I'd have to tell you. That was brave of her." I curled my feet under me. "Is there anything new in the Carrie Holgate case?"

"We're still waiting for DNA results on her unborn child. Fast-tracked."

"I thought getting viable DNA from the fetus was unlikely."

"But not impossible." He took another sip of his coffee. "They called in an expert at retrieving DNA in challenging circumstances."

"That's encouraging."

The sounds of our English garden were as mesmerizing as Orpheus's lyre. Frogs croaked. Crickets chirped. A rustling in the undergrowth revealed the movements of some small creature, making its way home. Safely, I hoped.

"You know I'm no technology expert," I said, "but I've been thinking about Edlyn Dark and her father's so-called warnings. Oh—and she won't see you. Ivor tried." I'd already told him about our visit and Ivor's attempt to contact the computer lab at the university. "The image of Grenville Dark said if the archaeologists didn't stop the dig, someone would die, and someone did—Dr. Sinclair."

"Are you saying the person who created the image knew in advance that Dr. Sinclair would be murdered—or did it himself?"

"I don't know, but Ivor and I actually heard the image say another body would be found, and it was Carrie Holgate. But how could he . . . *it* possibly know the CMBA would approve the test pit on the mound?"

"Coincidences do happen," Tom said.

"Twice?"

"You have a point."

"Tom," I said as two separate thoughts unexpectedly linked up in my brain, "what if the murder of Carrie Holgate nine years ago and the murder of Simon Sinclair really are connected?"

"You mean the same killer?"

"Not necessarily. Just connected in some way."

"Which points to the senior archaeologists. They were here in 2016."

"So was Alex Belcourt. And Peter Eley."

"Motive, means, opportunity," Tom said. "In both cases, all the suspects had the means and the opportunity."

"That's not true in the Sinclair case, Tom. Niall Nevin was working on his computer until the wee hours. Mark heard the printer. Why would he make up a detail like that?"

"He wouldn't unless they were working together."

"Do you believe that?"

"Not really. The problem is and always has been motive. We never did have a motive for Carrie Holgate's death. Now we know she was pregnant. That puts a different light on things."

"In Sinclair's case, everyone had a motive. Sinclair was blocking Mark Lambe's thesis and therefore his degree. He'd attacked Tamzin Oliver. He bullied Niall Nevin."

"And as long as Sinclair was alive, Celia Whybrew would never have a chance to know her daughter."

I must have groaned because Tom took my hand and squeezed it. "You have nothing to feel bad about, darling. This is about finding the truth. Just like your fourteenth-century woman. The truth."

"It's just so confusing."

"Uncle Nigel told me something once. A quote from the astronomer Galileo, I think. 'All truths are easy to understand once they are discovered. The point is to discover them.'"

Chapter Thirty-Four

Wednesday, July 9
Long Barston

The sun was out again, and the day promised to be one of those legendary English summer days.

The weather had been fine for so many days in a row, people were starting to take it for granted.

Ivor and I spent most of the morning emailing customers who we thought might be interested in the Roman antiquities auction but who might not have subscribed to the online catalogs. They weren't cheap. At eleven thirty Ivor left for an appointment in the village—a widow he'd dealt with many times over the years. They'd become friends. Nearly crippled with arthritis, she was slowly divesting herself of the antiques she'd inherited from her parents, the money allowing her to remain in her lovely, thatched cottage on the village green. She would give him lunch.

I'd promised myself to put Celia Whybrew and murder out of my mind, but my resolve was shattered when at twelve fifteen, I received a phone call from Duncan Price-Davies.

"Can you talk," he said, "or shall I call back later?"

"I can talk." I had to say something about Celia and the sooner the better. "Duncan," I said, feeling awkward, "thank you for keeping my name out of things with Celia. I wasn't sure you'd want to speak to me after that." I wondered if Celia had told him about her early pregnancy. He hadn't mentioned it.

"I admit I was angry," he said, "but it didn't take me long to realize that I was the one who'd volunteered the information about the journal articles. You didn't pull it out of me. And I'm not the only one at the university who knew about the incident with Sinclair. If I didn't tell the police, someone else would have done. I also realized that once I gave you the information, you had no choice. I appreciate you letting me be the one to tell the police."

I'd been impressed with Price-Davies before. Now I was amazed at his openness and honesty. Why Celia had stopped seeing him, I couldn't imagine. "I suppose you heard about Celia's arrest."

"She phoned me." He almost sounded pleased. "And I've phoned you because I have news. As soon as we hang up, I'm going to email you information from the eyre court records for the year 1348. Too complicated to go into over the phone. You can read for yourself. Rather than translate the Latin, which would take too much time, I've summarized the relevant portions."

"You mentioned the eyres before. I'm not familiar with the term."

"Eyres were the circuit courts in medieval England. Judges were periodically sent out from Westminster to preside over local matters. They dealt with all sorts of legal cases, especially serious criminal offenses and unexplained deaths. The records of the eyre courts were written in high Latin on rolls of parchment."

"Like the patent rolls."

"Exactly. The eyre judges were helped by county coroners who held inquests upon dead bodies, arrested suspects, gathered eyewitnesses, assembled juries, and administered justice."

"I look forward to reading what you've found. Can you give me a hint?"

"I don't think I will." He chuckled. "I want to see what you make of it. I will give you one interesting tidbit, though—to whet your appetite. You'll remember that the Wyck genealogy mentions an *R. Ufford* as the man who abducted Henry Wyck's first wife, Matilda. Turns out there's a problem with that. A Robert Ufford of Beccles was killed at the Battle of Crécy on the twenty-sixth of August 1346. Three days later, Wyck and his soldiers sailed from England. Upon arriving in France, Wyck wrote to his wife, Matilda. Here's the point: In September 1346, Matilda was still at Ravenswyck, recovering from an illness that sounds like a miscarriage, and R. Ufford was already dead. He couldn't have abducted Matilda unless he rose from the grave."

"Couldn't there have been another R. Ufford somewhere?"

"Yes. I searched. I couldn't find one anywhere in East Anglia."

"So why list the name of a dead man on the genealogy?"

"Think about it, Kate. Ask yourself why someone would record the fact that Matilda had been abducted in the first place?"

It took me a moment. "Oh, I see. To account for the fact that she'd disappeared."

"It's a possibility, isn't it? Lots of ifs here, but if Matilda was dead, and if the family wanted to keep it under wraps, they'd have had to account for the inconvenient fact that she wasn't around anymore. If they buried her body secretly in the crypt at St. Margaret's Church, no one would ever know except possibly the priest, and his living was in the hands of the lord of the manor."

"Who was Henry Wyck. But what about the servants, Matilda's lady's maid—assuming she had one?"

"Bribed. No one would try to contact the abductor. Someone who lived in a village forty or fifty miles away, like Beccles, might as well have lived in another country. It's all conjecture, of course, but when you look at what I've pieced together, I believe a picture emerges."

I was trying to see that picture. "So either people lied to Henry when he returned from France, telling him Matilda had been kidnapped, hoping he wouldn't ride off on his horse to get her back, or—"

"Or Henry killed her himself. This was the fourteenth century, Kate. Women were possessions, and the law protected the wealthy and powerful. If the lord of the manor returned home after two years to find his wife pregnant with another man's child, what would he do?"

His words hit me in the gut. *If a man, unable to father a child, returned from a two-month business trip to Southeast Asia to find his wife pregnant with another man's child, what would he do?*

I felt sick.

"Text me when you've read everything," Price-Davies was saying. "I'm still looking through the rest of the files—as I have time. Grenville Dark was a meticulous researcher. No stone unturned. It looks like most of the remaining files are legal charters, which isn't promising, but I'll at least pass my eyes over them to make sure we don't miss anything."

"Thank you, Duncan. I'll look at the files now."

* * *

The court records from Price-Davies arrived a few minutes later. He'd included a short introduction.

> *These are portions of the eyre court records for the year 1348. For background, after the victory at Crécy, Edward III turned his attention to the port of Calais, which would give him control of the Channel, and he issued the call for more soldiers. The siege began on the 4th of September 1346 and ended with the French surrender on the 3rd of August 1347. Military records, which I have not included, tell us Henry Wyck was severely wounded in the siege but had recovered enough to return to England in early February of 1348. According to the narrative we now believe is false, he arrived at Ravenswyck to find Matilda gone—abducted. In March of that year, he married for the second time. In November, he was found dead. One month later, on 22nd of December 1348, his new wife gave birth to a son, mere months before the bubonic plague reached Suffolk. Read the files for yourself.*

I downloaded the files. Price-Davies had summarized three separate court cases between Wyck's return from France in February of 1348 and his death later that year.

On the 17th of February 1348, Sir Henry Wyck charged his steward, one William Cogges, with theft, claiming he'd stolen two years' worth of rents. Cogges was caught in the act of flight. Having been found guilty, he admitted his crimes, stating that he believed Henry had died in France, and begged the court for mercy. He was hanged on the 18th of February 1348.

On the 20th of February 1348, Henry Wyck petitioned the Crown for an annulment from his wife, Matilda de Emeyse, on grounds of desertion, allowing him to remarry. His marriage to Julia Kirkeby took place one month later.

In the final case, Price-Davies provided a full translation of the brief court record.

On the 11th of November 1348, Sir Henry Wyck of this village hanged himself in his barn. His body was found and cut down by two of his servants, Thomas Robelyn and John Martyn, who gave witness. No one was suspected. The jury ruled felonious suicide. The land, goods, and chattels belonging to the deceased at the time of his self-killing are to be confiscated by the Crown.

Price-Davies had added a note:

As you probably know, suicide in medieval England was both a moral sin and a secular crime. In an unusual turn of events, the initial verdict of felonious suicide in Wyck's case was crossed out and replaced by a revised verdict of "accidental death while in a frenzied state, taken by madness," allowing his son to inherit. One can only suspect that gold changed hands.

Duncan Price-Davies was right—a picture was emerging, and when I asked myself which scenario best fit the facts, I found an answer staring me in the face. Not *the* answer, perhaps, but in the absence of further information, an argument could be made for a medieval love triangle.

While Henry was in France, his wife, Matilda, may have fallen in love with his steward, William Cogges. Perhaps William convinced her Henry was dead. Maybe they even believed it, and they may even have gone through some kind of marriage ceremony. At any rate, Matilda became pregnant, and when they learned Henry had survived his injuries and was on his way back to Ravenswyck, they planned to flee with as much of Henry's money as they could gather. Unfortunately for them, Henry returned in time to stop them. Did he kill Matilda in a fit of rage? Did he kill himself later out of guilt? No one would ever know for sure, but the poem he wrote, "The Pearl of Wyck," spoke of guilt and regret. If that was true, why hadn't William Cogges, at his trial, accused Wyck of murder? Maybe he had and he wasn't believed. Or maybe Cogges didn't know Matilda was dead and wanted to protect her.

Questions aside, the evidence suggested that Egemere Woman was Matilda de Emeyse, that she'd been murdered sometime in February of 1348, perhaps by her husband, Henry Wyck, who, later remorseful, buried her secretly with great care. He married again quickly, wanting to produce an heir, but wracked with guilt, took his own life before that heir was born. There was no proof of this, I reminded myself, and none of it answered the most puzzling question. Why had Matilda, if she was Egemere Woman, been interred with that priceless pearl?

I texted Price-Davies, thanking him.

It was time to report my findings to Alex Belcourt. How would he react? He couldn't possibly miss the eerie similarity between the deaths of Matilda de Emesye and his wife, Carrie Holgate.

Squaring my shoulders, I dialed Alex Belcourt's number.

Chapter Thirty-Five

Thursday, July 10
Ravenswyck Court

I'd made an appointment to meet with Alex Belcourt at three o'clock. He had only a small window of time as he had meetings all day and was leaving that evening for a weekend trip to Mexico, where his company owned a cardboard carton factory.

After ringing the bell, I was surprised to find the door opened not by Belcourt this time but by the butler, Hodgkins. "He's expecting you, madam. Follow me."

Belcourt was waiting in the library. The old portraits high on the walls seemed to look down on me with stern disapproval. I was delving into secrets they'd kept for more than seven centuries.

"Sherry?" Belcourt held a crystal decanter. When I declined, he pulled the stopper and poured himself a generous measure. He looked defeated, the skin around his eyes gray and the planes of his face slack. "What have you found?" he asked, but the question held no real curiosity. I understood. Now that his wife's body had been found, very little else mattered.

I can't make that better, I told myself. *All I can do is give him the facts. The truth Tom talked about.*

Using the printouts of the genealogy, the poem, the list of men killed at the Battle of Crécy, and the eyre court records, I laid out in chronological order the information I'd found.

He looked at me sadly. "I see what you're doing."

"Alex," I said, holding his gaze. I was going to have to be blunt. "I'm not doing anything except giving you the information I have. I realize the similarities to Carrie's death are strange, but it has to be one of those odd coincidences—nothing more. I suspect that Egemere Woman was Matilda de Emesye, the first wife of Sir Henry Wyck. I also think it's possible, even likely, that she was murdered by her husband or a member of his family, although there's no direct evidence and probably never will be."

"I didn't murder my wife, Kate." He looked and sounded exhausted. "I couldn't have harmed her no matter what she'd done. I would have given my life for Carrie. I loved her. I still do." He made a sound, a sort of choked sob. "Will this ever be over? Will I ever know the truth?" The pain in his eyes was almost unbearable.

I believed him. I really did. "Tom reread all the case notes, all the interviews. He's looked at all the evidence. There were no stranger sightings, no one from London, no one from Carrie's past."

"The police said that at the time." He looked at me, a quizzical expression on his face.

"It means Carrie was murdered by someone staying on or near the estate," I said. "Who was here in 2016?"

"I told you, I had only a few employees then. Three jobbing gardeners. Some women from the village to clean and do the cooking when Carrie was away on a shoot. And Peter, of course."

"Did Carrie get on with Peter?"

He looked confused. "Yes, of course she did. Peter was devoted to her. They'd bonded over the animals. Spent time together." His eyes narrowed. "Wait a minute. Are you implying that Carrie and Peter—" He shook his head, waving both hands in denial. "No, that isn't right. Don't even suggest it."

"All right, I won't," I said as calmly as I could, but I knew the suggestion had taken up residence in his brain. I regretted that. "Let's think about who else was here at the time."

"With the dig, you mean. The students had gone, but the team leaders were still here. The student supervisors, both young women—I can't remember their names—and the senior archaeologists—Sinclair, Niall Nevin, and Celia Whybrew. Niall and Celia had recently been awarded their degrees. Sinclair was about to take over as department head."

"Did Carrie get on with them?"

"You mean personally?"

"I suppose I do. Did she like them, work well with them? Admire them?"

"She liked Celia Whybrew. They were close to the same age. They went riding together sometimes, when we had horses."

"How about Dr. Nevin?"

"I think she was reserving judgment."

"Why do you say that?"

He shrugged. "I suppose because he was harder to know. Carrie was kind to people. She made allowances, but she wasn't naïve. I remember her saying once that Whybrew and Nevin were good at what they did, that they could make names for themselves if they ever got out of Sinclair's shadow."

"And Dr. Sinclair?"

Belcourt gave a short laugh. "She thought Sinclair was a brilliant archaeologist, but she didn't like him personally. She never said it in so many words, but I got the impression he'd tried it on with her."

"How would she have reacted to that?"

"She would have put a stop to it." He huffed. "When you look like Carrie did, you get used to men coming on to you. I remember it happened one night at the pub in Hartwell. Some oaf wouldn't leave her alone. Later, she said, 'You never have to worry about me, Alex. I know how to deal with men like that.'" His voice broke. "I should have worried."

Was he suggesting Carrie had become pregnant as the result of an attack? If that was true, why hadn't she reported it? Whatever the case, she'd overestimated her own powers. My thoughts went to the photograph of Carrie with Sinclair in 2016. "Did she trust Sinclair—professionally, I mean?" *He'd had an affair with Celia Whybrew. Why not the beautiful Carrie Holgate?*

"If she hadn't, I would hardly have invited him back."

"I know you've gone over this many times, but can you tell me again about the months you were in Southeast Asia? You said Carrie was tired—that was probably the pregnancy." He flinched, but I had to continue. "You got the impression she was unhappy, and you thought it had something to do with the dig. Can you remember anything else?"

"I've wracked my brain over it. She phoned me shortly before I was due home. There was something she wanted to talk about. When I asked her what, she said . . ." He closed his eyes, trying to resurrect an old memory. He opened them. "I do remember one thing. It isn't much. She said something was going on and I wasn't going to like it."

That didn't sound like an unplanned pregnancy. "Did she tell you what it was? Give you a hint?"

"No. I told her I was late for a meeting and could it wait until I got home." He pounded the arm of his chair. "*Stupid fool.*"

"You didn't know, Alex. How could you have?"

"I should have paid more attention. I was incredibly busy then. My company was on the verge of a major expansion. We were building our own factories overseas. I thought if I just put the company on a secure footing, Carrie would retire from modeling. She never really loved it, you know—modeling—but she was in such demand. They'd fly her around the world, dress her in designer clothes worth thousands. What she really wanted was to stay home, work with the animals, take part in the digs, create the museum. It was never about the money with Carrie." An odd look crossed his face. "Now that's brought something back. I haven't thought of it for years."

"A memory?"

"Of something she said. I can't say I remember her words, but I'm sure it had to do with money or finances and the dig."

"Do you mean the funding from the university or the CMBA?"

"I don't think so." He set down his cut-glass tumbler and stood. "I have her letters, you know—all of them, from when I was in Southeast Asia. I haven't looked at them since she disappeared. I could never bring myself to reread them. There might be something in one of them."

"Did the police ever ask to see the letters?"

"It never came up."

I thought of the letter that had solved an old mystery in Devon. These letters were private. I wouldn't ask to see them. "Would you reread the letters, Alex? If you find something, let me know."

"I'll do it now. I have time before I leave."

Afterward, I sat in the car and considered Belcourt's words. Carrie had been troubled, and at the time, Belcourt thought it had something to do with the dig—money or finances, perhaps. That led me to the missing finds lists and the image of Simon Sinclair on the Ravenswyck CCTV camera. Had Sinclair been stealing gold and Carrie found out? Had she confronted him?

It was only instinct, but I was beginning to feel even more convinced that the murder of Carrie Holgate and the murder of Simon Sinclair were linked.

Buckling my seatbelt, I pressed the starter button. A few sprinkles of rain hit the windscreen. The weather was changing—a stirring from the west, clouds gathering on the horizon.

Chapter Thirty-Six

Manor Farm

I had the evening to myself as Tom and his team were meeting with their counterparts in the Norfolk Constabulary. Public pressure to locate the Thetford killer was increasing. News reports were beginning to hint at incompetence.

At five thirty, I made myself a cheese omelet and ate it at the kitchen table with my black notebook open to the place where I'd written my revised list of questions. The first four concerned the murder of Simon Sinclair. The missing puzzle piece there was motive. Actually, it was more than a missing piece—the whole center of the puzzle was missing.

Mark and Tamzin had hated Sinclair, and with good reason. They'd scattered the fake pearls to harm his reputation, but had they hated him enough to commit murder? Maybe.

As for Niall Nevin, everyone agreed he'd been loyal to Sinclair, had admired him. Nevin said it himself, but loyalty goes only so far. At the Finchley Hall dinner, Sinclair had been baiting Nevin. Had the younger man finally reached the breaking point?

Celia Whybrew had the best motive for killing Simon Sinclair. Not only had he used her research and published it himself, he'd refused to give his consent to contact the daughter they'd conceived.

Any one of them could have done it. They'd all been at The Forge that night, but where did the snippet of an argument heard by Zach Valentine fit in?

You stupid fool. You've started again, haven't you?

You don't know what I'm up against. You'll ruin me.

According to Zach, the first speaker had been Simon Sinclair, but who had he been arguing with? What was this person up against and how would they be ruined? I couldn't think of an answer.

That led me to my fifth question—a connection between the murder of Simon Sinclair and the murder of Carrie Holgate. At least Mark and Tamzin could be ruled out in Carrie's case. They'd been teenagers in 2016. And I couldn't see any reason Celia would have had to murder Carrie Holgate. Alex said they were friends.

There were other possibilities, of course.

Top of the list was a romance between Sinclair and Carrie Holgate. I'd seen the photograph of them together in 2016. Sinclair had been an attractive man, especially nine years ago when he'd been leaner, more fit. He and Carrie had a shared interest in archaeology, and he had a reputation for charm when he wanted to use it. He liked the ladies, and Carrie Holgate had been a stunning beauty. Had Sinclair fathered her child, then murdered her to save his reputation?

I couldn't imagine Belcourt murdering his own wife, but I could imagine him taking revenge on Simon Sinclair. The problem was the nine-year time gap. First, how could he know Sinclair was the father of Carrie's baby? And if he did know it, why wait nine years? No—the shock on his face when the fetus was discovered had been real.

On the other hand, Peter Eley knew Carrie was pregnant, but Carrie had wanted him to believe her husband was the father. And again, there was the problem of the nine years.

So much depended on the DNA results. If the lab scientists were able to extract the baby's DNA after so many years in the ground, the father could be identified, and that would crack the case wide open.

Of course, the father of Carrie's baby might have been someone unconnected to any of this. Which would mean the motive for her murder was something no one yet knew or understood.

That brought up the pearls and Sinclair's ring. Had Sinclair really been trying to point the police to his killer? I couldn't think of another reason for him to have done those two odd things, and it did sound like something Sinclair might do. If he knew he was dying, making sure his killer was caught would have been a way of coming out on top. Sort of.

The agate intaglio in Sinclair's ring and its twin in the Roman earring was another mystery, one I hoped might be answered by Jeff Swift. If his posh client could tell us how he'd come to possess the matching earring, the police might have a solid lead. As for Sinclair ingesting the pearls, that seemed to point directly to the current excavation project and the fabulous pearl—the "Pearl of Wyck"—but that just brought me back around to Belcourt, Nevin, and possibly Peter Eley.

All speculation. No actual evidence.

I was puzzling over this, not getting anywhere, when my mobile lit up with a call.

"This is Kate."

"It's Alex. I just finished reading Carrie's letters." He cleared his throat. "One of them contains information the police need to know."

"Can you drop off the letter at the police station in Hartwell?"

"There's no time, Kate—honestly. I have business that must be wrapped up before I leave the country. At eight Peter's driving me to Stansted. My flight's at eleven thirty. It's tight as it is. The letter in question was the last one I received. I've taken a photograph of the relevant portion. I'll text it to you. Can you make sure the police get it?"

"You really should text it to Tom yourself. You're still a suspect. The police need to know you're not withholding information." I gave him Tom's number.

"All right. I'm sending it to you as well." I heard him let out a breath. "Thank you, Kate. And good luck."

The photo arrived in seconds. I opened it and turned the phone sideways so I could read more easily. Carrie's handwriting was small, neat, and regular with a few printed letters interspersed with the cursive. The image Belcourt had captured began in the middle of a sentence.

> *how busy you are, my darling, but when I tell you the whole story, you'll realize we must act. Something is wrong at the dig, and the person who should be most concerned says I'm imagining things. I'm not, Alex, I promise you. I can't possibly put it all in a letter, but last week I was working in the field office with one of the team supervisors—she's a bright girl, about to begin her PhD. During the second week of the dig, one of the students brought in a gilt silver cross found in the foundations of the Wyck Dower House near St. Margaret's Church. She's worried but afraid to speak up. She asked me if I have access to the finds lists. I told her not usually, but I could probably request a copy. She told me to look for the gilt cross. She says she's been part of two previous digs and she's sure someone is altering the digital spreadsheets and changing the descriptions of certain items. She begged me not to mention her name. I told her I'd keep my eyes open, but this needs you, darling. I can't wait to see you. I miss you, Carrie*
>
> I texted back.
>
> *Who did she mean by "the person who should be most concerned"?*
>
> He answered immediately.
>
> *Sinclair, I suppose. He was in charge of the dig.*

Altering the spreadsheets and changing descriptions—no one had mentioned anything like that in the interviews from 2016. Tom would have said something. Had this young PhD student, one of the supervisors, been afraid to accuse someone with power over her academic future? Duncan Price-Davies had called Sinclair "a force of nature," a person who liked to get his own way and generally did. If a subordinate got out of line, Sinclair would make sure they paid a price. Challenging him would have taken an extraordinary amount of courage, but Sinclair held no such power over Carrie Holgate. Just the opposite. She had the power to shut down the dig and damage Sinclair's reputation.

Who was this young PhD student, and would she now, after nine years, admit to keeping her suspicions under wraps? Carrie's letter had provided the first real link between the two murders nine years apart. In both cases, there were reports of discrepancies in the finds lists. I needed more information.

First, I emailed Celia Whybrew.

Do you remember the names of the two female student supervisors on the 2016 dig? Do you know what happened to them? I heard through Alex Belcourt that one of them said there were discrepancies in the finds lists. Do you remember that? I'd like to contact her.

Then I tapped out an email to Niall Nevin.

I'm sorry to bother you, but something has come up, and I'm wondering if you noticed discrepancies in the finds lists on earlier digs. Could someone have altered the spreadsheet or changed the descriptions without your knowledge?

Then I texted Tom:

Alex Belcourt sent you a text tonight. You're probably in meetings, but I think you should read it as soon as you can. Miss you. Love, Kate xxx

I'd just changed into sweatpants and a T-shirt when my mobile rang again. Thinking it might be Tom, I picked up.

It was Angela Foxe.

"Kate, I'm so sorry." She sounded out of breath. "Peter Eley just phoned. Hazel is in pain. He's worried something is badly wrong, and she means so much to Alex Belcourt. Could you possibly go with me? I know it's a lot to ask, and I wouldn't except I promised Edmund I'd call you if I needed help while he was away."

So much for an early night. "Of course. I'll be there in ten minutes."

"Wear your wellies, Kate. And old clothes. I'm sorry."

I was changing into an old pair of jeans when I got an email from Celia. I was surprised she'd answered so quickly.

I do remember the girl who made the accusation. Keely Armstrong. She's a lecturer now at Leeds. There was never any proof, and Simon made her feel quite a fool over it. The original lists had been destroyed. He blamed that on Niall, which wasn't fair. Typical Simon. Keely changed universities over it. Anyway, I emailed her. I'm sorry, but she refuses to talk to you.

I wanted to email Celia back, explaining how important it was to contact Keely Armstrong. Instead, I pulled up the website for the University of Leeds faculty. They didn't have a Department of Archaeology, but I found Keely Armstrong listed as a lecturer in the School of Languages, Cultures, and Societies. With her academic email. Which she probably didn't check several times a day.

With no alternative, I sent the young lecturer a message, explaining who I was and why I was contacting her:

I know you don't want to get involved, Keely, but it is rather important.

To my great surprise, she responded almost instantly.

I think there's been some misunderstanding. Celia never contacted me, and actually it was Celia herself who insisted I confront Dr. Sinclair. She was present when the gold was found.

Celia herself? Why would she lie about that?

Now I really was confused. But I couldn't think about that. Angela was waiting. So was poor Hazel.

I pulled on my wellies and headed for my car.

Chapter Thirty-Seven

Ravenswyck Court

Angela and I made it to Ravenswyck by seven fifteen. Peter Eley was waiting for us outside the house. "I've got her in one of the outbuildings. I'll drive you there, but I can't stay. I must get Mr. Belcourt to the airport in time for his flight. I'll leave the UTV with you and walk back."

"No problem," Angela said as we made our way toward the small utility terrain vehicle. "Tell me about Hazel. What's going on?"

"She's been restless, pawing the ground. Isolated herself from the herd. Lays down, then gets up like she's uncomfortable. Hasn't eaten."

"How long has this been going on?"

"Fifteen, sixteen hours."

"You were right to call me, Peter. I'll check her out. When I know something, I'll text you."

"Sorry," Peter said. "No mobile coverage in or near the outbuildings. I'll check back when I can. Or send Kate to the house. We have coverage there." He looked at me. "You can drive one of these, right?"

"Of course," I said, which may have been overstating things a bit. I hadn't driven a floor-shifter for thirty years.

We climbed into the open vehicle, which looked something like a heavy-duty golf cart. There were only two seats, so I climbed into the back and sat cross-legged, facing the way we'd come. Peter turned the key, and we took off with a lurch. I clutched Angela's medical bag against my side and held on to the metal roll bar with one hand as the vehicle bumped over the fields. The wind had picked up, and as the first drops of rain hit the ground, I released my death grip on the roll bar and pulled up the hood on my anorak. We'd gone about a quarter mile when I felt my mobile ping in my pocket. Someone had texted me—but we were bouncing around so wildly I'd have to wait for a better time to read the message.

The outbuilding where Eley had sheltered Hazel was a solid limestone structure, a barn, with a pine-planked door, two high, shuttered windows, and a roof that had probably once been thatched but was now clad with moss-covered tiles. Peter parked the four-wheeler near the entrance door. We climbed down and went inside.

Peter flipped a switch that lit up six or seven bare bulbs hanging from the ceiling. The space was probably twenty-four feet square with approximately a third of the space behind a shoulder-high partial stone wall. At one end, a ladder led to a loft. Hazel was leaning against the stone wall, arching her back slightly and breathing heavily.

"I see what you mean," Angela said. "Do you have water here?"

"There's a tap on the wall and a clean bucket if you need it."

"Thanks. I'll get started."

"That's grand." He looked at his watch. "Sorry—I must go."

I watched through the open doorway as he jogged swiftly toward the house.

Angela filled the bucket with water and added a measure of some blue liquid she had in her case. "Disinfectant," she said, sluicing her hands and arms up to the elbows. She dried them with absorbent paper cloths. "I'll need a mask and surgical gloves, Kate—and my stethoscope. Bring my case over if you will." She donned the mask and gloves and hung the scope around her neck. Reaching into the case, she pulled out a vial of liquid and a syringe. "I'm giving her a shot of antibiotics, in case she has an infection."

I watched as Angela ran practiced hands over the goat's head and neck, checking the eyes, nose, mouth, and ears. Using the stethoscope, she listened to Hazel's lungs and then her abdomen. She stood abruptly and stepped back, holding up both hands. "This goat's kidding."

"What do you mean?"

"She's pregnant. She's in labor. I can't do this. I can't be here."

"The baby?" I asked.

"Yes, it's too dangerous—Q fever, toxoplasmosis, listeriosis. I can't risk it." She backed up toward the partial wall.

"Are you sure? She doesn't look pregnant. Wouldn't Peter have known?"

"Goats can hide their pregnancies very well. Some get huge, bulging bellies, and it's obvious. But others carry their kids much more discreetly. It can be difficult to tell."

"Do you know how long she's been in labor?"

"Peter said Hazel's been acting like this for more than fifteen hours. That isn't good. She's showing signs of imminent delivery. I heard a heartbeat, but the kid isn't moving about. That means it's lined up for delivery. She should be making progress. There's a problem."

"Can you call another vet?"

"We don't have time. If we wait, we could lose the kid and the mother." She pulled off her gloves and rubbed her forehead with the back of her arm. "This is terrible, Kate, but I can't risk my baby. I don't know what to do." I saw her eyes fill. "She's probably been pushing for hours. She's exhausted." Angela adored animals. Her whole career was helping them live long, healthy lives, and now she had a horrible choice—consign the goat and her kid to a tragic fate or put her own child in danger.

"Can I help?" I asked. "I mean, I have no experience in this kind of thing, but you could walk me through it."

Angela moaned. "I can't ask you to do that, Kate."

"If you really have no other option, what do we have to lose?"

I saw desperation in her eyes. "Are you absolutely sure?"

"I don't think we have a choice. Tell me what to do."

"Okay." I could see her gearing up. "First, know that you'll never wear those clothes again. Sorry. Let's get some clean, soft bedding put down. There's straw on the other side of this wall. I'll pass it over to you."

When I had the bedding well down, Angela said, "Now we need to know what we're dealing with. This is the tricky bit. You're going to have to do an internal exam. First disinfect your hands and arms in the bucket—like I did. Dry yourself as well as you can and put on a clean pair of surgical gloves. That box right there. Don't touch anything. Use that large white tube in my case—yes, the one on top—to lubricate her back end and your right hand—you are right-handed?"

"Yes."

I must have looked anxious because she said, "The important thing is to stay calm. Start with a couple of fingers to see how wide she is. That's right."

I did as she'd instructed, feeling opposition. "She's trying to push me out."

"Entirely normal. Keep going in slowly until you can feel what's in the birth canal. It helps to close your eyes so you can concentrate on what you're feeling."

I felt around for a while. "I think . . . I think it might be the baby's rump. I can feel a tail."

"Okay—the kid is breech, blocking the birth canal. You can fix this. Gently push the kid forward and then try to slip your fingers underneath to find the rear legs."

"I feel them. What's next?"

"Which way are they pointing?"

"Away from me."

"Excellent. Now pull. Use constant pressure. This is going to be a breech birth."

I pulled but I wasn't getting anywhere. "My hand keeps slipping."

"The kid must be large, and Hazel isn't. Wish I'd brought my lamb-puller. Grab again, between the belly and the haunches. The rear end will come out first."

I tried again. And again. "I'm not strong enough. Is there anything else we can do?"

"This has to work, Kate. Try again. Give it everything you've got."

I tried again. Now I was in tears. "I can't do it. I'm so sorry."

We heard a rustling sound coming from the loft.

Angela and I looked up to see the pale, bearded face of a youngish man. "Let me try. Grew up on a sheep farm, didn't I? Helped me dad birth lots o' sheep."

"Who are you?" Angela asked.

I was pretty sure I knew the answer. "You're Derek, aren't you?"

He made a sound, neither yes nor no. "If you think you can help, you'd better come down and lend a hand."

Angela looked at me. "Who's Derek?"

"I'll tell you later."

Derek Quinn clambered down the ladder. He was medium height, wiry, in his early thirties, perhaps. His hair and beard were matted and his clothes filthy.

"You'll have to strip down," Angela said. "Remove your shirt. Wash with the antiseptic."

"I know the drill," he said. "Do you have gloves my size?"

"I should," Angela said. "Kate, see if you can find him a pair—largest I have. Help him get ready."

Ten minutes later, Derek had his arm inside Hazel. "Got it." I could see his muscles flexing as he pulled. After only a few minutes, a dark lump appeared, followed by legs, and then all of a sudden, the kid flopped out onto the straw in a mess of mucus and fluid. Derek put his hand inside the goat again. "Only the one."

"A big one," Angela said. "No way she could have delivered that kid without help. That's right, Derek—tend to Hazel. Kate, stand up. Rub the kid down with straw. Now take one of those paper towels and clear the mucus from around the head so it can breathe.

I did as she instructed.

"Now hold it up by the rear legs and gently swing it back and forth through your legs. Support the back with your other hand. This will dispel any remaining mucus."

"Done. Breathing." I was exhausted but felt a surge of elation. We'd done it.

"It's a female," Derek said.

"Present her to Hazel so she can start licking her clean. That will start the bonding process."

The three of us watched in awe as instinct kicked in and Hazel began her first moments of motherhood.

There was more to do, the afterbirth and the cleanup, but Derek followed Angela's instructions to the letter.

"I don't know what we would have done without you," I told him.

"Get cleaned up as best you can, Kate," Angela said. "We'll need to make a new batch of antiseptic liquid. Once we get the kid nursing, we can take the four-wheeler back to Ravenswyck. Peter should be back by eleven. He'll want to check on the kid himself."

Derek moved swiftly to block the door. "You're not going anywhere."

* * *

Angela and I sat on a bale of hay. Derek had offered some to Hazel, who was munching contentedly while her female kid nursed. She was an adorable little thing with a pink nose and a golden coat like her mamma. And healthy. She was standing now on her wobbly little legs.

"Hazel must have been pregnant when Belcourt bought her," Angela said. "Thankfully, it looks like the father was another Golden Guernsey. The seller probably didn't know."

"Do you have anything to eat?" Derek asked.

Angela got out a thermos of tea she'd brought and a tin of biscuits. She handed them to Derek, and he wolfed down the lot.

"You can't keep running, you know," I said.

I think Derek was about to argue with that, but our conversation ended when Angela let out a long moan. "Wow—that was a strong one."

"Braxton Hicks?" I asked.

"I don't think so." She gave me a meaningful look. "I've been having them for about an hour. Strong and regular. I think I'm in labor . . . oh!" She moved slightly. "I can't believe this. First Hazel, then me. That's all we need."

"Don't worry. Your first labor will probably take hours and hours." The look on her face told me that wasn't the most encouraging thing I could have said. "What I mean is by the time you need, ah, attention, Derek will have come to his senses and let me go for help—*won't you, Derek?*" I tried my authoritative mother voice.

"No." He stood, his arms crossed over his chest. "If you go for help, you'll bring the police. I'll be arrested and charged with murder. They won't believe it was an accident, will they? I've got form."

"*You* go for help, then," I said. "Leave us here. Find the nearest phone box and call emergency services."

"And pinpoint my location? I'll be on foot. They'll pick me up in no time."

"Take the four-wheeler."

"Oh, right—and that won't be easy to track at all, will it?"

I was getting angry. "What's *your* solution, then? Have you trained as a midwife in your spare time?"

He ignored that. "I need to think." He began pacing back and forth.

We were at an impasse, so I arranged the hay bales so Angela could have some support for her back.

"Maybe if I try to relax, things will calm down," Angela said—which was ridiculous, and we both knew it..

"Okay," I whispered. "Get some rest. I'll keep my eye on Derek."

With no clever ideas about what to do next, I remembered the messages I'd gotten in the UTV. I pulled out my mobile.

"Hey," Derek said. "Are you phoning for help?"

"I wish," I said. "There's no coverage out here—see?" I showed him my phone. "I'm reading my message, if that's okay with you."

As he didn't respond, I went ahead, glancing first at Angela, who had her eyes shut. She had a hand spread over her belly and was taking slow, deep breaths.

The text message was from Ivor.

Jeff won't tell me the name of his source. He did say the chap's selling off his late father's collection of Roman antiquities to pay for school fees. Embarrassed about it, hence the confidentiality. Jeff checked him out. He's legit. Jeff tried his mobile. No answer. Luckily, I can read upside down and have quite a good memory for numbers. 07894 520082. Looks like Norwich. If you call him, do not mention Jeff's name. Make up some plausible reason for calling. Ask him if he's still looking for a care home. Or tell him he won the Irish Sweepstakes. Just get his name.

School fees reminded me of Sinclair's daughter and her expensive boarding school. How long had it been since Jeff communicated with his source? I checked again for a signal. Still no bars. I slipped the phone back in my jeans pocket.

"How are you feeling, Angela?" I patted her leg. "Contractions?"

"Like clockwork." She grimaced in pain.

Another hour passed, and I was pretty sure the contractions were getting closer together.

Angela was in the middle of one, gritting her teeth, when I saw Derek looking at her with fear in his eyes. "Look," he said. "Give me an hour's head start. Promise me. Then you can go for help."

"I can't do that, Derek. That would mean leaving Angela here alone in labor. What if the baby comes? She'll need help."

The thought that I would be the available help scared me to death. At least Derek had birthed animals.

Angela's face screwed up in pain. After a minute or so, she relaxed and took a few breaths. "I hate to say it, Kate, but this isn't going to take hours and hours. My mom had quick deliveries. So did my sister. Runs in the family."

Angela was right. This baby wasn't going to wait for us to solve our Derek Quinn problem. I had to do something. "Derek, did you know Willow was on TV? She wants you to turn yourself in. She needs you."

"The police are using her to get to me."

"I don't think so." I decided to take a risk. "My husband is a policeman. He told me they've interviewed Willow. She and your little girl just want you home."

Derek gave me an agonized look. "Crap father, right?"

I'd finally gotten his attention. Time to hammer home the truth. "Willow told the police about Conor Pike, the assault. How you were defending her. She said it was an accident."

"Oh, right—and they believed her." He rolled his eyes.

"Actually, I think they did. You won't get off scot-free, but you could get a much lighter sentence if you turn yourself in. It was clearly involuntary manslaughter." I had no idea what the sentence for that might be, but I needed to give him a glimmer of hope. "Who knows? You might even get a suspended sentence."

"You think I'm falling for that?"

Angela was having another contraction, a hard one. "Kate," she gasped. "I need to get to a hospital. I can't have this baby here. Please—can you do something?"

"I'm trying, Angela." I really was angry now. If this stupid boy didn't see sense, he might cause another death. Nothing I'd said had changed his mind. I felt like screaming at him. I had to change tack.

And just like that, in one of those amazing bursts of clarity, I remembered something my mother told me once. I'd been dealing with a clique of girls in school who'd decided I wasn't going to be their friend.

"Have you heard of a thing called noncomplementary behavior?" my mother had asked me.

"No, what is it?"

"Noncomplementary behavior is doing what people don't expect. Doing the opposite. Responding to hostility with warmth. Giving someone who's hurt you a compliment. Being compassionate when you've been treated unfairly."

"That's not going to help," I'd said scornfully.

"How do you know? Try it."

I had tried it, reluctantly—and it worked. One of those mean girls was now one of my best friends. She'd flown all the way from Ohio for my wedding.

I had nothing to lose. "What's the name of your little girl, Derek? I saw her on TV. She's really beautiful."

"Rosie." I saw his Adam's apple bounce as he swallowed hard. "Poor kid. Father like me."

"I'll bet she loves you. Comes running when you get home at night, doesn't she?" *Could she even walk yet?*

He took a ragged breath. I'd hit the mark.

"Were you there when she was born?"

"Yeah—saw the whole thing."

"Do you really want Angela's little girl or boy to be born in this barn?"

I heard Angela croak a laugh. "Edmund says the best babies are born in barns." Her laugh was cut short by a strangled cry. Another contraction. They were coming closer now.

"Please, Derek," I said, speaking in a low voice so Angela couldn't hear. "This baby's coming too early. It might need oxygen. Are you willing to watch this baby die? Stay with Angela. Let me go for help."

A flash of light was followed by a crack of thunder. And rain.

I looked at my watch. It was eleven fifteen. Peter Eley would have dropped Belcourt off at Stansted around nine. That meant he should be back soon. Would he check on Hazel as he promised?

"We don't have much time, Derek. *Please.*"

"Go" was all he said.

"Bring clean towels," Angela added through gritted teeth. "And hurry!"

Chapter Thirty-Eight

Ravenswyck Court

The rain hit me like a slap in the face, instantly soaking my jeans and thin jacket—which were already damp and incredibly smelly from the birth of the kid. Pulling up my hood, I jumped into the driver's side of the UTV and turned the key. The engine roared to life, but in the dark, I couldn't see the shift pattern. Where was first gear? And where were the headlights?

After a couple of tries, I found the headlight switch, shoved the gear stick into what I hoped was a forward position, and took off in the general direction of Ravenswyck Court.

The lightning actually helped, illuminating the surrounding landscape for a few seconds at a time. Now that I was on my way to get help, it occurred to me that the house might be locked. Did the butler live in? I hoped someone would hear my knocking.

A vibration in my jeans pocket reminded me that I had my mobile phone. I was finally getting emails or texts, which meant—*yay!*—I had cell coverage and at least some charge left. With no time to waste, I stopped the vehicle, jammed it into park, and pulled out my phone. First, I called emergency services, explaining that Angela was about to give birth and giving them my best guess at directions to the small stone barn. Then I called Tom. Was he home and wondering where I was? He didn't pick up, which probably meant he was either still at police headquarters or possibly driving. I called him again, twice in quick succession, which was our signal. *You need to pick up.*

He did. "I'm sorry, darling. I'm staying in barracks tonight. Didn't you get my message? We're organizing a house-to-house search for Quinn."

"You can call it off, Tom. I know where he is." I explained. "The EMTs are on the way, but I'm really worried about Angela and the baby. What if the baby needs oxygen or something? Or—"

"Don't go there. You've done everything you could. I'm proud of you, Kate. Are you all right?"

"Fine." I found myself wanting to defend Derek Quinn. "I don't think he would have hurt us, Tom. He's not violent. He's confused, afraid, hungry, and exhausted. He's staying with Angela, which is a good thing if she does deliver the baby. It can't be that much different than sheep and goats, can it? Look, I'm almost at Ravenswyck Court. If I can rouse someone, I'll get some clean towels in case the EMTs don't make it in time."

"Okay—be there as soon as I can. I'll phone Edmund now. He can meet Angela at the hospital. And good luck, darling."

I made it to Ravenswyck Court. The rain had stopped. That was good. But the house was completely dark. There was a car parked near the museum entrance—one I recognized. It was Tamzin's little Renault Clio. What was she doing at Ravenswyck in the middle of the night? Something didn't feel right.

Another ping of my phone reminded me that I'd had messages. Quite a few of them. Someone had been trying to reach me. Sitting in the UTV, I quickly opened my messages.

Ivor had sent four texts followed by three missed phone calls. I scrolled to the first text and read the screen.

> *Kate, if you haven't phoned that mobile number I gave you, don't do it. This is really odd, but I heard from Edlyn Dark tonight. She found the computer guy's mobile number. No name, just a number. You're not going to believe this, but it's the same number as Jeff Swift's client*

07894 520082. Call Tom and let the police follow up. We don't know what we're dealing with. Could be dangerous.

The other texts were just repeats, asking if I'd gotten the first one. I tapped out a quick reply to the first text. *Got it.* Then I quickly forwarded the texts with the identical mobile numbers to Tom. I hoped he would read them right away.

My immediate concern was Angela. And Tamzin Oliver. What was she doing in the museum? Was Mark with her? Leaving the UTV where I'd parked it, I walked quietly toward the entrance to the museum and felt the hood of the Clio. Still warm.

As I approached the museum entrance, I heard the flapping of wings and felt the disturbance of air just over my head. *Ravens?*

The door was ajar. That was odd, too.

I pushed it open silently and went inside. "Hello?" I said in a small voice. "Is anyone here?"

No answer. The museum was dark, although I could see a faint light coming from somewhere further on. Maybe the inner office or the gift shop.

Turning my mobile flashlight to dim, I moved quietly through the darkened village street, telling myself the nightmarish wax figures looming up in the darkness were not alive.

Moving through the archway toward the displays, I called out, "Tamzin? Mark? It's Kate. I saw your car."

Silence.

Now I could see that the light was coming from the inner office.

I crept toward the door, holding my breath.

Dr. Nevin knelt in front of the open safe, a flush spreading across his face and neck. Beside him on the floor was a canvas gym bag.

* * *

"Dr. Nevin," I said, tempted to add the proverbial *I presume*.

"Ms. Hamilton." Nevin blinked at me, smiling nervously. "What are you doing here?"

"I could ask you the same thing," I said, trying for a light tone. "It's nearly midnight. I saw Tamzin's car outside."

"Borrowed it. I had some last-minute stuff to take care of. I'm leaving tonight." An odd look spread over his face. "What have you done to yourself?"

I looked down at my ruined shirt and jeans. "Birthing a baby goat. Sorry about the aroma." I pointed at the canvas gym bag. "Are you taking items out of the safe?"

He stiffened. "No. Well, yes, but only to deliver to the CMBA." More blinking.

"Does Celia know?"

"Of course."

He was a really bad liar. "May I see what you're taking?"

"Why?"

"Curiosity. Celia showed the CMBA board the pearl. What are you going to show them?"

"A few objects."

"All from Egemere Close? Medieval?"

"Of course."

The problem was I'd caught a glimpse of something as he'd slipped it into the canvas bag. It was a small silver bowl, and I was pretty sure it was Roman. What were Roman antiquities doing in the safe at Ravenswyck?

"Did you get my email about the discrepancies in the finds lists?" I asked.

"Yes, yes, I did. Sorry I haven't responded, but as I told everyone earlier, I know nothing about it. I work with the data provided to me."

I wanted to ask him about Keely Armstrong, but I couldn't put her at risk.

My mind raced as one thought after another flashed through my brain.

The box of gold in Sinclair's room—what if Sinclair hadn't stolen it but rescued it?

Nothing gets past you, eh, Niall? No funny business there. Sinclair's words at the Finchley Hall dinner came back in a rush. Had it been a warning? Had Sinclair begun to suspect Nevin of stealing artifacts?

The text Sinclair received at the Six Bells. The only person not in the pub that night was Nevin.

The deleted emails and messages from Sinclair's mobile. Who better than a computer expert?

You've started again, haven't you? What started again? The thefts?

Nevin's inexplicable opposition to the ground-penetrating radar and the test pit at the mound. I felt a cold wash of fear roll down my back.

Had Nevin opposed the test pit because he knew Carrie's body was buried there?

I swallowed hard. Was I jumping to conclusions?

I had no time to get to the bottom of it now. Angela Foxe and her baby were in trouble.

"You never said what *you're* doing here." Nevin narrowed his eyes.

"I'm sorry—it's Angela. Angela Foxe. You remember her—the veterinarian. She's in labor. Her baby's coming early. I called for an ambulance, but I need clean towels in case the baby arrives before the EMTs. Can you help me?"

"Where is she?" He looked confused. I didn't blame him.

"In one of the outbuildings. With a goat. Please help me."

What could he say? "All right, fine. I'll help you get towels, but it's almost midnight. I really must go."

Not if I can help it. "Of course. Thank you."

Women have tools that come in quite handy now and again. We rarely speak of them, but we all know they exist. I pulled one out now—the *damsel in distress*.

"Oh, dear. I feel light-headed." I put my hand to my forehead.

Nevin frowned. "Are you okay?"

"I'm shaking. It must be the stress. I don't think I can drive."

"You got here, didn't you?" He sounded cross.

"Barely." I put both hands to my head now. "I'm no good with manual transmissions." I turned the corners of my mouth down. "Could you possibly drive me to the barn? You can take the UTV and come right back. I'll wait for the ambulance and go with Angela to the hospital."

"Fine. I'll drive you there, but then I really must leave."

"Thank you. You're a lifesaver."

How was I going to explain Derek Quinn? I'd think of something.

We grabbed two armfuls of towels from one of the Ravenswyck bathrooms and ran to the UTV. Nevin was also carrying his canvas bag. He stopped and threw it into the Clio.

Taking off in the UTV, Nevin almost stripped the gears.

"You don't know how comforting it is to have you with me, Niall. I couldn't have done this without you." It was a bald-faced lie, but you are allowed, I reminded myself, to lie to killers. *Was Nevin a killer as well as a thief?*

We bumped over the terrain, once nearly hitting a stone wall and once almost upending the vehicle in a ditch, but we made it.

A loud, agonizing moan came from inside.

Chapter Thirty-Nine

"Angela, we're coming." I pushed Nevin ahead of me through the door.

Angela closed her eyes, gritted her teeth. *Ahhh.* She grabbed Derek's arm.

"That's right," he said. "Squeeze hard."

"I think you're in transition," I said, wracking my brain to remember how long that lasted. *Fifteen minutes? An hour?* I handed Nevin my armload of towels and ran to Angela. "Hold on. The EMTs are on their way."

"Who's that?" Nevin stared at Derek.

"Sheep farmer." Deflecting questions with useless information, I said, "He delivered the baby goat. See? Over there. Isn't she adorable?" She *was* adorable, making baby goat sounds as she nursed.

Nevin dropped the towels on one of the hay bales. "I really must go. Good luck." He started for the door.

"Wait," I said, hearing sirens. "It's the EMTs. We can't do anything until they get here."

Good thing he didn't ask why. I wouldn't have had an answer. But Nevin's moment of hesitation did the trick. The sirens screamed to a halt, the door burst open, and a team of paramedics clomped into the barn carrying emergency equipment.

Derek, clearly relieved, let them take over.

Nevin, whose way of escape was now blocked, retreated to the wall, as far away from both Angela and the goats as he could get.

There was a flurry of activity as the paramedics put in an IV. They were transferring Angela onto a gurney when we heard more sirens.

Tom and the police. Thank goodness.

Tom strode through the door, followed by DS Ren. He gave me a quick look but turned his attention immediately to Angela and the EMTs. "Will she and the baby be all right?"

"Right as rain," said a short, stocky fellow with bright red hair. "We'll get her to West Suffolk in Bury. Only twelve miles away. And if the little one doesn't feel like waiting, we'll welcome him into the world ourselves."

Welcome *her*, I wanted to say.

Tom was already texting Edmund with the location of the hospital.

I went to Angela's side as they were about to make their exit. "Good luck. Edmund is on his way."

I'm not sure she heard me.

DS Ren was quietly reading Derek Quinn his rights. All the fight—or more probably, all the fear—was now gone.

"Good luck, Derek," I told him. "And thank you. Angela and I will vouch for you."

Niall Nevin stood watching all this as if he'd wandered into some absurd play where none of the action or dialogue made sense.

"Niall was good enough to drive me here from Ravenswyck," I told Tom, giving him eye signals. "He's just about to leave the area."

"'All's well that ends well,'" Nevin tried a hearty tone. "Must go now. End of term, you know. Glad everything turned out so well." He began sidestepping toward the door.

DS Ren and Derek Quinn got there first. "I'm afraid you'll have to remain here, sir," Ren said, "until I have our prisoner secured."

"Of course, of course."

"It won't be long," Tom said. He followed Ren and the prisoner outside.

I heard the car engine rev and wheels screech as the police car backed up and drove off.

"Sorry," Tom said, re-entering the barn. "Do you mind if we ride back with you to Ravenswyck?"

"But I really have to—" Nevin was almost sputtering.

"I know—you have to go," Tom said.

"Could you call someone to pick you up?"

"Sorry again," I said. "No cell coverage out here."

"This won't take more than ten minutes. Kate's got her car at Ravenswyck. We'll drop you off, and you can be on your way. I'll drive."

Thank heaven.

* * *

All the way back to Ravenswyck, I wondered what Tom had up his sleeve. He knew I had good reason not to allow Nevin to get away, and even if he didn't know what that reason was, he trusted me. That was a scary thought. What if I wasn't right? That wasn't the only problem. How were we going to stop Nevin from leaving when we got back to Ravenswyck Court?

Tom needed to see what was in that canvas gym bag.

As it turned out, that wasn't a problem. Pulling into the Ravenswyck parking area, I saw that Alex Belcourt's big black Bentley had completely blocked the little Clio.

"Too bad," Tom said. "We'll have to get someone to move that big car."

The entrance door to Ravenswyck opened. The butler, Hodgkins, stood there, looking uncharacteristically disheveled. His long black tie was askew. But then who was I to make a fuss about sartorial correctness?

"What's going on?" Hodgkins asked, wrinkling his nose. "I heard sirens. Is everyone all right?"

"They are now—or they will be," Tom said.

"My car's blocked," Nevin said, "and I really must go." He was losing his cool.

"Peter has the keys," Hodgkins said. "I'll phone him now."

We all filed inside. Hodgkins made no comment about the state of my clothing, but he produced a tea towel and placed it on my chair in the Tudor drawing room.

"He made his exit, leaving Tom and me to come up with a conversation starter.

Tom got there first. "It was exceptionally good of you to help my wife, Nevin. Not the evening you'd planned, I daresay."

Nevin ignored this. "Is Eley here?"

"He must be," I said. "He parked the Bentley."

"Didn't he realize someone would need to get out?"

"He probably didn't notice the Clio," I said. "It is quite small."

Nevin scowled.

Hodgkins entered the room, carrying a tray of tea things. "I thought you'd like some refreshment while you wait."

"You got him on the phone—Eley?" Nevin asked. He was practically thrumming with nervous energy.

"Peter's dressing. He'll be here in a few minutes. In the meantime, would you like to pour out, Ms. Hamilton?"

"Of course." I reached for the steaming pot.

"None for me," Nevin said. He moved to one of the windows and stood looking out into the darkness.

"Kate," Tom whispered as I poured, "what's going on? Why don't you want Nevin to leave?"

"I think he's the killer—and the thief. He's got a—" I stopped whispering. Niall had turned away from the window. I gave him a big smile. "Won't be long now."

Nevin returned to the window.

"He's got a gym bag in his car," I whispered. "You need to search it."

"What about the texts you sent me from Ivor? The phone number of that titled chap who's selling off his father's antiquities and seems to have a computer-repair business on the side. Who's he?"

"One way to find out. Call him."

Tom pulled out his mobile, scrolled for a moment, then tapped the screen and put the phone to his ear.

A ringtone came from the direction of the window.

Niall Nevin stood, frowning at his mobile. "What's this?"

Tom held up his mobile, wiggling it in the air. "Selling off your father's collection of Roman antiquities to pay school fees? I didn't know you had a daughter, Niall."

Nevin's face turned white. He dashed toward the door.

"Tom," I shouted. "You left the key to the UTV in the ignition."

We heard the engine come to life.

By the time we made it outside, we saw the taillights bumping across the field. A shape appeared in the headlights. *Peter Eley*, coming to move the car.

To avoid striking him, Nevin wrenched the steering wheel to the right, but the sudden weight shift was too much for the vehicle. It tilted sharply and went over.

We watched in horror as the open vehicle rolled three times and burst into flames.

"Kate," Tom shouted as he raced toward the accident, "call an ambulance."

Chapter Forty

It was two-thirty in the morning. Tom and I sat in the waiting room of the A&E unit of the West Suffolk Hospital, waiting for the doctors to tell us if and when Niall Nevin could be interviewed. He'd been incredibly lucky. He'd been thrown clear of the vehicle, sustaining only a broken wrist and collarbone on the right side. I'm sure the impact didn't do his back any good, either, but the accident could have been much, much worse.

DS Ren had arrived shortly after Nevin was admitted. He'd changed his clothes and looked as fresh as a daisy. Oh, to be that young again. I felt like I'd been on a forced march for days. I looked and smelled like it, too.

Somewhere in that same hospital, Angela and Edmund Foxe were spending their first hours with their little girl, Scarlett Genevieve. Edmund had texted, saying mother and daughter were absolutely brilliant. Scarlett had made her debut a mere fifteen minutes after the ambulance had arrived at the hospital. She was eighteen and a half inches long and weighed a respectable five pounds, two ounces. Edmund had sent a photo, which made me cry. I was so thankful.

Now, however, I could barely keep my eyes open.

Tom nudged me. "We should spend the night somewhere. I'm too tired to drive home, and I'm expected at headquarters first thing in the morning."

I yawned. "There's a Holiday Inn Express about three minutes from here. See if you can book a room online." I looked at my watch. "It's two forty. Is it even worth it?"

"We'll both feel better after a couple hours' sleep. You can drive the car home in the morning. I'll get a ride with someone."

In three minutes, we had a room, but how soon we'd get out of the hospital was anyone's guess.

At three ten, one of the doctors informed Tom that he and DS Ren could have ten minutes with the patient.

"Why don't you go to the hotel? Ren can drop me off."

"I'm not driving alone at this time of night," I said, curling up on the couch and using Tom's jacket as a pillow. "You go interview Nevin. I'll wait for you."

I must have dozed off because the next thing I remembered was Tom's hand on my shoulder. "Wake up, love. Time to leave. You can go back to sleep when we get to our room."

"What happened?"

"He says he killed Sinclair, Kate. Nevin's a drug addict. Has been since his spinal injury five years ago. They gave him pain meds in the emergency room, so he's starting to make sense, but it's going to be a while before we can really question him. We'll know something tomorrow. Now, come on." He hauled me to my feet. "There's a bed waiting for us."

* * *

Friday, July 11
Bury St. Edmunds

At eight AM, DS Ren picked Tom up at the hotel. I rolled over and slept until ten thirty, after which I felt surprisingly human. After a long and very welcome shower, I reluctantly donned my filthy clothes and headed for home. The jeans and shirt smelled so terrible, I threw them in the trash, took a second quick shower, and changed into clean jeans, a white shirt, and my new white trainers.

I'd never been so thankful for clean clothes in my life.

Before taking off again for Bury, I texted Tom.

Can you meet me at the hospital? Scarlett Genevieve would like to meet you.

He texted back at once.

Wish I could. Give them my best. Nevin's been released from hospital. Formal interview with counsel at three thirty. Can you be here?

I texted back that I could, got into the car, and headed north.

The Friends Shop in the hospital's main entrance had a baby section. I chose a lovely soft white sleeper, the smallest they had, and a bouquet of pink roses in a vase shaped like a baby carriage.

Clutching my gifts and fighting back tears of gratitude, I took the lift to the maternity ward on the first floor, where a nurse directed me to Angela's room.

"Private room and all," I said, smiling as I knocked on the open door to announce my presence.

"That's what a possible livestock infection will get you," Angela said. "Come. Take a look at her." Angela was in bed, holding a tiny bundle in a pink blanket. Edmund sat next to the bed. Both were exhausted but clearly so entranced by their tiny daughter, they barely looked at me.

I put the flowers on the bedside table and handed my gift to Edmund as Angela partially unwrapped little Scarlett.

I looked, amazed, at her tiny fingers and thought of what my Norwegian grandmother said when she first saw my newborn son—"fresh from heaven." Scarlett was perfection itself—pink cheeks, a button nose, a rosebud mouth, and soft, downy hair. "Oh, Angela," was all I could say. Tears welled in my eyes.

"She's something, isn't she?" Edmund said. His eyes were shining with pride—and gratitude, I had no doubt. "The doctors say we can take her home tomorrow. They're keeping Angela and the baby here one more night to make sure there's no infection."

"Edmund's parents are on their way," Angela said, "and Hattie will be home the day after tomorrow." She blinked rapidly, fighting tears herself. "I can't thank you enough, Kate. I don't know what I would have done if you hadn't been there."

"You were the calmest of us all," I said, and then turned to Edmund. "You have quite a wife, you know."

"I'm well aware."

"Open the package, Edmund," Angela said. He did, and they exclaimed over the sleeper, which even in the newborn size looked enormous compared to Scarlett.

"She'll grow into that before you know it," I said. "Take lots of photos. They change every day."

"He's taken at least a hundred already." Angela laughed. "Everyone in the Anglican church has a photo by now."

Edmund blushed. "They told me to send pictures."

"Tom sends his love," I said. "He can't get away, but as soon as you're home, we'll stop over with supper."

"Just yourselves," Edmund said. "Vivian Bunn and Lady Barbara have already informed us that dinners, plural, are on the way, and Hattie will be cooking up a storm."

"Just us, then," I said, feeling a wave of exhaustion break through the adrenaline. "I'll go now. Tom's expecting me at the police station."

"What will happen to Derek Quinn?" Angela's eyes showed concern. She'd bonded with the young fugitive during those final thirty minutes in the barn.

"I'll let you know. I love you both—no," I corrected myself. "All three of you."

"The three Foxes," Angela said. "Sounds like a fairytale."

"It is a fairytale," I said, squeezing Angela's hand.

And the fox family lived happily ever after.

Returning to my car, I took a deep breath. Next on my schedule was Niall Nevin.

Chapter Forty-One

Bury St. Edmunds

The police station on Raingate Street was an imposing structure, built in the late nineteenth century in a sort of Jacobean revival style. I parked in the small side carpark and entered the visitors' waiting room, which was lined with posters urging folks to lock their cars, make sure their motor vehicle inspections were up to date, and make a difference by joining the police.

Tom met me and ushered me to one of their interview rooms. This time, instead of viewing the proceedings on a small computer screen, I'd be able to see and hear everything behind a pane of one-way glass. "DC Marsh will be with you," he said. "If there's something you want me to know, send her into the interview room with a note."

"Something I want you to know?"

"This has happened so quickly, we haven't had time to put together a coherent strategy. We will do that, but I want to interview Nevin now before he changes his mind about confessing. You've had more time to think through this, Kate. If I miss something, give me a shout."

As I watched through the one-way glass, Tom and DS Ren sat across from Nevin and his solicitor, a thin, bald, bespectacled man with sharp gray eyes. Nevin appeared calm, which surprised me. Maybe he was relieved. His solicitor had come prepared with a notebook, but he couldn't have had much more information than the police.

Only Niall Nevin knew what had happened on that misty night in June.

After the preliminaries, DS Ren began. "Niall Nevin, I'm arresting you on suspicion of the murder of Dr. Simon Sinclair. You do not have to say anything, but it may harm your defense if you do not mention when questioned something which you later rely on in court."

"DS Ren has explained your rights," Tom said. "Do you understand them, sir?"

"I understand." Nevin, who looked weary, sat up straighter. His right wrist was encased in a short cast and his arm had been immobilized in a sling. Other than a bruise on his right cheekbone, his face had somehow escaped visible injuries.

"Is there anything we can get you besides water?" Tom asked.

Nevin shook his head.

"Would you state your name, age, and profession for the record, please?"

"My name is Niall Gregory Nevin. I'm thirty-nine years old. I'm a professional archaeologist and lecturer at the University of East Anglia."

"Let's go back to 2016. The student archaeology project at Ravenswyck Court. In the hospital you said, and I quote"—Tom opened his black notebook—"'That's when this whole thing started.' What did you mean?"

"That's when I made my first mistake."

"We'll get to that in a moment." Tom closed his notebook. "First, what sorts of objects did you uncover during the course of that project—six weeks, was it?"

"Yes, six weeks. We found everything one would expect to find in a hamlet that was founded in the ninth century and existed until the plague reached rural Suffolk in the summer of 1349."

"Could you be more specific about your *finds*—is that what you call them?"

"That's correct. If you want details, I'd have to consult the spreadsheet."

"I have a copy of that spreadsheet here, sir." Tom took a packet of papers out of a file folder and handed it to Nevin.

Nevin flipped through the pages. "This is a list of several thousand objects—hoes, axe-heads, nails, hinges, and other iron implements and tools. We found hundreds of pottery shards, a few intact clay jars. Animal bones, textiles, fragments of leather and linen, bronze, copper, jewelry." He looked up from the pages.

"And gold?"

Nevin shifted uncomfortably. "Yes, there was some gold. Not a lot."

"In the form of jewelry?"

"Or jewelry parts, yes."

"Why isn't the gold listed on the official spreadsheet?"

Nevin glanced at his solicitor, who remained expressionless. "Because Dr. Sinclair and I culled out the gold before it was entered into the computer."

"Culled it out?"

"We separated it from the other finds." He looked embarrassed.

"You stole it."

"Simon called it *culling.* It was his idea initially. I'd joined the CMBA team in 2015, the year I received my degree. Sinclair had recommended me to the board. I idolized him. He was everything I could never be—charming, charismatic, able to chat to anyone about anything."

"When did the culling plan begin?"

"Late 2015. I'd injured myself pretty badly, my back, and Simon suggested I take charge of the finds lists for the summer work experience. He said I knew computers, and without having to do the field work, the actual excavation, I could recover more quickly."

"You thought he was being kind."

"I did." He made dismissive sound. "I realized later he was positioning me."

"Can you explain that?"

"He put me in that role specifically to alter the finds lists."

"What did Sinclair say—'Let's team up and steal some gold'?"

"Of course not. I remember his words exactly. He said, 'You know a lot of this stuff will end up in a storage bin somewhere at the CMBA. Why not let people enjoy it and get something out of it for ourselves at the same time?' I asked him what he meant, and he said, 'The really important objects are part of history. But no one cares about broken chains and empty bezels. All we have to do is put that sort of thing aside. Keep it separate in the safe. I'll get rid of it, and we'll share the rewards. All you have to do is make sure these superfluous items aren't listed on the spreadsheet. All the great archaeologists do it. It's one of the perks.'"

"You believed him?" Tom asked.

"I did—or I wanted to." Nevin looked at the spreadsheets again. He closed his eyes and pressed his lips together. "That's not true. The truth is I was afraid to say no. By that time, I'd seen what Simon could do to people who were disloyal. I knew he'd smile and say, 'That's fine, Niall. I asked, you answered,' but he wouldn't let it go. There'd have been reprisals, payback, but done in a way that could never be traced to him."

"So you and Simon Sinclair began stealing gold from the digs. Was that what you meant by 'your first mistake'?"

Nevin shook his head. "My first mistake was allowing myself to get pulled into Sinclair's web. I knew it was dangerous, but it was also exhilarating—being associated with a man like that."

"A man who stole gold."

"Not just gold. Other things, too. Simon would often point out certain items to me. That meant they weren't to show up on the spreadsheets or the summaries sent to the students."

"You thought you could get away with it?"

"We *did* get away with it—mostly. Every once in a while one of the students would ask about something they'd unearthed, and I had to come up with an excuse."

"Like what?"

"Usually I said the object was on another list."

"And they let it go?"

Nevin gave an odd, ironic smile. "They were afraid to take it further. They had their careers to protect, just as I did. In a lesser way, I was doing what Simon taught me. I'm not proud of it."

"When did the drugs start?"

"After my injury, I was prescribed painkillers—opioids. They were wonderful at first, pleasurable, a relief from the pain, but soon I couldn't live without them. After a while, my doctor stopped prescribing them, so I went to different doctors—those who don't work for the NHS. I ended up getting pills from several sources. That cost money, so I started borrowing, digging myself in further."

"Tell me about the night of Sinclair's death. We have a witness who overheard an argument at the dig site between Sinclair and another person. Was that you?"

"Yes."

"Sinclair said something about 'starting up again,' and you said, 'You don't know what I'm dealing with. You're going to ruin me.' Can you explain that?"

Nevin glanced at his solicitor. Was he hoping he would intervene?

"Things changed after the dig in Italy," Nevin said. "That was 2022. We were excavating a Roman village. A wall collapsed. I was injured again—this time it was a serious spinal injury. I was out for six months. By that time, I'd stopped taking painkillers, but they were prescribed again, and of course the addiction came back." He pulled out a handkerchief and mopped his forehead. "My doctor wasn't giving me enough to mask the pain. I couldn't work. I couldn't concentrate. I was desperate. Sinclair noticed—he always noticed—and he offered to get me more painkillers. He said he'd ask his doctor to prescribe them, and he'd give me the pills. That's what happened, which meant I was even more in debt to him than I'd been before."

"On the night of June nineteenth, he said you were 'starting up again.' What did he mean? Starting opioids again?"

"No. He already knew that. He meant the culling."

"Can you explain?"

"By early 2023, Simon had stopped providing the extra pills. He said his doctor was getting suspicious. I'm sure that was true, but it meant I'd have to find another source. Which I did—what else could I do? But this time my source was involved in organized crime, and the cost was exorbitant. Way more than I could afford. I'd inherited some money from my parents, but that was already gone, so I thought I'd do what Simon and I had done before—cull some of the gold from the digs and sell it myself. That's what Simon meant. I'd started culling again."

"But this time Sinclair wasn't involved?"

"No. He'd stopped culling in 2016. Said it was too risky. Students were starting to question the lists, and by that time, he was getting popular on the lecture circuit. Making real money. Simon liked money. He had alimony to pay, and his daughter was attending an expensive school."

"How did you sell the gold?"

"Online. On the dark web."

"And through Jeff Swift?" Tom asked.

Nevin's eyes widened in surprise. "That was only recently. I was desperate, and I'd begun taking greater risks, culling objects I knew were worth serious cash. The cybercrime unit from London was cracking down on the internet sales of stolen goods. I needed an alternative, and I met Jeff through an auction I attended."

I had to wonder at this point how an experienced and well-respected picker like Jeff Swift could be fooled—or would take a chance on stolen goods. It didn't seem right to me.

"What was your cover story?"

"*Ha.*" He gave a mirthless laugh. "I told Jeff I was selling off my wealthy father's collection of antiquities. It was partly true, which was helpful because I'm sure Jeff did his due diligence. My parents weren't titled, but they were wealthy, and my father did have a collection of antiquities. That's how I got interested in archaeology in the first place. It was all gone by that time, of course—the money, the collection."

"How did you convince Swift to keep your name confidential?"

"That was easy. I borrowed Simon's story. Told Jeff I had school fees to pay—a child no one knew about. I told him I'd lost my inheritance in a failed investment scheme, that I was embarrassed about having to sell the collection and didn't want anyone to know about that—or the child."

"He believed you?"

"I know what people think of me." He scoffed. "I don't come across as clever enough to make something like that up."

"You've been . . . *culling* again since when?"

"I started in the summer of 2023."

"And ended?"

Nevin's mouth twisted. "The nineteenth of June."

"The night Dr. Sinclair was murdered, yes. Let's talk about that night, June nineteenth." Tom was getting to the main event now. "The archaeologists went to the Six Bells in Hartwell. You stayed at The Forge to finish up some computer work. Was that the truth?"

"No. By then, I'd realized Simon was checking up on me. He'd been taking inventories of the safe at the field office and the one at Ravenswyck Court. I wanted to explain, beg him not to say anything. I thought he'd understand about the painkillers."

"Walk us through what happened that night."

Nevin took a drink of water, wincing from the pain in his arm. "I went to the field office to retrieve a box of gold I'd hidden there. It was gone. I panicked because I needed more pills. That's when I realized Simon must have taken the box, so I texted him around ten fifteen and asked him to meet me at the dig site."

"How did you persuade him? It was late."

"That was the weird thing." Nevin's brow furrowed. "I noticed someone had left a mallet near one of the trenches. I went to investigate and saw the pearls. It was so strange. I still don't understand why someone would do that. I saw immediately that they were fake, of course, but then I realized it was the perfect excuse to get Simon out there. I texted him and said I'd found pearls in one of the trenches. I knew that would pique his interest. I was right. He texted back and said he'd meet me there as soon as he could. He arrived just after midnight. I showed him the pearls, and he laughed at me. 'Overreacted as usual, old man.' He said it had to be the protesters, vandalism. That's when I asked him outright if he'd taken the gold from the safe. He said he had, and that I had to stop culling. I begged him to let me have the gold—just once more. I told him if I couldn't get the pills, I was going to go crazy—or die. He said that was my problem. I was the one who'd got himself hooked." Nevin was sweating. He took another drink of water.

Outside the interview room, DC Marsh and I exchanged glances. So many things were falling into place. One thing that didn't was Nevin's computer. It had been active during that time, and Mark Lambe had heard his printer working. How would he explain that?

"Did you plan to kill him?" Tom asked.

"No, I swear." Nevin shook his head violently. "I just wanted to reason with him. I told him I'd do anything. He wouldn't listen. And I just . . . lost it. I shoved him into the trench."

"Then what did you do?"

"I panicked and ran. I couldn't believe I'd done it. Somehow I made it back to The Forge. Went to bed."

Tom didn't tell him about the pearls Sinclair had ingested—or about the time it took for Sinclair to die. That would come later.

"What did you do with Dr. Sinclair's mobile phone?"

"Took it, of course. He'd been emailing and texting me about the finds lists. He knew."

"Where is the mobile now?"

"I don't know—honestly. I deleted the incriminating data and took it apart. Over the course of a few days, I discarded the components, bit by bit, at a number of locations."

"And you deleted the same data on Sinclair's computer."

"Of course. That very night. It was easy."

"Tell me about the next day, when you met my wife and Mr. Tweedy at Ravenswyck Court. You suggested everyone should look for Dr. Sinclair at the dig site."

"I knew the body would be found, so I said Simon was probably at the dig site and we should meet him there. I also knew my DNA would be all over it."

"That's why you jumped into the trench?"

"Of course.." He lifted his chin. "I'm not sorry."

As I'd been listening, an idea had occurred to me. I scribbled some words on the note pad Tom had left there, folded it in half, and handed it to DC Marsh. "Take this in to him."

I watched through the one-way glass. "Excuse me, sir." Marsh handed Tom my note and exited.

Tom read the note. His eyes glanced briefly in my direction.

"How did you feel about Simon Sinclair?" Tom asked, slipping the note into his folder.

"How did I feel about him?" Nevin's lip curled in disgust. "He was the devil himself. When I realized how he'd drawn me in, trapped me, controlled me, used me, I realized I hated his guts. I was glad I'd killed him."

Tom was silent for a moment. Then he said quietly, "Did you feel that way about Carrie Holgate as well?"

The blow landed.

Nevin broke down completely. "I'm sorry. I'm so sorry. I never meant to kill her."

"My client needs a break." His solicitor stood. "Now, please."

Chapter Forty-Two

During the break, Tom brought me a paper cup of the station's coffee, which was strong enough to clean silver.

Tom perched on the edge of one of the desks.

"How did you know he'd murdered Carrie Holgate?"

"I didn't know. I suspected. Remember I said I thought the two murders might be connected? There were similarities, the most obvious being that they both occurred at Egemere Close. The nine years separating them was puzzling, but when I learned that in both cases, there were accusations of missing objects and altered finds lists, I decided that couldn't be a coincidence. Someone had been stealing artifacts, specifically gold, and the only people with access to both the safes and the finds lists were the team leaders. Tamzin and Mark weren't part of the dig in 2016, so if the two murders were connected as I suspected, the killer had to be someone else. Initially, I assumed Sinclair himself was the thief. The box of gold in his room seemed to prove it. The problem was I couldn't figure out why someone would murder him over it. Why not just turn him over to the police? I did wonder if Sinclair had been the father of Carrie Holgate's baby and if someone killed him because of that, but then I learned about the argument Zach Valentine overheard. Sinclair accused the second person at the dig site that night of 'starting up again.' If he meant the thefts, as I suspected, the culprit could only be Celia Whybrew or Niall Nevin. Celia had a motive for wanting Sinclair dead, but I couldn't believe she'd killed Carrie or was involved in stealing gold from the dig. That left Nevin. Carrie must have suspected the thefts. Her letter to her husband implies it, and that put Nevin in danger. He hated Sinclair, and with good reason, but he couldn't have hated Carrie. Now that we know about Nevin's drug addition, it makes sense. He was desperate, but he's still human.

Tom squeezed my hand. "We need a confession. He's going to have to tell us himself."

The interview with Niall Nevin recommenced at four PM. Nevin looked as if the life had been sucked out of him, leaving a husk as fragile as eggshell porcelain. His solicitor sat beside him, expressionless, grim, and, I imagined, resigned. We all knew where this was heading.

"Niall Nevin," Tom said, "I'm arresting you on suspicion of the murder of Carrie Holgate. You do not have to say anything, but it may harm your defense if you do not mention when questioned something which you later rely on in court. Do you understand?"

"Yes." Nevin sat slumped in his chair. "Let's get it over with. I don't feel well."

"All right. I'd like to go back to the student excavations in 2016. You've already admitted your cooperation with Dr. Sinclair's plan to cull—to steal—certain objects, especially gold. When did Carrie Holgate confront you?"

Nevin put his head in his hands. "Just before her husband was due to arrive home. She said she'd figured out what had been going on, and she was going to tell him. She said she wanted to give me a chance to confess, that it might reduce the charges against me if I cooperated with the police and testified against Sinclair. I begged her not to say anything. I promised to put everything back, make it right. I remember the look on her face." Nevin choked on a sob. "She said there was no way I could change her mind." Nevin was breathing hard now, struggling to get the words out. "I was in trouble. I hadn't had any painkillers that day—I was out of them. I was confused, aching all over, shaking. I realized my hands were around her neck." He sobbed. "Her face . . . I closed my eyes. I pressed and pressed until she went limp."

"Where was this? When did you meet?"

"The field office caravan. After hours."

"How were you able to deal with her body on your own?"

"I couldn't. My back." He wiped his eyes with his fists, like a child. "I called Simon. I didn't know what else to do. He helped me bury her body on the mound. I was a mess, but Simon put everything back so carefully no one would ever have known the ground had been disturbed."

"You didn't take Carrie's gold and emerald necklace. Why? It must have been worth a fortune."

"I said we should." Nevin swiped at his face. "Simon still had enough sense to tell me that if we ever sold the necklace, even on the black market, it could be traced back to Carrie and then to us."

My throat closed. I pictured that beautiful young woman—happy, brave, kind, gifted—her life extinguished for drugs.

"What happened then?"

"Simon told me that was the end. We couldn't continue culling. It was too risky. I told you, he'd already started making money on the lecture circuit."

"And the drugs?"

"I decided to get clean." Nevin gave a brief smile. "I checked myself into a rehab facility. It was the hardest thing I've ever done in my life, but I did it. And I did my best to forget those years and move ahead. But Simon kept reminding me—in subtle ways no one but me would understand. The message was clear—*I own you now.* Simon used me to do the research for his talks and journal articles. In the end, I was practically writing them. He loved the money and the fame as long as I did the work."

"But you'd started using drugs again. When was that?"

"I told you. After my serious injury at the Roman village in 2022. Things were even worse the second time. That's when Simon agreed to get me more pills. He could see I was falling apart, and he needed me to do his research. Then he stopped giving me pills, and I was forced to find another source."

"I'd like to go back to the night of June nineteenth," Tom said. "Dr. Sinclair accused you of culling and said you had to stop."

"He said if I didn't, he'd tell the police I'd killed Carrie Holgate."

"But wouldn't that have meant incriminating himself as well?" Tom asked. "He helped you bury her body on the mound."

"I told him that. He just scoffed and said no one would believe me. He was probably right."

"You said you shoved him into the trench," Tom said. "You mean you shoved his body into the trench."

"His body?" Nevin looked confused. "No, I'd grabbed his lapels and was shaking him, begging him to help me. And then without actually deciding to do it, I pushed him backward into the trench. He must have hit his head because he lay there, not moving. I knew I'd killed him."

"When did you hit him with the mallet?"

Nevin looked at his solicitor. "What's he talking about?"

"Dr. Sinclair was killed by a blow to the back of his head with a mallet. We found the weapon."

Nevin stood, almost knocking over his chair. "But that means—" He put his good hand to his mouth. "That means I didn't kill him?"

"Take a seat, Dr. Nevin," Tom said, leaning forward. "Let me get this straight. You're telling us you pushed Sinclair into the trench, but you didn't hit him with the mallet?" He glanced at DS Ren.

"Yes, that's what happened. I thought . . . I was certain I'd killed him. The next day, when I saw all the blood, I figured he must have hit his head on a rock or something."

"What did you do after you pushed him into the trench?"

"I told you—I ran. I thought I heard someone coming."

"What exactly did you hear?" Tom's voice was as sharp as cut glass.

"Footsteps. I wasn't sure, but I wasn't going to stick around and find out."

"Did you see anyone? Hear a voice?"

"No, nothing. The mist was so thick I could hardly see my own feet. How I made it back to The Forge, I'll never know." Nevin's eyes widened. He opened his mouth but no words came out for a good ten seconds. "Someone was there that night. And that person—that person killed Simon." He laid his head on the table and sobbed.

Tom joined me outside the interview room. "At some point, we'll ask him about Edlyn Dark and the grief bot, but first we have to address the murders, take his statement, and get a medical professional to assess his condition."

"How about his computer that was supposedly working all night?"

"Yeah—that, too."

A wave of fatigue washed over me. "I don't know how you're managing to stay awake. I'm going to drive home while I still can."

"Be safe. I don't know when I'll be home. We're back to square one in the Sinclair murder."

As soon as he said the words, I saw it. I understood. The puzzle was nearly complete. One piece only was missing, and I recognized the shape of it. I knew who'd killed Simon Sinclair. The only person left. And it made me sad. "No, Tom. We're not back to square one. Remember what Sherlock Holmes said—'When you've eliminated the impossible, whatever remains, however improbable, must be the truth.'"

"What do you mean? If it wasn't Nevin, are you saying it was Celia Whybrew after all?"

"I don't think so." I pushed my hair back, summoning what mental energy I had left. "Who is the one person who never did and still doesn't have an alibi for the night Sinclair was killed? Who admitted to seeing lights at the dig site that night?"

Tom stared at me. "Peter Eley. But what motive would he have had?"

"We've talked about it and around it since the beginning. Carrie Holgate was the motive. Peter loved her. He knew she was pregnant, and he knew the father couldn't be Alex Belcourt. He must have assumed it was Simon Sinclair. I think he went to check out the lights at the dig site that night, thinking the nighthawkers were back."

"I see what you mean. He must have heard Sinclair and Nevin admit to killing Carrie."

"He may have suspected before, but that night he knew."

Tom opened the door to the outer office. "DC Marsh, you're with me." Holly Marsh, the youngest and newest member of the team, looked up from her computer, surprised to be singled out. "We're going to arrest Peter Eley," Tom said. "I'll be charging him with the murder of Simon Sinclair."

* * *

Tom made it home by eight. He'd texted to say he'd buy a couple of ready meals from the Tesco near the roundabout on the way. As I unpacked the Tesco bag, Tom said, "Eley confessed right away. Went with us willingly. As you said, he saw lights at the dig site and went to investigate, thinking it was nighthawkers. He planned to scare them off, but when he got there, he realized it was Sinclair and someone else instead."

"He didn't know it was Nevin?"

"No. The mist was so thick that night, he couldn't be certain, but he knew Sinclair's voice and heard him talking about burying Carrie Holgate's body. That sealed it for him, for Eley. He found Sinclair in the trench, on his knees, trying to stand. The mallet was there. He picked it up and smashed Sinclair's head in. Sinclair never even saw him."

"That was it?"

"He threw the mallet away, went home, cleaned up, and went to bed. He says he slept well for the first time in nine years. He's not sorry, and he's ready to take his punishment."

"Oh, Tom. Peter said he wished he could have died in Carrie's place."

"He really loved her, but that didn't give him the right to take a life, no matter what the provocation."

"Of course not."

"Sometimes solving a case is satisfying. Sometimes it's not. The truth is what matters. Ultimately, Simon Sinclair was responsible for the ruining of more than one life. I wouldn't like to die with that on my conscience."

"No." I took a kitchen scissors and opened the meal packets. "What about Nevin?"

"It took about an hour for Nevin's pills to kick in. The good news is as long as he's on them, he can process what's happening to him."

"The bad news?"

"We now have a duty of care. It will take a whole team to manage his addiction. Right now, my job is to make sure he's fit enough to be questioned and to go through a court proceeding. He's charged with the murder of Carrie Holgate, and he's a material witness in the murder of Simon Sinclair."

I spooned the contents of the meal packets onto two plates and put them in the microwave, one at a time. "Was Nevin able to tell you about Edlyn Dark?"

"Oh, yes. He went into a lot of technical details about a computer back door, which I won't bore you with."

I laughed. "You mean you had no idea what he was talking about."

"Completely lost." Tom gave me one those half-smiles I fell in love with in Scotland. "Good thing Ren is young. He explained to me later that a back door is a program installed on a computer to give someone a covert way of remotely accessing that computer without the normal authentication protocols."

"I see—sort of. Nevin wanted the files in Grenville Dark's computer—all the research he'd done." I carried our plates to the table. "There's a bottle of water in the fridge."

"Actually, it was Sinclair who wanted the files." Tom poured two glasses of chilled water. "Sinclair knew about Grenville Dark and his research into the history of Egemere Close. He also knew the old man had died before he could publish his book. Sinclair intended to publish a series of articles that would take advantage of the notoriety surrounding the discovery of Egemere Woman. That would lead to more paid lectures. There was talk of a book contract. But he needed Dark's research, so he told Nevin to steal the files."

"Which Nevin did because he had no choice."

"Nevin emailed Edlyn Dark, pretending to be a history professor at the university and asking her if he could read her father's manuscript. She refused point-blank."

"When was this?"

"Last spring, shortly after the body was discovered. Edlyn told him she intended to publish her father's work but was having trouble accessing the files."

"He offered to help."

"He was more clever than that. He told her there was a computer lab at the university that helped people in the community with computer issues, and if she contacted them, they'd send someone out to see what the trouble was."

"I suppose he gave her his own mobile number."

"You got it. She called him. He pretended to be the university's repair service and said he'd come right out. They'd only emailed previously, so she didn't know his voice or what he looked like."

"What did he do when he got to Edlyn's cottage?"

"The first thing was to complete the needed updates. The old computer was seriously out of date. Then he sent the files and the uncompleted manuscript to his own computer. Then he deleted everything. At the same time, he installed the back door on the old computer, which meant he could access it at any time. Over the next week, Nevin transferred the rest of Grenville Dark's files, documents, and images to his personal computer, and he used the back door to install a bot to mimic Edlyn's father."

"But it was so realistic, Tom. How was that possible?"

"AI, artificial intelligence. Ivor was right about that. Nevin had everything at that point—not only the papers and correspondence Edlyn's father had written during his lifetime, including letters to Edlyn, but also extensive audio files of his lectures plus images and photographs. Nevin fed all the data into his AI model and trained it to mimic Grenville Dark."

"So the bot incorporated his image and learned his voice and speech patterns. But what about the warnings about disturbing the dead?"

"Nevin added those himself, incorporating material from a society in London that exists to prevent historical exhumation."

"What was his purpose in stopping the dig?"

"To prevent the CMBA from excavating the mound and finding Carrie's body, of course."

"Yes, I see. Which is why both Sinclair and Nevin were keen to keep the team away from Mark's mound."

"Mark Lambe had been making his case about the plague pit for some time. Sinclair and Nevin feared the board would agree."

"But the protests weren't focused on the mound," I said, a forkful of chicken tikka masala balancing in mid-air. "In fact, I'm not sure Edlyn Dark and the protesters even knew about Mark's proposal."

"True, but all Sinclair and Nevin needed was a group of protesters. They hoped the threat of public protests would convince the CMBA board not to authorize any further excavations in or around Egemere Close. In fact, they were ready to sacrifice everything they'd done there in order to keep anyone from finding Carrie's body."

"Celia told me Sinclair had been lobbying to have this year's student experience at a Roman villa near Oakham. Just think, Tom. If Sinclair had gotten his way, they'd never have found Egemere Woman." I shook my head in amazement. "I did think it was strange Sinclair was so opposed to Mark's theory, even after a plague pit had been discovered in Lincolnshire. And I noticed that Nevin tried everything he could think of to prevent the radar and test pit on the mound."

"They knew Carrie's body was there." Tom put down his fork. "Nevin asked how we figured out he was involved."

"What did you tell him?"

"The truth. You recognized the second earring in the auction catalog."

"How did he explain the matching intaglio in Sinclair's ring?"

"That was interesting. Nevin said they'd found the pair in the excavation of the Roman village in Italy—a matching pair, undamaged. Sinclair wanted the stones. They'd be worth a packet, but a perfect pair like that would also have given rise to questions. Where had the earrings been found? How had they ended up on the market? They couldn't have that, so Sinclair decided to split them up."

"Even though it meant they'd bring in a lot less cash."

"According to Nevin, Sinclair was becoming more cautious at that point. And he'd taken a fancy to the image of Mercury, who among his other gifts, was thought to be the god of eloquence and communication. Sinclair saw the ring as a kind of charm. He palmed the ring as he was dying, hoping it would point us to Nevin."

"Sinclair assumed it was Nevin who'd hit him with the mallet?"

"Probably. He never saw his assailant. As he was bleeding out, and assuming it was Nevin, Sinclair did two things he knew the police would puzzle over and investigate. The pearls were meant to point to the archaeology team—you understood that early on—and the ring was meant to point to the thefts."

"And ultimately to Nevin."

"Injured as he was, I'm amazed Sinclair had the wits to think at all. How did Nevin manage to create the impression his computer and printer were working that night?"

"Because they were. He'd programmed everything in advance. Something to do with self-modifying codes, programmed delays, and transitions. Beyond me."

"One thing still bothers me—Edlyn Dark's warnings of death at the site. Obviously, the threats came from Nevin, but they started before Sinclair's murder and before Nevin knew the CMBA would authorize the test pit on the mound."

"The timing of the deaths was pure coincidence. The warnings were meant to frighten and motivate the protesters—Edlyn in particular. In order to rally the protesters, she had to really believe the spirits of the dead at Egemere Close were going to exact revenge."

"Poor Edlyn. She lost her father, his research, everything."

"Not true." Tom gathered up our plates and utensils and put them in the sink. "She still has her father's book and his research. All the files are on Nevin's computer. We have a team looking through them as we speak."

"We need to tell Edlyn, Tom. She deserves to know the truth."

Chapter Forty-Three

Saturday, July 12
Ravenswyck Court

No one could say the last two and a half weeks had been uneventful. I was more than ready to return to my old routine at home and the shop, although I still had questions about Egemere Woman and the Pearl of Wyck. I might never know who she was for sure, but my biggest question was still the pearl. Why had someone—Henry Wyck?—forfeited a fortune? If guilt had pushed him to take his own life, I could see that an earthly fortune would have meant nothing to him. Still, I had the feeling there was more to it than that.

Tom, Ivor, and I had been asked to meet Celia, Mark, and Tamzin at Ravenswyck Court that morning at ten thirty. They were still in shock over Dr. Nevin's arrest, but the silver cuff had been delivered from the restoration company in Cambridge. Celia would be taking it back with her to Norwich for another meeting of the CMBA board, and she knew Ivor and I would want to see it in all its glory.

We picked Ivor up at the shop and made the twenty-plus-minute drive to Ravenswyck. The horse chestnut trees lining the drive were in full bloom as they had been every summer for nearly three hundred years. Soon their showy, pinkish white candles would give way to spiky husks that would eventually shed the shiny, reddish-brown conkers that were the essence of autumn in Suffolk. Out of the corner of my eye, I thought I caught the sight of a large black bird taking wing. A raven? If so, I hoped those harbingers of doom would finally abandon Ravenswyck and move on.

Belcourt met us at the door. "Welcome, friends." He looked better than he had twenty-four hours earlier, but I knew it would take him a very long time to process the discovery of Carrie's body and all that it meant. Tom had notified him of Niall Nevin's and Peter Eley's confessions, and he'd had a visit from a victim liaison officer, who would keep him informed of the court proceedings. How Belcourt felt about Peter Eley's act of revenge I couldn't imagine. I'd texted him my condolences and told him I would email my final report on Egemere Woman in a few days.

Once more, we rode the creaky old elevator down to the recreated village and museum. In the inner office, Celia, Tamzin, and Mark stood with their backs to us. Hearing our approach, they turned, and I saw the trauma of the last few days on their faces. Two and a half weeks ago, there had been five on the archaeological team. Now there were three.

"Come, have a look," Celia said. She put one arm around Tamzin and rested the opposite hand on Mark's shoulder. Sinclair had called her a mother hen. It was true, and the young people needed her at this moment. Mark was dressed uncharacteristically in gray trousers, an open-collared white shirt, and a navy linen sports jacket. Tamzin was even more uncharacteristically dressed in a cotton eyelet shirtdress in a flattering pomegranate color.

The now-gleaming cuff rested on a square of felt. Celia handed us each a pair of white cotton gloves. "Thank you for recommending we have it professionally cleaned. Now we can see the details, and yes, the heads are the Twelve Apostles. The symbols are clear."

She was right. Peter had the crossed keys symbol above his head. Andrew had a fish, and James a scallop shell. Each of the Twelve could be identified by the emblems associated with them in medieval art, and with the exception of the identical blue glass eyes, each face was also distinctive. I was glad to see the Cambridge restorers had left a light patina, which enhanced the beauty of the design.

"I suspect this was a talisman," Ivor said, "carried into battle to ensure divine protection. A common practice in the Middle Ages."

"Which begs the question," Mark said, "why was it buried with Egemere Woman?"

"If only we could ask her," Tamzin said. "Being present when her coffin was opened was the most thrilling moment of my life. It's just so awful that—" Her face crumpled, and Mark took her in his arms.

"We're sorry for what you've been through," Tom said. "You know by now that Dr. Nevin has confessed to the murder of Carrie Holgate, and Peter Eley to killing Dr. Sinclair." He glanced at Belcourt, who'd so far been silent. "If any of you feel you need to speak with someone, a counselor, we can arrange that."

Celia drew me aside. "I lied to you. I'm sorry."

"About Keely Armstrong, yes." I'd forgotten about it. "Why?"

"To protect Niall, I suppose. At the time, Keely had suspected him of stealing gold, and I wanted to know for sure before I said anything. Foolish, I know. I've told the police." Then she said, in a voice loud enough for everyone to hear, "Kate, would you like to show your husband the pearl?"

"Yes," Tom said without hesitation. "Kate's described it, of course, but seeing it would be a great privilege."

I hadn't counted on this. As Celia eased the pearl out of its leather pouch, I focused on breathing normally. *In and out, slow and steady.* Against the dark felt background, the pearl gleamed, the beauty of its pure white luster pulling me in.

A wave of heat rose in my body. My heart kicked up, and my mouth went dry. *Oh man.* I tried to pull my eyes away, but they wouldn't cooperate. I could hear myself breathing hard. Tom must have heard it, too, because I felt his hand on my back, steadying me.

Fear, terror.

An image rose in my imagination—not Egemere Woman but Carrie Holgate's bloated face, horrible in death, her beauty erased as she fought to breathe.

A tiny mewling sound escaped my lips. I cleared my throat and closed my lips as tightly as I could. I didn't dare look at Tom.

I have to tell him. This has to end.

At last, Celia was tucking the pearl back into the leather pouch. "This has been a horrific time for us," she was saying, "especially Mark and Tamzin. We will come to terms with it in time. I won't say there's a silver lining because that isn't true, but I do have an announcement that I believe will be most welcome." She turned to Alex Belcourt. "I've been waiting to announce this until we were all together. With the permission of the Crown, the CMBA board has agreed to house all the artifacts unearthed at Egemere Close—past and future—in the Ravenswyck museum, where they belong."

Everyone applauded.

"Thank you," Belcourt said, his voice filled with emotion.

"When do you leave?" Tom asked the archaeologists.

"This afternoon," Mark said.

"I'm meeting Mark's mother this evening," Tamzin said. "Vivian and Lady Barbara bought me this dress. Do you think I'll pass muster?"

I thought she looked adorable and said so. The fact that she'd styled the eyelet shirtdress with a black leather corset belt, black-and-white striped tights, black combat boots, and a rhinestone tiara gave the outfit that uniquely Tamzin flair.

Mark took her hand. "She's going to love you."

"Do you have plans?" I asked Celia.

She looked a little embarrassed. "I'm having dinner with Duncan tonight. Duncan Price-Davies. He's recently got in touch. We're old friends."

And maybe more than friends again, I thought. *How nice.*

"We'll be back in September to excavate the mound," Mark said. "You're all welcome to observe. We just might find that plague pit."

We all thanked him.

I would follow their progress, but I had a feeling our paths wouldn't intersect a second time.

* * *

Our next stop was the rectory. Angela and the baby had arrived home that morning, and Edmund had texted, saying Angela was ready to show off little Scarlett Genevieve.

"Do you want to see her?" I asked Ivor. I'd never seen him around babies or children.

"Best keep our eyes on them," he said with the barest suggestion of a wink. "You know they're planning to replace us."

When we arrived at the rectory, Edmund answered the door, looking every inch the proud first-time father. "Everyone's up in the nursery."

"Everyone" turned out to be Angela, Vivian, and Lady Barbara, who was holding Scarlett and cooing.

"She's an attractive newborn," Vivian said as if pronouncing a verdict. "You'll have to get her on a schedule as soon as you can, Angela dear. That's the secret—a schedule."

Lady Barbara and I exchanged a glance. We'd actually had babies.

"Would you like to hold her, Ivor?" Angela asked.

"I believe I'll wait until she can talk," he said, which made us all laugh.

"How about you, Kate?"

"Of course." I took the tiny bundle in my arms, remembering vividly the feel and the smell of my son, Eric, and my daughter, Christine, when they were infants—that never-to-be-forgotten blend of milk, soap, and diaper-rash cream. Scarlett began to whimper. I bounced her gently, which only made things worse. "Maybe you should take her, Angela."

"Let me try," Tom said. I handed Scarlett to him, realizing I'd never seen him with a baby. He held her upright, tucking her head under his chin, and began to stroll around the room. She burrowed against his shoulder and immediately fell asleep.

"You have the touch," Edmund said. "You'll have to give me lessons."

I noticed that Angela's eyes were at half-mast. "I think Mum needs her rest," I said. "And the new parents need time alone."

"She's a bonnie baby, Edmund," Ivor said. I noticed the wetness in his eyes.

"Come on, you two," I said to Vivian and Lady Barbara. "We'll have plenty of time to see Scarlett in the days and weeks ahead."

"Yes, indeed," Lady Barbara said. "Francie will deliver a meal tonight, Edmund. One less thing to worry about."

"If you need a babysitter," Tom said, "Kate and I would be delighted."

"Watch out," Edmund said, herding us all downstairs. "Kate might get ideas."

Tom laughed uproariously.

We all said goodbye, and Tom and I headed for my car.

He pulled out his phone, looked at the screen, and frowned. "A text from my mom." He pulled it up and stopped walking.

"What is it?" I asked. "Is she all right?"

"She's met a man." He looked at me, his forehead furrowed. "She says she's in love."

* * *

Manor Farm

When Tom and I got home, we were still speculating about the text from his mother, Liz. "Did you answer her?" I asked Tom.

"Not yet, but I'll have to. What should I say?"

"That you're happy for her and looking forward to meeting him." It was an easy answer and the right one, but I shared Tom's concern. Liz Mallory was an attractive woman in her youthful sixties. I could understand how she might attract the attentions of an eligible man, but we'd recently been through a similar experience with our friend, Sheila Parker, who'd been taken in by a captivating online boyfriend and lost thousands of pounds in the process. Tom began tapping out a response. "I'll postpone judgment until I meet this chap who's swept my mother off her feet. He must be quite something."

He must be something, all right, I thought but did not say. *Like a potential con man.*

"Let's enjoy what's left of the afternoon," Tom said. "We haven't had a real weekend in weeks. It's a lovely day. Why don't you go out to the patio? I'll pour us a couple of glasses of prosecco. I feel like celebrating with the brilliant woman who played a pivotal role in the solving of two major cases."

"You don't have to tell me twice," I said, grabbing a cardigan.

Tom and I were sitting quietly, taking in the beauty of our back garden, when my phone pinged with a text. It was Duncan Price-Davies.

> *"No stone unturned" is the phrase of the year, Kate. I told you the rest of the files Grenville Dark consulted were legal documents, concerned with mundane things like property rights, laws, and resolving disputes. I was wrong. I believe this particular document holds the key to the mystery of Egemere Woman. You'll see from the photograph it was written in a Gothic cursive script on parchment and attested to by four men. Two of the names will be familiar to you. Thank you for giving me the privilege of working on this. And I must say, Grenville Dark did a fine job with the modern English translation. I couldn't have done better myself.*
>
> *Must go now. Dinner with Celia. Wish me luck. Duncan*

I showed the text to Tom. "I'd like to read these on my computer."

"I'll make dinner. What do you say to a vegetable omelet and a green salad?"

"Perfect," I said, reaching over to kiss him. "I'll be in the sitting room."

Opening the files on my laptop, I saved them to my desktop. Then, carrying the computer, I settled myself on the sitting room sofa, drew my feet up under me, and began to read.

The first file was a digital photograph of a very old document, handwritten on parchment with four red seals attached to the bottom with ribbons—a legal document, witnessed by four men.

The second file was the translation.

The Confession of Henry Wyck
Translated into Modern English by Grenville Dark
BA (Hons) History; MA (Hons) Medieval History; MLitt Medieval English

Testimony by Father John Wickham of the Church of St. Margaret, Egemere Close, Thomas Robelyn, tenant of Ravenswyck, John Martyn, tenant of Ravenswyck, and Robert Fogg of Hartwell of a confession statement by Sir Henry Wyck of Ravenswyck Court, Egemere Close, concerning the death of his wife, Matilda de Emeyse.

On the 1st day of November in the Year of Our Lord 1348, Sir Henry Wyck of Ravenswyck Court, in a state of mental anguish and suffering from madness, in hopes of God's mercy, did make his confession before these witnesses, who testify that they heard Sir Henry Wyck relate the following:

On the 3rd of August 1347, while entering the garrison at Calais, Sir Henry came upon a French knight whose armour had been pierced by an English longbow. Left behind when the French troops abandoned the garrison and in great pain, the knight pleaded with Sir Henry to spare his life, in return for which he would give him a powerful talisman to preserve him in battle and guarantee his future happiness. "What is this rare object?" Henry asked. "First you must swear to spare my life," said the knight. "I swear it on all I hold sacred," Henry replied and found the precious object beneath the knight's padded undergarment. Suspended from a silver chain around the knight's neck was a leathern pouch containing a magnificent pearl, the like of which Sir Henry had never seen nor imagined. Possessing the talisman and being unwilling to sacrifice his horse for what was surely a dying man, he unsheathed his sword. "Pray do not do this, sir," said the knight, "for if you break faith, the pearl will be to you a curse rather than a blessing." To his shame, Sir Henry ran him through.

Two days later Sir Henry was thrown from his horse and nearly disembowelled by his own dagger. His wound was declared to be mortal. However, after many months he recovered, and having survived, convinced himself the wondrous pearl had made him invincible.

He sailed for England in early February of 1348, longing to reunite with his wife Matilda de Emeyse, who because of her piety and great beauty was known as the Pearl of Wyck. Instead of a joyous reunion, he found her married to his steward and with child. She wept most piteously, begging him for mercy and claiming she had thought him dead. In a fit of madness he killed her and laid her in the leaden coffin prepared for his own body, intending to bury her secretly in the crypt of St. Margaret's Church. It was then, overtaken by remorse, he remembered what the French knight had said. Desiring above all things to be free of the curse now resting upon him, he placed the pearl in Matilda's coffin along with the silver amulet he had carried into battle.

We testify this is a true and accurate account.

Declaration of Father John Wickham, Church of St. Margaret, Egemere Close, Thomas Robelyn, tenant of Ravenswyck, John Martyn, tenant of Ravenswyck, and Robert Fogg of Hartwell.

I sat there for a long time, contemplating, as I had nearly a month earlier, death and grief and the strange turns life sometimes takes. *Someone had loved her, and someone had wanted her dead.* In the end, they were the same person.

"Dinner's ready, Kate." Tom's voice from the kitchen came with the comforting assurance that all the pain and guilt contained in the historical records would not, *could not* touch us. If there had been a curse, and I wasn't one to believe in such things, it had been buried seven centuries ago in a leaden coffin. Finally the loose threads of history had come untangled, and generations would marvel at it. The archaeologists had been given the privilege of unearthing the body of a woman brutally murdered along with her unborn child in 1348. I had been given the privilege of learning her name and telling her story.

"Coming, darling." I picked up my laptop and made my way into the heart of our home. A page had turned. A new story was being written.

Chapter Forty-Four

Sunday, July 13
Hartwell

Since my last visit, the citizens of Hartwell had posted new signs:

> *Tours of the Plague Village & Museum. Enquire at the Six Bells.*
> *Two-bed self-catering cottage to let.*
> *Room with ensuite. Book now.*

Now that the museum at Ravenswyck Court was set to reopen, the citizens of Hartwell were gearing up for an influx of tourists. Their village offered the irresistible combination of ancient history, an exceptional stately home and museum, three graves, and three murders.

Tom and I parked in the pub's overflow lot and walked to The Old Schoolhouse. Edlyn Dark had reluctantly agreed to see us.

Entering Edlyn's front garden, we saw the curtains twitch. She opened the door. "I don't have much time so make it quick."

"We will," Tom said. "There are things you should know, and we have what I hope you will think is good news."

Inside Edlyn's dim parlor, we found Zach Valentine slouched in a chair. He gave Tom a wary look. "Are you going to arrest me?"

"No, Zach," Tom said. "There are no charges against you. You helped us with our investigation. We're very grateful to you." Tom took a seat beside him. "I'd like to recommend you join one of the detectorist clubs in the area, though. Do things the right way."

That seemed to satisfy him.

"What is it?" Edlyn said, her hands on her hips. "I don't have all day."

"Right," Tom said. "The first thing we want you to know is how truly exceptional your father was."

I could see she was softening. "I've known that all my life."

"Now everyone will know it, Edlyn," I said, "because the police have the complete manuscript of your father's book about Egemere Close."

"The police have his book? Why? How?"

"It's a complicated story," Tom said, "and it begins with your father's computer. The technician you called in lied to you. You deserve to know the truth."

"I know the truth," she said. "Father was with me, and now he's gone."

"Not quite," Tom said in a gentle voice. "Is it all right if we sit? This may take some time."

"Yes, of course. Zach, bring in the tea."

I took one of the brown geometric-patterned chairs. Tom sat beside Edlyn on the sofa. Slowly and carefully, he explained to her about the fraud Niall Nevin had perpetrated. "He used your father's data to create his image and his voice. That's why it sounded familiar to you—because it was."

Edlyn's hands were in her lap, but I could see them clenching and unclenching as she struggled to comprehend—and to accept.

Zach brought in the tea tray, which, as before, had been ready and waiting for the hot water to be poured. Edlyn had even made shortbread, which told me that despite her defiant attitude, she'd been looking forward to our visit.

As I poured the tea, Edlyn listened to Tom, her lips compressed. When he'd finished, she said, "So what you're saying is Father was never really here."

"Not from beyond the grave, no," Tom said kindly. "But he is still with you in a sense. As Kate said, the police have recovered your father's manuscript and all his files from Nevin's computer. Nothing has been lost."

She looked down. "This man, Nevin, took advantage of a silly old woman."

"Not a silly old woman," Tom said firmly. "A woman who'd suffered a great loss, which made her vulnerable. Niall Nevin wasn't a nice man, but he had problems of his own, and those problems caused him to do unconscionable things. He will have to answer for them."

Edlyn nodded slowly, breathing in and out. "You have all Father's files, you say? His book?"

"We do. And as soon as our team has finished with them, they're yours to do with as you wish."

"You can publish your father's book as you planned," I said. "Everyone will know what a talented historian and author he was. His book will be in the library and all the local shops, I'm sure. His work will be acknowledged for the remarkable achievement that it was. That's one way to live on, isn't it?" Edlyn was listening, so I continued. "The most important thing is that he'll live on in your memory. You had a good and loving father. So did I. Not every girl can say that." Privately, I decided I'd ask Alex Belcourt to acknowledge the work of Grenville Dark in the museum, and I thought he would willingly agree. I could imagine some kind of grand opening of a new Egemere Woman exhibit with photographs of the local historian and maybe Edlyn herself there to cut the ribbon.

"Father had been working on that book for more than ten years. Always hoping to find more information."

"Then perhaps you can do that for him," Tom said.

"Would you read it?" she asked me. "You'll know if it's ready for publication."

"Of course," I said, doing mental fist pumps. "I'll have my husband's sergeant send me the file. As soon as I've had a chance to read it, we can get together and talk."

"Well." She reached for a piece of shortbread. "I'll need help with the computer stuff."

Zach brightened at that. "I can help you, Eddy. I'm pretty good with computers."

* * *

On the way back to Long Barston, Tom and I drove along the Roman-straight road, passing woods, leafy glades, and open farmland. Quintessential Suffolk. Some people prefer more dramatic landscapes, but I had come to love the gentle beauty of fields and hillocks and the towers of far-off churches rising above distant woods.

"Stop here for a moment," Tom said. We'd reached a vista that looked out on a patchwork of fields—pale yellow barley setting off the glossy, emerald-green sugar beets. Getting out of the car, we leaned against a five-bar gate and breathed in the fresh scent of greenery and distant livestock. "I'm glad this one's over," he said, "or almost over."

"What will happen to Nevin and Peter Eley?"

"Mandatory life sentences, I imagine. Chance of parole."

"And Derek Quinn?"

"I don't know. Quinn has no previous form as an adult. If he gets a sympathetic judge, he might get a minimum sentence—two years with community service, maybe less?" We heard his ringtone. "That's Ren. I'd better take it."

Tom listened, interrupting only to say, "Got it. . . . That's definite? . . . Right." When he ended the call, he said, "We got DNA results back on Carrie's baby."

"Oh?" I felt a frisson of fear. "Do they know who the father was?"

"They do, but Belcourt should be the first to hear it. Do you mind?" He shoved his phone in his pocket. "Come on, we can turn around and drive back to Ravenswyck."

Fifteen minutes later, we were knocking on the door of Ravenswyck Court.

"This is a surprise," Alex Belcourt said, beckoning us in. "Good timing as well. I'm leaving for Manila later this evening."

"We have news," Tom said. "Could we sit somewhere?"

I saw Belcourt's body tense. He must have realized we had news that would change his life.

We followed him into the large formal sitting room. "Can I get you something to drink?" he said.

"We won't be staying that long. Kate, why don't you start?"

"Last night I read the translation of a file that was found on Grenville Dark's computer. Egemere Woman was Matilda, the first wife of Henry Wyck. He was her killer. I'll send you the file, and I'll also include it in my final report."

"I look forward to that," Belcourt said, "but could you tell me—"

"There's something else," Tom said. "More important."

"The baby."

"We got the DNA results about an hour ago."

Belcourt's face turned pale. He swallowed. "Tell me."

"*You* were the father, Alex," Tom said. "The results are clear. *You* were the father of Carrie's baby. You know vasectomies aren't one hundred percent reliable. No wonder Carrie wanted to wait until you were home to tell you."

Belcourt sat there for several long seconds. Then he began to weep.

Chapter Forty-Five

That evening, at home, Tom and I did the things we normally do on the weekend. We made dinner together, watched an episode of *Antiques Roadshow*, and sat on the patio, listening to the crickets chirp as the sun turned the sky from pink to coral and finally lavender.

Everything should have been fine. Tom's murder cases were solved. I'd completed my research into the identity of Egemere Woman. Alex Belcourt could finally put the past behind him and maybe even move forward.

But everything wasn't fine. There was something in Tom's face I couldn't ignore. *He'll tell me when he's ready.* But when the sky had finally turned dark and he still hadn't told me what was weighing on his mind, I decided to ask.

"Tom, what's wrong?"

"That getaway we talked about earlier. I want to book us in for a week, maybe two."

"That would be lovely. I'd like nothing better. But I didn't think you could take any more time off for a while."

"Time off isn't a problem."

"Really? Okay, then. How about the first week in August—right after the Scottish auction?"

"I can do that." His eyes flicked to me and then away. "I have something to tell you."

"I have something to tell you, too."

"You go first."

"No, you."

"All right. I want to spend time with you, alone. Just the two of us."

This was starting to sound weird. "I'd like that, too. You know that. 'Nothing in the middle of nowhere' is my kind of place."

"Like Devon." He nodded slowly as if coming to a decision. "The thing is, Kate, I've been suspended from duty."

I sat up. "*Why?*"

"Amy Cartwright. She filed an official complaint, accusing me of circumventing police procedures, of purposely damaging her reputation, and of endangering the public—you, Kate."

I couldn't believe what I was hearing. "Does she have a case?"

"I don't think she'll win in the end, but she'll try. And until then I'll have nothing to do. I want to spend that time with you. Just the two of us."

I took his hand. "All right. I'll clear it with Ivor. And it's good timing, because it won't be just the two of us for very much longer."

Tom's mouth dropped open. He turned toward me, his hands steepled over his mouth. "Kate, darling, are you *pregnant*?"

I laughed. "No, silly. I told Angela we might be able to take one of those springer spaniel puppies that were born last month. If you agree, of course."

He took me in his arms. "I love you, Kate Hamilton. What should we name him—or her? We'll need a collar and a leash and bowls and—"

I watched his face light up.

I will have to tell him about my so-called gift. But not now. Not tonight.

Acknowledgments

The inspiration for this story came from a stunning archaeological discovery in Cumbria, England. In 1981 a series of excavations by Leicester University at the ruined Benedictine priory at St. Bees uncovered a lead coffin. When opened, the coffin revealed a medieval body, so well preserved it might have been recently buried rather than six hundred years earlier. The man's nails were manicured, his fingerprints intact, his organs sound, and much of his blood still liquid. Forensic tests revealed that "St. Bees Man" had died a violent death.

Since then, DNA testing and genealogical research have identified him almost certainly as Sir Anthony de Lucy, who was killed on a Teutonic crusade in 1368.

I was mesmerized, and unable to get that story out of my brain, decided to make a similar discovery the centerpiece of my sixth Kate Hamilton Mystery.

As always, I have many people to thank. Zoe Stansell of the British Library provided important information about medieval documents. Dr. Keith Briggs, visiting lecturer at the University of Oxford, set me straight on the topic of rural plague pits. Dr. Matthew Hefferan, teaching associate in Medieval and Early Modern History at the University of Nottingham, provided welcome information about medieval Suffolk and the Battle of Crécy.

For particulars about the forensic examination of St. Bees Man, I consulted Dr. Ofelia Meza-Escobar of the School of Biomedical Sciences at the University of Birmingham and Gemma Craven of the

British Association for Biological Anthropology. Sarah Wisseman, a fellow author and archaeologist, was kind enough to read the portions of my manuscript dealing with excavation procedures.

I have used their information in a fictional setting. All errors are mine alone.

I also want to thank Joyce McClennen, secretary to the late P.D. James, for scouring my manuscript for misplaced Americanisms, and my dear friends and beta readers, Lynn Denley-Bussard and Grace Topping. Their wise counsel and advice proved once again invaluable.

I am grateful as always for Faith Black Ross, my editor, and for the entire team at Crooked Lane Books who have supported and encouraged me during the writing process. Thanks also to my agent, Paula Munier. Without the help of all these generous people, this book wouldn't exist.

Last, I wish to thank my husband, Bob, for his unfailing patience and support. I love you.

Soli Deo Gloria